D0658812

Where the Light Remains

A Novel

Hayden Gabriel

A TOUCHSTONE BOOK
Published by Simon & Schuster
New York London Toronto Sydney Singapore

TOUCHSTONE
Rockefeller Center
1230 Avenue of the Americas
New York, NY 10020

First Touchstone Edition 2003
Originally published in Great Britain in 2002 by Pan Books
An imprint of Pan Macmillan Ltd.

For information regarding special discounts for bulk purchases,
please contact Simon & Schuster Special Sales at 1-800-456-6798
or business@simonandschuster.com

Designed by Michelle Blau

Manufactured in the United States of America

10 9 8 7 6 5 4 3 2 1

Library of Congress Cataloging-in-Publication Data
Gabriel, Hayden
[Quickening Ground]
Where the light remains: a novel / by Hayden Gabriel.—1st Touchstone ed.
p. cm.
Originally published: Quickening ground. London: Pan, 2002.
"A Touchstone book."
1. Women—England—Cornwall (County)—Fiction. 2. Cornwall (England: County)—Fiction. 3. Farmers' spouses—Fiction. 4. Married women—Fiction. I. Title.
PR6107.A22Q53 2003
823'.92—dc21 2003045719

ISBN 0-7432-4314-5

For my mother

Acknowledgments

Grateful thanks to the following institutions and individuals for help with the research and writing of this book:

BCC Archive, Plymouth; Birmingham Museum and Art Gallery; Bristol City Art Gallery; Cambourne School of Mines; Cornish Studies Library, Redruth; the Courtney Library and Cornish History Archive, Truro; Tony Brooks, Geevor Tin Mine, Pendeen; Bill Greenhalgh Musical Instruments, Exeter; Gwenap Pit, near Redruth; Helston Folk Museum; Brian Humphrys – Antiques, Penzance; W. H. Lane, Fine Art Auctioneers, Penzance; David Messum Fine Art, London; Meteorological Office, Bracknell; Morrab Library, Penzance; National Maritime Museum, London; Penlee House Gallery and Museum, Penzance; Plymouth City Museum and Art Gallery; Plymouth Local Studies Library; Python Pictures, London; Royal Cornwall Museum, Truro; RNAS Culdrose, Helston; Sotheby's, London; the Laycock Collection, Torquay Museum; TV South-west archive, Plymouth; Wayside Museum, Zennor; West Cornwall Art Archive and Jamieson Library, Newmill, Penzance; West Country Studies Library, Exeter; the Wren Trust, Okehampton.

Ben Batten, Pam and Noel Betowski, Hazel Burston, Simon Butler, Mike Chalwin, Jon Cook, Julian Cooper, creative writing class UEA (1995–96), Tom Cross, Nicky and Bill Davenport, Caroline Fox, Terry Gifford, Todd Gray, Iris M. Green, Francis Greenacre, Gill Gregory, Ted Grimes, Alwyn Hall, Melissa

Hardie, Jonathan Holmes, Mike Izzard, Russell Celwyn Jones, Paul Lawley, Stephen Lloyd, Jonathan Mathys, Debra Myhill, Jean Nankervis, Joanna Newey, Nigel Payne, Richard Perryman, Michael Praed, Richard Prince, J.C.C. Probert, Louise Quayle, Roasbel Rayner, Mary Reeves, David Rivington, Trixie Rowe, Nicky Smith, Imogen Taylor, Simon Trewin, Jill and Dave Try, Janette Turner Hospital, Ru Wellings, Eric Wilson, and Richard Wood.

Especial thanks to Doris Cooper for her subtle editorial understanding; Roger F. S. Thorne for his authoritative guidance on Methodism in southwest England; to Andrew Motion for his insightful tutelage during the creative writing M.A.; and, by no means least, to my mother and Frances Fraser for their unerring supportiveness.

Where the Light Remains

One

West Cornwall
1886

Munro waits at the rear of the chapel, chafing slightly at Claira's lateness and the stiffness of his collar. He peers through the finely bubbled glass. Heavy rain clouds gather and the light is failing, but still she does not come.

Beside him, the minister catches his eye, *don't worry, she'll be here.*

Munro purses his lips. He runs his mind over the arrangements, as if they might somehow be assembled at the wrong time. Absurd. The chapel's full. Practically the whole village has turned out *and* his brother, come down from Truro. Everyone here but Claira. His life feels suddenly out of kilter. He thinks of the yard at Trethenna, empty of him; thinks of the cow gone off her feed, of the wind rising and the clouds that gather. He twitches his coat. It will be dark at least an hour before time and, besides the ceremony, there's the gathering to be had. And, dear God, let her be here soon.

Drawn, inexorably, to stand next to Munro, Mary Bellham sees his face in profile, set. He moves and his elbow catches hers and the energy of his unrest jumps across at the contact so that he stumbles out apologies for his clumsiness and, unable to hold his eye, she must turn away, tilting her face, birdlike to the window, then to the timepiece at her waist, daring to allow herself the small thought, *perhaps she will not come.* Her hands fly to one another. Knuckles squeeze white. It's not just her. Others have had such thoughts. She heard the women, on the way in, talking of it. How the thing is bound to end badly. Assuming it ever gets started. How it's too close to Christmastime for a wedding. And then, such an unlikely match, what with the girl's family and her being so much younger than him—almost *sixteen years* younger—and him so well-to-do he could have had his pick. For weeks now there's been talk of it. Whisperings of which Mary Bellham has heard snippets and quashed with a stare, but now, in these last minutes, she can no longer subdue the thought.

Perhaps at last he will see sense. Really, perhaps she will not come.

Munro peers again through the glass. Where in Heaven's name is she? Yesterday he'd felt so sure of this marriage. Driving the horses to plow over stubble, his feet had been firm in the furrow; at each step willing the next day nearer.

Returning from the fields, Jed had been there, ruefully displaying wet clothing as silent protest against the newfangled pump. Munro had shown him again how to work the thing—so much faster to use than the well. And in that moment, easing good water from the good earth, Munro had felt his body primed and strong. By his design the pump was there, by thought and sweat he'd brought the little miracle about. Though hushed air hung heavy under a gunmetal sky and the chickens hunched together against the weather, Munro felt himself quick and vital. With the guidance of God and his own steady hand, he seemed a fulcrum around which his life was turning. Excitement had surged and—as he crossed to take the harness from the horses—his lips had formed their countering prayer, the plea, again, for humility and calm.

Perhaps that's it, he thinks, turning from the window to pace the chapel floor: he has not been sufficiently humble. *How can a man take fire in his bosom and his clothes not be burned?* He feels the sour churning of his stomach.

"Here we are," the minister says and Munro looks up to see. At last, through the blurring glass there is movement. The carriages make silhouettes, black against thunderous gray. Figures descend and Munro feels his pulse quicken at the sight of his soon-to-be wife, borne slowly towards him like some pale flower head on the foliage of her family, who circle behind her in a dark wreath.

It is then he senses something is wrong.

He glances quickly round the Wesleyan chapel, drawing reassurance from its familiarity, the warm light of the lamps, the roundness of those heads yet bent in prayer, the expectation in others' glances; then he looks back out to the advancing party. It's too much of monochrome. There seems something almost funereal in their approach.

Munro goes to move towards them, but the minister's face registers nothing wrong and then Mary Bellham is before him, holding his eye now, willing him to understand something he does not.

"I will play for you then," she says in answer to his frown.

"Thank you, Mary," he manages and she turns to take her place at the harmonium, even as a single figure detaches itself from the bridal group and hurries towards the chapel, black coat billowing in the rising wind. Munro recognizes Claira's neighbor and opens the door to admit him.

"What is it, Jack?"

He looks to the ground. "Her father, at last."

Munro catches his breath. "Not dead?"

The man nods. "Scarcely an hour since."

Those in the chapel, aware of some disturbance, begin themselves to stir.

"Then we can't go on here."

"She won't hear of stoppin'. Says her father would want as much."

"Why ever was no word sent?"

"There's been no time. I'm here as soon as I could be."

As Munro nods his understanding, the chapel door opens and the bride's family are among them. Notes are struck upon the harmonium, stumbling at first, then stronger.

Munro has never seen her so pale. The color has drained completely, even from her lips, so that her wanness matches the stuff of her dress and he is reminded of the white waxen roses of Christmastime. Numbed, her family move past him and on into the chapel, the mother pausing, silently, to greet Munro. Then Claira stands before him and—even in this paleness—her beauty takes his breath. God, that such a creature will be his; save that her eyes, today, don't seem to see and he tumbles into their deep vacancy; dark wells in the pallor of her face. She reaches out and he takes her hand so icy in his hotness and it is she who seems dead, a specter in his grasp and won't she stop, won't she warm herself he wants to ask, can he not comfort her, but no words come and they walk together down the center aisle and he cannot be sure how it is she moves.

And so they wed.

Throughout the ceremony she remains remote. Remote too through the sad celebration, the wedding wake at Trethenna, where the guests drain quickly away as the news spreads and darkness gathers. At last, when they have all gone, she speaks, the first Munro has heard from her that day apart from the words required by ceremony. No, she cannot eat, nor rest, can think only of seeing her father. So Munro takes her, bundled in the jingle, through the wildness of the night, to her village six miles hence.

Claira stands at the foot of small, steep stairs. She has lived here all her life and yet she does not know these stairs, sees them as if for the first time. She places a hand on the banister, knowing she must ascend to her father, her dead father, who lies above. Her husband stands at her side. She thinks he is a kind man, although she does not know him. If she turns round, she will see her family, Beattie, Samuel, Jethro, Hannah, William and their mother, in black, round the fire. Liquid dazed eyes. If she turns round she will see herself at the foot of the stairs. Sickness, dizziness. She does not turn round.

She does not climb the stairs. She floats them. She floats up the stairs and into the dark room where two candles burn by the mirror and her dead father lies on the bed. There is a noise of footsteps on the wooden floor. They are her footsteps, so she cannot be floating. She nears the bed, wedding gown shroud-white. There he is: beautiful and gone; his face so like and empty of him. She kisses his cheekbone. It is colder even than hers. And hard. There is a rocking. It is her body. There is a low moaning. It comes from her body though she does not ask it to. She feels a movement of the floor. Her mother is there, bringing something. From a distance Claira hears her, but cannot make out the words. She tries very hard, concentrating on her mother's mouth. *This is yours now, Claira. He wanted you to have it.* Her mother presses something into her hands. It is his fiddle and the horsehair bow. She cradles them. They are warm to her touch.

Munro takes her home, through the darkness, to Trethenna. By the time they arrive Claira is shivering and Munro begins to fear for her, she seems so inert.

"Best get to bed," he says to her unfathomable eyes, then realizes she doesn't know where to go. Her trunk is in the hall still. He watches while she takes her night things from it, then he leads her up the stairs. They pause on the landing at the door of Munro's room. His big bed is visible, but he cannot think of her there tonight.

"Mrs. Jago made up a bed in the attic for John Trehearne, only he went home when . . . he went home after all. You had best get to bed up there. I'll bring a hot water bottle."

He opens the door to steeper attic stairs and watching her ascend, is reminded of seeing his brother's children go up to bed. Her wedding garb, bedraggled now, seems suddenly a nightgown; the fiddle, still clutched in one hand, a child's beloved doll. He wonders if she can be trusted with the lamp.

A few minutes later he brings the bottle. The attic room is dark. He has left his lamp below thinking hers would still be burning, but she has doused it. In the low light he stands, straining his senses towards the area of darkness he guesses she occupies. He listens for her breathing, but cannot hear for the wind against the side of the house. He steps nearer. Dimly he makes out the shape of her, curled tightly in the bed, and a darker patch, her hair, and surely the fiddle, yes, the fiddle too on the pillow. Softly he moves closer. With care he stands the bottle at his feet, hesitates, then reaches out to move the instrument, only to find she's holding it still. What's he to do? Halting his breathing, he begins to release her fingers from their grip on the fiddle's neck. Fine-boned fingers he uncurls one by one. Carefully he lifts her hand, warmer now, the wrist so narrow in his handling. Sliding the instrument away, he moves to put it aside. With a clunk it locates the washstand next to the bed and he draws sharp breath in fear of waking her. And will she not hear the thumping of his heart? She does not stir and he lets the fiddle rest on the slate surface and begins to breathe again. Just her wrist now to place down without her waking. In the dark he feels her hand's weight and the knuckles rounded against his palm, smooth against the roughness of his skin: her own dead calm held in his strange unsteadiness. The room and the sound of the wind are lost to him. Disembodied, he becomes this touching of hands. Like the carrying of eggs—new-lain warm—or the weight of a stillborn lamb's head; limp: the hand of his new wife in his.

She stirs and draws deep breath and he holds his own; heart pounding again to think she might wake. Moving her hand to the pillow, softly he releases it there. Another moment's hesitation, then he lifts the covers and places the bottle beside her, near enough to warm, not near enough to burn. Gently, he tucks her in.

For a minute longer he watches, then, like the shock of unexpected lightning, a flicker of annoyance darts round the room. His thoughts reach out to catch its meaning, to glimpse what's revealed in the flare. What *exactly,* his crossness demands to know, is he *doing*? Taken a wife to wait on her, has he? To stand at her bedside, as if moonstruck or mazed; lovesick in the darkness while she sleeps. He wants to protest, but the barb hits its mark and he straightens and turns and strides from the room, clattering down the dark stairs.

In the kitchen, he jettisons a cat from the table and turns the lamp up bright. Loosening his collar, Munro sees Mrs. Jago has left supper heating through. The table is laid for two. One place for him, another for his bride. Aunt Eadie will have eaten hers already and then taken herself off to bed. He hasn't checked. *Has* he? He hasn't looked into Eadie's room to check she is all right. What *is* it makes a man so forget his duty? Swiftly he walks down the passage, opens her door and, seeing the elderly woman well settled, crosses to the bedside and turns out her lamp.

Pacing back to the kitchen, he prods the turf on the fire. The old lady has not had much of a day of it. He places furze on the flame to blaze, then lowers the pot nearer the heat. Not much of a day for any of them, come to that. And as for his wife's mother. He thinks of the strain on her face tonight. A day that's seen her daughter married and her husband dead. Not unexpected, of course, his death. A merciful release, the state he was in. And foul this one. No matter how much the linen had been washed and the boards scrubbed, their cottage had been thick with the reek of him; sickening under the camphor and cloves. They'll surely bury him as soon as may be. A funeral then. At the chapel by dint of his widow's attendance. Munro sighs, wondering however such a man could hope to rest with his Maker.

Checking the contents of the pot, he burns his fingers.

"Owww!"

The hot lid crashes.

Going to the larder, he scoops a pat of butter and smears it on the burn. He sees the dirt-ingrained cracked skin and pauses, thinking of her hand; how, curled in sleep, it nested in his.

Crossing back to the hearth, he swings the pot away from the heat.

He doesn't much feel like food.

Tugging on boots, he goes out into the night. The wind's backed westerly. There'll be more rain before dawn. The lantern splutters as he treks to the byre.

There's a sick cow needs tending.

Two

West Cornwall
1986

"Shall we have a look at the outbuildings? There's a particularly fine byre."

"What's a *byre?*" Howard mouths to his wife, behind the estate agent's back.

"It's the cowshed," Claire whispers.

Howard looks at her. Pulls a face. "Oh. That *will* be useful."

The children clatter after them down the bare stairs; their footsteps booming round the empty rooms. Claire catches them on their way through the kitchen, makes them wait while she does up their jackets.

"No more racing around in here, you two," she says, quietly. "Go and explore the garden, only, stay away from the well. Okay?"

"Okay."

They charge out after the men and Claire leans against the back-door frame and watches them; thinks of the way they must leave from the house in St. John's Wood: always with an adult and wary of traffic, onto gravel and pavement to the pedestrian crossing; tarmac to the park, where every inch of ground is known, every blade of grass pressed by the passing of feet.

She sees them run, now, where the orchard rises towards the

bigger hill. Blundle Hill, she thinks it's called. She scans her eyes along the sweep of landscape. God, it's beautiful. Raw and unforgiving. Imagine it—waking here day after day with this much space and this much sky. She feels the delicious fearfulness here: space and emptiness and wild air and silence.

She counts the houses she can see from the door. Two at the end of the valley, one across from Trethenna and, if she cranes her head to the left, another farm. All tucked below the moor-line.

She ought to catch up with Howard and she crosses the yard past his BMW, the swirl of clouds mirror-imaged on the hood where—beneath the black luster—contracting metal ticks and she stops; listening to what else there is to hear. Only breeze. No traffic noise, but there—as the wind shifts—the sound of tinny music. She traces it to the tractor poised on the hill's ridge. Gerry Rafferty, isn't it?

Between the sax and guitar of "Baker Street," the farmhand drains his tea. After he fires up the tractor, music drowns beneath the engine's thrubbing.

"You missed the byre," Howard says, sauntering back from the yard and turning her to the house again. "He was right though. It is a *splendid* byre."

Claire looks at him, trying to gauge his irony, then lets it go as she sees he is flaking paint from a window frame.

"Some of these are in desperate need of attention," he tuts.

"I could do that," Claire offers.

Howard raises his eyebrows.

"Didn't know you were a painter."

She thrusts out her chin.

"There's quite a lot you don't know about me."

He laughs; aims a flick of a finger at the end of her nose.

"Trouble with you is you're an incurable romantic. The house is in the country, so never mind the dry rot."

She slides an arm round his waist.

"Do you hate it so much?"

"No, I don't hate it. Goodness knows, there's nothing to be had in terms of a decent town house down here. And structurally it seems quite sound. I think it'd be a good investment for a year or two. The estate agent's gone now, but he seemed to think the seller would accept my offer."

She grins up at him.

"You've put in an offer?"

"Pleased?" he asks.

"Yes."

"But, Claire, if we *do* buy this now, you know it'll be just the three of you here for a time, until the Clarendon projects in Surrey are a bit more established."

"But the retirement apartments?"

"That'll mean some time down here," he agrees. "But the country clubs will be the main thrust of it in Cornwall and we won't be starting those for another twelve months."

Claire purses her lips. "It's back to schools again, Howard. I don't want to start Nathan at a school in London and then have to pull him out a few months later and expect him to start all over again somewhere else."

"Okay. But I won't be able to join you for a while."

"Weekends?"

"Yes. I'll probably make it down at weekends."

They find the children in the garden, playing by the well. Nathan is jumping to the lawn from the well's raised edge while Damien swings all his weight on the water pump, which does not budge.

"Come on. We're going now," she calls, her voice losing its battle against the nearing tractor's racket, but the children run anyway, following their parents to the car, Nathan wide-eyed at the tractor-monster, so close now at the field's edge.

The driver turns in Howard's direction. Their eyes lock. The engine noise is deafening. Howard nods to him; this must be the little man the estate agent told him about who rents Trethenna's land.

The boys clamor to be lifted to see and with surprise Claire watches as Howard indulges them, helping them up to a good foothold; lifting them at the last so they can peer over the wall. Suddenly silent; the children's faces are awed at what their father shows them: the power and din of the massive tractor, red; the cruel blades of the plow coming shiny from tumbling earth as gulls scream, reeling.

Claire files a different image: the cameo of close heads, watching; the children's eyes shining; their faces flushed with running and the freshness of air.

She holds the moment to her. Treasure and good omen.

Three

The rain has been relentless. Three days now and the land struggles to shrug off the excess. Through the downpour, Munro's farmworker walks home from Trethenna to his cottage nearby. The lane has become a hectic stream. Water dams up behind each footfall and Jed paces steadily downhill. Mud has washed away, exposing rock. He stops and surveys the damage, turning his back to the weather, as cattle do. If he can divert the deluge into the ditch now, there'll be less mending for him to do later. For several minutes he works, his thin frame hunched inside his coat as he bends to lift rocks, placing them across the flow. It is a repeat of work he did yesterday and the day before, but any defenses break down against this flood and the job must simply be done again.

Jed straightens himself and looks to see if his labor has been successful. With the heel of his boot, he gouges wet earth from the lip of the ditch where the water is not yet flowing freely. He might need to come back with a spade. He waits in the rain to see. Not there yet. Using his hands now he breaks the turf, scoops out more mud, and the backlog of water he has created bursts through with a tumble of small rocks and silt. Bending again, he rinses his hands in the icy water, sluicing out grit from his fingerless gloves.

He stops at the cottage gate. His cold hands fumble at the buttons of his fly and he relieves himself into the fast-flowing water in the ditch.

At the cottage door he pauses. The prayer he utters is rounded with use, as familiar to his ear as the door latch to his hand. He takes off his gaiters, heavy with wet, and leaves them in the porch to drip.

Once inside, he hangs his wet clothes high in the fireplace and takes down a dry sweater, pulling it on over the shirt that clings to his shoulders. The fire is nearly out and he stirs the embers a little before adding more furze, then lowers the kettle nearer the heat. He wonders briefly about eating, then dismisses the idea. More important things to do.

He goes to the corner of the room, his socks leaving damp footprints on the flagstones. Opening the cupboard he takes down an empty paper bag, the one his tea came in. He steps back to close the door and notices there is a mouse in the trap he has set on the bottom shelf. He stoops, round-shouldered, to pick it up, works the mechanism to release the little body which he tosses to the fire where it lands with a hiss. Third one this week. It's the wet that brings them in. Collecting a knife from the table drawer, he pads softly upstairs.

The day is dark with rain and he crosses to the window. Resting on the sill, he uses the knife to slit the bag along all three edges. His hands are cold and the cracks in his skin reopen and seep. One piece of paper he puts aside, that will do for next week; the other he creases carefully down the middle before slitting it in two with the knife. He reaches inside his sweater, into the breast pocket of his damp shirt for the coins. Three shillings and a sixpence. He wraps two shillings in the paper and puts the remaining one and six in a black leather pouch that already holds two half-pennies. Picking up the wrapped coins, he tosses them lightly in a cupped hand. They make no sound.

The needle and thread are in the drawer of the washstand. Jed opens the waxed-paper packet and clicks his tongue when he sees that the needle has begun to rust. He had thought it would stay sound in the drawer. He looks at the granite round the window. The plasterwork has come away and the green growth has spread, but two feet in, at the turn of the wall, the stone is drier and he rubs the needle against it there, sanding the rust away on the wall's roughness. Picking up the reel, he breaks off a length of cotton. Hampered by the low light, it takes him several attempts to push the end through the eye. His fingers do not feel the thread.

The narrow bed is neatly made and he pulls back the blankets and untucks the sheet to expose the straw mattress. Pushing the knife in till it penetrates the seam, he cuts through a few inches of stitching. Blindly, he inserts a hand. The cloth bag is soon discovered among the straw and he fumbles the drawstring open and pushes the two wrapped coins in. There is about the bag a fatness that is worrying. *It is easier for a camel . . .* Quickly he resettles the straw . . . *to go through the eye of a needle than for a rich man to . . .* He withdraws his hand and sets about sewing . . . *than for a rich man to . . .* The seam here is greasy with handling yet, for all his poor hands, the stitches are neat and small . . . *than for a rich man to enter into the kingdom of God.*

There is a knocking at the door. He starts and his hands become still. The rain drives hard against the window. He listens, his mind drenched with the morning: empty fields at daybreak, heavy with their burden of rain; the rabbit in the snare, ragged fur tangled with debris; wet hair matted on the heads of cattle as they watched from the byre for his bringing of hay; birds, low lying and silent in dripping hedgerows. And he has seen Munro today, said all that needs saying. There's no one, today, to knock on his door. He can't have heard it; his hands resume their sewing. There is another knock and a voice calls. He listens. It's Munro's wife. It is. The boss's new wife. He lodges the needle safely in the seam and tucks the bedclothes back round.

As he goes downstairs, the air seems strangely charged. It cannot be; she is only at the door. But no. He arrives in the kitchen and finds she has let herself in and closed the door behind her. He hesitates at the foot of the stairs and smooths a hand over his sparse hair. Here's his home with someone else in it. A woman. She stands near the door, taking the hessian sacking from her shoulders and shaking the rain from it. You would think in this weather she would tie back her hair, but he can see that, beneath the wet scarf, it is loose still. A strand of it sticks to her neck. She takes a basket from under the coat he recognizes as Munro's. Her face is pale against the coat's darkness and the darkness of her eyes.

"Mrs. Jago said to bring you this."

She hangs back by the door, then takes a step into the room, propelled by the need to put the basket on the table. She removes the oilcloth covering and uses an inner cloth to lift out the hot cooking pot she has brought.

"Shall I put it over the fire?"

"Mrs. Jago shouldn't fuss so."

"I think it's still hot, but she said to put it back on the heat if you had any."

There is a dewdrop at the end of his nose and a tracing of broken blue veins in his cheek. The cottage looks clean enough, but there's a smell she can't identify that's something more than damp.

"How was Jed?" Mrs. Jago asks as Claira returns from her errand. The uphill walk back to Trethenna has put some color in her cheeks. Worth sending her out just for that. "Did he have his fire lit?"

"Yes. It wasn't very hot, but there was plenty of furze in the corner."

"Oh, he always has plenty of furze, all right. It's just he seldom burns any." She smiles at Claira. "Only the Lord knows why. He has all the fuel he needs as part of his wages and Munro's always the Christian in keeping him supplied, but still he doesn't use much."

She passes Claira a cup.

"Could you give that to Aunt Eadie? It's the tonic she has before her meal."

Claira takes the cup to the old woman, who sits at the hearthside, then looks to see what needs doing and finds clean crockery to put away.

"Oh, thank you, dear," Aunt Eadie says, looking at her daily medicine, as if surprised.

"I sometimes think," Mrs. Jago continues, "that given the chance, Jed would live on prayer and bread and water."

"Jed's a God-fearing man," says Munro, coming, that moment, into the kitchen with a brace of rabbit to hang in the larder. Bedraggled heads, dead eyes glazed, dangle by his muddied gaiters.

"And so was my husband God-fearing," Mrs. Jago laughs, "but he would never go cold. I know of no scripture says a man should go cold."

She takes the rabbits from him.

"That's three today," she says, "Jed left one this morning *and* there's two already hanging. They must be throwing themselves in the snares."

"Poor beggars are pleased to come in out of the rain." He tuts. "If he must get rabbit for us, how I wish he would shoot them, not set these wretched snares."

"He does it as a favor to us."

"I know."

He nods to where Claira stands, her back to them now as she gazes through the window.

"How has she been?" he asks his housekeeper.

"Quiet," Mrs. Jago replies.

They keep their voices low, but need not, for Claira is quite lost. A milk jug still in her hand, she stares out of the window where the rain runs and she is a child again, peering through the wet for her father to come home. *Here he is.* Through the dark runnels she can see the red flash of his neckerchief and the tall broadness of him and his gait faintly lame from the taming of too many horses. She runs out into the rain and, laughing, her mother scolds after her,

Claira you'll catch your death, and then she is lifted, swung high, *hello, pumpkin,* carried against the breadth of his chest, her arms tightly round his neck, rough against her skin, and the smell of tobacco from his jacket.

Mrs. Jago says quietly, "Poor child."

Munro nods. "Yes, but I don't know that brooding helps. She would be better for being busy."

"There's no accounting for grieving. She'll be back to work soon enough. It's in her nature. Just think how she worked last haymaking."

Caught unawares, Munro's mind is instantly swamped with it. Claira pitching hay high onto the wain, her hair, flying from her bonnet, made gold in the summer light as she forks. He remembers her absentminded wiping of hayseeds from the sweat on her face; the symmetry of her grin as she called to her sister; the day's dirt ingrained in the muscle of her boyish arms revealed by pushed-back sleeves; the bareness of her throat as she tilted her head to drink; the narrowness of her waist his hands would span.

He bends to fumble with the buckle on his gaiters.

"I don't doubt but what she did," he grunts to the sole of his boot.

"I just think of my Mary when her father died," Mrs. Jago says as Munro straightens. "She probably took it worst of all. It's hard on a daughter—if they've been close."

Munro nods and Mrs. Jago moves past him to rest a hand on Claira's shoulders.

"There's food nearly ready," she says.

The face that Claira turns is wet with unacknowledged tears. Brought back to herself, she blinks her eyes.

"Thank you. I should wash."

The stairs are so different. Polished, with a turn in them, so much wider and not so steep. And then there's the banister, polished too, a dense wood of a type Claira has not seen before; silky to the touch; the balustrade foreign in its turned solidity. She pauses on the landing at the door of Munro's room and dares to look in at the heavy furniture and the rich reds and blues of the rug by his bed. She's seen a rug as rich once before, in the rectory one day when she went into the town with her mother. Now, as then, she wants to go into the room and touch, but dares not.

Claira walks on and the sound of her footsteps changes as she passes the empty rooms. Empty rooms. She has been here three days and they are still a shock. Most of her life, there have been eight living in a two-bedroom cottage and now she lives in a house with empty rooms. There are three on this floor and another one next to her room in the attic. Disbelieving, she stands in the doorway of the first, unable to come to terms with the oddity of indoor space. Shards of memory are prompted by the taste of it and she concentrates until she recollects the whole: a cottage in the village after the family had moved out. Her mother had helped and Claira, seven or eight years old, had wandered around the increasingly deserted rooms where ceilings seemed suddenly high and her small feet gained the eerie power to make hollow echoes rebound. She remembers noticing, for the first time, scuffed paint on the stairs caused by the passing of feet that would no longer tread there.

Claira looks into the second room. Curtains, faded and thin from years of sun, hang at the tall window. It feels a husk of a room where time has passed, washed by different light.

The third room, towards the back of the house, is smaller than the others and the window, facing the prevailing weather, is smaller too. Even though the rain beats against the pane, this room seems somehow more welcoming. She ventures a step inside and finds the wall warm to her touch and realizes the kitchen chimney must run up through here. In the warmer air, her face feels tight from earlier tears and the weight of grief swamps her again and the tears renew unbidden and she runs on up to the attic and they will stop, won't they, these tears that just flood from her and these strange sobbings that take her shoulders for their own, they will stop soon. It's been weeks now, stifled crying under bedclothes, her sisters in the same bed in fitful sleep, his pained breathing groaned in the room next door, and willing him to be better and live and willing him to die and be free of his crushed body black from the falling of rocks underground and his shoulders so beautiful still and his belly swollen black and swollen his chest, purple-ribbed and him so strong and whole only weeks before the stench of him rotting alive and let him die, let him die quickly.

Quickly she tips water from the ewer into the bowl and plunges her face into the coldness and pulls back gasping for breath and scooping water up to her eyes, rubbing hard, then takes the towel and rubs hard with that too and the physical buffeting drags her mind to the present.

Water has splashed onto the glass-fronted photograph that shares the washstand. A picture of the family before William was born. She picks it up, not letting her eyes rest on the image of her father. As she wipes the wet away, her own face is reflected back to her, strange and strangely swollen. She lays the picture on the narrow bed and begins to wash her face again, more gently this time, forcing her mind to mundane detail. She must ask Mrs. Jago if there is a table she could use for things that shouldn't get wet. And the room needs cheering. She likes its cream simpleness and the sloping ceilings, which remind her of the only other room she has ever slept in, and she likes the view from the narrow window across Blundle Hill, but she will ask her mother if she can bring her rag rug and a bedcover. She towels her face gently dry and presses her cold fingers against her eyes before hanging up the towel and turning to leave, shivering a little in the cold air.

She has hung the fiddle on the wall near the door and she stops and lets a finger glide across the belly of it. Her father's pupil, she has played for twelve years. The fiddle was his for thirty. In places, the wood has been polished to a smooth sheen: there, where his shoulder supported, there, where his sleeve rubbed, there, where his hand held.

In the kitchen, Munro arranges cutlery on the table. Mrs. Jago, crossing the room with a dishful of steaming potatoes, stops when she sees he is laying places for four.

"Oh," she says, "I was thinking of going home."

Munro looks up. "Someone sick?"

"No."

She places a mat on the table and puts the pan down.

"No trouble, is there?" It would have to be something exceptional to warrant her going back midday in this weather.

"Nothing like that. I just thought perhaps it'd be best for me to go home mealtimes from now on."

"Why would you do that, Mrs. Jago? You have eaten at this table for the best part of ten years."

"I have. I just thought—now you've taken a wife . . ."

"No, Mrs. Jago," Munro says, looking at her across the table. "There is no reason to change things. It is not something you have to consider."

Returning to the kitchen, Claira hesitates in the doorway.

"All's well and good, then," Mrs. Jago says, returning her mindfulness to the stew.

Four

Days spent in painting snowscape. Bramley wakes to the white excitement of it. See how snow throws up light from the ground! Bright and softly round the model he has dragged early from her home, quickly before the light goes, diffused through condensation on conservatory windows; her sleep-puffy face a perfect mimicry of mourning.

The light! How can he make paint match it? And snow! Full over fields, snow lies. Against the trunks of sparse trees it clings. Hedgerows run over snow-covered fields like the embracing arms of a harbor, like the span of distant bridges, hazy through white and light and the crystal film of water droplets on the window.

There will need to be more. Thought out so far: the black of her mourning, the landscape's pallor, the pallor of chrysanthemums. Yes, there will be the weary green of sheltered plants and the light this snow rebounds. But there needs to be more.

Walking back to the village, he sees it. A conservatory where dead leaves have been left to lie. Cupping a hand to glass, he peers. Wonderful. A dreamlike drift of them, left from autumn, curled and crisp. In the light of his painting, their pale fawn would glow gold, supplying the color he seeks.

In haste he knocks at the cottage door.

So there's another tale, then, to gossip over garden walls. The artist—Mr. Bramley— who called wanting dead leaves and a sack to gather them in, only gently, so they would not spoil.

Eyes widen.

As if there could be any spoiling dead leaves that should, long since, have been swept out and put on the bonfire.

"Did 'e take 'en, then?"

"Oh yes, though I sent 'im off to find 'is own sack. Thought it might be the last I saw of 'im, but no, back 'e trotted, pleased as punch and brought me a mullet by way of thank you."

"Well, *that* was nice, then."

"George does like a good mullet."

Eyes laugh.

"More than dead leaves, I should say."

Five

There is excitement in waking, these first mornings: even in the way the sun filters through curtains, even in the way the curtains move, like breathing, to the open window. Think! The possibility of sleeping with the window open! And then—the quality of air that comes through! Waking first—and early—Claire draws deeply on its sweetness, quietly, not wanting to wake Howard. Moving here is like discovering a new lover, she thinks, silently leaving the bed: the fresh perfection of the unfamiliar.

Her feet find the polished wood of still-strange stairs, then the coldness of flagstones in the hall. Cold, too, the front-door latch, clunking open to her stealthy fingers, letting in the morning slant of sun. The phone rings loudly in the stillness so that she jumps and grabs the cordless thing, taking the handset out into the garden.

"Well, well? How is it?"

"Emma!"

"How's Cornwall?"

"I miss you!"

"Don't change the subject."

"I'm sure it'll be *dreadful* in the winter," Claire says, grinning, barefoot on the lawn in sunlight and her nightshirt.

"You rat! It's wonderful, isn't it?"

Claire curls her toes, feeling dewed blades of grass between them. She laughs. "That would depend on what you find wonderful," she says, stretching one arm above her head and freeing her eye to roam where fields rise, green upon rolling green, then up onto the thrust of moorland; the frown of rocky outcrop and the feathered heap of clouds that gather against blue. "I think it's brilliant. I'm just hoping you'll come and visit soon and see what you feel."

"We'd love to. Spirelli's after the school run is not the same without you," Emma says over the mounting scream of approaching sirens that must pass down the street before conversation can continue. "I bet you don't get woken by *those* now," she comments once they've gone.

"No, but I *did* get woken by the dawn chorus for the first couple of days," Claire says, earnestly. "It's really *loud* here."

"Oh, my heart *bleeds*. Woken by birdsong. You'll have to get together with the Neighborhood Watch and shoot the little blighters. Are the children liking it?"

"I don't think Neighborhood Watch has arrived here. Not enough to watch, I suppose. Yes, the children are loving it. You should see the change in them, Emma."

"Turned into Tarzans?"

"It's certainly hard to keep them indoors, these days. I have to drag them in for meals and I don't think they've watched TV at all since they arrived."

"The mind boggles."

"I daresay it will wear off."

"Does it all meet with Howard's approval?"

Claire circles her foot lightly over the tips of grass.

"Ah *hah*," Emma says. "I'll take your hesitation as a negative. There was bound to be a fly in the ointment somewhere."

"Let's say he's looking forward to the business challenges."

"That sounds like Howard. I expect he'll come round to the rest. In any case, he's still going to be in London and Surrey a lot of the time, isn't he?"

"He is for a while, yes. And I'm feeling terribly guilty because I'm going to use the extra time it gives me to do something entirely for me."

"Not drawing, Claire?"

"Drawing, Emma."

"You did say you were going to make it a priority—outrageous woman."

In her hand, charcoal hesitates. Daunting, daunting. She tries to reach back to all she learned—the foundation year she never followed up; the classes at uni outside her degree course; the study in summer schools; the sense she had that one day she might make a painter. A painter! It's like thinking about someone else. Claire looks at the marks she has made on paper. No charisma. Too tight. This landscape is so . . . *vibrant*.

Nathan zooms the plane past her ear and down along the table edge.

"Wow!" she says to mirror his excitement; smudging lines she meant to leave clean.

"Neeoooow," says Nathan, whizzing the toy over her shoulder.

"Hang on, Nath . . ."

"Neeooow," says Nathan.

"Listen, rascal, I just need a few minutes."

"Can we play the flying game?"

"In a little while. Where's 'Copter?"

Nathan turns to rummage in the box of toys they've brought outside and Claire wastes hard-won seconds watching him. He's leaner now and his rounded limbs have been browned by the sun and his hair made blonder. She watches the way breeze moves his hair, like the way it ruffles hay fields at the foot of Blundle Hill. He stands a moment, his head, in sunlight, framed by the backdrop of rippling grass.

"I can't find 'Copter," he says.

"I think I saw him under the table."

The boy goes onto all fours to crawl underneath.

"Mind your head when you come out."

A spear of malevolent sound, the noise hits them with physical force. In fields animals race from its path. Claire feels it as a blow to the back of the neck.

Fighter jet. That's all.

But her muscles have jumped, jerking her knees so that she jolts the table. Tumblers of orange juice tip, flood her drawing, drip through wrought iron to the child beneath. Nathan screams. She reaches down to him, drawing him out and up, onto her knee.

"All right, sweetheart? *Noisy* plane! Did you hurt yourself?"

"Yes!" he says emphatically and she has not to laugh at the tragedy of his tear-stained pouting as she reaches a Kleenex from the box, dabs the orange juice that's soaked his shirt and, sensing her giggle, he nearly laughs too, then thumps his fist against her shoulder and cries some more, laughing, and she hugs him and rocks him; stifling her laughter in his hair.

It's in the evening when the longing is strongest, the children tucked away and sleeping. Guiltily, she smothers it, bad mother, pacing the kitchen floor. Selfish to want her own time; craving the lush pull of charcoal in drawing; the embrace of space and air and outdoors. Selfish. This didn't happen when they lived in St John's Wood. Not like this. Selfish. The children might wake, Howard might ring, there's more unpacking to do; the day's chores hardly started. From the window, she sees shadows flow over the meadow; as surely as they would flow through her onto paper.

And they do.

They do.

In the garden now, her board thrown down against rock and railings as the heavens darken, heart thumping as she draws in a race against failing light, quickly, quickly, she pushes the drawing till, catching up, she grins: her paper resonant.

A second phase where she becomes the medium, translating shadows cast on the hill; following where darkening clouds lead.

And so, of course it happens that, as she needs the figure for scale and for something else she cannot name, he appears, jogging towards her through the sun's rays, lean silhouette of a man upon the path on Blundle Hill.

Quickly her hands work to set him down, or rather to suggest him, merging as he does into landscape; melding, as he does, earth, air, sun.

Six

Watery sun seeps through the little window. Claira jolts awake. She scrambles from bed, and her breath hangs on the cold air as she throws on clothes before hurrying downstairs.

Aunt Eadie's in the kitchen. Putting away the breakfast things, she clutches china and her long skirts in one hand, while the other searches for support to get her across the room. Claira's mortified. Munro will have done two hours' work already, then come in for breakfast and gone out again and all the while Claira slept and here are others doing her work for her. She takes the china from Eadie's unfirm grip and places it in the dresser.

"Thank you, dear," Aunt Eadie says.

"I am so late. I am sorry."

"Late? Are you?" Eadie says, passing Claira more crockery.

"Where is Mrs. Jago?" Claira asks in the same moment that the plates slip from her hand and fall to smash on the flagstones. Fragments of china hit the hem of her dress and Eadie's ankles, exposed below her gathered skirts. Claira curses herself.

Stupid girl!

The tears brim.

Don't cry. Don't cry. No use crying over spilt milk.

She clenches her fists.

So stupid! It would have been better to leave the old woman to it, she's far more capable than you are, bursting in late and getting it all wrong.

Just how much do you think these china plates cost?

And never mind letting your tears flood, for goodness' sake look to the elderly aunt.

"Everyone all right?" Mrs. Jago asks, coming into the kitchen, duster in hand. "Have you been trying to do too much again?" she asks Aunt Eadie as Claira helps the frail woman to a chair.

"It was me who dropped the plates," Claira says, kneeling to pluck out shards of china snagged in the wool of Eadie's stockings.

"Was it, dear? Never mind."

"And I was so late. I am sorry."

She fights tears that begin again to gather.

"You weren't late. We all thought you needed your sleep." Briefly she pats Claira's knee. "Let's get this cleared up. There's breakfast kept warm for you. Then you could come and give me a hand with the cleaning."

The flagstones in the front parlor have been swept already. Looking through the smaller side window, Claira can see Mrs. Jago beating rugs she has hung over the line. Dust rises in pale sunlight.

A basket of cleaning things has been left by the hearth. Claira rummages through it. Polish for the brass fender, cloths, beeswax, a tin of a whitish cream. She looks round the room. That will be to feed the leather top of the writing table and the bigger desk she has seen through the door of his study. She thinks of the furniture at home. Scuffed pine. She stands and runs a finger along the edge of the desk. It's like the banisters: silky. The leather top is the same green as the fabric of the huge sofa with its rounded arms and buttoned back. There are buttoned-back chairs too. Heavy. Solid. She imagines Aunt Eadie and Munro sitting here in the long evenings. Perhaps they read the Bible that rests, hugely, on a table by the sofa. She tries to imagine being there with them and cannot.

Enough. It may be a hundred times grander, but dust still falls and wood still needs waxing.

Finding the right materials, she sets about it.

In search of Mrs. Jago, Munro pads through from the back of the house, silent in stockinged feet. His mind—full of the outdoors still—responds with the force of habit to the rustle of skirts he assumes are his housekeeper's and yes, there is her basket and . . . and no. No. It is not Mrs. Jago at the polishing. It is his wife. Unnoticed he stops in the doorway, watching the tumble of her hair and the push of her waist as she polishes his furniture.

Quite absorbed, Claira pauses to run a finger along the newly polished wood and he uses the moment to step into the room. Still she does not hear him. As she resumes her work, the sway of her hips sets up the sway of her dress. Surely she *must* hear, he's so close now. And then she does and she jumps in surprise, flashing dark eyes to him, exhaling sharp breath as she looks away. He looks away, too.

"I—I didn't mean to start you."

"No, no. I just didn't hear you."

"I was looking for Mrs. Jago."

"She was in the garden a while since, beating rugs," Claira says, pleating the cloth she holds and looking towards the window.

"Do you—do you like the . . ." He indicates the table she's been working on.

"Oh. Yes."

Glancing round the room, he tries to see it in the strange light of her vision.

"This is my mother," he says, pointing to a small portrait in a heavy gilt frame.

"I thought it must be."

"*Did* you?" he asks keenly and she blushes under his scrutiny and looks down; tilting the edge of her shoe into the groove between flagstones.

"Yes. Your eyes are the same," Claira says, turning her own eyes back towards him so he is the one, now, who must look away and he simply has to: her mouth looks like perfectly ripened fruit.

"I haven't seen her for a long time."

"So I heard."

"Well, ten years."

"Does she like it in . . ." And she can't quite bring herself to say it, in case she doesn't get it right and anyway, can it be true that this man is here, yet most of his family are at a distance she cannot even imagine?

"In Africa?"

"Yes. Does she like it . . . in Africa?" Claira pushes out the syllables and, now it's spoken, the tale seems more likely. After all, there are plenty of miners from her village gone to Africa and America and Australia. Only Munro is so unlike them.

He shakes his head. "I don't think she does like it, no."

"Is that why you came back, because you didn't like it?"

He smiles.

"It wasn't that simple."

He takes a step away from her and reaches up to the high mantelshelf.

"Have you seen this?" he asks, bringing down a wooden box.

She shakes her head.

"I wanted . . ." He sits down on the chesterfield, then immediately gets up and fumbles on the mantelshelf for the key. "I wanted to show you," he says, seating himself again.

He looks up at her where she still stands, so that she pulls up the footstool and sits in front of him, childlike, as if waiting at her father's knee for the tale he is about to tell. Her throat tightens at this new version of an old comfort and she wants to complete the ritual: to rest folded arms on his lap and have him kiss the crown of her head.

He has turned the key in the lock and, opening the lid, lowers the box down to her so that she can see. It is half full of yellowish subsoil. Gritty. Dry.

From his position above her, Munro sees her head bowed before him. Her mass of dark hair is still tangled from sleep and it's shocking to him: how she leaves it loose. Light from the window catches the gold in it and he tries to imagine what it would feel like between his fingers or against his face. *To have and to hold . . .* His eye wanders over the rise and fall of her breast and he feels his penis stir. *To love and to cherish . . .*

She lifts her face to him and he cannot meet her openness.

"It's from Africa," he says, dropping his eyes to the box, which he shifts onto his lap, plunging his fingers into the gritty earth. "Hold out your hand a minute."

He gazes into unfocused middle distance as his fingers work through the subsoil. After several moments searching, he comes up with something between his thumb and forefinger that he holds briefly to the light before depositing it in the palm of her obediently outstretched hand.

"There," he says, resuming his search.

She looks down at the fragment, a small pebble, dusty and unremarkable, then back up at him as he deposits a second, even smaller stone.

"What do you think?" he asks.

She thinks that she is cold. She thinks that she can feel warmth from his leg near hers through the good, thick corduroy she cannot believe he wears about the farm. She thinks she doesn't understand what game he is asking her to play and what answer he wants her to give. Moreover, she feels cold on the inside, a heavy coldness like metal or ice; the weight of her father's deadness. What does she think? Nothing. Rather she aches with the need to curl round this numbness and have Munro's warmth curl round her too, shutting out the world and the cold and the hurt in her gut.

"They are diamonds," he says.

She looks at him and then at the stones, where they lie, forgotten in her hand.

"Are they?" She'd thought diamonds were supposed to be

shiny, not like these poor pebbles. "Is this what you went to Africa for?"

"Yes," he laughs as she hands the stones back to him. "I suppose you've seen prettier on Porthcurno beach."

And it's this little moment Mrs. Jago sees as she shows William James into the room. And it's news of this little moment he'll take back to Claira's mother. Despite the strangeness of their brief courting and the tragedy on their wedding day, the new bride and groom are at one, seemingly.

"William James is here with a message for you, Claira," Mrs. Jago says from the doorway, rugs over her arm.

Claira jumps up and spins round to face the visitor, who sees something he won't report. She's pale as death. He comes into the room, twisting his hat in his hands.

"Your mother sends her love to you, Claira, and her greetings to your husband and all and she's asked me to tell you the funeral's set for the day after tomorrow at eleven o'clock."

Claira nods, her mouth tight.

"Thank you, William," she says. "Will you have tea before you go?" She makes a move towards the kitchen, then stops as she passes Munro, looking up at him, her face screwed into a frown.

"I broke some plates this morning," she says.

" 'Course, it mayn't be any good," Mrs. Jago says to Claira the next day, undoing string from the brown paper parcel she has brought. "And there'll be plenty of altering to do. I had to take it in 'fore I could wear it and there's not half as much of you."

The kitchen's on the cusp of late-morning limbo; the dairy work done and lunch cooking itself. Munro, pulling mangolds, isn't due back for an hour.

Mrs. Jago parts the brown paper, then layers of tissue until the dress is revealed: black silk.

"Oh!" says Claira, seeing its fineness. "It's very beautiful."

"Oh, I remember this," Aunt Eadie says, touching a clawed hand to the thing. "It is a *beauty*."

"Nothing but the best for Lady Treloar."

"It wasn't *hers*?" Claira asks.

Mrs. Jago nods.

"She sent it to me when my husband died. He'd always served her well, she said, and 'e had. Not that she was more than one of his customers. He was prompt for her as he was for all. Put her out once, though," Mrs. Jago says, eyes shining at the memory.

"Her nephew'd been driving too reckless, dropped a wheel in a rut, broke three spokes and the felloes an' all. Her ladyship sent straightaway for my husband to have him mend it, said she wanted the vehicle that evening and must have it done that day; no *mention* that it were the Sabbath. He sent back he'd be pleased as Punch to do it at dawn on the morrow, but he'd not break the Lord's day for her nor nobody."

"What did she say?" Claira asks as Mrs. Jago lifts the dress free of the paper and lays it on the table.

"Said he was quite right and it'd been wrong of her to ask it and seven o'clock the next morning'd do very nicely."

She looks at the dress.

"What do you think?"

Claira reaches out to touch the richly stitched bodice, the six carved buttons at the wrist of each sleeve. The silk is gathered and sewn into fine ruching and she can't see how this elegance could fit the grief she's so far known. She looks at the plain black garb she's worn since her wedding day.

"I don't mean to say there's anything wrong with what you wear now," Mrs. Jago continues in the face of Claira's silence, "I just thought, for the funeral, it might make you feel—"

"Yes, yes. You're right."

"I'm sure Munro would have got you something made, only what with the wedding and then the funeral being arranged so quick, there's been no time."

Claira lifts the garment and holds it up against her body. The silk whispers as it moves.

"I think this could be perfect, if it can be made to fit," Claira says. "It would be wonderful to have something special to wear. Thank you."

Mrs. Jago beams her pleasure.

" 'Course, I'll have to take the skirt of it from the bodice," she says, tucking the thing round Claira's waist, "then undo the side seams and sew it up again."

"*You* will?"

"Yes. Unless you want to do it."

"No, I . . ."

"Perhaps we could *both* work on it," Mrs. Jago says.

"Oh *yes,*" Claira agrees, feeling tears threaten. "Thank you. Are you sure you won't . . ."

"Want it again?" Mrs. Jago finishes for her. She shakes her head. "Heaven forbid that the Lord will see fit to take any more Jagos yet awhile, and even if he does"—she pats her hips—"I've taken comfort from my food since Henry Jago was called, so I'd never fit the thing now."

And then Munro is there, padding in from the back door, his face smeared with grime: sweat wiped with a soiled hand.

"What's to do?" he asks, seeing the women huddled together.

"Hold it up again," Mrs. Jago says, dodging behind Claira to draw the dress close about Claira's waist. She turns Claira to face Munro, to give him the full effect and Claira sees his lips part as he looks at her draped with the silken thing. His eyes widen and she blushes and turns her head to one side, holding the dress to her shoulders and wishing she could drop it and she would, but Mrs. Jago's grasp is so firm and Claira doesn't want to let her down, only—for pity's sake—where is she to put her eyes?

"What do you think?" Mrs. Jago asks, hearing no comment and popping her head out from behind Claira; the ventriloquist or puppeteer. "What do you think?"

Munro nods his head.

"Her father would have been proud of her, I'm sure."

"So he would," Mrs. Jago says, releasing Claira at last. "Would you get the sewing box from the parlor?" she asks, smiling as Claira turns. "There's scissors and needle and thread."

Seven

Stir linseed oil into viscous black paint. Wipe fingers on the oily rag, smeared with color from the cleaning of brushes.

More work yet to do on the figure, the fabric, the long mourning black. Bramley's palette knife pushes and flattens; mixing paint. Push and flatten. Hands work while the eye takes in. All right at the edge where chrysanthemums lie, but sketchy still where the folds are near the feet. Good, where the light falls and there, where the stitch pulls, no need to bring her back, then: the dress, left for him. But there's the trouble: where the fabric lies on the floor.

Deep breath and slow the breathing.

This brush?

No, narrower.

He takes another from the jug.

Better.

Flex the bristles. Load a little paint.

This area first. Then work down the flow of it.

Reach out. There then. Brush on canvas.

Eyes flick to black fabric. Over the tuck and crease of it.

Work deep, the tuck and flow and crease of it.

Eight

The patch of sunlight grows dimmer and longer on the table. Claire moves so her hands are again within it, squinting as she oversews the end of the thread.

If he left Surrey at two . . .

She snips another length of cotton from the reel.

. . . and it's five or six hours' drive . . .

She's lost the needle a moment—there it is.

. . . then he'd expect to get here at about eight.

She picks the needle up. Threads it.

Of course, he may have been delayed leaving and *he'd want to stop for something to eat . . .*

She knots the end of the cotton and the needle glides through fabric again.

. . . so add another hour at least.

She glances at the clock.

Ten to ten. He'll probably be home any minute.

It's getting uncomfortable, focusing on the stitches. She reaches out and turns on the lamp, a little promise broken with the flick of a switch: he said he'd be home well before dark.

Traffic's probably bad.

She wonders what Howard will think of her new purchase. It keeps very good time, she reflects, checking it against her watch for the umpteenth time that day. And she loves the slow, measured tick . . . tock . . . and the color of the long wooden case: the rich tones that only aged wood attains. There's a danger Howard will think it ridiculous. Something nearly as tall as he is just to tell the time and you have to remember to wind the thing and then there's the ancient mechanism—whatever happens when it goes wrong? But he might like it. He might. It fits so well here.

She draws back to look at her stitches. They're still small and regular, so she'll keep going for now. The clock begins to strike the hour and she smiles to herself. It's a lovely, mellow tone. The floor upstairs creaks: old boards on old beams: Damien turning in his bed as the clock rings *eight . . . nine . . . ten . . .* The sound fades and she listens to hear if the chime has woken them. All's quiet, but she'd better turn it off overnight.

The little door is opened by a brass loop handle that falls flush with the facia when not in use. Inside she finds the lever the man showed her and slides it across. She hears a car on the lane, but it passes.

Well, all right, she laughs as the most recent of her drawings punches her in the eye; so they *are* getting stronger. The latest of this series, propped on the dresser, is again the sweep of fields, the rise of Blundle Hill. In the bottom corner this time, the running figure of a boy; arms wide in a gesture of defiance and pleasure, made tiny by landscape and the race of clouds. She laughs. Emma's right. The move here is turning her children into Tarzans.

She flicks through the pad. So many drawings already. Each one in some way more confident. Or perhaps just less subtle. And she thinks of the tutor she had on the foundation course. How good it would be to touch base.

Closing the sketchbook, she puts it in the drawer and goes back to the table, picking up the fabric. Then she gets up again. There's another work of art to visit.

The painting had been in the shop where she bought the clock, or rather, it had been in the storeroom and she had seen it when she put her head round the door to call the man to make her purchase. It had been stacked on its side with half a dozen other pictures, leaning one against another, behind furniture and cobwebbed to the wall.

"You've a lot more stock here," she had said to the man as he shuffled through.

"Want to look?"

"Yes."

In this room, the pretense at antique shop disappeared entirely. "House clearance mostly," the man said, at her neck. Ten in the morning and she could smell the whisky on his breath.

"I'd like to buy the clock," she said.

"Yes? Well it's a lovely piece."

Left alone while he took the clock to her car, Claire shifted vinyl and Formica to get to the paintings.

Just curious.

There was nothing she thought special, until the last and, having seen the last—an enchantment half guessed at through griminess—she felt she had to take the painting home.

Opening the study door, Claire steps quietly in, flicking on the inadequate light. It's a real mess, this picture. Quite large, she thinks again. Only just fit into the BMW and she'd had to clean the car out afterwards. And look at that tear in the canvas. Silly idea probably. Two hundred pounds' worth of a silly idea. Claire takes hold of the picture to turn it to the light and leans the painting at an angle against the wall, holding the eye of the young woman who, standing in a wood, is caught in a movement of turning. Even through the surface grime, her eyes chime out. The head is backlit through trees on a dipping horizon. The light filters, too, through the woman's mass of hair. Slanting light, from a setting sun. The burgundy dress flares with movement. There is something in her hand—a water pitcher, perhaps. It is here that the canvas is torn and birdshit has collected. Claire lets out breath she hadn't realized she had been holding. Imagine it. Birdshit. In the store, the painting had been beneath the beam where swallows nested under the tin roof. Perfect place to collect their muck. The frame is caked with it and the canvas would have gotten more if the other pictures hadn't been stacked in front. A real mess. Still, Howard can't be too cross. She'd spent her own money on it—the dwindling account from before she stopped working. She'll have to get the painting to a restorer to see what can be done. They might be able to identify the signature. There's a date, too, in the corner. 1887.

Moving closer, Claire takes the torn canvas and tries, gently, to straighten it, wary lest the thing might crack. Looking up, she finds painted eyes upon her.

In the kitchen, Claire sews on an hour or more, the needle going in on tick and out on tock, pull the thread through, tick . . . tock . . . The rhythm frees her mind to wander and the painting's image is before her and she wonders who put brush to canvas, who the artist's model was. The depth and darkness of eyes.

Nine

Claira's eyes widen to the evening dark. For company and spark, she throws more furze on the fire and watches it flame, briefly outshining the lamp at her elbow. Soot on the chimney catches light and glows, rippling. Armies on the march, her father used to say.

Altered now, the dress hangs by the chimney to air. Claira runs a finger down the black silk of its skirt, hears the fabric whisper.

But for her, the house is empty, the others gone to chapel. Munro, observing Claira's pallor, had said perhaps she should stay in the warm, although frail Eadie was determined to go. Before they left, Munro had opened the Bible on its table in the front parlor and told Claira that she might read in their absence. After they had gone, Claira wandered through to see which section he had put out for her and raised her eyebrows at his choice from Proverbs. *Who can find a virtuous woman?* Turning to inside the front cover, to the list of family names, she had been shocked to find her own name there, newly written in his sloping hand.

The crackle of the furze has died down, and the tick of the clock cuts back into the silence. Claira has never lived with a clock before and she crosses the room to inspect it.

Holding the lamp high, she sees the clock face has images etched onto it: fishing boats at the foot of St. Michael's Mount. There's a curved section at the top from behind which a painted full moon peeps. She sees it through the reflection of the lamp in the clock's glass front and through the reflection of her own pale moon of a face. Sometimes her eyes focus on one moon and sometimes on the other. The painted moon has a smile and wide eyes and her moon hasn't; for now.

Claira wonders if the real moon has risen and she goes through to the back door and then she does smile as she steps out under hundreds of stars, brilliant in a cloudless sky, too early for the moon. Orion strides. She draws her shawl more tightly against night air that's crisp with cold. No wind stirs. The babble of the brook in the valley sounds like voices. In her kennel, Jess fidgets and whines then, at Claira's footfall, there's the thump of her wagging tail on the boards.

Going back in to the lamp and firelight and their dull glow on stone and wood, she feels the strange weight of deserted rooms close about her and realizes she has never once in her twenty years been alone in a house. She paces round the kitchen, trying on the emptiness like a new dress, feeling it trail behind her. Then suddenly the tick of the clock sounds like another's footsteps, dogging her, and she spins round, heart thumping in the same moment that she chides herself for being ridiculous. But a decision's been made and she snatches the lamp from the table and runs from the room.

Shadows flail as she pushes aside darkness with the halo of light. Her footsteps echo on the attic stairs and she feels her body carve through colder air.

In the attic the fiddle takes a little time to tune. Claira closes her eyes. With selfless ritual, her body is poised round the instrument and she could cry for the joy of satiny wood in her hands, but that the notes are more important. Once the thing is tuned, she picks up the lamp and clatters down the stairs clutching the instrument to her. Where shall she start? Munro's room? No, no. The kitchen first. She races on down.

Drawing herself to her full height, Claira finds the clock is still the taller. She gathers her body taut and begins to play. And her father would be pleased, she knows, at the way she attacks the beginning; the pace and drive punchy from the first. She closes her eyes, feeling the wave of music bludgeon the timepiece, overlaying rhythm with rhythm, and she turns, sends the swell to lap round crockery lined in the dresser, to flow round black pans that hang, and the sound fills the room to overflow, seeping into the larder and the cheeses on the shelf. And she plays in the fireplace and her music's alight now, rising up through the chimney and out into starry, still air, where it hangs. Then she stops and listens, grinning now at the room's charged crackle. She supposes the clock still ticks, but cannot hear it for the singing of her blood.

In the parlor next she feels music fly from her; the power and pulse of it surge over the Bible and whisk round portraits and furniture. She tilts back her head and laughs, and the sound is like surf on the wave of the reel as it crashes on the rocks of the hearth, sending up rainbow spray in the light. Light—she wants more and, putting aside the fiddle, she takes up a spill to give flame from her lamp to the candles on the mantelshelf. Then she's in the hall and on the stairs and even into Munro's room, lighting everything that will. The lamp in the dining room, the lamp in the hall, three wall candles behind glass at intervals on the stairs, the lamp by the bed in Munro's room and the candle by his mirror. There is nothing to light in the empty rooms, so, when she runs downstairs for the fiddle, she fetches the kitchen lamp too and brings it back up, placing it on the windowsill in the biggest empty room at the front of the house.

And so she plays on the landing, but falters this time and stops, shocked by the sense of all that space and the power of her notes to fill it. In the vibrant air the echo ricochets back to her, forceful and strong, so that she dares not begin again. She supposes Munro's room will be quieter, so she tries and finds her cadence there, the soft rug and furniture absorbing the sound. And she's a teenager again, playing at her parents' bedside, *Listen Daddy, listen. Is this right? Is it?* Perhaps one day she'll play to Munro here, only he won't know if it's right or not and she must rely on her own learning: fully fledged now.

Still playing, she turns and walks back to the landing, confronting the space. Though the resonance is huge, she drives it now.

She settles in the empty room, bearing the brunt of the music bounced back to her. Backing up the rhythm with her foot on the floorboards, she feels the house a drum: a vessel for her to resonate.

Eyes closed, she bathes in sound, floats in it, warm and vital. In its fullness it seems as if others play with her and she thinks of the times her father's brothers were traveling through. They would go to the inn at the crossroads to play and, once, she had been allowed to go too, although her mother was angry. But it had been wonderful, the fiddles and drum powering through the evening, though the rain beat never so hard against the window. Claira had hugged her knees by the fire, watching these men, her father and uncles, so strong and unshakable and she vowed one day *she* would play like that. And now she does, she supposes, as she makes a faultless link between one reel and the next, hearing the thing take off, the lilt somehow held delicately between her hands or more, her whole body, somehow her whole body is . . .

There's a footstep into the room and it makes her jump so hard, the bow flies from her hand, clattering to the bare floor. It's Munro and she laughs and swoops to pick up the fallen thing.

"You did make me jump," she says, amid the resonant slow fade. "I had no idea you were home. How long have you been there? Can I make a hot drink to warm you?"

He takes a step into the room, slowly. Looking round.

"What's this then?" he asks.

"I was playing," she says, quieter now.

"It isn't what I left you home for."

"I . . ."

"If I had known you had energy enough for this . . ." He steps round the room like a once-caught cat. "I don't know what to say," he comments. "My room"—he indicates with his hand—"all the lights. At first, as we came along the lane, we thought there must be a fire." He looks at her, sees that her eyes shine and her face is flushed though the room is cold. *Like a woman possessed.*

"Did you read the passage I left for you?"

"Yes."

"And?"

"My mother often read it to me."

"*Did* she!"

"Yes," and she begins to quote it. "*Who can find a virtuous woman? For her price is far above rubies. The heart of her husband doth safely trust in her so that he shall have no need of spoil. She will do him good and not evil all the days of her life. She seeketh wool, and flax, and worketh willingly with her hands.*"

Steadily the words chant from her tongue and he is amazed at the way they flow from her, her knowledge more thorough than his own.

"*She maketh fine linen and selleth it and delivereth girdles unto the merchant. Strength and honour are her clothing and she shall rejoice in time to come. She openeth her mouth with wisdom and in her tongue is the law of kindness.*"

Surely she'll stumble.

She does not, but feeling the strength of his scrutiny, she lowers her gaze, her voice becoming quieter as she recites.

"*Favour is deceitful and beauty is vain; but a woman that feareth the Lord, she shall be praised. Give her of the fruit of her hands and let her own works praise her in the gates.*"

Her eyes, as she finishes, are cast to the floor.

"Perhaps you had better come downstairs," he says, quietly.

She glances up to find him looking at the fiddle and she looks at it too, where it hangs in her hand, half hidden behind her skirts.

"I'll . . . I'll take this to my room," she says.

Leaving her the lamp to light her way to the attic, Munro douses other flames on his way downstairs.

Ten

Now, that *is* Howard's car, surely—the scrunch of tires on the drive and his engine stopping. Ten past eleven. Claire jumps up and fills the kettle, then sits down again, wishing she could feel nonchalant. She picks up the sewing.

He swings into the room, tall, dark-suited man of the world, and her tiredness is gone. He lets his briefcase thud to the floor, followed by his suitcase and an enormous *kite*.

"You've bought a *kite*!" she says, putting the sewing down.

"I have. Oh and you've bought a clock."

"I have. All the better to tell how late you are."

"Yes. Sorry about that."

"Has it been horrid?"

He stretches. "Oh, you know. Extra meetings scheduled and then the traffic was appalling."

"Hard luck. What do you think?"

"Sorry?"

"The clock."

He regards it. "Lovely," he says, stretching again. "Where'd you find it?"

"A little shop in a little village in the middle of nowhere. I took the children out to St. Ives and came across the place on the way back. I bought a painting, too."

"Oh?"

"It's in the study. Coffee?" she asks, reaching out to tuck an arm round his waist. He pats her hand briefly, then disengages himself, moving away from her as he leans down to pick up the kite.

"Mm. Coffee'd be lovely."

He pulls the kite from its packaging.

"Have a look at this," he says.

"It's *wonderful*," Claire says as the fabric spills from the polythene sleeve.

"Do you think they'll like it?"

"Oh yes, I'm sure they will."

The colors are gorgeous, pink and lilac and pale blue and it's obviously a thing of quality, well made of rip-proof fabric.

"I thought we could fly it at the weekend."

"That'd be fun, Howard," she says, taking down the French press. "So how was Surrey?"

"All right. The manager really *is* a bit of a pillock, but I think I managed to impress upon him that it's not *actually* his place to rewrite Clarendon's employment policy."

Howard takes his jacket off and puts it on the back of a chair.

"I said to my father when he hired him I thought he was trouble."

"How was your dad?"

"Pleased I went."

"He phoned last night."

"Really?"

"Yes. Seemed to think you were coming straight home after seeing him yesterday."

"*Really?* He *does* get his wires crossed these days. You knew not to expect me, didn't you?"

"Oh yes, I told him you had meetings today."

She places the coffee and mugs on the table and rests a hand on his shoulder where he's tense sometimes and begins to rub his neck, only he stands up, moving her away and picks up the material she's been working on and says, "How are the curtains coming on?"

"Okay."

He flounces the fabric out, his back to her, and it's as if he's hiding his face and he *is*, he *is* hiding his face.

"Howard, are you all *right*?" she asks, dropping a hand on his arm, wanting to turn him. It's then he explodes.

"For *Christ's* sake, Claire!"

And she gapes at his angry shrugging.

"Of *course* I'm all right."

He steps from her and paces down the room.

"What's the matter?" she asks.

"Nothing. I'm tired, that's all. It's been a *really* busy few days. I can't just come back here and . . ." He runs his hands through his hair. "And play happy-bloody-*families* from the minute I walk in the door."

"I'm sorry."

"I just need time to . . ." He flings his arms wide. "Time to *adjust*. All right?"

Turning from his pacing, he sees the hurt on her face and crosses back to her. He presses tight fists against his eyes.

"I'm sorry, I'm sorry," he says in his turn.

Taking her by the shoulders, he briefly brings her to him, then moves her away again. He exhales sharply.

"I'm tired," he says.

Taking his jacket from the back of the chair, he draws a line through the air in a gesture of finality.

"I think it's best if I have a shower and then go to bed."

Claire nods, then finds her voice. "Okay."

Sinking her weight onto a chair, she hears the sound of his feet on the stairs. She brings her knees under her chin, wrapping her arms round them.

He didn't drink his coffee.

Resting her head on her folded legs, gently she rocks in time with the ticking of the clock.

Eleven

Using the leather thong she's fixed to a hook in the wall, Claira hangs up the fiddle. The thought of facing Munro again slows her movement and she finds herself tidying round, delaying and before she knows it, she is tipping water from the ewer into the bowl, beginning the ritual for bed. She can always go down once she has washed her face, except that next she finds she wants to undress and sponge herself, making the most of being warm enough to bear the water's cold and the coldness of the air. Her belly contracts as the water runs, but she makes herself stretch tall in the frozen space, her body, warm still, soaped and lean. She grins.

There's a cocoon to be made of the little bed and she curls into it, blankets over her head, breathing in the warmth of her own breath. Her flesh smells good from washing; tingles from warm, on cold, on hot. As she cups her breasts in her hands, her body shivers once, before the warmth builds again and she feels her nipples tighten against her palms. Liking them like that, she fingers their taut buttoning, and feels her vulva clench as she catches deep breath. *William Penfold!* her mother's voice whispers from childhood, *You'll wake the children.* Her words bubble with giggles and—smothered—her father's deep laugh replies, and Claira doesn't want to listen, but how can she not, for the wall is thin as card and, but for it, she could reach out and touch them, they lie so close.

Flipping the blankets clear of her head, Claira leans to blow out the lamp and in that instant hears the door open at the bottom of the stairs. A footfall scuffs across the landing. She drops back into the bed to listen and a spring rings out protest and she hears her heart thump. There's light under her door. She pictures Munro, lamp in hand on the landing below, looking up. He wouldn't come upstairs though, would he? She holds her breath as the seconds slur. Then the light moves, then another footfall. Closer? No, away. Away. She hears the door shut quietly to.

In fetid sleep, there's the need to run and his legs won't work and they won't work! they won't! though he stabs the ground with all his effort, they scarcely move, they slide, yet it's vital—he knows it is and he lifts his head, slow as if drugged and it won't lift, but he slews his eyes enough to see and fire! That's it! For the love of God—the byre's alight! Brilliant in the darkness. Then he is beside it, among the scream and stench of burning cattle.

Not all alight?! Not all?!

He wrenches the gate, but cannot shift it and he looks to see where it sticks. He groans out. *Devilment!* A milker has her head thrust through, charred tongue out. He hears the fizz and pop of eyes. Under her deadweight, the burnt gate gives; releasing the thunder of burning cattle trampling.

Then, above the clamor, there's music from the house.

"Claira!"

He screws his head round to see flames blaze from the upstairs rooms, yet still the music comes. And then he sees it, in one window: black shadows flickering in the sickly orange light.

So that's where she is.

And then he is there too, on the stairs. Above the crackle and roar of fire her music pounds, as if she orchestrates the blaze, and he does move now, inexorably towards her, though his skin must scorch.

Quite naked in the flames she stands, golden, bright, her hair alight and the fiddle in her hands. She pauses from her playing and walks towards him, smiling. Her breasts sway at each step; at each step her thighs brush and part. Gasping for breath, he feels his phallus rise. She's almost upon him and he cannot breathe, the heat, he backs, her breasts will smother him, his penis surges; huge.

Crying out, Munro wakes, throwing blankets aside; sweating and soaked in the wet of his coming.

The minister is in need of more tea and Claira takes a cup from the trestle table and gives it to him. And he's obliged to her and, nodding and smiling his thanks, he holds the saucer and her gaze, whispering a few words, bringing their heads closer together.

The chapel hall is packed with mourners. Standing with Mary Bellham, Munro watches his wife through the throng and wonders, again, how this marriage will ever be consummated. Not as she takes herself to her room can he bring himself to intercept her; nor in the mornings when he sees her tousled still from sleep. And now this side of her: an elegant containment. Untouchable, it says. Of course, to be a marriage, it must be done. In the eyes of God, it must be. Perhaps when her grief is quite gone.

"She looks so charming," a florid-faced farmer's wife says, coming to stand by Munro. And she does, Munro thinks, as he sees Claira look demurely down. The dress is remarkable on her and her hair is brushed and braided today, tucked beneath the little black bonnet. There's color in her cheeks from walking and grace in her poise. "She really is a credit to you. Isn't she, Miss Bellham?"

"Indeed," Mary Bellham says, her mouth twitching briefly to a smile.

"Of course," the farmer's wife continues in a whisper, as if confidentially, " 'tis a shame we haven't seen her in chapel. But we will soon, I'm sure."

"Oh yes," Munro agrees, watching Claira, looking, for all the world, like the devoted follower taking comfort from her minister.

Claira's mother, Ellen, looks up as her daughter approaches. *You look well,* Ellen's eyes say, *you look handsome and I'm proud of you.*

You've been courageous, Claira's eyes return.

"Shall we go outside?"

Linking arms, mother and daughter walk towards the door.

There is warmth in the December sun and, in its blaze, Claira sees again that the sleeve of Ellen's mourning dress seems faded against her own black silk. She hugs her mother's arm the closer.

In the lane, horses stand, tied to the railing and dozing in the sun or reaching down to crop the short grass. The women pick their way between carriages, then pace together, as they did for an hour or more this morning from cottage to chapel, behind the coffin. Walking mourning; the singing of hymns, the footfalls had fitted, unbidden, the rhythm. And all the while the sun streamed down and Claira saw sweat on the necks of the bearers, till six took the places of six like clockwork, though her heart skipped a beat: *don't drop him.*

No one had gone to the mine this morning, and winding through steep streets, the procession had grown. Singing swelled as villagers came from their doors. And farmers had come, black-dressed: men her father sold horses to.

The two women stop by the grave. The soil has been heaped in already. The sun on their faces is warm and they think of his body beneath the weight of earth.

"I never thought to see his grave so soon," Ellen says.

Claira squeezes her mother's arm, then releases it as Ellen kneels. Newly silver hairs shine on the crown of her praying head. Claira rests fingers on her mother's shoulder. In silence, Ellen's lips move.

Then the feeling is there again, the one Claira has had all morning: the feeling of being watched. She looks across the chapel yard to see Munro at the gateway, looking. Looking as the mother prays and, noticeably, the daughter doesn't. Claira sighs, thinks of going over to him; turns again to find him gone.

At the foot of the hedgerow, a thrush scraps through leaves. Gray fieldfare eat from a flush of red berries.

"I wonder if you would call and have a word with my wife," Munro says to the minister, their boots scrunching the gravel path. "If you could find the time, it would be a great help to me."

"Mr. Richardson, it would be a pleasure. How is your wife settling down?"

"It's about just that. You'll remember we spoke before the wedding about how we felt my wife would surely return to attending chapel and come with me after our marriage."

The minister nods his agreement. "Yes, I remember."

"It doesn't seem to be happening."

"I see. This unfortunate business of her father's death . . ."

"Yes. Extraordinary timing and I have made allowances, but nonetheless, it seems . . ." Munro stops walking and looks at his companion. "It begins to seem as if she's being willful."

"I see."

"I came back from chapel the other evening—I had said she should stay at home, she seemed to be ailing. When I came back I found her . . . ." Munro glances about him. "I found her playing her fiddle at the top of the house as if the Devil himself were after her."

"Good Heavens!"

"It was strident enough to carry halfway down Blundle Lane." He flips gravel aside with his boot. "Then, when we came to Trethenna, near every window was lit and I could see her upstairs, the lamp on the windowsill and her shadow across the ceiling."

Through the December sun, a fleeting shaft of dream-image glows and is gone. Munro frowns, easing his shoulders.

"I thought if you could have a word with her about her attendance, she might see sense."

"Of course. I'll call early next week."

He smooths the sleeve of his coat.

"Is everything else all right?"

Munro glances at him.

"Oh, she works well," he says. "Works hard, in fact. She is learning the dairy from Mrs. Jago, who says she is very quick to pick it up and thorough. It's her not attending chapel I'm worried about. I would ask our minister from the Wesleyans, only as she did attend here, you know her ways and she would be more likely to listen to you."

The minister nods. "It is an advantage of being here for an extended term. It gives me a chance to get to know my flock. Though I have to say," he continues, pulling at his long whiskers, "she has not been seen in chapel these past two or three years now. Of course, her mother never misses, nor her brothers and sisters."

"But the father never came?"

The minister looks at him.

"The christening of his children and the burial of one."

"Not other than that?"

"Never."

"However did they sort it between them?"

"I cannot answer you, only to say that it's not something Mrs. Penfold has ever troubled me with. The opposite in fact."

"How do you mean?"

"I broached the subject with her, once. She—politely—made it clear it was not something I need concern myself with."

He gives Munro a brief smile.

"I respected her wishes. She is a good woman, and besides, I felt she had had enough trouble of the marriage from her own family."

"Not here again today, I see."

"Her parents? No. I don't suppose you saw them at the wedding either, did you?"

"No."

The minister catches Munro under the arm and they turn and walk back towards the chapel.

" 'Be ye not unequally yoked,' " he intones. "It's not just religion it applies to. Ellen Carrack's parents said they would disown her if she married William Penfold and they did. It must have been a big sacrifice for her."

He stops and looks at Munro.

"But that's history," he says. "What matters now is getting your wife back to chapel."

He touches Munro briefly on the arm.

"Don't worry. I'll come and visit her. We'll make it a matter for prayer."

Twelve

Leafing through pages, Frank Bramley finds again, the drawings of the face he did when snow was on the ground. Breath escapes him. Yes, yes, there is *much* more there than he has painted. The light coming up through the window from snow onto her face is really quite strong. And, the hair is better, too. More disheveled. More as if in the abandonment of grief. He should have referred to these drawings earlier. He thought he remembered them well enough, but he was wrong.

"You are too tidy today," Bramley says over the drumming of rain on the conservatory roof. Through cracked glass, water drips into a bucket. His model, standing to rest from her pose, has her back to him. She makes no answer. She gazes out of the windows, her shoulders hunched in protest at the cold. She should have come yesterday. Yesterday was sun and—with yards of precious canvas spread outside in approximation of snow—he had managed to create something like the direction of light he wanted. Only, being the Sabbath, she would not come, leaving him to check details of light on the window frames and the plants, in place now. He clicks his tongue. Rain and Methodists. Cornwall is cursed with them and this week he suffers both.

At last she turns. She does look cold. He holds the drawing out to her.

"If you could loosen your hair," he says.

So she sits in position, unpinning her hair, messing it a little with her fingers. But the light is useless. He thinks of sending her home and working just from the drawings, but really, the day is too dark even for that. He sighs out.

"It would seem God is not willing for us to work on this today," he says, reaching into his pocket for coins for her.

Once they are in her hand she is through the door and gone.

"We'll try again tomorrow," he calls after her into the rain.

Thirteen

"I'm just about to set off from Truro and I wondered if you'd like to meet up on the coast somewhere. I know how you love the cliffs. I thought if you bring the kite, we could fly it. What do you think?" Howard asks on a phone line, local and crackling with static.

Gracefully, Claire accepts the peace offering.

"The children are just eating, but I expect they'd love to come in a little while."

"Good. Shall I see you in about an hour? That place we went to before on the north coast. Something Head."

"Gurnard's Head," Claire supplies.

The finger of land stretches out into the sea. In the distance thunder rumbles and the air crackles with the threat of rain, yet it's sunshine they walk in, slanting richly through the gunmetal gray.

"Can we fly the kite now?" Damien asks, turning from where he scampers ahead.

Claire sits in sunlight in long grass as Howard and the children go about the men's business of preparing the kite. Howard watches her watching him. It's good to exclude herself like this and to see him taking trouble with the children: even as penance. And she must do penance too. She's not sure what yet. Certainly she must make a point of not crowding him when he comes home from being away.

The children's voices reach her, raised with excitement at the kite's launching. Its pinks and purples chime against the sky's gray and the flash of white tail is like the lightning that streaks out to sea.

Fourteen

The fire is slow to stir into life. In her nightdress, Claira prods the ashes, shivering in the dimness. Walls recede into shadow and the gray dullness pressing on windows: the mizzle that passes for dawn. She thinks of her mother waking and of her father's body; buried. There has been rain overnight.

She turns her thoughts back to the fire and works the bellows once more. The turf glows then fades, too feeble for the furze to catch. Surely she'll not have to start afresh with the tinder? She pumps the bellows and pumps them, then steps back.

There's nothing to cry about.

Her fingers are gray ash, so she smears the tears with the back of her wrist.

It only needs a little patience.

She sets about making passages for air, gently with the poker: to kindle, not douse. The cold creeps up her legs. She hears cattle low in the byre. Jed must be there already, bringing feed to them. Munro will be down any minute then and she had hoped to have this finished and be back in her room.

Her strategy with the fire pays off and, as she hears his feet upon the stairs, a little flame leaps. She wraps the overgown more closely round her nightdress; draws, again, her wrist across her eyes. The furze catches and flares and she feels rather than hears him come into the kitchen and stop; seeing her there.

"You'll catch cold, woman," he says gently.

She nods, keeping her back to him, keeping down the tears. "I just wanted to rouse the fire first," she says, busying herself with lowering the kettle back over the heat.

He has to walk nearer in order to go out and she feels him hesitate behind her and she, too, stills. Not three feet in it. Tears battle her body tense. There would be such comfort to be had at his breast.

"We'll, the three of us, to chapel this morning," he says. It's almost a whisper.

She bends and half turns, picking up more furze from the little pile by her feet, making sure her hair tumbles about her face, but still he catches sight of the red round her eyes: she has been crying again. With compassion his hand moves; then stops.

"Will Jed not come with us?" she asks, her back once more to him. Her arms jar as she breaks stubborn furze.

"Samuel Grey calls for him Sundays."

"Ah."

He watches as she stacks fuel on the fire. She'll smother it, won't she? She looks heavenwards and for an instant he marvels to see her praying, then he shuffles at his stupidity.

She is not praying.

She is waiting for him to go.

"We need to leave at nine then."

"Right."

She's run out of things to do with her hands and she must find something or the tears will come and taking the lid from the kettle, she peers in to check water she already knows is there with vision, in any case, blurred.

"I'll have the trap round the front by five to."

"Right."

Going out to the grayness and cattle, he glances back as he closes the inner door. Through the isometric patterning on the glass, her pale form flickers as she flees the room.

The clock face says it's ten to nine. The clock glass says Claira's face is puffy, her eyes hardly visible in swollen surrounds, her skin scorched red with tears.

Don't fuss. It's all right. It'll be all right in a minute.

She walks across the kitchen, seeking cool corners now, waiting for the silk she wears again to work its magic. She fingers the filigree stitching at her breast, like a touchstone or talisman. It does not work. But then, the surprise is that it did work yesterday. Who'd have thought such a flimsy skin could contain this welt of grief? An image from childhood springs into her mind. Squirming rats in a hessian sack and her brother shouting, *Quickly! Drown them! Drown them before they get out!*

If only.

The dress simply *must* work. She knows the horse and jingle wait ready. Munro will be changed and downstairs soon. Then there's the little journey to the chapel and then all the faces. Strangers. She makes herself pace the room as if that might evoke the feeling of the day before.

The doorway tells of Aunt Eadie's approach: the slow tap of her cane on the flagstones, the creeping tide of her skirts. She emerges, raven black in Sunday best and Claira goes to help her to her chair.

"Thank you, dear. You're coming to chapel this morning, then. That'll be nice. Oh dear."

Their heads have come level and even Eadie's poor sight registers the change in Claira's countenance.

"Oh dear. It *is* a sad business. And him such a young man, all considered. Can I help in some way?"

"No, no. Thank you." Claira says, spinning away from her. Not sympathy, not that. Nothing guaranteed to open the floodgates more quickly. "I do not mean to be rude, it is just—"

Hearing Munro coming downstairs, she stops, turns to look out of the window. Images swim and she knows the battle's lost.

"All ready, then?" Munro asks, striding into the room.

There are moments of silence when Claira senses some little unspoken exchange takes place.

"I think perhaps . . ." Aunt Eadie says just as Claira turns to them and Munro's jaw drops at the red distortion of her face.

"I'm sorry," Claira pushes out, knowing it won't be long now before she is overtaken. Grappling to control her voice, she shrugs her shoulders and says as the tears flood, "I don't want to cry anymore."

She feels a laugh bubble up and her face twists in ugly grimace. They watch. Disabled.

"It is just . . ." she continues, gulping breath between each phrase now, "we did . . . everything we were . . . supposed to do . . . and it seems so . . ." She shrugs again, rubbing her fists across her eyes. "It is so . . ."

Throwing her hands away from her face, she gathers all her effort.

"I cannot believe . . . we will never . . . have him back."

That is it, she realizes. *That* is the thought which has skulked beneath the surface since waking. She will never see him, or speak to him, or hear his voice again. Ever.

As Munro watches, her arms twitch and he thinks she will fold them, and she does, for a second, before her hands continue the movement to her shoulders and her head comes forward, pushing her face into the crook of an arm. Slowly Munro unravels what he watches: his wife is trying to embrace herself. He steps towards her, only Eadie's nearer and struggling to get up from her chair and he finds his movement diverts itself to catching the old woman under the elbows; helping her to her feet. Two unsteady steps bring her near enough and Munro watches as Eadie reaches Claira, puts out frail arms to embrace her: doing his comforting for him.

Munro grips the back of the chair Eadie sat in. It scrapes across the floor.

"All right, dear, all right," the old woman croons. "You'd best stay home. P'raps go back to bed. Probably the best place for you."

And Munro watches as Eadie turns her about, gives her the handkerchief from her pocket and walks her unsteadily to the door.

Claira's descent into sleep is like flying or falling or like the way a bird glides only into nothingness, a dreamless, silent slide.

Fifteen

Such beautiful sleep. Claire surfaces from it slowly, coming by degrees to an awareness that it is the middle of the night, that her body is evenly warm and stretched out, luxuriously, across the bed.

Where's Howard?

Still clumsy with wakening, she reaches out to check; before the thought filters through that he's in London. She turns over: the pleasure of clean linen on naked skin and space to expand into.

The faint red glow from the clock beside the bed reads 3:42. The curtains are open and the window slightly ajar. The night reaches in, damp and mild and bringing with it, on a soft breeze, the low moan from the lighthouse. Fog. She can feel the dampness in the air that stirs about her face. She really ought to get up and close the window, but the foghorn calls again; a long, sad note that takes time to trail away and she finds herself sleepily listening, waiting for the next sounding, which comes, melancholic. Her body is utterly relaxed; her drowsy mind intent only on fixing the point at which the voice of the breeze is left without its sonorous overtone. There? Yes. The sound of air alone now, lazily sighing through sycamore trees outside the window. It does sound like a sighing, this flow of breeze through wet leaves. She listens for the lower note of the foghorn, but it does not come; only the resonance of a breathing darkness.

There *is* a breathing.

Her attention draws itself back into the room and she laughs quietly in recognition, reaches a hand out of bed and locates the soft fur of the cat, curled up on the chair. Quiet enough to hear a cat breathe. He lifts his head to her touch and begins purring, raucous through the silence of the night. Claire's lips form themselves into a smile. The cat in the bedroom. Howard would have a fit. She wonders how his time in London is going. He's been so tense lately.

She gets out of bed without turning on the light and begins to rescue her dressing gown from beneath the cat, then leaves it where it is, feeling her way to the bedroom door without it. As she's awake, she'll just go and check on the children.

In darkness she crosses the landing. From the depths of the dark stairwell a tangible calm reaches up to her belly. She stops; gives herself to it for a few seconds, then moves on, guiding herself to the children's bedroom by keeping one hand on the granite wall.

Damien is half out of bed as usual. She takes hold of his arm, which is hanging to the floor, crosses it over his chest and lifts him back into the center of the bed. Her face touches his warm body, picks up the healthful smell of him. She draws the duvet lightly back in place. Now Nathan. Her hands reach out in the darkness and lightly touch his sleeping form. The shoulder, the hip, the duvet clear of his face; he's fine.

Toeing LEGO aside with bare feet, she crosses to the window and leans on the frame, nosing out into the darkness. The moisture drifts in, cool on her face and shoulders and breasts. Poised there, she can hear Nathan's even breathing and, outside, the soft stirring of foggy air. She wonders how far the fog reaches. How far the tender blanket spreads.

She lingers, listening to drops of water dripping from fog-drenched leaves and to the plaintive sound of the foghorn. Such balm: it seems sacrilege to shut it out. But the breeze pushes in and the curtain that drapes itself against her thigh is languid with damp.

All right. All right.

Yielding to the voice of reason, she slides the casement closed.

Heart thumping now, Howard's breath comes in short gasps. Sweat lathers the small of his back. He jerks a foot behind to rid himself of the duvet, feels his belly slide on hers, his penis caught between them. He draws a sharp breath, feels the upward thrust of her hips and, pushed against him, the hardness of her nipples. He wants to laugh. Her urgent readiness, snared beneath him. He grunts out air—*Louisa, Louisa*—lifts his face to clear his mouth of her hair. Blood beats in his head.

She shifts beneath him, the heat of her seeking him. *For God's sake, Howard* hissed in his ear.

"Still then."

Though she's stretched already, he knees her thighs wider, shifts and locates her straightaway, thrusts easily in, easily, lifting her, ramming hard home and—hearing her cry out—drives on faster: gaining oblivion with the giving of seed. And release. Oblivion. Release.

Spent, he drops his whole weight on her, lying widthways across the bed.

As the pounding of his heart subsides, he hears laughter and raised voices filtering up from the darkened street and from the gutter, the clatter of a beer can; kicked. He opens his eyes and his vision is filled with red numerals—3:42—vivid then pale as the flash of red neon enters the room. Now vivid, now pale. Now vivid, now pale. His steadying breath chimes in with the timing.

Sixteen

The paint is as petals are. Creamy, white. Each petal to be laid down on canvas; all seen, or only part, to make a whole, rounded, beautiful flower head. The petals are as paint is. Creamy, white. Each one—Bramley touches fingers lightly on the head of the flower at his side—each one has a tensile resistance.

Drinking in detail from reality, he moves his brush from palette to canvas; looks up to scrutinize his last brush stroke.

Drink in detail from reality. Move brush from palette to canvas: scrutinize.

A different rhythm from the last few weeks: the snowscape, the arched frame of windows over, the figure, the fabric of her dress; his breathing rhythm different, too.

He pauses to change tone where petals curl into shadow, still stark against the black of her mourning garb.

Drink in detail from reality. Move brush from palette to canvas: scrutinize.

Essence of chrysanthemum.

Chry-san-the-mum.

Littered on the floor at her feet.

Littered on the ledge at her knees.

He works now on the one in her hand, the next to be braided into the chain.

Brush to petal-paint to canvas.

Seventeen

"I had no choice on Sunday, but to leave her at home. She was too troubled to go out. I offered that Eadie or I should stay too, but she wouldn't hear of it, said she would just go up to bed. I went upstairs when we got back from chapel and she was dead to the world. Slept six hours straight through, plus whatever she had the night before."

"There is God's merciful blessing in such sleep," the minister observes.

Munro nods. "I cannot help but wonder—"

Hearing her footsteps in the hall, he stops.

"I shall have a quick cup then leave you to it," Munro says beneath his breath, as the door opens and she comes in bringing a tray of tea things.

Claira's busy: calling on her mother's poise. The china *will* stay on the tray. She *will* walk with her head high. She *will* greet her husband's visitor with grace. She smiles a little at her own determination.

The Primitive Methodist minister polishes pince-nez and puts them back on his nose. She really has grown into a strikingly beautiful woman, he thinks—so his task will be simple. In order to remain beautiful, beautiful women know they must please. And this one in particular, hoisted as she has been from such lowly beginnings, will be especially keen to keep favor.

Claira's never seen anyone drink a cup of tea as fast as Munro, who then says he must just go and see to . . . to what? What was it he said? As he closes the door behind his haste, she hears the clink of the door latch dropping home. Metallic.

Munro's in the kitchen garden when, fifteen minutes later, Claira comes to him. He had been deep in his own thoughts and her presence is sudden and the first thing he's aware of is that the little garden, gray on this gray day, is changed and made colorful, for all her black garb. He looks up and his heart quickens its beat.

"The minister is about to leave," she says, sliding her eyes away from him.

"Oh, I'll come back in," Munro says, throwing weeds he has pulled onto the compost heap in the corner. "You have done wonders tidying up out here," he adds.

She doesn't reply and, walking beside her as they cross back towards the house, he notices her gait is different. What is it? Her steps are faster, more jarring and her arms are folded. And then he has the chance to observe it at slightly more of a distance because, instead of continuing with him, she takes the turn in the path towards the yard.

"Are you not coming back in?"

She halts and throws a glance at him. No—it's *not* a glance, it's a *glare*. His wife has glared at him. Anger.

"Thank you. No," she says. "I've seen enough of the minister for one day."

"Ah," he nods. "Did you not like what he had to say?"

"You knew, then, that he had something to say?"

For a second Munro hesitates, shifts his weight from one foot to the other before the conviction of the rightness of his action comes to his rescue.

"I have been concerned for you."

"And what has *that* to do with the minister?"

She accompanies the word "minister" with the throw of a hand towards the house and he sees the color has risen in her cheeks before she turns on her heel and begins to walk away from him. Her skirts rustle with her anger and he finds himself wanting to laugh at this fire contained in such a tender frame.

She turns again to face him.

"Perhaps," she says, pacing backwards away from him, "you could try talking to *me* next time."

"All right," he calls, feeling his heart beating harder now, "perhaps next time I will. In the meantime, it's the minister's job to be concerned for your soul."

Her eyes widen.

"My *soul* is my own business, thank you."

"It's my business *too*," he retorts, feeling the heat in his face, "and I'll not have you idling at home when by rights you should be at chapel."

She stops her movement to stare at him.

"I went to chapel long enough to know I do not care for it."

"You do not *care* for it? You will *do* as you are told."

"You are *not* my father!"

"No!" he roars. "I am your *husband*!"

For a second she glares at him, the next she's gone; wheeled round and running to the footpath, flying up and over the stile then on up the hill. Through the gray he sees her shoulders bobbing and the flare of her hair.

For a time there is the surge of righteousness, pumping hot through her veins and the solace of the strength of her body as she runs up Blundle Hill, heart thumping, lungs drawing deep the moist air. The minister's words echo in her head. *Self-possession is the ruin of many of us. To be possessed of the Devil is a misfortune and to be pitied, but possessed of ourselves* . . . his neat mouth had formed a silent "o." She stops to spit him out. As she runs through moist air, her skin makes moisture too, till there seems such a narrow divide between the mist and her. Perhaps she will simply meld into mizzled air; be free of her body and of men. Perfect.

That Munro should have brought the minister in. Colluded with him. Contrived this little trap. On reaching the rocky outcrop, she wheels round to face the direction in which she knows Trethenna lies.

"How *dare* you?" she flings from the height of the hill.

And the fog wraps round her words and her.

She thinks of going home—to her mother's home—the six miles nothing to her. But even as her feet find their way, she knows she cannot go back there now and she turns to follow the stream down, through the wooded valley.

The dip in the landscape envelops her, folds her in undergrowth, soft beneath fog-heavy breeze; the freshness of ivy and lichen, drenched. Her dress drenched. She feels strong, but all the time cooling and growing in the certainty of having to return. She loses track of time, only knowing from her stomach she has missed food at midday and then from the darkening air that it is sundown. Her body shivers. The humiliation of having to go home.

A lantern hangs high in the stable door where Jed and Munro bed down the horses. From the dark perimeter of the yard, Claira wonders if she might be able to reach the house unseen, but her movements alert the dogs, who bark and circle her, unnerved by her silent approach from this angle, in this darkness, at this hour. She knows two of the dogs can be trusted, but the walleyed third is frantic and threatening and she stills herself, suffering him to come to her, thrusting his muzzle at her skirts, while she holds her breath; waiting to see if it's his teeth she'll feel next.

The men stop shaking out straw and peer out from the circle of lamplight and then Munro steps forward as he picks out her white face floating in the darkness.

Jed busies himself.

With a word, Munro calls his dogs to him. He looks at her, her eyes wide, hair wet and sticking to her head. As his own eyes adjust to the dark, he sees her dress is wet through, the hem heavy with muck.

"There is soup in the pot," he says and she gathers her skirts and her dignity, muddied, and walks by him and on to the house.

There's warmth now, in her feet. Hot food in her belly. Dry clothes on her back. Her gaze, unfocused, is filled with the cream of the attic lit by her candle. Through the stillness, there's an awareness of a minute movement at the edge of her vision. She takes the trouble to bring her sight back to her service long enough to comprehend that the movement belongs to a spider, anchoring its web in a groove of the paneling, before she lets her gaze again slide. All the while, her hands and ears work through their ritual, checking together, the violin's tuning.

The bow next, picked up from beside her on the bed, is tensioned with no change to her gaze. She brings the violin to her shoulder, interrupts the movement to briefly nudge her face against the silken wood of its belly, before nestling the instrument home.

A note then. Play it.

And she does, one note in the dim light, then she stops, listening to the way the sound carves into silence. She wonders if Munro will hear. At the edge of her consciousness an awareness forms that she has to learn not to care if he does.

She takes a deep breath, then pushes out three long, slow notes and hears them flow across the floor, lap at the walls and door and roll back again, back. There's a melody asking her to be played. She has part of it in her head—the rise and slow push of it. Half a dozen notes. What is it? She plays them. Oh yes, of course. The tune her father composed and named "The First William" after his son who had died in infancy. She had listened to the rawness of it as her father pieced the thing together, then heard it grow to something solid and beautiful. Claira had been shy to ask if she could learn it, but her father taught her, gladly.

Calmly, and with conviction now, her fingers seek the notes; firmly, finely, the bow makes them sound.

Through the floor of the attic, a little of Claira's music seeps and from beneath the attic door it flows gently out and down where it meets a pocket of Munro's discontent, loitering on the dark stairs. Saddening and stale, these remnants are no match for this wave of sound, which simply overwhelms them, effortlessly dousing embers, before flowing on down the main stairs, where it meets Munro himself on his way to bed. Weary, his eyes are downcast, watching his feet by the light of the lamp in his hand. Then his head jerks heavenwards. It is his wife; playing the violin. To hear the better, he stops on the stairs and, lifting his lamp, he peers through the darkness as if the sound from above might somehow be visible or as if he might see her. Foolish. He lowers the lamp and listens, letting the anthem wash over him. If this is the voice of the Devil, then he speaks with a calming—no, Heavenly, actually; Munro makes himself face it—a *Heavenly* tone.

He wonders what it sounds like in the attic and he pictures her there, the soft light, the room full of her music. Perhaps her hair is dry now, falling down her back. Perhaps as she plays she has her eyes closed. The lashes on her cheek. And if he went to her? His mouth tightens itself. All would be broken. He cannot. Still he listens. And, as he listens, the piece ends, a long, low sonorous note and Munro, transfixed as the silence floods back in, catches himself hoping there will be more. There is not.

Slowly, he takes himself to his room.

At first light, Claira stands in the hall, outside the kitchen door, hesitating at the sound of Munro inside. She can hear the soft scrape of his feet on the flagstones and the clink as he puts the lid on the kettle.

She has taken her time dressing. Partly to put off this moment and partly following some instinct to guard herself. Her hair is braided, tight and close to her head. As her mourning garb still hangs by the chimney where she left it to dry, she has put on an old dress and buttoned the high-necked garment all the way to the collar. She has grown since she made it, so the sleeves are too short and she stands in the doorway, now, tugging at her cuffs, trying to cover the exposure of her wrists.

She starts abruptly as the sound of Munro's feet draws near the door. Her hand darts towards the door handle. She mustn't be found dallying in the hall. Her heart thumps hard, but his feet pass by and on into the larder. She thinks of turning and going out of the front door and would, but for the realization she could only repeat yesterday's lesson.

Claira grasps the door handle and enters the kitchen as Munro comes out of the larder. He has not heard her arrival and jumps in surprise and she jumps too, the timing of her entry having brought her into sudden and too close proximity, so that he moves away a step and backs into the doorjamb, catching his elbow on the metal latch. He stifles his cry, not wanting to reveal himself hurt and she averts her gaze to the floor and hurries to the fire, dropping to her knees to tend it, only he has done it already, so she must scurry to find herself other business that will let her keep her back to him while he busies himself with the breakfast things, so she can't do *that* and what *next* then?

The chicken bucket. *That* would do it!

As a drowning man grabs rope, she seizes the thing and heads for the back door.

The first few minutes of the day gotten through.

Eighteen

The second outbuilding is crammed full to the door. Peering in through gloom, Claire leans against the door frame and sighs. More junk. Odd lengths of timber and old tools and what looks like old leather work and a couple of car tires and, there, some kind of metal framework she can't identify. Rusty. Filthy. And isn't that a bicycle?

Sickly, but tough-looking brambles have forced their way in. They reach through the broken window and through gaps between the roof and the walls, binding the stuff together. Excellent shelter for rats. Behind the debris, she can see the curve of what could be a chair's back. It's not a rocking chair, is it? She bobs down to get a better view, but other things block the way. She'll say it is for now. A rocking chair. Something of interest to work towards.

"Wherever shall we begin?" she asks Nathan as the boy runs up.

She tugs at the nearest planks of wood. Rotten edges come to pieces in her hands. Gathering fragments, she takes them to the bonfire she has lit. Determined to help, Nathan trails her, his hands full of the decaying crumbs.

"Mind you don't get splinters, Nath. Put your gloves on, like Mummy has."

Returning to the outbuilding, Claire pulls out a hoe, its edge eroded with use. She stops and takes off a glove to feel properly the hoe's wooden handle. Dryness and dankness have opened wide the grain. She runs her fingers along the smoothness and wonders about the hands that wore down the wood: whose hands they were, which summers they worked.

She takes the hoe and the plank and places them on the fire, watching the way the flames lick round.

"Won't it be full of worm?" Howard asks on the phone from London. "Rotten, too, I shouldn't wonder."

"Not if it's made of hardwood, will it?"

"I don't think rocking chairs *were* ever made of hardwood, were they?"

"I don't know. I assumed this one must be to have survived. It looks quite unusual. I think the rockers are on a kind of platform and then there's been some upholstery, too—a center panel on the chair back."

"Oh well. If it keeps you happy."

"Howard, I'm trying to sort things out."

"What did you say?" Howard asks over crackle.

"I said, I'm trying to sort things out. Tidy up a bit. I thought you'd be pleased."

"Yes, of course I am. How are the children?"

"Oh, they're fine. I'm sorry if you think getting the chair out is a waste of time."

"I *don't*, Claire. How's Nathan getting on at playschool?"

"Fine. He's been such a brave little boy—meeting all the new children. He came home with paint in his hair yesterday."

"Oh dear."

"Some child had decided to extend their artwork. We had a few tears when I arrived, so we went and spoke to the teacher about it."

"Hadn't she noticed?"

"No."

"That's not very impressive."

"Too busy, I suppose. Anyway, we sorted it out and there's been no problem since. He couldn't wait to get out of the house this morning. Damien has been saying he needs a computer at home because he can't stay on the one at school for long enough. The school has been really helpful with his reading."

"Good."

"He has a new friend now called Josh. They seem to go everywhere together."

"Good"

"Will you be late home on Friday?"

"I'm afraid I'm not sure I can make it on Friday at all."

"Oh, not again!"

"Meetings, I'm afraid. Saturday, too. And it hardly seems worth coming all that way for just Sunday, so I'll probably spend the day with Mother and Father."

Claire traces a finger along beading at the edge of the clock case. It's nicely rounded. Fits gently under the fingernail. Runs the length of the thing. On both sides.

"Claire?"

"Yes."

"I thought you'd gone."

"No."

She loves the noise it makes. Such a measured, deep, tick . . . tock . . .

"Cheer up," Howard says. "We knew it would have to be like this for a while. And you were the one so keen to move sooner rather than later."

"We didn't say it would be weekends, too."

"It's not for long, Claire."

It takes her two days to reach the rocking chair. As she nears her goal, Claire begins to slow down. Catching ever closer glimpses of the chair's pocked brokenness she works on, her face turned to the floor. Her hands at last reach the chair and she drags it out into the sunshine, bumping it across stony ground. Two struts in the chair's back are broken, the pieces missing. Upholstery on the seat and down the center panel is well rotted and—home to earwigs—the remains of the stuffing stink. Damp has loosened wooden joints and there's a history written in varnish and paint. Pink, bile green, cream, yellow, black. And Howard was right, there is woodworm. Futile exercise. The thing is clearly past it.

Arrested now, she stands in the yard. Covered in dirt and cobwebs, she stares at the chair, or rather stares past it. Seeing nothing present, she battles against this minor defeat: the hole in the dam through which the sense of a larger futility threatens to burst. Sun shines on her and the child who plays at her feet. A breeze moves down the valley and into the yard, fans the flames of the bonfire, chases the smoke as it rises, ruffles the hair on the heads of mother and child, offers the blond in it up to the sun. Claire does not stir. Only tears begin to brim. Furious, she jams a fist across her eyes, smears the muck and tears down her face. Determined not to let Nathan see, she fights to smother this silly distress.

Of course it's reasonable of Howard to stay in London.

Of course, it is.

Standing next to the chair, arms wrapped round herself, gently, from foot to foot, she rocks.

In the vastness of the skies, a buzzard circles Blundle Hill, sees and dismisses the woman and child: specks in the largeness of landscape.

Nineteen

It's a Thursday evening, but Jed is in Sunday best when he calls. Eadie and Munro are so dressed too, as is their custom for chapel on Thursday and Tuesday evenings. Claira is in the attic room, but Munro takes it as a good sign this time, for—as he was changing, he could hear her movements on the floor above him—perhaps she was changing too. She has seen sense then. She is coming with them.

The clock strikes half past.

Munro fidgets then paces the floor.

"Time we should be gone," Eadie says from her chair by the fire. The tick of the clock orchestrates silence: . . . tick . . . tock . . . tick . . . tock . . .

Still the three wait.

Aunt Eadie brushes unseen specks from her chapel black.

Jed gives himself to the Testament he pulls from his pocket.

The sound comes of Claira's feet on the stairs and then she is with them, dressed again in mourning garb. She walks with measured pace and her head held high, but instead of going to the door, she moves towards the spinning wheel in the corner. Seating herself at the little stool, she reaches into the basket to pull out a handful of the fleece, then, unhooking the combs from where they hang at the basket's rim, methodically, and with her back erect, she begins to tease out the wool.

Muscles at the side of Munro's face twitch and he hears his

breath gather itself into a snort. This, then, is her idea of compromise. She will not idle her time at home. Here she is for all to see, calmly and efficiently going about her work. It is simply that she will not come to chapel.

Munro helps Aunt Eadie to her feet.

Without a word the three depart.

As they leave and when they have gone, Claira does not falter, but continues her work, combing the wool until there is a little pile of it. Then she begins to spin it, her hands drawing the fineness out. And still she does not falter, even as a tear runs down and splashes, ignored, to her breast. Her countenance is calm. She will spin and comb and wind the wool. She *will*. And she does for the two and a half hours they are gone. And when Munro and Aunt Eadie return, the balls of wool are there on the little table next to where Claira still sits. Evidence of her industry.

There are many such tasks in a farmhouse kitchen that can be accomplished in such a span of time with outcome that is measurable in produce. New socks can be knitted and old socks darned, rabbits can be skinned and gutted, chickens plucked, old linen can be charred for tinder, torn shirts mended, buttons sewn on, smocks can be sewn, clothes can be ironed, eggs boiled and pickled. The list is endless and Claira kept adding to it. Work to keep her away from chapel. And if, from time to time, her fingers flew through their work, she would let herself go to the attic and bring down her fiddle to the empty room and play, but watchfully now, one eye on the lane for the first sign of their return.

Sundays were more difficult. Freedom bought with industry during the week was not an acceptable regime for the Sabbath. Sometimes Claira sat herself at the parlor Bible, she would—after all—*read* the Bible, though much of it she was familiar with already. Sometimes, too, she would wear the black silk—a mark of respect, but no, the tilt of her head answered Munro's unspoken question, she had no intention of going to chapel. Every time before he left for worship there would be this silent exchange, he would seek her out, his mouth tight as his eyes demanded to know her intention and she would return his gaze with steadfast calm.

I am remaining here.

The lengthening days helped her cause, for Sabbath or not, lambs will be born and ewes must be watched and it is not such great work to watch through chapel hours. And despite himself Munro was grateful for her vigilance, her quickness in clearing suffocating membrane, her deftness in pushing heads back in, finding legs to come first. And then there is calving. Cows, too, must be watched.

He was grateful. And moved.

In spring sunlight he had come upon her with orphaned lambs in the orchard when they scarcely had any need to be further tended. He had been drawn there by her singing and had approached unseen to find her brushing out her wet hair to dry in the sunshine, singing to herself and stopping to call to the lambs as they rushed and gamboled and mounted the fallen tree trunk, then ran to her, surrogate mother, so that she had to push them away and stand or be overwhelmed, laughing and shaking out her hair in the sun. Lithe and slender she stood. An innocent he named her then and uttered a prayer of thanks to God that he could watch her from his hiding place and feel himself moved, not roused.

A stable limbo, then.

Chapel-less, sexless.

It could almost have been all right.

"She can't be *made* to come here, that's for sure."

"Why ever not?"

"What's 'e to do, drag 'er screamin'?"

"Yes. If there's nothing else for it. She should be ashamed. Man like that. She should be proud to be with 'en."

"Why don't she come then?"

Shoulders are shrugged.

"Who can say, staying alone like that. Queer, I call it."

"I've heard it's playin' 'er fiddle she does when 'e's away."

"Just like her father—no mistakin'."

" 'E was a good man though."

"Maybe was, maybe wasn't. 'E never darkened the chapel door neither."

"You'd think Munro'd make her."

"Maybe he ent man enough to."

"How d'you mean?"

A nose is scratched, a voice is lowered. Heads come nearer.

" 'Tis said she's sleepin' in the attic still."

"No!"

"What! Not bedded after all this time?!"

"Ssshhh!"

"Who's saying she is, then?"

"I can't tell."

" 'Tis tittle-tattle then."

" 'Tisn't."

"*Who* then?"

A voice is lowered further.

"Molly that helps to milk went upstairs to look and, finding nothing of Claira's in his bedroom, took off up the attic stairs and—sure enough—all her things is up there."

Breath is drawn in.

"Well I never."

"She 'ad no business poking and prying."

"Business or no don't alter the fact of it."

"Ssshhh!" says one, for up the center aisle the subject of their discussion walks and from their glances, Munro knows it's he who is talked about and the substance of their gossip is an easy guess.

Helping Aunt Eadie from her pew, Mary Bellham also notes the women's talk. For weeks now she has noted it. At first it had been simple to rise in unspoken indignation. Now, she's not so sure. She feels there is some truth in her own growing notion that it should be Munro's wife who helps Aunt Eadie down the aisle, not Mary Bellham, spinster of the parish. For years she has done it. Her illness that coincided with the news of Munro's forthcoming marriage had been simply that. Coincidence. And she *is* better now. *Quite* recovered.

The women's eyes are on her. Not that she cares a jot for their opinion, she thinks as she takes Eadie's hand and tucks it into the crook of Munro's arm.

"I just need a word with the minister," she says by way of explanation before walking off.

Twenty

"Good heavens," the little man says, peering over half-moon glasses. "Do you know what it is you have here?"

"A wreck of a painting?"

"No, no. Not a wreck. No. A little worse for wear, certainly, but—unless I'm much mistaken . . ." He moves the angle lamp so that it shines more directly on the corner of the painting. "Certainly all the signs are . . . Unless I'm mistaken . . ."

Claire watches as he inspects the canvas. "Can it be restored?"

"Restored?" He looks at her. His glasses and bald pate catching the light. "Yes. Nearly all paintings can be restored with differing degrees of success. This might cause something of a problem." He indicates the bird mess. "Nothing leeches color more." He straightens up. "You've no idea who the painting is by?" he asks.

Claire shakes her head.

"Well, I really don't think there can be any doubt about it. I was almost sure just from the image, but the signature—look at that." He indicates the lettering to her. "Elizabeth Armstrong, almost for sure."

Claire looks blankly at him.

"Not heard of her," he comments. "You will have heard of the Newlyn School painters, I expect?"

"Oh yes," Claire says. "Stanhope Forbes and—don't tell me—Bramley. Frank Bramley. I saw work of theirs in the Tate not so long before we moved down. They were based in Cornwall late last century, weren't they?"

"Among many others. Elizabeth Armstrong was one of the Newlyn School. She married Stanhope Forbes. This is one of hers almost certainly. If that's the case, this is a significant find."

Twenty-one

The vulval labia are moist and swollen, easing themselves open. Ebenezer moves round to peer; pushes his hat back to scratch his head.

"She couldn't be more ready," he says.

"Yes, yes," Munro says impatiently.

In a tight circle, he pushes the stallion away from the mare.

"I'll bring him up again. If we've no luck this time we'll call it a day."

"Per'aps he's gettin' too old."

"He never is," Munro retorts, walking the cob smartly away. "'Tis his first mare of the season that's all."

"The Good Lord help 'im with 'is last then!" Ebenezer chortles.

Munro chooses not to hear. The spring day is unexpectedly warm and he wipes a hand round the back of his neck, wishing he had left off his jacket.

Then Claira is there, the flutter of her skirts catches his eye. On her way to the henhouse, she carries a bucket of scraps and a basket to pick up eggs. That's all he needs: Claira as witness. He'll wait till she passes, but she stops by the gate and puts down her basket. He hears the bucket handle clank down.

"Come on, Munro. Let's not keep my mare dallyin' all day."

There's nothing else for it. Munro turns the cob and marches him towards the mare, but it's hopeless. The cob's penis, unsheathed, merely hangs by his thigh. He is clearly not about to perform.

"Ah well, we tried," Ebenezer says.

"I hope he isn't sickening for something. Perhaps try him another day."

"I don't know, Munro. I want this mare in foal the soonest. Don't really want to wait till she comes round again. Might have to take her to Samuel James's stallion."

Then Claira is with them and taking the cob's halter rope, which Munro relinquishes with a nod.

"He may as well go back in the stable."

Claira walks the cob away in a wide arc, slowly and talking to him and letting him stretch his neck and rubbing his crest with the heel of her hand, releasing bound muscle. She stops him and stands in front of him, his head lowered, and she works his crest more and behind his ears where it is hot beneath the halter she eases, talking. He shakes his head, rubs his face against her torso. The same size. His head and her torso. And she walks him on again, another wide arc, back to the mare whom he sniffs, who calls to him. And Claira seeks Ebenezer's eyes. *Ready?*

Thinking back, it was the lift that shocked Munro the most. As the cob mounted, Claira remained level with the mare's hindquarters and, as the stallion came down on the mare, in one smooth movement, Claira put out a hand, cupping the shaft of the penis, raising it the last necessary inch or two, then removing herself from harm's way as the weight of the cob plunged forward. Smooth. Slick.

Ebenezer is all congratulations. Claira gives a brief smile, eyes downcast, then goes back to the gate and her bucket and basket while Munro catches up the cob.

An Innocent, he had named her.

"Well," says Ebenezer, pleased as Punch and thinking what a tale it will make, "she 'as 'er father's way with horses, no mistake."

Twenty-two

Claire rakes ashes together. Even now the bonfire is not quite out. Last night she had looked down from the attic, seen the red smolder still in the darkness and had come out beneath a sky teeming with stars to make sure the thing was safe.

Up before the children, in this early sun she sees how the patch of black has eaten into green. She works the rake. There's metal among cinders to sift out and discard.

"Hello," a voice calls and she jumps to see a man coming over the stile from the footpath into the yard. She half closes her eyes against light to see who it is; silhouetted. There's something familiar, but she can't quite . . .

"You're a brave woman," he calls. "No one has dared to tackle that outbuilding for decades and here's you . . ." He dips from light into the shadow of the building to peer in through the doorway and Claire can only gain an impression of him, tall, spare. "And here's you emptying the place so soon."

She sees movement as he ducks his head beneath the doorway, the raising of an arm to rest on the frame, the ducking out again. She glimpses trainers and long muscled calves: out jogging, then.

"It must have taken you ages," he says, walking towards her, out of shadow, but against the sun still. She sees his fluid gait; loose-limbed. And then she has it. The man in her drawing, coming out of the sun.

"Two days," Claire says, shielding her eyes.

Seeing her discomfort he sidesteps so that she, too, can quarter-turn. She sees he has dense white hair. He looks very fit.

"It must have been a lot of work." He smiles easily. "I'm Nick Franklin. I live at the first cottage down the lane. I've been meaning to drop by and say hello."

"I'm Claire," Claire says, shaking hands. "I recognize you, Nick. I have to confess I've drawn you already."

"*Have* you?"

"Yes."

"Oh, *that's* what you were doing—ferreting around in the dark the other evening."

"Ferreting around?! That was serious artistic endeavor, I'll have you know."

He rests eyes on hers, a second. "I'm very pleased to hear it," he says and she finds her heartbeat quicken and why should it do that and what does he mean—he's pleased to hear it—and she replays his phrase looking for irony only she doesn't find any and instead finds she is laughing. Audacious man.

"I *suppose* I could make you coffee."

He grins. "No. Thank you. I have to get ready for work. May I call again when there's more time?" he says, turning away already. "Oh, how was the rocking chair?" he asks, before she's had time to reply.

"The rocking chair? How did you know . . . ?"

"People have been meaning to dig it out for years. Rather a beauty from what we could see."

"Once, perhaps, but well past it."

"Really?"

"Yes. Lots of worm and bits missing and so many layers of paint."

"Yes, but all sortable. It's amazing what can be done. Do let me know if you need a hand restoring it. I've a friend who's just brilliant with that sort of thing."

Claire flicks the rake against charred ground.

"A little late for that, I'm afraid."

It takes a second for realization to filter through and even then, he must have it confirmed.

"You haven't put it on the *bonfire?*"

Claire flinches.

"I suppose it was *mine* to do with as I saw fit."

Across the sunlit air eyes lock. Claire raises her chin.

Slowly he nods, says quietly, "Yes. Yes, of course it was. Anyway, if there's anything I can help with, let me know, will you?"

"Thank you."

He is gone then, moving from her in a second: loose-limbed, loping, animalesque.

Twenty-three

They are like a sea of golden hands, these leaves that curl and froth at her feet. For days he has buried himself among them, tracing each tip and vein, learned to love their shadowy cupping, their knuckled rounding, their holding in and reaching out.

Drawing back, Bramley sees that they do the job he wants them to, in color and metaphor and season: gold against the black of her mourning dress, an empathetic sea, between vital green and winter snow.

Reaching for the rag, he cleans the paint from his brush.

It won't do. He is messing now. Adding little touches: the painting finished, not wanting to let go.

It has been a matter of love, being in it.

It must go, of course. And very soon. *Weaving a Chain of Grief*. To London and the critics. He takes a step back from it and nods his head. He thinks it will withstand both.

At the window again, the robin taps and flusters: fighting his own reflection.

Twenty-four

It does become easier—allowing herself time. It's true, she can't go physically far, has to tether her activity to within calling distance of the house and the sleeping children in it and—of course—it doesn't always work: Damien will wake, or Nathan needs to talk through his day again, or the weather makes painting outdoors impossible, or the light is dull. Even so, she's carving out time. And she is *painting* now. On one of the canvases she's bought. Ridiculous price. She'll have to make her own, she thinks, stretching back from her work and yawning.

Claire, this is not going well.

That's right. It isn't.

Perhaps you could stop watching yourself.

It's only because the materials are not familiar yet.

Taking a virgin palette knife, Claire scrapes away oil paint she has placed on canvas, wipes it off on a rag. Seeing what remains, she grimaces.

What a muddy mess.

Primordial swamp from which something extraordinary may emerge.

Hah.

Using turps she thins the swamp. Good, in any case to begin on colored ground.

Settle, now, settle. Give yourself to the landscape. Background, forget, ignore the process. Just do.

It's only when Nick has been through that she can. Another to add to her list of distractions: children, weather, light and Nick. Unbidden, her eye traces the path where it traverses the shoulder of Blundle Hill, every few moments seeking out the bobbing of *his* shoulder, the rounding of his head, emerging behind rising ground. There. There he is. A little later tonight. Her eyes burn to fix the mark of his limbs against landscape. Unbidden, her lips part as she watches his movement down the hill—jogging with such even pace over such uneven ground—like the flow of water he runs; there to where the path forks. He takes the turn and is lost to her.

Sighing out, she loads more paint onto her brush.

Twenty-five

Nathan screams as the train pulls in and the brunt of noise blasts through him. Claire laughs in the din and scoops him up, hugs his little body against her own to lend it weight.

"I said it would be loud," she calls, her lips brushing his ear. He clings to her, turning in her arms to watch the engine as it passes.

"It's all right, it won't leap off the rails. Come on, let's find your dad."

These days apart probably do them good, she thinks, her stride alive as she walks down the platform to meet him. In rays of light through the filigree of ironwork, scattered pigeons fly from her feet.

A man gets down from the train wearing Howard's clothes and Howard's face, only much older. He expects to take a taxi and does not look for a welcoming party and Claire sees the unguarded countenance, downcast as he steps from the carriage. He turns away towards the rear of the train and it is left to Claire to follow him along the platform. Wrestling with the shock of his round-shoulderedness, her own gait becomes less certain. She calls his name, but—dreamlike—the sound is lost.

The passengers flow past in the opposite direction and she supposes he must know of some other exit, but he reaches the guard's van and stops there, allowing her to catch him.

"Are you all right?"

He turns abruptly at the sound of her voice and the frown is replaced by a wry smile and he holds her eye a second.

"What are you doing here?" he asks. Nathan reaches out to him. Howard ruffles his hair.

"We came to meet you. Are you okay?"

The doors of the guard's van rattle and are opened from within. He looks away.

"Yes. Fine. I've been asleep on the train. Had a whisky soon after Plymouth and slept the rest of the way. Not ideal, in fact—I had some papers to go through."

"How did it go?"

"Okay," he says. "Good."

Claire puts Nathan down on the platform.

"Look, Nathan," Howard says. "I've brought something for your mother."

The guard, clattering parcels to the edge of the carriage, brings Howard's purchase from the back of the van. A rocking chair, bound for the journey in corrugated cardboard.

"Howard!"

"I know how sorry you were about the other one."

Claire blushes. Her folly in burning a restorable antique is something she has kept to herself.

"You weren't supposed to see this until it was home and unpackaged," Howard says, placing the chair down out of harm's way. "Which car did you come in?"

"Yours."

"We should be able to fit it in then."

"Howard, how kind of you to think of this."

He smiles briefly. "Don't be daft. Shall we go?"

When she brings the coffee through, Howard is standing, leaning against the edge of the window and staring out into the garden, one knee on the window seat.

Putting the mugs down on the table, she watches him draw deeply on his cigarette and thinks of the smoke curling inside him:

lethal caress. His tight mouth clamps the tip and he draws the poison down like a drowning man finding air: as if his life depends on it. She always feels it as a physical pain: watching him smoke. Suddenly she wants him in bed; wants to slide her hands over his breast as if she could dissipate this hurt he does himself. She crosses to where he stands and without dislodging him, tucks herself into the crook of his body and kisses him on the mouth. The sting of the cigarette's bitterness is on her tongue and from his breath comes the scent of a deeper harm.

"Come to bed," she says.

He drops an arm round her shoulders and, with his other hand, holds the cigarette away from her so it will not catch her clothes. He rests his head on hers and says quietly, "I've got work to do."

"Come to bed," she says and he feels himself stir. He moves to stub out the cigarette and, as he takes one last drag, his chest is brought close and she pushes her face against his warmth, shunting his shirt collar aside with her cheek.

She goes ahead of him, dumping her clothes on the bedroom chair before crossing to close the curtains. The late evening sun filters through and the room Howard enters is a dimly pink cocoon; his wife's body silhouetted against the rose light. He sees the outline of her full breasts, as she turns to pull the duvet back and, as she leans, the fall of her hair. He hangs back near the doorway and Claire steps towards him, holding out a hand to draw him closer, and his mind presents an image from the night before: Louisa reaching out to catch his arm in emphasis of some point or other and—in the equivocal instant Claire's hand touches him—he has to resist recoil; rounding the energy into an embrace; hiding his face in her neck.

"Claire. I'm really tired."

"I know. I just want you to come to bed and unwind," she says, her hands undoing his shirt buttons. "We don't have to make love if you're too tired. But I'm going to be *really* stubborn about one thing." Briefly she kisses the bridge of his nose. "I think you're working too hard and you need to stop for today."

Sliding the shirt from his shoulders, she tries not to notice the beauty of him and sits, instead, on the edge of the bed, flicking through the memory of the days he's been away; seeking detail that might detain him. Her hands undo the fastening of his trousers.

"I didn't tell you. I think the painting I bought may be by someone well known, after all."

"Yes?"

"I took it to a restorer who recognized the style and the signature, said I should take it to Lanes, the auctioneers who deal with stuff from the Newlyn School."

"Oh, good. Might it be worth something?"

"Could be once it's restored—oh—and Damien's school's starting a scheme where they send work home that's to be done with help from parents," she mutters.

She slips his trousers and underwear down. With childlike obedience, Howard steps from them.

"It'll only be three times a term. I forget what they call it. Integrated learning, or something like that." The curve of his breast is at eye level. She draws a quick breath. "I think it's a good idea, don't you?"

"Yes. I suppose so." Louisa fills his consciousness and he wonders Claire can't feel her presence leaching out of him. "Although I should have thought it the school's job to teach, not yours."

His skin feels drenched with her. He's showered twice since then, but he's still not sure the scent has gone and he brings his fingers to his face to catch the smell of them. He thinks it's just soap and perhaps an overlay of tobacco. He runs his hand through his hair.

"Oh, they're not really asking us to teach, just trying to keep the communication going between school and home."

She lies back onto the bed and lifts the duvet high and he crawls into the cavern she's made and feels it gentle round him.

"That's better," she says, lightly kissing his forehead. "That's better," and she slides farther up the bed until her breasts are level with his head and his face is drawn by their heavy warmth and his mind replays the thrust of Louisa's tight little tits. His chest tightens. The tension in his shoulders sharpens; knowing Claire's readiness and his own flaccidity, his hands at her waist where he might, now, draw her to him.

Claire eases her body gently from him; gently strokes the hair from his forehead.

"Ssssshh."

"I'm sorry, Claire." He shoves his head between her breasts.

"Ssssshh."

"I'm sorry."

"Howard. It doesn't matter."

His jagged breathing sounds like sobbing and she enfolds his head and rocks him.

"It's all right. It's all right."

From the children's bedroom, a high-pitched wail, "Mummy!" followed by distressed cries. Claire disentangles herself and grabs her dressing gown as she leaves the room.

In a pool of green and orange, Nathan, flushed with fever, has been sick in his bed.

Twenty-six

"Oh yes," Mrs. Jago says, "the Missionary meeting's a big occasion. 'Course, the prayer meeting and tea at Trethenna beforehand's a big occasion too. All three ministers'll be there. You've only met the one that married you. And then there'll be them that's invited from the circuit."

Thunder rumbles, nearer now, and she stops her plucking to glance over her shoulder at the gathering of gray clouds. By her skirts in sunlight, white feathers float and settle.

"I should think we'll just about get this done before the rain."

"And what am I to do?" Claira asks, stopping, to look at Mrs. Jago.

"Oh, there'll be plenty to do, these birds to be cooked and vegetables to be lifted and puddings to be made," Mrs. Jago replies, pulling feathers from the breast of the bird.

"No, no. I don't mean the getting ready. I mean—what am I to do at the prayer meeting?"

Mrs. Jago glances at her.

"As Munro's wife, there'll be plenty for you to do then," she says. "Serving food to the table's an honor and no mistake and there's many a woman in the parish would be pleased to be in your place."

Using her foot, she draws the sack of feathers nearer to her.

"Then there will be hymns to join us in"—she looks at Claira—"and prayer."

Claira looks down at the duck; dead and nearly naked on her

aproned lap. She holds the twisted head with one hand and pulls at the short stubborn feathers of the neck.

"I do pray," she says.

"Do you?"

"Yes. Just to a different God."

Mrs. Jago's hands falter, then resume their work. The hairs at the nape of her neck rise.

"Or at least," Claira continues, "it is probably exactly the same God, only he likes healthful places best. I never find him in chapels and black books."

"Claira!"

"But I do find him on moor tops and in valleys and by the brook down the lane and in wind and in rain and in sunshine. And music," she adds, glancing at her companion.

Mrs. Jago rises from her seat. Feathers fly and flurry about her. She puts the naked bird on the metal tray at her side.

"The Lord's hand is to be found in many things," she says, picking quickly at down stuck to her clothing. Then she adds, "I expect this is your father talking."

"No, it isn't," Claira replies, then thinks further and says, "Well, perhaps some of it is. He did say, when you have traveled a long way and seen several different religions, it's difficult to understand why one should be right and all the others wrong."

Mrs. Jago winces.

"Lord knows what Munro would say if he ever heard you speak like that. He's traveled far enough and never found reason to change his belief. On the contrary, he always said 'twas one of the things that kept him safe in foreign lands."

She stuffs feathers into the hessian sack. Loose ones chase and run from her hands.

"What goes on between husband and wife is none of my business," she continues, "but you've asked me a question, what should you do at the meeting, and I've given you my answer—you should rise to the honor bestowed on you."

She looks at Claira.

"And while I'm about it I'll say this, Claira Richardson. Your husband is a good man and it's cost him dear, your not comin' to chapel and I think it would do you no harm if you were to accompany him in future."

"And pray in chapel words I do not mean," Claira says quietly, looking up to where Mrs. Jago stands above her.

A heavy drop of rain lands on the back of Claira's hand, another on the duck's cold flesh, several more on the slab by the tray where they spread; soaking into and darkening the stone.

Twenty-seven

For a small village, it is quite a large hall and when Claire and Howard and the children arrive, there are fewer than twenty people in it. At the door, three teenage girls giggle in a huddle, casting only a cursory glance at the tickets Claire proffers.

"*Who* was it who sent us the tickets?" Howard asks again.

"Nick Franklin," Claire says. "He put them through the door the other day. He lives in one of the cottages down the lane."

Greenery drapes the sloping wooden ceiling beams and bales of hay form makeshift seating.

"Look, Damien. A castle," Claire says, pointing to a square enclosure of bales at the end of the hall, opposite the musicians.

Needing no second prompting, Damien throws himself across the bales, landing on his knees in shooting position with two other boys he knows from school. Claire recognizes the faces of the two women who must be the boys' mothers. They smile across at her and Claire thinks about going over to say hello, but she can see they're deep in conversation; perhaps later.

Nathan hangs behind Claire's skirts, kicking his toe against a raised knot in the wooden floor.

Claire leans down to lift him, to stop the sound in the echoing space.

"Do you want to bring him over here?" Howard says, moving to the bales.

"Look at the musical instruments, Nathan."

As the musicians tune up, they laugh at the pennywhistle player, who's demanding beer by knocking on the closed serving hatch of the kitchen, which tonight doubles as a bar.

"Go away," a voice calls from behind the screen. "We don't open for another ten minutes."

Nick's voice. Claire feels her face flush. Wishes, suddenly, they had stayed at home.

The pennywhistle player only knocks the harder and then Nick's hand appears round the door clasping a freshly poured pint, so that the other musicians protest favoritism and a fiddle player runs to open the hatch himself and there Nick is, then, shifting crates of bottled beer.

Pouring pints for the players, he sees Claire and smiles and—when he's finished—wanders over to meet Howard and the children, so that Claire finds herself introducing them. Howard and Nick. Nick and Howard. These men she has held separately in her head; meeting now.

"Kind of you to let us have tickets," Howard is saying, shaking hands.

"My pleasure," Nick says as he sits easily down, not on a bale, but on the floor, so that his head is level with Nathan's. Specks of dust fly in the shafts of evening sun as Nick pulls handfuls of hay from the bale; greenly gold in the light's rays. The hay's scent rises sweetly round them.

"So, how's Cornwall treating you, Howard?" Nick asks, beginning to weave the pieces of hay purposefully around one another.

"It's treating me well, although I haven't had time to see a great deal of it yet—apart from Falmouth and Gwendever Head."

"I hear you're planning a golf course out at Gwendever."

"A country club, in fact."

"We certainly don't have one of those around here," Nick comments, looking back down to his hay work as Nathan steps forward to see what he is doing. "You did well to get planning permission. Bit of a battle, wasn't it?"

Howard narrows his eyes. "Not especially," he says, measuring his words. "The planners were a little slow to catch on about the benefits of having a prestigious country club in the area. Missed the socioeconomic point for a time. They got there eventually."

Nick continues working the hay and Howard finds himself having to speak to the back of Nick's bowed head.

"Claire mentioned you called round the other day."

"Yes, just dropped in to say hello. How are you settling in?"

Nick looks up, addressing this last to Claire.

"Very well," she says. "I love the house."

Nick smiles gently.

"I've always thought Trethenna exceptional."

The hay in his hands is taking shape—crude, but recognizable as the head, neck and forelegs of a horse. When he has fashioned the body and hind legs, he fishes a large needle from its lodging inside the lining of his fleece and a reel of thick cotton from the pocket of his jeans. He threads the needle and quickly binds the ends of the horse's legs, forming hooves.

He nods towards the teenagers on the door. "I've been teaching those girls how to make these wretched things all day and I can't seem to stop," Nick says. "Fund-raising stall next Saturday. I'm beginning to feel like a TV presenter."

He laughs and becomes the ventriloquist, putting the horse in the crook of his arm.

"This is one I made earlier," the horse says and Nathan moves forward to take hold of it, so that Nick removes it from his reach.

"I've not quite finished—what's your name?"

"Nathan."

"I've not quite finished, Nathan. One more minute," he says, threading the tail through and Claire finds herself watching the beauty of his deft, long-fingered hands.

"I should have thought hay is something of a fire risk in here," Howard says.

"Definitely," Nick agrees. "That's why there's a total ban on smoking." He looks steadily up at Howard.

"Expecting many tonight?" Howard asks.

Damien, hot from playing with his friends, runs over to see what's going on. Nick looks up and smiles at him before replying.

"Oh yes. Give it another hour and this place will be packed."

"Really?" Howard says, his voice rising to ring round the hall's vacancy.

"This is Damien," Claire interjects, quickly.

Nick stops his activity and proffers Damien a hand. The boy looks at it and then, realizing what is required of him, shakes hands.

"Hello, Damien, I'm Nick."

"What are you doing?"

"Making a horse for your brother," Nick says, tucking in the last strands of hay before handing the toy to Nathan, who, shiny-eyed, whispers an unprompted thank-you.

"Shouldn't we pay you for it?" Claire asks.

"Thank you, but no."

"Can I have one?"

"Damien!"

"No. Not today," Nick says. "I've got to get back to the bar. You could however come and meet Sam. If you're lucky, he might let you play the bodhran—that's his drum. Would you like to do that?"

"Ye-ah!"

"Yes please, Damien," Claire corrects.

"Yes please," he repeats.

"Is that all right?" Nick asks Claire.

"Yes, of course. Thank you."

Picking up the remnants of hay from where he's been working, Nick gets to his feet. And Claire finds herself watching him again. His easy agility.

"Come on then, Damien," Nick says. "I do hope you enjoy the evening," he calls back over his shoulder; his hand ruffling the hair on Damien's head.

An hour later, the hall is packed and nearly everyone dances; the wooden floor vibrating to the rhythmic pounding of feet. The caller is good, patient and clear, and the band—three fiddlers, the bodhran and pennywhistle players and a rhythm-mandolinist— plays jigs and reels with a compelling cadence. Though she's only on apple juice, Claire feels intoxicated: the energy and drive.

"Won't you dance, Howard?"

"What about the children?"

"I could ask one of the mothers from Damien's school to keep an eye on them for a few minutes."

"No. You dance with Damien."

Claire hesitates.

"Go on."

Their set is chaos—a jumble of bodies in the wrong place at the wrong time, their only salvation the gallop when they join hands and charge down the room. There are three children in the group and the adults all take care to keep them on course, except that no one seems to know quite what the course should be. They throw back their heads and laugh at the uproar, haul each other back into place, the wrong place, in fact, and laughter halts them again. Claire's belly begins to ache with it as she muddles the Basket with the Star. In a blur of movement she catches sight of Howard's face as he watches from the sideline and immediately feels foolish, but hands take her, move her on. *Quickly! The gallop!* Damien laughs, eyes shining, cheeks flushed. Everyone changes partners once more and Claire dances with a farmer, rotund, high color and callused, rough hands. His arm round her waist, he spins her too quickly and the room spins with her as she's passed on again. Next a woman, thin-wristed, Claire's sure they've gone wrong, but the woman calls in her ear, "It's all right. I'm being a man, to dance with my daughter." Only her daughter seems to have ended up in the next set. Never mind. Last time—the caller warns. Concerted effort. A scrabble to find first partners and go through the steps. Last chance to get it right, so they do. In the final strain of music, breathless, they bow to each other, smiling at the camaraderie of their little triumph.

Struggling to carry three pints of beer through the crowd, a young woman almost bumps into Claire, who recognizes her as another of the mothers from playschool.

"Sorry."

"It's okay. Shall I carry one?"

"Oh. Yes please." Claire helps ferry the drinks, destined for the musicians and then speaks to the woman—how good the music was, what a fun thing it was to do. All the while, the bodhran player, the woman's partner evidently, lightly touches the back of his lover's lower leg, catching his hand there in a habit of tenderness, he sits while she stands, balancing his beer on his knee as he carries on a conversation with one of the fiddle players. A little girl comes up to them, their child, Nathan's age.

"I didn't realize you'd taken up waitressing," Howard remarks as Claire rejoins him. "Nathan's been fractious," he says as she sits down.

The cue to leave.

"Perhaps we should go," Claire offers.

Nathan's soon asleep, but Damien won't settle. For the third time, Claire takes him back upstairs. It's really endearing that, regardless of the space they have available, the boys have chosen to share a room, but at times like this it can be a trial.

"Come on, trouble, back to bed. *Quietly!*"

"I'm not tired."

She looks at his bright eyes and sees the truth of it. Still high on dancing.

"And," he protests, "*why* did we have to come home?"

With a glance towards Nathan, she puts a finger across pursed lips. "Ssshhhh. Get dressed," she whispers.

"What!?" Damien exclaims and she clamps a hand over his mouth and speaks in his ear.

"You mean 'pardon,' not 'what,' and I said you could get dressed, only Nathan's asleep and Daddy's reading the paper, so you're not to disturb either of them. Get dressed *quietly* and we'll go outside."

In collusion now, he tiptoes to his clothes.

The evening sun casts long shadows as they start out on the footpath.

"We probably won't go all the way to the top," Claire says, slowing to read the information board, which has appeared in the last few days. "It's a good job it's not Sunday," Claire says, reading. "Apparently in the last century they thought that the stone circle here was made when girls danced on the Sabbath. 'People believed the maids incurred the wrath of God and were turned to stone,' " she reads aloud. "Just think, if it'd been Sunday today, the village hall would have been changed into a heap of rubble."

"That's *stupid*," Damien says, kicking a pebble. "Come *on*."

"Race you," says Claire, beginning to run.

High on the granite outcrop they sit, looking back down over scrub to rich valley fields. The stone is warm to the touch: storing the day's heat. They settle into the angle of rock, cocooned in hard coziness. A sliver of new moon and the evening star hang in a sky tinging green as it fades.

"I'm going to fly to the moon when I'm older."

"Are you? That'll be exciting."

Damien shifts to lean against his mother and she puts an arm round him.

Lights from cottage windows punctuate the landscape.

"Who lives there?" asks Damien, pointing to one of them.

"Mrs. Laity. She works at the hospital."

"And who lives there?"

"Don't know, Damien. Haven't met them yet."

"Who lives there?"

"Where?"

"Over there by the trees."

"That's Dennis, the farmer."

"Dennis who?"

"I don't know his other name. He just said he was Dennis."

She points to another light.

"I think that cottage over there is where Sam and Kate live. You met Sam at the ceilidh this evening—the bodhran player. They've got a little girl the same age as Nathan and she's going to bring her round in the holidays."

"Not a *girl.*"

"It'll be nice," Claire says. "She's got an unusual name."

"What is she called?" Damien asks.

"Sky," Claire says.

"Sky?!" Damien exclaims.

"Hmmm," Claire confirms.

The boy picks up a stone and strikes it against the rock.

As the twilight deepens, buildings that aren't lit blend into darkening land. More stars appear, more than Claire can remember seeing before. She rests the flat of her hand on warm rock, the boy tucked, warm, against her.

"Who lives there?" asks Claire, nodding towards Trethenna, scarcely visible, cradled in the valley's fold.

"Damien and Nathan and Claire and Howard."

One feeble light shows: Nathan's lamp.

Damien yawns and snuggles closer.

"Can we stay here all night?"

Claire laughs. "I don't suppose so."

"Why not?"

"It would be too cold and Nathan would miss us and Daddy would too."

Damien sits up. "*Would* he?"

"Yes."

He leans against her again and bangs the heel of his shoe on stone.

"Why is Daddy always so cross?"

"He isn't."

"Yes he is."

"No, Damien. He's just very busy and tired and has a lot to worry about."

"He's cross."

Claire gives him a brief hug.

"I think, unless we go home soon, we won't be able to find our way."

She stands and pulls him to his feet.

"Now be careful, it can only be an hour or two before it's Sunday, so no dancing on the way down or you never know what might happen."

They start to move off when Claire hesitates.

"Wait a minute."

She helps him up onto a rock so that his head is the same height as hers and he too can catch the breeze that comes from the village behind them.

"What?"

"Listen."

Across the fields, under starshine, comes the distant tune of fiddlers.

Twenty-eight

"Listen."

"What is it, dear?"

"Can you not hear it?"

Mrs. Jago listens hard but, between the striking of hooves on rab and the rhythmic squeaking of the carriage she can hear nothing exceptional.

Mary Bellham pulls the horse to a halt so abruptly that the animal's hind feet slide.

"*Now* can you hear?"

Mrs. Jago turns the collar down from her ears and pushes her scarf inside her coat. The horse stamps a hind foot and snorts, tossing her head and jingling her bridle, but there, though torn to fragments by the boisterous wind, the sound is unmistakable: Claira upon the fiddle.

"Oh, is *that* all," Mrs. Jago says with an easiness she does not truly feel. "She's taken to playing in the barn recently, that's why we can hear her from here."

She turns her collar up against the spots of rain the wind flings at them.

"A cheerful tune on a blust'ry day."

"How can you *say* it?" Mary Bellham retorts, releasing the horse, which goes forward into a trot. "And no wonder she plays in the barn. Munro could hardly have her play in the house."

She catches at the reins as a bird darts from the hedge and the mare shies.

"You will have noticed Samuel James was late for chapel yesterday. Flew past here at half past nine, said he heard her playing as if the Devil Himself was spurring her on."

"I don't suppose she means any harm by it."

"Doesn't mean any harm? On the *Sabbath*? Florence Jago, I think she has turned your head. On the Sabbath? Waits till Munro's taken himself to chapel, then gets straight to her playing. Harm's done whether she means it or no. And I've not seen *her* in chapel since the wedding, have you?"

The swaying of the trap is the only answer she receives and she grunts her satisfaction of a point rammed home.

She slows to let Mrs. Jago down at Trethenna. The sound of the reel is easily heard now.

"I'll thank you for the ride," Mrs. Jago says, "and, as for the other, we must all answer to God."

"Oh, that we must," Mary Bellham says, flicking the horse into motion.

Twenty-nine

Molly the milkmaid always sniggers. Claira had thought the girl would show more respect coming into the house and on holy business, too, but no. There she stands, by the kitchen door, with Rachel and Sarah, whispering and giggling and nudging her companions and looking across at Claira.

Claira blushes hotly. She wishes the thing would just get started, but there are eight people, or more, still to arrive and the ministers are not here yet. She runs a thumbnail across the fabric at her wrist and looks away from Molly's tittering.

Munro comes in from answering the door to Mary Bellham and Molly straightens: becomes demure smiles and little curtsies.

Claira goes into the larder.

Low light filters through the mesh on the tiny window and the cool air is clammy, smelling of cheese. She sighs and leans against a shelf. The babble of voices from the kitchen is muffled by the door. She wonders how long this part of the meeting will last before they move on to the chapel. Two hours? Three? Fiddling with the beads that weight muslin over the milk jug, she makes them hit against one another. Click, click. Click, click. She begins to count the jars of bottled plums.

"There you are," Mrs. Jago says, thrusting open the door. "Jed is looking for you."

"Jed?" Claira asks, fumbling to arrange the muslin cover, but Mrs. Jago has already gone.

Claira wades out into the room.

It's more full now, perhaps twenty people. She can see tall Jed; head and stooped shoulders above the others. Molly and Sarah have gone off somewhere, leaving Rachel on her own. Claira ventures a smile at her, but she blushes and looks down, as if guilty.

Then there's Mary Bellham to pass.

"Good afternoon," Claira says, brightly.

Mary Bellham turns from her conversation with Aunt Eadie.

"Oh," she says quietly, "good afternoon."

Her eyes slide away.

Claira moves on, reaching familiar Jed. An island.

"Hello," she says. "How are you?"

Jed touches his hand to his forehead and shifts his weight from one foot to the other.

"Well, by the grace of God, thanking you."

"Mrs. Jago said you wanted to see me."

"Yes," he says, "I have something for you."

He reaches inside his jacket and Claira thinks how much of it there seems to be and how little of him: as if his tall frame was once much fuller. She sees his shoulders hunch round his thinness. He cannot have been eating enough. He brings out a package wrapped in brown paper. As he gives it to her, Claira sees the veins standing out on the back of his hand; big and blue.

"For me?" she asks.

He nods and shuffles, looking down from his height at the parcel in her hands, watching her open it.

The crumpled paper smells of his cottage. Inside there's a pouch of black velvet. Immaculate. The two women talking at Claira's elbow cast an interested eye towards it. Claira flips the lip of the pouch open and draws out a Bible bound in white leather. The gilt edges of the pages glisten.

"Munro was saying you didn't have one."

"I—I didn't, no. But, Jed, this is . . ."

The women nod and smile, *very nice,* then look at each other, *it should be for the husband, surely, to give such a thing.*

"Well, Jed, thank you," Claira says. "Thank you. I'll put it upstairs, out of harm's way."

Like milk in the mouth that turns out, suddenly, to be sour, the attic room feels tainted. Claira stops in surprise and looks round, listening. What is it?

Dismissing the notion, she places the Bible in its pouch in the drawer of the washstand. She will have to speak to Munro about it later. She feels sure Jed can ill afford such a gesture. She wonders at his motivation. Perhaps he, too, is concerned for her soul. Then she freezes again for her mind has resolved its earlier feeling of strangeness.

She wheels round to face the little table by the bed. Such a blatant emptiness. The photograph has gone. How could she be so slow? Coming into the room, it is ritual now to rest her eyes on the image of her family. How could she not have noticed straightaway?

You must have put it somewhere else, a voice reasons, though she knows with certitude she has not. Then the horsehair bow yells to her from its hook next to the fiddle. How could she not have noticed that, too? It's hanging all wrong. There can be no doubt, then. Someone has been in her room.

Crossing to the fiddle, she takes down the bow, marveling to see it turned upside down, the hook distending the line of slackened horsehair. Tensioning it, she straightens the fibers, then slackens them again before rehanging the thing—as she always does—so its weight rests on the curved wood of its heavier end.

She turns and searches for the picture and finds it. A corner of the frame, facedown, is visible beneath the bed. She picks it up. The glass is smashed. A piece of it falls and rattles to the floorboards. She looks at the pattern of the break, the tight web of cracks in a nucleus where it must have hit something hard. The bed end, perhaps. The impact has hit her mother's shoulder and her face is quite ground away, except the mouth, where a splinter of glass has jabbed in and somehow protected it. Her father's face—Claira releases breath—it seems her father's face is all right.

Regardless of where glass falls, she turns the frame facedown and shakes it. Turning the picture back towards her, she cries out, for, after all, his image, too, is spoiled. What she had taken as just a crack in the glass was more: a deep scratch in the picture, right across his face. As if someone has crossed him out. She digs splinters of glass from the image with her fingernails, holding back tears. She wonders who it was that did this. And straightaway the answer comes: Molly and Sarah. It must have been.

"Claira! Claira!" Mrs. Jago's voice is on the stairs.

Claira jumps up and goes to the door.

"There you are," Mrs. Jago tuts from the landing below. "The ministers have come and Munro would like to introduce his wife to them."

The kitchen is brimful now. The voices hush as Claira walks in and the knot of people round the ministers falls undone. Claira feels her heart rush its beating. She recognizes Andrew Maddocks, the minister who presided over the wedding. Two other ministers stand at his side, solid and rotund in ministerial black. Munro is there and will not look at her. Molly, Rachel and Sarah watch in their huddle.

"This is my wife," Munro says as she approaches. Then he does look at her. "This is Mr. Pascoe and Mr. Summerhill."

Claira curtsies, politely, but Henry Pascoe takes her hand, too, holding it in both of his. She feels dwarfed by the hugeness of him.

"I'm very pleased to meet you," he says, smiling down at her and seeking her eyes. "I hear you play the violin very well."

The silence in the room solidifies. People stand like figures in a waxworks.

Claira's hand has quite disappeared inside his. He looks at her, his pale eyes direct and she looks back; heart pounding.

"Not as well as my father once did," she replies.

Henry Pascoe smiles again.

"Although we cannot ask you to play in the chapel," he says, "we were wondering if you would be kind enough to accompany our hymns here today. No harmonium, you see, and I am afraid we might go out of tune without you."

Claira looks at Munro to see if he knew of this. The color has risen in his face. He did, then.

"Of course, I could, if you would like it," Claira answers.

"Good," he says, releasing her hand.

"Come then," Andrew Maddocks says. "Let's make a start, shall we?"

"There's a man who knows how to make his mark," Mrs. Jago says as the room returns to hubbub.

"Well, I'm not at all sure it's seemly to have the fiddle playing the Lord's hymns," says Mary Bellham.

"It's not the *Lord's* hymns as I've ever heard her playing," Molly whispers in her threesome.

"What you sayin', Molly Dacre?"

"Ssshh, now, Molly."

"I've heard what I've heard and if it were holy, then I'm a billy goat."

He has done it again then, Claira thinks as she runs upstairs to fetch the fiddle. Her anger mounts with every step. He couldn't speak to *her,* oh no. Just as before, he has consulted the minister; gone behind her back to talk about her. What is it that a man will speak to his minister before he will speak to his wife? How *dare* he?

Reaching the smaller, attic stairs, she wrenches open the door.

And then this public display, she thinks, as she charges up the stairs, this public bringing of her to heel. She gives a rueful laugh at the tactic. How could she have said no?

She bursts into the attic, sees the ruined picture on the bed. No retribution. Her word against theirs. In any case she cannot be sure it is them and they will hardly confess to it.

She takes the fiddle from the wall.

Oh yes, but she will play for them.

Claira comes to stand next to Molly and waits for prayers to be over. Her teeth ache from being clenched. Henry Pascoe looks across at her as he announces the hymn. Claira gestures that she must listen to a verse to pick up the tune. She does. It is simple. Idiotically. By the end of the verse, she has it in her head and then it is an easy matter for her to transfer it to the instrument. As they begin again to sing, Claira starts to play, stridently, confidently and ever so slightly out of tune.

Standing next to one another, the ministers sing with gusto and in the opposite corner of the room, Molly sings with gusto too.

When all are sweetly join'd . . .

Playing in Molly's ear, Claira sends the notes slurring out, nudging Molly ever more off-key and out of time.

True followers of the Lamb . . .

Sarah and Rachel take their pitch from Molly and from the fiddle and the two old dames beside them are swept along, too.

The same in heart and mind . . .

Claira drives the music on. Even Mrs. Jago is with her.

And think and speak the same . . .

Just how long will they let themselves be led before they stop to question this insufferable racket? Forever it seems. It's effortless.

And all in love together dwell;
The comfort is unspeakable.

Mary Bellham looks over her shoulder. Standing in the middle of the room, she's caught between the two versions of the tune. There's a pause for the beginning of the next verse. Slipping back into tune, Claira fills in, then begins the process again.

By the end of verse five, much of the room sings to her fiddle.

The riches of his grace

In fellowship are given . . .

Just the ministers hold fast to the tune. Voices begin to flounder. Glances are exchanged. Claira nearly falters when she sees Munro. His face is white and he is staring at her. Let him. Molly continues to sing; with fervor and off-key.

He fills them with the choicest store,

He gives them life forevermore.

The silence that follows the hymn is absolute; then cracked . . . tick . . . silence . . . tock . . . silence . . . tick . . . silence . . . tock . . . Eyes are on Henry Pascoe. He nods his head graciously to Claira.

"Thank you, Mrs. Richardson," he says.

Claira inclines her head to him.

Henry Pascoe turns to Munro and says, "I don't suppose there's a chance of a cup of tea, is there?"

Murmuring breaks out.

"There should be two hymns more yet," whispers one.

"Not with that unholy din, there shouldn't."

Chatter rises. Mrs. Jago goes to take the kettle from the fire. People part away from Claira as she places the fiddle high on top of the dresser. Munro leads the ministers through to the dining room.

"It may not be my place to say it, but I don't know what it is you're thinking of," Mrs. Jago says, taking down a huge teapot from where she has left it to warm. Claira says nothing and busies herself, bringing out the food they have prepared that morning and putting it onto trays. Cold meats, cheeses, cold boiled potatoes, bowls of salad, hard-boiled eggs, bottled beetroot, fresh-made bread, a dish of butter.

Though the dining table is large, not everyone can be seated at it and those who cannot must sit at two smaller tables brought in for the purpose.

As Claira brings a tray of food, she sees the empty chair at Munro's right, the balloon-backed "O" left vacant for her. They are waiting for tea until Munro's wife is there to pour it.

"Let Mrs. Jago bring the rest now," Munro whispers up at her and she takes her place at his side, keeping her eyes downcast on the task she must do, hoping her hands will be steady. For a moment there is pleasure in knowing Molly's little table will be the last to receive tea, but it is short-lived as she fills the cups, the image of the ruined photograph in her mind. Drops of tea splash, staining the tablecloth.

It feels as if the meal will last forever and Claira gives up all pretence of eating, seeing to the visitors instead. She would rather do that than be part of the gorging. The food coming from Trethenna's kitchen would feed her family for a fortnight. It sickens her, watching it so quickly devoured.

When at last it's time for them to go to the meeting in the chapel room, Claira has quite withdrawn into herself, so that she feels it is someone else standing next to Munro at the front door wishing their visitors good-bye. In any case, they speak to him, not her. It helps, feeling invisible. Their eyes glide over her to fasten on him. And he, too, will be gone to the meeting soon. She clings to the thought. The place empty of them all.

She helps Mrs. Jago clear crockery from the table. For a while she works, then stops to listen to the silence of the house. He has gone then. While Mrs. Jago is in the dining room, Claira takes the fiddle from the top of the dresser.

If she had looked up as she crossed the yard to the barn, she might have seen the jingle still in its shed, or glimpsed through the stable door the cob still in his stall, tied where Jed has left him harnessed. But, inconsolable, she has her head down, hair loose again and freed from the silly hat she must wear at tea, so she does not see beyond the cobbles at her feet or the tightness round her heart.

Soon, in the barn, she is bathing in music.

Upstairs, leafing through the papers he must take, Munro hears the sound of her fiddle. He stops and listens. It's that tune again. The one he heard her playing in the attic. Even through this distance he can hear the deft precision of her skill. He expels the breath he has been holding. There was a moment, this afternoon, when he thought her unable to play that which was asked of her. The assured complexity of her playing mocks him now as surely as her deliberate dissidence mocked them all earlier. He feels his heart thump with the truth of it. He snorts as he gathers up the papers. He will take them all. He will be late otherwise.

Running down the hallway, he nearly knocks into Aunt Eadie, struggling somewhat as she carries out the table linen.

He takes the burden from her and shoves open the door into the kitchen.

"Not helped you to clear up then?" he asks of Mrs. Jago.

"Oh!" Mrs. Jago cries out as he strides through, "she did to start with, yes."

The music needles in from the barn. A reel now. She has changed the tune to a reel. Lively. Pushing. The slam of the door cuts through it.

There is a blindness in anger, and thinking back, Munro never could remember the action of leaving the room, nor crossing the yard to the barn. It was a reaction, unreasoned, like the charging of a bull.

Claira meets the charge head-on. It is not bravery. There is only one door to the barn and his anger fills it. And besides, the speed with which he approaches allows her no time. One second she is quite lost in the reel, the next he is almost upon her.

In Munro's head a voice of conscience calls—*this is Anger, show Humility before the Lord*—but it's too late, for this *is* anger, slowly gathered anger, dammed up during the months of his marriage: he is carried by its bursting as so much debris by a flood. Yet through the deluge something in him fights. Seizing it between them, his conscience and his fury draw time out into long, slow seconds in which he struggles to wake from this nightmare, in which his anger *will* be satisfied. In determined horror he sees his arm swing back, sees her white face open before him, mouth and eyes stretched wide. Even during his hand's slow hurtle, the question forms itself in his head, why does she not defend herself?

She is rigid. Rigid and rooted, as the impact hits her face. It knocks her backwards, arms spread wide. At the corner of his vision he sees the fiddle fly from her hand, sees it strike the cobbles and crack—springing in round itself like a mousetrap, triggered. Claira, the luckier, lands on straw.

"What is it you *do*?" Munro bellows, hearing the voice of his anger fill the barn.

"What *is* it you do?"

But his question rings in the silence and his conscience takes it, turns it deftly and delivers it back to him, dropping it at his feet, with Claira, in the straw.

The calf, frightened by the skirmish to the back of his pen, comes forward once more. Saliva trails from his muzzle as he pushes his nose out through the bars to sniff at Claira, the bringer of his milk in strange relation now. She is clutching her face, her mouth stupidly open, taking breath in gulps.

In Munro's head a chant starts at the sight of her, flung back in the straw. *Like the dog you beat for chasing sheep. Like the dog you beat for . . .*

The calf stretches out his neck. His muzzle reaches Claira's head and the trail of saliva clings to her hair as he searches her for milk. He begins to mouth her hair and Munro takes a step nearer to move him away. But the calf strains towards him; it is Claira who cringes.

"Oh my God."

He cannot believe it and he repeats the action, reaching out a hand to her. The calf snuffles towards him; Claira backs in ungainly shuffle and there's a cry too, high-pitched and strange.

Like the dog you beat for chasing sheep.

Without trace, the coward, his anger, slips out through the door.

Munro drops to his knees, pushes the calf's head back through the bars; hears a low mumbling: his voice. It isn't a prayer, or not his usual sort, more the tone that speaks than the words: the way he would talk to still a young horse fearful of the strangeness of harness. He blinks his eyes to see her more clearly and only then knows he is crying.

Slowly he reaches out to her, with gentleness dares to take her upper arm, carefully he brings her up onto her knees and then to her feet. She seems unable to let go of her face, seems unable to take her hand away, and gently he turns her so that, when he draws her to him, he will not hurt her further. Crying still, he gathers her in; his solidity rounding her slenderness. And he can make out his words now, "I am sorry. May God forgive me, I am sorry, I am sorry."

"Let me see," says Mrs. Jago, come from the house and at his elbow, suddenly.

Munro releases her a little and an "Oh!" escapes Mrs. Jago when she sees Claira's face.

"Quickly," she says, turning Claira towards her. She puts her fingertips on Claira's cheekbones, then with the heel of one hand, jolts Claira's jaw back to center. They hear her cry out, hear the grating of her teeth. Munro catches her as she faints.

Thirty

"We can't go down there, surely?"

The offshore breeze mocks, tugs her hair forward, invites her simply to step from the dizzying height to where the sea sucks at the boulders below. A voice in her head sneers, *Go on then*. Against her will, Claire rocks onto her toes and has to put out an arm to catch her balance.

It takes about fifteen minutes to get to the bottom. The steep path does need care and there are places, even steeper, where the soil gives way to boulders they must climb down. And there's a stream to cross. The water trips over stone, overgrown in a cavern of fern and goat willow and deep dripping mosses that lag the rocks.

At last the beach. Released from the need to watch every step, the children run on. And it *is* extraordinary. A small sandy cove hardly visible from the top of the cliffs that rise steeply from the beach; the tide far enough out for the waves to seem benign. And, further reward for their struggle to be there, they have the cove to themselves.

Kate's waiting, apologetic.

"Sky gets so excited coming here, I'd forgotten how she charges on. I'm sorry, Claire, I guess the path's a bit alarming if you don't know it."

Claire smiles. "No harm done and besides, what a treat to be brought here. We'd never have found it ourselves."

"It's amazing, isn't it?"

They walk to where Kate says the sun stays longest, trying to outwit the huge cumulus clouds that heap the sky today.

Claire nods to where the children are, already busy digging in the sand. "I did wonder if Sky might feel left out, being the only girl."

"Don't think so." Kate laughs a mother's proud exasperation. "Being left out isn't really her style."

Claire grins. "It isn't, is it?"

"Talk of the Devil."

"Can we go swimming?" Sky asks, simultaneously running up and removing her sweatshirt.

Kate shakes her head.

"No, Sky. Look at the waves. It's too rough today."

Sky utters the long, drawn-out ooooh of protest, accompanied by a gesture that's almost, but not quite, the stamping of a foot.

"Go and say 'oh' to the waves, not to me. I didn't make them lumpy," Kate says and Sky runs off, leaving her sweatshirt in the sand. Ten seconds later, she's calling again, jumping up and down and looking out to sea this time. Kate gets to her feet.

"It's Sam," she says, waving.

"Who?"

"Sam."

"Your husband?"

Kate smiles down at her. "Sky's father."

Claire gets to her feet and sees that a small open fishing boat has come into view, traveling across the mouth of the cove to bright marker buoys. If she screws up her eyes, Claire can see that there are two men on board. In yellow oilskins, a figure waves.

"He's come ashore here before now."

"Really?"

Kate nods. "He won't today. The conditions have to be just right."

"I didn't know he was a fisherman."

"Only some of the time. Depends on the weather and the price of fish."

She looks out to sea as she speaks and Claire sees her face, flushed, and her eyes shining as she waves to him. And Claire looks away from the joy of it: blinding now she's grown used to her own pale light.

Kate settles to reading, once in a while raising her gaze to the children. Claire watches the progress of the little boat moving steadily from buoy to buoy. She takes her sketchbook out of her bag.

She's sorry the boat couldn't land. She'd liked to have met Sam. Liked the look of him at the ceilidh. It would have been good to see him here, to have the boat get nearer, till all the detail could be picked out: the name on the bow and the way the boards run and their faces getting clearer. She tries to imagine the way the prow would slush into the sand, the excitement of the moment when the vessel was suddenly no longer afloat and could safely deliver Kate's man to her, his oilskins encrusted with salt. And fish gut too, she thinks. Probably they gut fish on the boat, don't they? Certainly the gulls are wheeling round.

She flips the paper over to a clean page. Daunting today: white paper and the scale of the landscape and where to begin.

Sidestepping, she checks the children. They seem to be playing really well together. Damien's voice is occasionally heard in strident protest, but perhaps that's no bad thing, as long as he's fair with it. Her eye takes them in as they huddle round treasure they've found on the beach. Lovely shape. She puts pencil to paper. They move.

Of course they move. Children playing generally move.

Kate's more static.

"Mind if I draw your foot, Kate?" Claire asks, inwardly chastising herself for the cop-out: dodging landscape like that.

"Be my guest," Kate says, drawling her words as she speaks and reads at the same time.

It's rather beautiful, Kate's foot. Leaning back against a rock, Kate has it supported on her other knee so it's not much below Claire's eye level. She wears handmade Indian leather sandals—how *did* she get down the cliff in those?—and, round her ankle, a string of tiny beads, red and gold. The ankle's slim and brown and the fine downy hairs are blond. How ever to do justice to those with this lump of black lead she has in her hand.

Not so much of a dodge after all.

Don't panic, Claire. Think bone and sinew and covering flesh and light direction and shadow.

One more check of the children and she starts to draw.

Thirty-one

Dear Claira, Claira reads and straightaway it occurs to her that it's only the second time she has known him to use her name. In the officialdom of the wedding and now here. She glances up at Mrs. Jago, who's putting a tray of breakfast things down on the wash-stand and wonders if she already knows the letter's content. *Dear Claira,* she reads again, *I have asked Mrs. Jago to give you this letter in the morning, by which time I will be gone from Trethenna. I must go away tonight and think about what I have done and pray for God's guidance and forgiveness. I do not know how you will ever be able to forgive me. I certainly shall never forgive myself.*

Claira looks up as Mrs. Jago sits on the end of the bed, waiting for her to finish reading. *I shall stay with my brother, Edwin, near Truro, Mrs. Jago has the address. If you want for anything out of the ordinary, you should send there for it. I cannot tell how long I shall be gone. I have spoken to Jed about the farm and with Michael and Joseph to help he should manage. Mrs. Jago will see over the dairy. I know how hard you work, but, Claira*—and she raises her eyebrows at the use, again, of her name—*my only wish is that you should rest and return to health. I have asked Michael to take word in the morning to your Mother that you are not well . . .*

"Has Michael left yet?" she asks quickly.

Mrs. Jago nods, but Claira hears the dogs barking with excitement and she tumbles out of bed, feeling her legs strange, her back and neck stiff. She goes to the little window, throwing it open and yes, there he is crossing the yard, the dogs at his heels.

"Michael!" she calls and her jaw screams at her so that she has to clutch it.

"What is it?" Mrs. Jago asks.

"I do not want him to go."

"Why not?"

"I do not want him to." Claira turns again to the window.

"You're not to hurt yourself," Mrs. Jago says. "I will tell him." And she calls down the message while Claira finds the letter, on the floor under bedclothes she dragged there in her haste.

. . . with Michael and Joseph to help . . . will see over the dairy . . . to take word in the morning to your Mother that you are not well although I have not found the courage to own what ails you.

As God is my witness, I swear I shall never again do such a terrible thing. I have never before felt so sorrowful for something I did. Beneath this there are three or four ink marks, as if his pen had been put to the paper and taken away again; then there is simply his name. *Munro.*

"I'm to call the doctor if he's at all needed," Mrs. Jago says.

Claira attempts to shake her head, but finds her neck too stiff.

"No. Thank you. I'm all right."

She folds the letter and tucks it under her pillow.

Mrs. Jago lifts the bedcovers and indicates that Claira should lie down.

"I've the strictest instructions that you should rest."

And Claira finds herself pleased to have support for her head on the pillow.

"I've brought some breakfast for you. Will you have something to eat yet?" Mrs. Jago asks, tucking the bedclothes round.

"In a little while," Claira says. As Mrs. Jago turns to leave, Claira, her back to her, adds, "Thank you for what you did yesterday."

There are three days of limbo—a sort of numbness in which the sunlight moves round the little attic and Claira cares only to slide under the bedclothes and sleep some more or, if wakeful, watch how shadows move their way across the wall.

At some point she notices the bow has been hung back on its hook next to the empty one where the fiddle used to be. It's upside down again. She stares at it hanging there. No point in moving it now that the fiddle is . . . Slow, fat tears come to blot out the thought.

At intervals Mrs. Jago arrives with food, and leaves with the chamber pot and Claira says little and even feigns sleep.

On the fourth day she wakes and, curled on her side, hooded by bedclothes, reads the letter again. When she's finished, it occurs to her she should find somewhere safe to put it, somewhere no one but she will be able to find it. She will soon. She lies back and brings into focus the sentence that has hung about her these last few days:

I have never before . . .

A bumblebee stumbles in through the open window and blunders drowsily round the room, striking the sloping ceiling. Claira's eyes follow it.

I have never before felt . . .

Drawn by light, the bee bumbles back to the window where it bangs against glass. The opening is so near to it, the breeze fresh.

I have never before felt so sorrowful . . .

From the yard comes the sound of a dog yapping. Jess. The noise she makes when a cat is teasing. Claira shifts in the bed.

I have never before felt so sorrowful for something I did.

Casting the covers aside, Claira swings her legs over the edge of the bed. She tries tilting her head from side to side, then raises her shoulders a little and drops them again. Once on her feet, she stretches her arms high. Her body feels much freer now. There's a jug of water Mrs. Jago has left and a plate of bread and butter.

Claira pours a glass of water and drinks it down. Eating; the butter is rich on her tongue. Her jaw copes.

Crossing to the window she looks out at the day before blowing and scooping the bee towards the opening. It fumbles and frets round the window bar before dropping and finding its way out where it is taken high by the breeze, a black speck against blue. As she watches she wonders what it is that pushes such a man as Munro to his most sorrowful of things.

"What day is it?" Claira asks, minutes later, dressed and in the kitchen.

"Monday," Mrs. Jago answers, her eyes wide.

"Good," Claira says.

A day to get her strength back.

Helping Aunt Eadie down from the jingle, Jed's not quite quick enough to notice her dress is caught on the last step and Claira darts forward with a whisper of black silk to release Eadie's garment before it tears. She hears rooks caw and thinks of them rising from the treetops as she spends time arranging the hem of Aunt Eadie's dress. Then there's nothing else for it, but to turn and go in as Jed is busy securing the cob and Aunt Eadie needs an arm to help her up the path.

Slow on the gravel, Aunt Eadie's even slower on the chapel steps. Holding her arm, Claira makes sure Eadie's feet find firm footing. She studies the lichen on areas of stone seldom trodden on. The steps are smoother in the middle, polished by the passing of feet. In the corner of her vision, skirts sweep by, then the black shoes of a man approach—polished to a high shine—and hesitate, before moving on.

In the doorway, the sun is warm on her back, the air from the chapel interior cool.

"Good evening," an elderly voice says and Claira half looks up but Aunt Eadie does the answering for her.

"Good evening, Mrs. Boase. A very fine one 'tis, too."

Eadie's cane makes a different noise on the wooden floor. Claira knows heads turn as they make slow progress down the aisle. The murmur of conversation stops. Claira feels the old woman tighten her grip. There's a surprising strength there. She feels herself nudged and realizes it is Aunt Eadie now who is guiding her; showing her where to sit.

Then someone lightly touches her other arm and Claira looks up in surprise. On his way to take the service, Henry Pascoe nods briefly and smiles at Claira.

"Good evening," he says and then to Eadie, "Good evening," and he takes the hand that holds her cane. "How are you today?"

"Well, thank you, Mr. Pascoe, by the grace of God."

"Good," he says. He smells of soap and clean linen. His frock coat flurries as he moves on to talk to others and Claira is grateful for the attention he takes with him.

During the service, Claira studies the kneeler and waits for the calling out to begin. In the Primitive Methodist chapelgoing of her experience, it was always one of the things that caused her greatest agonies: the public display of a religious fervor she did not share. It seems not to be happening here. Perhaps later.

She lets her eye wander over the heads of the soberly dressed, over the plainness of the walls. They *are* plain, it occurs to her. No gilt stenciling here. The wedding had passed in such a blur she can scarcely remember the place, but now there is time to take in detail, she can see that everything in this Wesleyan chapel is much simpler than she is used to: the wooden furniture plainer, the pulpit lower, less ornate. It seems at once both more humble and more dignified.

The service ends with no more calling out than the communal responses and amen.

As she leaves, Aunt Eadie stops to chatter. Mary Bellham catches Claira's eye and raises her eyebrows before turning away.

On the way home, Claira has the reins. Up the hill from the chapel, warm breeze is in her face, sneaking out hair from beneath her bonnet. She drives the cob at a spanking trot; the reel in her head chiming in time with the beat of his hooves.

Thirty-two

"They shouldn't *put* these here, *should* they?" Nathan protests as he struggles to climb the rocks on the way back up the cliff path.

"Don't be a noddle," Kate says, pretending to box his ears, then lifting him swiftly to the next foothold. "Nobody *put* them there."

Claire smiles, she likes this woman, likes her affectionate rudeness with someone else's children, but still she comes, gently to her son's defense: "I suppose," Claire says, "living where he has, up till now everything he's ever bumped into has been put there by someone or other."

The climb takes half an hour. Already tired from play, Nathan finds it tough going, becomes tearful at the stubbing of his toe and even Sky needs the biscuit break they have halfway. They find dry rocks by the edge of the stream and Claire takes Nathan on her knee. She's glad to stop too, feels her own pulse settle. All this exercise. She might even lose a bit of weight.

"You all right, Nathan?" she asks, hugging the boy. His hair is sandy and sticks to his head with sweat. "Here, have some juice."

"Can I see your drawings again?" Kate asks.

"Yes," Claire says, surprised, fishing the sketchbook from her bag.

A strange rendezvous, she thinks, looking round. Two women and three children in this hidden place, the sky almost blotted out by goat willow and the canopy of undergrowth. It occurs to her that no one knows where she is. If someone were to want to find her, Howard she supposes she means, if Howard were to want to find her, he wouldn't begin to know where to look. She imagines the phone at home; ringing in the empty house.

Damien wants another drink and she pours him one. He's sitting by the edge of the stream, plunging his hands through waterweed, laughing when he finds his fingers covered in water snails, showing them to Sky, who laughs and splashes him.

"Hey, monster!" Kate says. "Go farther away if you want to throw water around." Then to Claire, "These are good."

She closes the sketchbook and passes it back.

"Not especially," Claire says, moving to take it from her, only Kate doesn't relinquish it.

"These are *good,*" she repeats, quietly emphasizing the word and Claire wants to back off from the contact, only Kate won't let her, holds on to the sketchbook with *oh but you will look at me* resistance and their eyes meet and Claire sees that Kate's are the same green as the foliage round her, green and flecked with amber—like camouflage, except they are so direct . . . *I'm waiting, Claire* . . . and insistent . . . *this is really important* . . . and Claire yields and Kate's mouth, firmly set, molds itself into a solemn smile.

"Trust me," she says, then lets the sketchbook go and laughs. "I may have flunked out of St. Martins, but I know quality when I see it."

"You went to St. Martins?" Claire gasps.

"Relatively briefly," Kate says, wryly. "Couldn't cope with the hothouse. Anyway, if you don't believe me about the drawings, you should show them to Nick. Show them to him anyway."

"Nick Franklin?"

Kate nods.

"Why him?"

"He *didn't* flunk out."

"Don't tell me he went to St. Martins, too?"

"The Slade, in fact. Teaches art at the college now."

"Really?" So that's why he approved of her artistic endeavor. That's why he looked so intensely at her. That's why he . . .

"Is it so surprising?" Kate asks.

"No. No."

"You mean you've not seen his work then?"

"No." A painter. Nick, a painter.

"I'm surprised, there are quite a lot around—those that aren't up-country or abroad. I'm sure he'd let you see his current work sometime. Are you all right, Claire?"

Claire sweeps a strand of hair from her face. "Yes. I'm fine. I was just thinking though, I couldn't possibly trouble him with my stuff. I should think it's the last thing he needs: other people pestering him with their work."

Kate shakes her head. "He'd be pleased. It's a way of life for him."

Claire reaches round Nathan to begin to pack their things away. "Hey, young man," she says, gently. "Don't go to sleep on me. We've got some more climbing to do before we get home and I can't carry you up here."

Nick, a painter. Why hadn't he said?

"I haven't seen him for a long time," Claire muses aloud.

"Nick? He's away. Always goes off at this time of year."

"There have been plenty of cars outside his house."

Folding Sky's discarded clothes, Kate nods. "Holidaymakers. Nick moves out and lets the cottage—well, both of them—he owns the one next door, too. Goes off traveling and leaves the letting to an agent who does the changeovers."

There's the sudden flurry of undergrowth and, from the path above, a stranger's feet break into the space. High-tech trainers, male legs, fit. Then the rest bursts through—hellos—awkward—both surprised by the presence of the other; the picking up of things from his path where they've spread themselves, proprietorial; then he's gone, the searing white of his shorts and the red of his shirt left on the retina.

It's only ten minutes' drive home, but bundled in the back of Kate's Beetle, the children are soon asleep.

"Sorry," Kate says, briefly patting Claire on the knee.

"What for?"

"Being heavy about your drawing."

Claire laughs. "You were, weren't you? I don't remember when I was last so severely told off."

Kate smiles across at her.

"Sorry," she repeats, stopping while a rabbit in the middle of the lane considers its predicament. Kate turns pale eyes to Claire.

"I mean well," she insists. Her hands fly in emphasis. "It's just one of the things I'm worst at is keeping quiet when I see potential going to waste. Or even worse: put down."

Reaching a decision, the rabbit hops into the hedgerow. Kate drives on.

"D'you know what I mean?" Kate asks, taking her eyes from the road to search Claire's face for understanding. "Women are especially prone to it—the *oh I couldn't possibly* syndrome: martyrdom really."

"How old are you?" Claire asks.

"Twenty-six. You?"

"Thirty-seven."

"What of it?"

"Nothing." Claire laughs. "Merely incensed I didn't think like that at twenty-six."

Thirty-three

There's a letter with the parcel the carter delivers. Addressed to Claira, it says simply, *I would have word you are well.* The hand is firmer on the page, which—despite the lack of signature—she reads as a sign that Munro is more himself.

The parcel takes the form of a rough wooden box and Claira carries it out onto the yard to seek Jed's assistance in opening the thing. Three-quarters made, the rick of furze they have been building stands abandoned. They must be collecting the next load. She goes into the workroom for tools that might help her. Hammer and chisel come quickly to hand. Whatever can Munro have sent her? More religious admonishment? Sauntering back to the box, she kicks a stone with the toe of her shoe, then sits beside the box and looks at it. Opening it wouldn't be difficult, but she lets the tools clatter to the ground at her feet. Perhaps she will wait for Jed after all. She picks at the edge of a fingernail.

Mrs. Jago comes from the house with two buckets for water.

"I'll do it!" Claira calls and jumps up to take them from her.

"Not managed to open it yet, then?" Mrs. Jago says as Claira pumps.

"No."

The water swooshes into the pails. Bubbles chase and rise as it crystal-clears against the wood.

The women look up at the sound of a cart turning into the yard,

Jed and Michael. The vehicle is piled high with faggots of furze they have cut and bound.

"We need your help, Jed," Mrs. Jago calls, then, as Claira lifts the buckets, "I'll take those in a little while."

"It's all right," Claira says, heading for the house and kicking herself for not just getting on with opening a box she knows will yield in moments. There will be an audience now.

She returns to find Jed has half the lid off and is easing open the second half. A curious Michael absentmindedly fingers the long curls of wood shavings that have spilled out onto the yard.

"There you are," Jed says, giving the lid a twist to free it of the last nail.

"Whatever is it?" Mrs. Jago says.

Jed pushes the box towards Claira, who begins to part the packaging. China? Glass? Her hands contact oilcloth and she finds an edge and opens it. Beneath that, plain black cloth, soft. Wanting to know now, her hands are impatient as she seeks an opening. There's a smoothness and a hard, beaded edge. Her heart begins to thump. Surely, he would not, would he?

She finds a way to move the cloth and her hand flies to her mouth.

It is not merely a fiddle she finds.

It is *her* fiddle.

Repaired. Intact.

For a second she cannot move, then she reaches in and lifts the instrument clear of the box.

Thirty-four

The library is in a refurbished building—Victorian—with high, high ceilings and wide windows high on the wall and a windowed central dome—as if, at some stage, it has been an exhibition space. Now books line the walls and a gallery has been put round to house nonfiction.

"Here, Nathan. Here's the children's section," Claire says, turning into the alcove and browsing the books with him, so that it's only when she turns back that she sees the painting at the end of the hall. From the top of the doors to the ceiling it reaches, from wall to far-reaching wall: sea and cliffs; the rich weight of rock; granite abstracted; sea slurred to sky and there the outreach of rock that could be a natural or a man-made harboring—the nature-culture boundary blurred. And she holds her breath to see it, the size of the thing—how to paint on that scale and keep such poise and balance: smears of paint like lichen layered, a vibrancy of sunlight suggested, an essence of outdoors brought in. And she has seen the style before—where was it? Truro—the triptych in the bank.

"Do you want that book, dear?"

Claira jumps at the voice. Realizes she has wondered towards the painting and the checkout desk, looks round for Nathan, there he is, back in the children's section at the play table. In her hands she holds a book of Babar the elephant.

"Yes. No. I don't know. Sorry I was looking at the painting. It's stunning."

"We like it."

"May I just . . . ?" Claira indicates the picture and her desire to get closer.

"Just leave the book on the counter and pick it up when you've finished."

Abandoning *Babar*, she goes nearer to peer up at the signature—just initials: N.F.

At the other edge of the painting she finds it—the little plaque, the title, the date, the name: Nicholas Franklin.

Thirty-five

"This is Mummy and Daddy's room," Sky informs them from the landing, with an imperious wave of the hand. "And this is the bathroom," she continues, pushing open the door so everyone may see. Then—opening the door to another bedroom—"This is where Daddy sleeps when Mummy isn't talking to him."

On the stairs, Claire grins at Kate.

"Your daughter will go far, Kate."

"But *not* as a diplomat," Kate laughs, shaking her head.

"And this is my room," Sky continues. "You can come in and look at my toys, if you like." Like lambs, Damien and Nathan follow her in.

"How does she *do* that?" Claire asks as the door swings closed behind the children.

"By being a thoroughly bossy little tyke," Kate replies. "Want a cuppa?"

"Lovely."

"Mind your head on the way down," Kate says, descending the steep, narrow stairs, ducking beneath the low beam.

From the medley of objects on the crowded shelf, Claire takes a piece of ceramic work and lets her hands explore it. It's like a sea urchin or a seedpod, a giant poppyhead. It's a bit gritty; dust from the Aga, and she smooths the surface of it back to the glaze's dull sheen.

"Do you mind Earl Grey?"

"I love Earl Grey."

Carefully Claire places the piece back on the shelf where it can again prop up the photo of Sam and Kate at the beach, Sky's second place running race certificate and a postcard from Thailand.

"I bet Sky is proud of this," Claire says, indicating the willow and colored-tissue butterfly whose three-foot wingspan hangs from the end of the shelf.

"She is. I would rather it went somewhere where it doesn't hit me on the nose every time I do the washing up, but apparently that's the only place for it. Something to do with the window."

"So the light comes through it?"

"I think that must be it."

Claire pushes the thing so that it swings parallel with the pane. Light dapples through plants that climb over the outside of the window and through the red and blue of the butterfly's wings.

A cat winds itself round Claire's legs.

"Oh, push him off if he's a nuisance, Claire."

"He's fine," Claire says, picking up the cat and taking him to sit on her knee at the table. "How long have you been here, Kate?"

"To collect all this junk?" Kate laughs, coming from the Aga to the table with tea. "About ten years."

"It's lovely," Claire says, stretching back in the wicker chair. And it is, she thinks. Every inch of space a warm chaos that speaks of their lives and their loves together, the denlike quality of the room's low light, the mellowness of so much wood, the low, beamed ceiling.

"I mustn't get too settled," Claire says. "The painting I told you about—"

"The Elizabeth Armstrong?"

"If it *is* an Elizabeth Armstrong. Anyway. It's due back from the restorers today. He said he'd be here after four-thirty. What time is it now?"

"Four o'clock."

"Perfect. Will you come and see it?"

"You bet."

Thirty-six

"Happy, Lizzie?"

"Good heavens, Forbes. That must be the third time you have asked the poor girl within the hour."

Elizabeth laughs. "What shall we tell him, Frank?" In the back of the jingle she pulls a face of serious contemplation and then pronounces, "I care not for the ruts in the road, but the quality of light," she continues, casting an arm through the gold of early evening, "is heavenly."

"And the company?" Forbes persists.

Frank Bramley tuts and raises eyes in mock appeal to the divine.

"Most certainly the best I have had since lunchtime," Elizabeth says, with which answer Forbes must content himself as the lane takes a turn downhill and he must concentrate and slow the pony to a walk in order to safely navigate the road.

It *is* heavenly. The hedgerows heavy with dense walls of wildflowers, the air heavy with the scent of bluebells; the golden light, the sound of a stream running as it descends near the edge of a wood. And then Elizabeth sees her, in the little clearing; her startled movement catches her eye. She touches Forbes on the elbow.

"Could we stop?"

He turns round, concerned.

"Must you get down?"

"I must."

While he brings the vehicle to a halt, Elizabeth lifts the lid of the hamper and finds a water bottle that is empty. As she steps from the vehicle, she leans towards her companions.

"Extraordinary, wouldn't you say?"

"Pardon?" Forbes issues, then, "Oh yes!" as he sees the woman Elizabeth refers to. Against the sunlight, slanting from the skyline between the trunks of trees, they see her slender figure flit then freeze.

Walking uphill towards her, Elizabeth's alerted senses stretch themselves to capture detail. The light falls so, the long shadows of sunset thus. No light at all touches the face: that will have to be dealt with. Her torso is as willowy as the trees she is among.

As she draws near, Elizabeth uses an undulation in the terrain as a reason to alter course slightly. The woman turns to keep the stranger in full view, allowing the sunlight to catch her face, high-cheekboned, elfin, such finely drawn features; dark, dark eyes. She looks wary, like an animal who might at any moment run. The limbs are fine, a doelike litheness. One hand is tucked away from view. She's concealing something behind her skirts.

"Hello," Elizabeth calls and, receiving only the slightest nod for an answer, indicates, with her bottle, the stream that runs between them and asks, "Is the water sweet here?"

"Yes."

"May I take some?"

Eyebrows are raised in surprise.

"The water is everyone's."

Elizabeth laughs. "You look so at home here, I feel I have to ask your permission."

She squats down on a rock at the edge of the stream to fill the bottle.

"Not there. From the middle, where it's fast-flowing."

"Thank you," Elizabeth says and leans farther out. "Do you live nearby?"

"Yes. Not far up the lane."

"I am sure if I lived nearby, I would visit this place all the time," Elizabeth says, getting to her feet and taking in more of her surroundings.

"Would you?"

"Mmmm," Elizabeth murmurs, attempting to commit light and landscape to memory.

"Why?"

"Why? Because it is the type of place I love. Magical. Beautiful and mysterious at the same time."

Claira rests her eyes on Elizabeth's and for a moment the two women look at each other. A little smile forms on Elizabeth's mouth and is mirrored on Claira's. Then Elizabeth tilts her head to one side.

"In mourning," she comments.

Claira touches the garb.

"My father," she says.

"Ah," Elizabeth says. "Mine, too, died when I was about the age I would guess you are now." She nods softly. "A lamentable business."

Again; the purposeful meeting of eyes; a drinking deeply of one another.

"There are orchids," Claira says.

"Are there? Where?"

Claira nods downstream.

"May I see?"

Claira crosses the stream, balancing on stones and Elizabeth sees it is a violin and bow she carries.

"They are just here," Claira says, taking a few paces downhill to a little clearing where the plants grow.

"Lovely!" Elizabeth exclaims, sitting down among them and inspecting their faces so that Claira laughs at her and Elizabeth laughs too and hugs herself round the knees.

"I shall *have* to come back here."

"Will you?"

"Yes. It's perfect. I'm a painter and this is exactly the type of place I like to paint. And you," she grins up at Claira, "you are perfect too. Do you think there's any chance I might paint you here?"

"Paint *me*?"

"Yes," and she gets to her feet. "How rude of me. I haven't even told you my name. I'm Elizabeth Armstrong," she says and holds out her hand.

Claira takes it and says, "I'm Claira Penfo—Richardson. Claira Richardson." And she curtsies a little and blushes her confusion, and Elizabeth touches her arm and turns to walk back upstream.

"I am afraid it would be very arduous for you, sitting for me, but that it's a lovely place and I could pay you a little and we would have a lovely painting to look forward to. What do you say?"

"I don't know," Claira says. "I would have to ask . . . I would have to ask my husband."

"Would you do that?"

"Yes, although he is away presently."

Elizabeth nods. "Perhaps if I could give you my card. I have one on the jingle." Then, seeing her companions approach, she exclaims, "Good heavens, the menfolk, I am afraid I had quite forgotten them!"

"Sorry, Lizzie," Forbes calls ahead. "We were getting concerned about the amount of daylight as we don't know the road."

"You are quite right to interrupt. I had forgotten the time. This is Mrs. Claira Richardson. Claira, this is my fiancé, Stanhope Forbes, and our friend Frank Bramley."

"Charmed to meet you, I'm sure," Forbes says among the shaking of hands.

"I am hoping Claira will sit for me," Elizabeth says as they walk on towards the jingle.

"You should, you know," Forbes says to Claira. "She is a very fine artist. One of the best. She would paint you wonderfully." He indicates the violin. "Come here to play, have you?"

Claira glances quickly at him. "Yes."

"Well, lovely place for it, I am sure. Saves annoying the folk at home," he laughs. "Thought about taking up the cello myself. Not quite sure what the landlady would think of it though."

"There you are," Elizabeth says, taking a card from a little leather case. "I shall be moving to St. Ives before long, but my mail will be forwarded."

Claira looks at the card. An address in Newlyn.

"In fact, Claira, if you give me your address, I could write and let you know my new one. Or you could just give me the house name as it's just up the lane here and we do know where we are, don't we, Stan?"

"Oh, rather," Forbes confirms.

"It's Trethenna," Claira says.

"That's a pretty name," Elizabeth says, taking a pen from the same leather case to write it down. "Is that how you spell it?"

"Yes. Perhaps if you pass this way again you would like to call in."

"Oh, lovely!"

"Only," Claira adds hurriedly, "not on a Sunday."

"Heaven forbid," Forbes intones.

Elizabeth prods him on the arm. "We would love to call and see you. Thank you. Now we should be going. It has been a great pleasure to meet you, Claira," Elizabeth says, smiling at her.

"And you," Claira says.

As the jingle pulls away, Elizabeth turns to wave a farewell. And there is the glade and the stream, but Claira has quite disappeared.

Thirty-seven

"There you are," Claire says, at last finding Nathan in the sitting room.

Then the painting takes her breath again. How different this room is with it. How charged.

Claire goes to where Nathan sits, eating crisps and banging his heels on the sofa. "Not crisps again, Nath," Claire admonishes, sitting beside him. She puts an arm round his shoulders and snuggles him closer. "After these, no more until the weekend. Okay?"

"Damien had some."

"Oh, *did* he? Well he's banned until the weekend, too. Anyway, what are you doing in here? You were so quiet, I couldn't find you."

Nathan crunches on crisps.

"Did you come to see the painting again?" Claire asks.

Nathan munches on and nods; points a salty finger at the Armstrong painting. "Is she an angel?" he asks.

Claire smiles. "I don't think so, no, but I know what you mean." What is it, through his child's eyes, that makes this image seem angelic? Backlight, like a halo; arms in movement, away from her sides, radiant hair. The restoration has done such work. Claire had expected the painting to look different on its return; had expected a certain increased clarity; a revealing of further detail perhaps; an improvement in depth of color. But not this. "Is she an angel?" is not a question Nathan has asked before. His response, then, to the subtlety revealed. A sense of the ethereal.

Nathan scrunches his crisp bag.

"Okay, rascal. That packet needs to go in the bin," Claire says, holding him close-captive now, turning her face to bring her lips to his hair. "And a certain grubby boy," she continues, letting her free hand hover in a threat of tickling, "who should *not* have been eating crisps in the first place"—Nathan squirms and giggles in her grasp—"and who should *not* in *any* case have been sitting in *here* and eating them, needs to go and wash his greasy mitts *before* touching anything else." Claire lets her fingers contact his ribs. "Okay?"

When he has gone, she sits on a moment, still in the marvel of this painting in this room, thinking back to its return today, how, pied-piper-like, the delivery man had led them, carrying the painting in its wrapping into the house, while she and Kate and Sky and the boys followed on. And then the unwrapping. The color and the clarity and the good repair so that it's possible to see now—it's a violin the women carries, not a water pitcher at all.

It does amaze her, this image revealed: the model's heavenliness so solidly grounded. She thinks of her own work, the image of Nick, emerging out of sun and landscape: flesh and stone and sun and air. Thinks of how much she still has to learn. Perhaps Nick will come and see this painting. She imagines it: Nick the painter—as she now knows him to be—Nick the art tutor, returned from traveling and standing at her side looking at the gorgeousness of this work. A little smile plays on her lips.

Thirty-eight

"I shall know my way up here soon," the carter says, grinning down at Claira and Mrs. Jago once he has turned his vehicle in to the yard. He jumps down and begins to untie the tarpaulin, thrown over his load against a day that threatens to spot with rain.

"Whatever is it this time?" Mrs. Jago asks.

"You'd think it urgent, judging by the message I had that I was to make no mistake, but to be sure and meet the train from Truro and bring this here posthaste," the carter answers, taking his time over the knots. "Had to laugh when I saw what it was."

"Is there a letter?" Claira asks.

He shakes his head. "Not this time."

Claira frowns a little. Perhaps she should have written more in the reply she sent him. She had thought for what had seemed like hours and had simply ended up by writing: *I am well, now.* And then, underneath, signed her name.

With practiced movement the carter flicks back the tarpaulin, then shins up the wheel, glancing to see if Claira is watching him, but he's disappointed. He picks his way between the boxes and farm implements awaiting delivery.

"Per'aps if you two ladies would be kind enough to take this between you," he says, beginning to hoist something towards them.

Not a box at all this time. As the thing comes into the women's reach they realize that, beneath the thick padding, what has arrived is a rocking chair.

While his horse eats from her nosebag, the carter sips the tea Mrs. Jago brings him and watches as Claira takes off the packaging in the yard.

Beneath the bound hessian there's straw. Beneath the straw, soft cloth. As the chair emerges, the carter gives a long, low whistle.

"What a beauty," he says. "Per'aps I do see now why he didn' want it left about the station."

The wood of the thing is rich and richly polished, the high back elegant in its arching, the seat and central back panel thickly upholstered. The rockers rest on a platform, a sprung mechanism there to aid the rocking.

"Never seen one quite so handsome, I must say," Mrs. Jago agrees. "Won't you try it, Claira?"

"Me?"

"Surely. 'Tis yours after all."

"*Is* it?" she says.

"Of course. Who else did you suppose it for?"

Claira runs a finger over the silken wood. She thinks of her trunk in the attic room, the scuffed, ancient article the only piece of furniture she owns. Would Munro have sent her such a thing as this?

"Perhaps it's for Aunt Eadie," she says.

Mrs. Jago looks unconvinced. " 'Tis possible, I suppose. There was no name given you?" she asks the carter.

He shakes his head. "No."

"Where shall we put it?" Claira asks.

"Seems there's no doubt it's intended for the parlor," Mrs. Jago says. "Think how the fabric matches what's there already."

"Oh yes, of course."

"Besides, it's too grand a piece for anywhere else."

Before they can make protest the carter has lifted it for them and is taking it towards the house so that Claira runs to open doors before him and he has the pleasure of watching her.

"Oh no," Aunt Eadie, brought to make an inspection, says. " 'Tisn't for me. They're lovely to look at, but I never could tolerate the things for sitting in and Munro knows it. He always wanted one for me and I always said no."

"There," Mrs. Jago says. "It's surely for you, Claira."

"I suppose it must be," she says, though in the parlor next to the fireplace and, dark against the pale flagstones, it seems even grander and less likely to be hers.

Mrs. Jago picks up the carter's cap from where it's dropped from his pocket. Giving it to him, she moves towards the door and says, "You must have many more calls to make, judging by your load."

Left alone, Claira rests fingers on the arm of the chair, then pushes down a little and releases. The chair rocks to and fro, to and fro, and she's surprised how long the movement sustains itself. And then, as chairs are meant to be sat in, she slides onto it and it's lovely how well it holds her and it's a pleasure to rock so and she smiles to herself, then looks at Munro's chair opposite: empty.

"How is it?" Mrs. Jago asks, popping her head round the door.

"Like swing boats at the fair," Claira laughs.

Thirty-nine

Squatting, Claire rolls the stone along, like a wheel. I hope you're worth it, she thinks, pausing to catch her breath. She brushes earth from the stone's rim, her hands in tough gardening gloves, several sizes too big. Then suddenly, the weight's all wrong and she has to fight to stop the stone falling on its face.

"Now that *would* be stupid," she says aloud as she struggles, aware that, if it were to fall, the pointer, the prong—further undermining her strength, she giggles at her *hopeless* attempt to find the right term—the *finial* might be damaged. End of sundial. But she wins the battle and balance is regained. Although, really, she hasn't thought it through well enough. What's she going to do when she gets it to the front of the house? She rolls it on regardless, an undignified wide-legged, bent-double shuffle.

Once there, she lets the stone drop safely onto its back. There's just enough sun for a shadow to be cast and she finds her watch beneath her glove and checks the hour, then rotates the sundial until the shadow falls on present time. Half past two. She supposes it's as simple as that. And she finds herself smiling at the delight of low tech, then laughs at her own wonderment. Little things.

Of course, she can't just leave it on the ground. A mother's momentary panic-vision presents itself: her child tripping over and being impaled and she resolves to move the thing before the children come back. But that's enough sidetracking for now. She'll think what to do with it while she gets on with the afternoon's real task. She walks across the front garden to where she's been working, taking brambles from the hedge. There's quite a pile already.

With a fork she gathers the briars and takes them to the backyard to dry out for burning. The breeze moves with her, buoying her along. Returning, fork empty, she pauses, breathes deep the wind where it comes from Blundle Hill, laden with the scent of earth, wet from overnight rain. It begins to feel like autumn. Already the trees in the valley are changing color. She sees movement on the road at the shoulder of Blundle Hill. A figure, walking. Claire turns to fetch more brambles, then more again and each time the walker's nearer and she can see he's tall and carries a rucksack. Then he's disappeared round the dip and curve of the road.

What she needs, she supposes, stepping aside as one of the brambles she forks takes a swipe at her ankles, is a stone base of some sort, to raise the sundial out of harm's way. Yes, a stone base would be ideal. She wonders where she could find one the right size.

"Hello," a voice calls and she glances up to see the walker on the lane.

"Hi," she calls back. She shoves her fork into the roll of brambles again, then realizes the walker has turned in to the drive and is striding, with long gait, towards her. Recognition clicks. "Nick!"

And in the moment of her realization, he bends to kiss the side of her face and she smells sun and travel and good sweat on his skin.

"Nick! I hardly recognized you!"

He draws back and ruffles his hands through his thicket of white curls. "It's the shaggy-dog look that throws people," he says, smiling and letting his eyes rest on hers. His face is tight and lean and brown. "You look well," he says.

"And you. Where have you been to get so brown?" Against a deep tan and the whiteness of his hair, his eyes now seem a startling blue. "And fit. You do look disgustingly fit," she laughs pulling away for a mock inspection of the ridge and groove of his muscled legs; seeing, too, the way the hip strap of his rucksack pulls, unhindered, across the flatness of his belly. "Dis*gust*ingly fit. I take it you've been hiking."

"I have. In France. One of the *grande randonée* footpaths. Do you know them?"

"I know of them. Tough going, I should think."

"Heaven on earth. I've been walking and drawing, or possibly drawing and walking, but either way it's been heavenly. Once or twice I made myself walk barefoot on a stony track just to . . ." His eyes laugh, watching her widening face, as he searches for the right expression. "Just to ward off the sense of impending perfection."

They laugh. "Oh, there's nothing *worse*," Claire emphasizes.

"Absolutely. Dangerous state."

"Quite. And nothing like a cut foot to remedy things."

"Exactly so. As long as it's not too bad a cut. Wouldn't want to snooker the whole thing."

"No, no. Just enough pain to feel you're having to work a bit."

"Precisely."

When she brings the tea, he's sitting on the grass by the side of the garden furniture. He gets to his feet and moves towards the table.

"It's all right, Nick," she says. "Sit on the grass if you'd rather. I don't think it's too wet, is it?"

She puts the tray on the ground.

"How's it been here for you?" he asks as she pours the milk.

"Good. The children love it and so do I. Howard's not too keen—not that he's been here very much—so, as we were saying, just enough pain to feel I'm having to work a bit."

She passes him tea and finds him studying her, his pale eyes calmly intent and she wonders what on earth possessed her to

give this report on the state of her marriage to a near stranger and at so little prompting. She looks down, snatches a tall stem of grass.

"I'm surprised you said yes to a cup of tea," she continues, quickly. "I should have thought—being so near—you'd be anxious to get home."

"I am in some ways. In other ways it's often an anticlimax, to stop traveling. Quite nice to postpone the moment of arrival." He smiles across at her. "You look well, Claire," he says again.

Spoken by his voice, her name sounds unfamiliar, like something exotic he's brought back from afar. The grass she's wound round her fingers snaps. "Thank you. I am well. It suits me here." She throws the broken pieces down. "So. How was the hike?"

And he tells her then, quietly, of six weeks of walking, putting one foot in front of the other in rolling countryside with all he needs on his back; he tells her of the weather, mostly kind, except for a few nights of rain on his tent. He tells her of staying in one place for days when he's driven to draw; of eating when he's hungry and sleeping when he's tired; of the coolness of streams emerging from the hillside; of mountains emerging above the hills; of interrupting his solitude with a stay in a farmhouse once in a while; of walking on, twenty miles or two, depending on how he's feeling and the way his drawings are.

With eyes half closed she pictures him, solitary figure, climbing out of beech woods onto higher hills, the certainty of a path before him and his body's strength.

"I'm never quite sure if I walk between drawings, or draw between walks." He smiles.

"May I see?"

"The pictures?"

She nods.

"Oh, that's enough of me, don't you think? And there aren't many here. I post them to a friend as I go."

But she insists, and he digs them out of his rucksack, where they are rolled inside a rigid plastic tube.

"Tough old mollusk of a rucksack; might have guessed it held a pearl or two," she says once the drawings are out on the garden table.

By her side, he laughs. "Smelly socks, I can guarantee. Not so sure about pearls."

"There's such a *wealth* of work here, Nick. They're gorgeous."

"Oh, I *am* in trouble, then. Not much room for the gorgeous in the eighties."

"Will you sell these?"

"Oh, well, some of them I'll frame and sell. This one, probably, and this one." He indicates a big drawing, a close-up of hedgerow and grit and gravel and leaf mold and another hectic drawing of woodland. "But the rest here are mostly working drawings, towards paintings I'll produce this winter."

She lets her eye take them in, his drawings an oasis for her, so that she drinks deeply from long-felt thirst. He talks little of them, a word here or there, his low voice quiet and warm, like the sun, now, warm on her back. Outstretched to the drawings on the table, his arm is so close it almost touches hers as he moves the drawings on top of one another and her skin sings at the minute movement of his body, in warm, close parallel to hers. Unbidden, she feels her body yield towards him: the subtlest shifting of weight.

A robin lands nearby on the shoulder of the garden fork, before flying down to search over earth she's upturned with the pulling out of roots.

She sees Nick's hand move from the table towards her . . .

"Claire, I . . ."

. . . and—married woman—she pulls herself away; turns to face him, then can't meet his eyes, looks down, backs off a pace.

"I saw your painting in the library," she says, hurriedly, so that it's his turn now, to look away.

"Yes?"

"I loved it. Wanted to bring it home. Even before I knew it was yours." She laughs awkwardly, looking away still.

He smiles, watching her, then looks to the drawings again, beginning to gather them together. "Bit of a big bugger to bring home. It's a while since I painted that one."

"Twenty-two years."

"Is it? I suppose it must be. I don't do much that size these days."

She swoops down to gather tea crockery onto the tray.

"You haven't really said how things are with you," he says. "Done any painting or drawing yourself?"

"Oh, some," she fudges. "I've been busy with the children, mostly. They just love it here. Howard has been very busy at work. In London much of the time. We've hardly seen him, really. He'll be back this weekend, though. His parents are coming down, hence I'm trying to sort the garden out a bit."

"And I'm stopping you. Sorry."

"Oh no. It's good to stop and oh, Nick—how could I forget?" and she abandons the tea things and begins to walk to the house, turns back to call him. "It's my most exciting bit of news."

"What is?" he asks, laughing at her reverse gait and the way she tilts her head to one side.

"Come and see. I've bought a painting."

It is still remarkable to her, opening the sitting-room door on the spell this painting casts—how the image fills the room, again the sense of the outdoors brought in. She loves the way the burgundy and green chime, the strong assurance of beauty, of a priceless moment caught. Still the thrill of it runs up her spine. And now to have Nick here and watch his face open in wonder.

"Oh, my God, Claire. I had no idea."

He takes a step nearer.

"Well, it's an Armstrong, isn't it? Elizabeth Armstrong?"

"It is."

"But that's incredible. Wherever did you find it?"

"In the storeroom of an antique-cum-junk shop."

"You wonderful woman," he says, standing to face the painting.

"I had no idea who had painted it," Claira says. "Hadn't even heard of Elizabeth Armstrong."

"Then you will have come to it with an unbiased eye. It's an *excellent* example of her work."

"That's what the auctioneer said."

"You've had it valued?"

"Yes, but I preferred it when I didn't know how much it's worth."

"I know what you mean."

"*Do* you?"

"Yes. You value the thing for its artistic and aesthetic merit. The financial side of the equation merely complicates matters."

"Pre*cise*ly, Nick. Precisely," she says, thinking if only Howard could see that point. "How did you know it was an Armstrong?"

"The setting is typical of her. And the use of backlight to frame the head in that way. It's just glorious, Claire. What's the date of this one?" he asks, peering at the figures beneath the signature.

"1887."

"A couple of years before she married Stanhope Forbes, then. Elizabeth was prolific. Other Newlyn School women who married artists stopped painting in their own right, but not Elizabeth. Her work still appears every now and then. Well—as this one has. Much of it goes to collectors in the United States, but there's quite a lot in of her work in public collections. I stood in front of a picture of Elizabeth's in Sydney not so long ago—on display next to one of Stanhope's." He smiles at the recollection. "I hadn't expected to find them there. It was like bumping into old friends—all that time and geography away."

He goes closer still to inspect the canvas's surface.

"It looks in pretty good shape, too. What was it like when you found it?"

"Dreadful. The restorers have done such a good job."

"What a find, Claire. A once-in-a-lifetime find." He smiles across to her. "Precious, precious thing. It's gorgeous, isn't it?"

"The house has felt very different since it arrived," she says.

"I bet," he agrees immediately, engaged again in his close inspection.

"No. I mean, *really* different."

He stops his scrutiny of the painting to look round at her. "So that every day you wake with an awareness of its presence in the house and you come to visit it and find something different and the same every day and it becomes an anchor to you and a source of energy to draw upon." He grins at her. "*That* sort of different?"

And she laughs at this man, summing up her experience with such exactitude. "Yes, Nick. Something like that."

"That's quite a homecoming," he says, in the garden again to pack the drawings away and she wants to ask him something and can't quite bring herself to and she ought not, no, she won't bother, then her voice says, "Nick?"

"Yes?"

"A favor."

"What is it?"

"If I promise to keep them well out of the way of grubby children and the cat and whatever"—she takes a breath—"could I borrow a couple of the drawings for a day or two?"

"Why?"

She meets the keen inquiry of his eyes.

"I just want to live with them. A couple of days. That's all."

He nods. "Which ones?"

"The big views of landscape."

"You *have* been drawing, haven't you?" he says, pulling out the work she's suggested and passing it to her.

"Yes." She laughs. "Easier without you around, running through my landscape every evening." And she hopes he'll pick up on the little joke, only he doesn't, leaves instead a silence in which the meaning of her words mutates, while his eyes rest on hers.

She looks down. "Thank you for these," she says of the drawings, "I'll take them indoors straightaway."

"Is that the time?!" Claire exclaims, looking at the sundial as she returns to the garden.

"Could be," Nick says. "Although these things are not fantastically accurate." He squats opposite her, the dial on the ground between them. "So soon passeth it away. So we are gone," he says, quoting the dial's axiom, rather than reading it to her.

Claire looks down, runs her finger over the faint letters let into the brass and finds it an exact quotation. His eyes are on her, kindly. "Bit of a grim reminder," he says. "But I suppose we do all need reminding." His fingertips touch the sundial stone—balancing himself.

"How did you know . . . ?"

"The sundial was here when I lived here, Claire. "

"You used to live *here*?"

"I did, with Helen—my wife—and our son, Ben. We owned Trethenna and the two cottages down the road—the ones I still have. Property was so cheap then, they practically gave the cottages away. No roofs, mind you."

He smiles at the memory, his eyes steadily on her.

"When was all this?"

"Quite a while ago. Helen was pregnant when we moved in. Ben was fourteen when they moved away. He's twenty-three now, so, quite a while."

"It must be strange for you, coming here," she says, sitting on the ground, so that he sits, too, the dial between them.

"In some ways, but there's been so much water under the bridge since then. Ben is grown up and you are the third family to have lived here since we moved out. And although we were happy at Trethenna, there were difficult times, too."

"In what way?"

He shrugs. "We were both so busy. I was teaching full-time then and Helen had started a business retailing craftwork. Quality stuff, but very different from where I was, which was fine, except that I had a lot to prove then—as an artist." He laughs. "God, I was horrible."

"Were you?"

"Impossible, I should think. Archetypal angry young man, forever fighting the corner of my personal aesthetic—which needed doing in some ways."

"Did it?"

He nodded. "My values were very different from those of the mainstream art world then. Still are." He laughs. "I'm just more laid-back about it these days."

"Less to prove."

"That and . . ." He searches for the explanation. "I don't feel I have to defend my personal aesthetic anymore. It's survived the test of time. I know the value and meaning of it for me—regardless of what the rest of the world thinks—and it's a sound meaning. Of course, it was *easier* once my work had started to sell."

"Did it take long?"

"I spent quite a while bashing my head against the wrong gallery wall. Then I found a gallery in London who acknowledged the worth of good drawing and weren't fazed by me working figuratively sometimes and nonfiguratively at others. That was a real breakthrough—and then opportunities came up to show elsewhere: Holland, Germany, France and later on America."

"And where was Helen through all this?"

"At home with the baby, initially." He grimaces. "I said I was impossible. Still. I was working hard. Teaching, renovating

Trethenna, putting roofs on the cottages before they fell down; painting. A lot. Painting a lot. At college all hours—I used to paint there then, before I got a viable studio going here. I think it was that which was the final straw for Helen."

"What happened?"

He laughs. "Irony. Irony. She went off with a gallery owner."

Claire laughs. "Oh nice one."

"It's so good to be at the stage of life where I can look back and see the silly side."

"So you sold Trethenna when you two split up?"

"Yeah. I needed to pay Helen her due and in any case, it was too big for just me, so I moved into one of the cottages which I'd done up by then."

He smiles. "By the way, it's in the shrubbery."

She frowns. "What's in the shrubbery?"

"The base."

"For the sundial?"

He nods. "In the shrubbery."

She looks at him, then scrambles to her feet and crosses to the bushes and begins to rummage through them. "Where?"

"A little farther to the left."

"I don't believe a word of it," she says, then, "Oh. Well, what's it doing in there?"

He laughs, getting to his feet. "Never knew anyone who could keep on top of these shrubs. Nor anyone who could be bothered to dig the base out."

"It does look very well entrenched. I'll just have to put the dial on it there for today. I know the sun won't get to it, but more important, the children might not get to it either. You couldn't help me lift it, could you?"

"I'm sure I can manage it on my own. Might be easier, in fact."

"Sure?"

"Yes," he says, squatting to lift the thing. And it does seem easy for him and she parts the bushes while he brings the stone, hugging it to his chest. She backs into the shrubs, holding them aside for him and, as he leans to deposit the dial, she glimpses the tautness of his breast under strain, brown-skinned with a scattering of white hair in the cleft. There's beauty in his arms too, their tensile, easy strength.

"Mind yourself on the finial," she says, reaching out to disengage his shirt, which has caught and threatens to tear as he carefully lowers the stone into place.

And he looks up at her, from where he is entangled, his arms still round the stone of the timepiece, patient as she performs the little rescue and she might feel ridiculous, backed against the greenery tending him, except the face he turns is rounded with gentleness.

Released, he straightens up and she sees his features soften, so that she drops her gaze away from his openness and hears herself say, "Thank you. I'd have found that a struggle."

Brushing the dust from his hands, he turns away, holding the greenery aside for her to exit. "I'm pleased to help," he says.

They look back at the sundial in situ. He runs a finger down the central pointer.

"You can't call that a finial, you know."

"Can't I?"

"No."

"What is it then?"

"Not sure. Begins with 'N,' I think. Not a finial, anyway."

With practiced ease, he swings the rucksack onto his shoulders, fastening the hip strap as Claire walks with him to the gate.

"On to the next little era," he says. "Your children must be back at school soon."

"Yes. Nathan's starting full-time the week after next. I shall have to look for work once he's settled."

"What sort of thing?"

"I was Howard's father's personal assistant in London. I think that's going to translate into secretarial work down here. It's how Howard and I met—when I was working for his father."

"Ah. An office romance."

Claire laughs. "An office pregnancy at least. We're just lucky it's worked out as well as it has."

He glances at her. "Has it worked out well?"

She balks at the question. Its directness. His audacity.

He merely stops, turns pale eyes to her, says evenly, "Has it?"

"Yes. Yes. I . . . Nothing's perfect, but yes. On the whole we work things out."

He gives a small smile. "Good."

"We'd hardly have had a second child—or a first, for that matter—if we hadn't felt . . ."

"Of course not. Good."

Good? Good? He has a nerve and she twitches the hair from her forehead, her umbrage waiting for a better answer while she feels the blood rush to her face. He drops his gaze, white curls blowing gently across his brow; hiding hooded eyes. For several seconds she waits while he says nothing. Then he looks up and again catches her wrongfooted; for her annoyance melts at the sadness she sees.

"Sorry," he says, managing a rueful laugh. "Put it down to homecoming. I'm never my most subtle when I return from being abroad. I should know by now, the transition always takes me off balance for a little while."

Like Howard, she thinks, and turns away, confused.

"No harm done."

Watching him walk down the lane, she notices how immediately he adopts an easy rhythm and she wonders how many miles he covered in his six weeks away. And then, good grief, there's Kate coming round the corner already, bringing the children home from the party and Claire's not done half what she had hoped to.

The old VW stops as it draws level with Nick. Kate jumps out to welcome him and they hug each other in the road, a great-big-bear-of-a-hug and then the children tumble out of the car, Damien and Nathan and Sky, and she sees Nick ruffle the boys' hair and lift Sky to him.

The wind takes their voices away from Claire and it's funny watching them, a silent movie of greeting, the man, the woman and the children, looking, for all the world, as if they were a family.

Forty

Eadie retired to bed half an hour before the sun. Mrs. Jago, Jed and Michael have long gone home. Trethenna's westerly rooms are washed gold by the last rays. Tangible peace.

In the attic Claira stands and bathes her body. Naked, she raises an arm and soaps herself, squeezing lather from the sponge, drawing it down her arm then across, beneath and between her breasts. A breeze stirs in through the open window, moving softly round her body. Her hair is piled high and pinned and she brings the sponge and squeezes it behind her neck, then catches the water that runs to the small of her back, rubbing it round.

The door is pushed quietly open and a cat pads softly in, crosses the floor and jumps up onto the bed into the patch of sunlight Claira's shadow moves across.

They look at each other, Claira and the cat. The animal blinks slowly, lifts a paw, licks the inside of it and begins to clean his face.

Claira rinses the sponge in the bowl of cool water, takes the soap and makes fresh lather. Soaping her belly, she sees its reflection in the little mirror, the slant of her navel in her belly's firmness, and lower, the bush of hair, dark against her paleness. The sponge follows down the line of her groin. She hesitates, then turns her body away, so the mirror does not witness. Quickly, she washes.

She takes the bowl to the window and tips the contents out onto the slope of the roof, pausing to watch how the water runs, then looking out at the folds of landscape, green and gold in the evening light. Across the valley, hay has been made and in the fields they are working, still, to bring it in. She can see a wain piled high, figures moving round it and the speck of a dog. Jed was saying today, Trethenna's meadows are ready. Perhaps the fact that hay needs making will bring the farmer home.

A gust of breeze breathes onto her flesh and, wet, her nipples rise.

Filling the bowl with water from the jug, she rinses off the soap, then tends to the washing of her feet. Soaping between her toes, she is reminded of washing her infant brother's feet and she smiles at the memory of the chaos of bath night, the jumble of bodies and the clean nightclothes and the hugs and the squabbles and the tucking into bed.

Picking up a towel, she dries herself, then shakes out a nightgown, crisp from its starching, and slips it over her head.

"Come along, cat," she tells him, scooping the animal up and taking him downstairs.

"Go on. Find a cozy bed in the barn," she says, depositing him outside the back door.

Through silence marked by the tick of the clock, she pads back, barefoot on the flagstones and pauses by the dark corridor to Eadie's chamber, then stands and listens. No sound.

The door of the parlor squeaks as she opens it. She peers into the room's heavy stillness at Munro's chair and the rocking chair in silent conversation.

Up the stairs, into fading gold light diffused through empty rooms, she passes, then pauses; retracing a step or two.

Munro's room, to the back of the house, is darker, facing north, the window small. Her feet feel the cracks between polished floorboards, then the soft tufts of his rug. As she looks round, sensing the undisturbed air, her toes find the fringed edge of the carpet and curl round it, pick it up, drop it; curl round it, pick it up, drop it.

The washstand holds his shaving things and she wonders how he is managing without them. There's a razor, a cutthroat, and, hanging from the side of the washstand, a leather strop to sharpen it on. The razor's bone handle is worn smooth with his use. There's a shaving jug on the washstand, too, holding soap, and she leans closely to it and inhales, only gently, yet instantly her mind is filled with the sense of him. For several moments, she rests her hands on the slate top and lets herself stay that way, bent forward and breathing him in.

Like the furniture downstairs, his wardrobe is dark and silky. Her hand hesitates by the opening. Then she pulls at the handle and the door yields to her and she opens it farther, slowly, till it's wide. Neatly ranged, his clothes hang: dark suits and jackets at one end, trousers in the center, shirts at the other end. She thinks of her father's garments. Two or three changes. She fingers the sleeve of the jacket in front of her. The thickness and quality of it. One of the suits is very different from the rest, a much thinner fabric; loose-woven. Perhaps something he wore in the heat of Africa. She brings her face among his shirts, but smells only the starch Mrs. Jago—for it does seem to be her, still, who sees to his clothes—has used on them and a faint trace of the lavender that hangs from the rail.

The lamp on the bedside cabinet is polished and, as she approaches the bed, she sees the distortion of her nightgowned reflection in it; her lower torso hugely distended, tapering to tiny shoulders and a dot of a head.

In the failing light, the white of two pillows looms. She touches the cool of the nearest and wonders if Munro has always slept like that, with two pillows side by side, or whether it was an arrangement he'd made approaching his marriage. Or perhaps Mrs. Jago saw to it.

Claira takes the covers and turns them back: a neat V. This then, by rights, is where she should sleep. She lifts a knee to the high bed, then stops; puts her foot to the floor again. Reaching down to the hem, in one movement she sweeps the nightgown up and over her head, letting it fall to the floor. She feels a slight dizziness. The lamp reflects an image of her belly, hugely rounded under weighted breasts. Sliding herself between cool sheets, she feels her true body reaffirmed as the covers settle over her; slim torso, taut to the crisp sheet, breasts reaching up as she breathes in deeply. Her back sinks into the feather mattress as she sighs. Rolling onto her side, she takes the second pillow and pulls it to her, embracing it lengthways against her body; placing a bended leg over it.

Forty-one

"She makes such a charming mother," says Howard's mother, resting a hand on his knee, and showing her teeth to Claire in a smile. "Didn't I always say she'd make a lovely mother?"

"I don't remember you saying anything of the sort," Howard's father mutters into his gin.

"Oh, but I *did*, didn't I, Howard?" she pursues, patting her son's knee in emphasis.

"I believe you did," Howard says, getting up from the conservatory table.

The gold charms at his mother's wrist click together as the bracelet slides down her arm.

The evening, too, is gold, filtering in through the woody grapevine.

"Will you have another drink, Mother?"

"Lovely, darling," she replies, passing him her glass and the bracelet falls back again, click, click, click. "You're so *patient* with them, Claire. I'm sure I couldn't be."

"I don't really find they demand much patience."

"*Don't* you? I should have thought children *always* do."

Nathan, in his pedal car, chooses that moment to crash into the table leg. Cutlery and china jangle. Howard's mother puts her hand to her throat, where the skin revealed by the low-cut dress is tanned a deep brown and scattered with slurred dark freckles. With red nails she fingers the gold at her neck.

"Nathan," Howard says, "you've been told not to bring that in here, now please take it outside." He pulls open the door that leads from the conservatory into the garden, but a stone has become lodged beneath the door and he can open it only so far.

"I don't want to go outside."

"Go *outside*," Howard says, forcing the door. The stone grates along quarry tiles.

"I don't want to go outside."

Claire gets up. "Supper's nearly ready, Nath. Do you think you could go and tell Damien to switch his computer off?"

Nathan looks up at his mother's retreating back, then gets out of the pedal car and runs indoors behind her.

"Oh *damn*," says Howard's mother, "I've forgotten to take my wretched tablets." She looks across at her husband. "Do you think you could get them for me, Douglas?"

Douglas puts down his glass. It makes a loud clink as it catches the edge of a plate. He scrapes back his chair.

"Where are they?"

"Where I always keep them."

"You *poor* darling," Howard's mother says as soon as her husband has gone. "How ever will you cope when you have to spend more time down here?"

"I expect we'll manage."

"Well, Claire *obviously* loves it, but I shouldn't have thought there would be enough here to satisfy *you* for long. What *ever* will you *do* with yourself?"

Howard stretches his back, stiff after his bending to retrieve the stone from beneath the door.

"Work mostly," he says, throwing the pebble outdoors before crossing to the side table to finish pouring the drinks.

"You're *bound* to miss the city *dreadfully,*" she says, taking the glass he offers her. "What ever do people *talk* about in Cornwall?"

He laughs. "As far as I can make out it seems mostly to do with the price of cabbage. And the quantity of fish and tourists."

"How *ghastly*. I'm sure I couldn't put up with it for a week. Still it's not been all bad. That painting Claire's bought. What a bonus."

"Isn't it?"

"Nice little windfall. Could come in very handy." She pats him on the knee again. "There need to be some compensations, living right out here. I know Claire was keen, but really. Even small things like buying a paper must be a nuisance. Which reminds me, Douglas *must* have his Sunday paper tomorrow. I don't suppose they deliver out here, do they?"

Howard shakes his head. "I'm afraid not."

"How far is the nearest shop?"

"Four miles."

"Seriously?"

Howard nods.

"An eight-mile drive just to buy a paper," she observes. "What a chore, Howard."

"I suppose we'll get used to it."

"Well that's *very* stoical of you, darling."

Conspiratorial, she leans towards her son, resting her body against the edge of the table. He sees the freckles at her breast stretch and bulge with the movement.

"I've made your father promise," she whispers, "that as soon as these Cornish ventures are established, he'll whisk you straight back to London."

"I can't find them," Douglas calls, coming back, that moment, into the conservatory.

"What do you *mean* you can't find them?"

"I can't find them. I don't know where you've put them."

"They're where I always put them, by the side of the bed."

"No they're not."

"Yes they *are*, Douglas."

"Well *I* couldn't see them."

"Oh *really,*" Howard's mother says, thrusting her glass onto the table and pushing herself to her feet. "It's simpler to fetch them myself."

Douglas exhales a long breath and lowers himself into a chair. "What is it we do when we marry, heh?"

Howard swirls the drink in his glass. Evening sun catches the ice.

"I don't know, Dad. What is it we do?"

Douglas shakes his head, then looks over his shoulder.

"Listen, Howard. We ought to have a chat."

He runs a finger down his moustache and says quietly, "It's about that time—a while ago, now. I've been meaning to talk to you. You nearly landed us both in it when I phoned Claire expecting you to be here and she sweetly informed me that you had meetings in Surrey, when I'd seen you off myself the day before."

"Yes. Sorry about that."

"It was a sticky moment, I can tell you. Had to play the forgetful old duffer, which I daresay is not so far from the truth these days, but really, Howard."

"You're right. Sorry."

"I won't moralize—"

"Good."

"Because, as I have *ample* reason to know, marriage can drive a man to distraction, sometimes, but I must say, I am a bit sorry."

"You really needn't be. I'm sure I can handle it, thanks."

"But that's my point, Howard. You very nearly *didn't* handle it. And—even if we can't be in love all the time—"

Howard shifts in his seat.

"—we can at least be compassionate. So I hope you will, Howard, be compassionate towards Claire. To your wife. To the mother of your children. She's a good woman. Works hard. Always worked hard for me. Conscientious. Very devoted to the kids. And to you."

"I know."

"Anyway. I'm sure you'll have to get on with this other thing. Get it out of your system and then come home." Douglas drains his drink. "Anyone I know?"

Howard shakes his head. "No."

Towards the end of the meal, the children are excused from the table and sent out into the garden together. As Claire brings dessert, Damien comes back in with an envelope bearing her name.

"What's this, Damie?"

"It was in the bushes on the sundial," he says.

There's a little hushed expectancy as Claire opens a letter found in such a strange place. Inside, a piece of paper with the words "It's a gnomon" written on it. Claire's face softens in realization before she drops the paper on the table and picks up the pie server.

"Who's it from?" asks Damien.

"Nick, I suppose," says Claire, cutting through the soft belly of glazed fruit. "He walked past the other day when I was moving the sundial. We couldn't think of the right name for the pointy bit and he's written to tell me it's called a gnomon."

"How *very* considerate of him," Howard's mother says. "Don't people round here usually put letters in the letter box?"

Claire hands her mother-in-law apple tart: homemade with lashings of cream.

"The first of the cookers," Claire says and smiles. "The children picked them from the orchard this morning. It's far too early, of course, but Damien was very keen, so I've just used plenty of sugar."

In the kitchen aftermath of the meal, Nick's letter sits among the debris. Claire cleans round it, plates and cutlery to the dishwasher, leftovers covered and placed in the fridge. Wanting to wipe the surface clean, she has to move the envelope, so, really—as it's in her hands—she may as well look at it again.

"It's a gnomon."

She finds herself trying to read the character of the hand. She thinks of him bothering to look the term up and then writing it down for her and wandering up the lane to leave it where she'd find it the next time she looked into the shrubbery to ponder what to do with the dial. She smiles to herself as she fills the kettle, then takes a pen from beside the telephone.

"Well," she writes beneath his statement, *"you did say it began with an 'N.'* Then, beneath that: *"Nick. I must get your drawings back to you. They've been so useful, thank you."*

Finding an envelope in one of the kitchen drawers, she seals the note inside. She goes to crumple the old envelope and pauses a moment, liking the look of her name in his sloping hand.

A voice of conscience clears its throat: *Aahh, meanwhile, Claire, everyone's waiting for coffee and it's high time the children were in bed.*

She tosses the envelope into the waste bin; takes cups down from the shelf.

In dream she walks through long grass, the sun hot on her skin, the voice of water in a stream. She searches the tree line. She would paint the lie of landscape here if Nick were in it. She catches movement she knows is his at the edge of the stream she walks towards; steps up to him in the dappled light of trees. Look, his eyes insist, and, turning to the deeps, he has only to dip his hands to come out with the flicking silver of a fish and the spray of rainbow droplets in the sun. Closer, she sees fish mouth and gills gape wide in straining. *Put him back now. Put him . . .* Letting him go, the vital body spurts from his strong hands. He rounds on her, his kiss is close and firm and long and her body rises to be caught by his wet hands.

She surfaces awake in heated unremembering: dream fragments stream from her like water running fast through fingers.

Forty-two

"Your family are here!" Mrs. Jago calls, coming back to the kitchen from the knock on the door.

"Surely not!" Claira gasps, putting down the dough and rubbing flour from her hands.

"Oh, but we are," Claira's mother says, smiling and coming into the room followed by Hannah and Beattie holding William by the wrist, then Jethro and Samuel, all grown.

"What?" says Eadie, rousing from a doze by the hearth.

"How wonderful!" Claira says, and hugs her mother, trying to avoid marking her with flour and then hugs her sisters and her brothers, daubing dough on young William's nose.

"Oh, good gracious," Eadie says, realizing and Ellen goes over to her, bobbing down and holding her hand a moment.

"Hello, Miss Richardson, how are you? We are something of an invasion, I'm afraid. I don't think you can have received our message."

"Message?" Eadie asks.

"To say we would like to call and see you," Ellen says, looking towards Mrs. Jago.

"No, we didn't, I'm afraid," Mrs. Jago says.

"I sent it with Henry, the carter. He came by our house a few days ago and was pleased to tell me he was to deliver a chair to Trethenna and I asked him to say we would like to call today and to bring word if it wasn't convenient."

Mrs. Jago laughs. "Too taken with the lady of the house to remember any such sense as that," she says.

"With me?" Claira asks, surprised.

"He was, Claira," Mrs. Jago replies. "In any case it's no matter. We were about to put our baking in the oven, so your visit is timely."

Crossing to the hearth, she opens the cloam oven and rakes out the hot ashes while Claira finishes putting dough in tins and Ellen and Hannah help with the clearing up and Beattie lifts William to peer at the clock while Samuel and Jethro go to inspect the new chair.

"How are you, Claira?" Ellen asks, as they lay the table together, stopping to give her daughter a hug.

"I am well, thank you."

"Your husband is from home, I hear," Ellen says, sweeping a strand of hair from Claira's face.

"Yes," Claira answers, dropping her gaze. "He is staying with his brother near Truro."

"And when is he expected back?" Ellen asks.

"I am not sure."

"Oh," Ellen says and then raises her daughter's chin to look in her eyes, only William barges up with something he has found: a letter opener with an ivory handle carved in the shape of a lion's head.

"Put that back, young man," Ellen says and so the moment passes and then there is tea.

William sits himself at the head of the table.

"No, William, not there," Hannah chides him, but Eadie indulges him.

"He's doing no harm," she says, coming—with Ellen's help—to the table.

"And besides," Beattie says, pushing his chair so that the arms of it meet the table, "if we capture you like this, I think there's *some* chance we might know where you are for more than a few moments at a time."

"I think," says William, once they are all seated, "that when I am older, I shall live in a house like this."

They laugh.

"Oh *will* you?" Ellen says. "Well, for now eat your tea or you won't grow to be older."

There is bread to be buttered and there are home-smoked ham and salads from the garden that Claira's grown and how the weeds do come through this year, how good the cream is on the scones.

Tea flows with talk of Hannah, taking classes at Sunday school and she *does* remind Mrs. Jago of her own Jane, so like her at that age and—*don't do that, William!* And how are your hens laying, Mrs. Penfold? And *what are you laughing at?* Not that story again, Samuel: the Penfolds' neighbor, poor man—sleepwalking twice this week; rode his horse in his nightshirt Tuesday. And, you might laugh, Jethro, but his wife was quite beside herself.

So nobody hears Munro arrive. Not the carriage that brings him, nor the greeting of the dogs, nor his foot upon the step. For a moment he stands, undiscovered behind the patterned glass, seeing his kitchen full.

"I had a feeling I should have hurried," he says, coming into the room. "It rather looks as if I have missed tea."

As the silence falls, it's Hannah who reacts first, jumping to her feet and pulling William's chair away from the head of the table. "Now you *shall* have to move," she says.

Then Mrs. Jago is up too, finding an extra plate for him and Beattie begs the boys to shift their chairs in, how's a body supposed to move round the room with them sprawling so? Only Claira remains quite still and silent. Here he is then. She hadn't remembered him so tall.

"How lovely," Ellen is saying. "We were missing the master, but rather a noisy homecoming for you, I'm afraid," she says as she and Munro shake hands.

"It is good to see the room so used and I am pleased to think Claira has had your company in my absence."

"Oh, only today," Ellen asserts. "We were not aware you were from home until a few days ago."

"No? But I sent word to you the day I left," Munro says, looking towards Mrs. Jago who nods towards Claira, who, on seeing their communication, looks away.

Ellen smiles. "Another message gone astray, then. I sent word we should like to come today, but it never arrived and so *we* arrived quite unexpected. Indeed, I am sure we should be going and leave you to settle home in peace."

"Not at all," Munro says, seating himself in his chair. "You are welcome to stay for as long as you will. There is, however," he continues, adopting a gruff tone and turning to face William, whom he takes by the shoulders, "there is, however, a penance to do for anyone found sitting in my chair."

William visibly shrinks.

"In this case," Munro says, turning back to the table and taking a piece of bread. "In *this* case," he repeats, helping himself to salad, "the person in question . . . let me think."

William waits, agog.

Munro lifts the teapot and swirls it round to see if there is any tea left.

"Ah yes," he says, finding it empty. "In this case, the person in question shall make the next pot of tea."

He turns to where the wide-eyed William stands. With serious gaze, Munro hands him the pot. "If you are very lucky," he says before he relinquishes it, "Mrs. Jago will help you with the kettle."

"Good heavens, Claira!" Hannah cries, "did you take out the heavy cake?"

Claira leaps to her feet.

"I had quite forgot it," she says, rushing to the oven as there is a knock on the door that Mrs. Jago will answer if only Hannah will watch William with the kettle.

"It *is* a day for callers," Eadie says.

"Someone for you, Claira," Mrs. Jago says, returning to the kitchen. "Elizabeth Armstrong and her mother. I've put them in the parlor as we're very domestic in here."

"Who is this?" Munro asks.

"Someone I met last week," Claira says, not able to look at Munro's eyes. "A painter."

"Perhaps you could introduce me," Munro says, getting up from the table.

Claira glances up at him, trying to gauge his response, there by the door, holding it wide for her.

"I . . . yes, of course," she says, going out ahead of him.

As they leave the kitchen, Ellen raises her eyebrows to Mrs. Jago, who gives a grim little smile. Yes, it acknowledges, that is the first communication between husband and wife since he returned home and no, that is not unusual.

Forty-three

No, no, no, Claire chastises herself. *That one simply will not do. It doesn't fit. Don't quite know why, but it doesn't.*

She takes the drawing away from the others and puts it face-down on the kitchen table before rearranging the remainder to fill the gap that's been made.

"My turn!" Damien's voice sings in from the yard, through the open doors. "My turn to hide, now."

From the lack of screams, Claire assumes the game is going well and lets herself continue the process of seeing what she's drawn this summer. She turns the discarded drawing faceup again.

Why doesn't it fit? Different style, but the standard is the same. It's as good or bad as the rest of them.

Yet it seems right to throw it out. She looks back at the others.

Content then. Simple as that.

The others are mostly figure in landscape. The one she's thrown out is still life.

Is that it? It seems she must involve the human figure. No, no. Why not throw out the study of rocks and vegetation at the beach, then? Why not throw out the undergrowth and goat willow? Their content doesn't fit, but the concept does. "What is it? The *natural* fits, but the man-made doesn't, is it back to that again?"

"Seems it must be," says Nick, who, finding the doors open and unable to make himself heard has wandered into the kitchen.

Claire spins round to see him propping up the doorpost. "Nick!"

"Unless, of course, you're responding to the tone of them," he says, taking a step into the room.

"Don't you ever knock?" Claire asks. She moves in an attempt to block the drawings from his sight, but there are too many. He's the last person she would want to see these now.

"I did. Three times," he says, looking past her at the work. "It *could* be resonance. Look at the strength of these, compared to the one you've discarded."

She feels herself squirm as he comes closer to them. It seems too personal. Too raw. Her arms move to physically turn him away. She folds them across her breast.

"The majority are *much* more vibrant," he continues, indicating one she drew by the stream on one of the excursions down to the beach. The small figure of Sky is almost swallowed by the swirl of undergrowth sweeping around and over her.

"The odd one out is much more passive. Technically good, but only that, really. Academic, dry. Whereas these . . ." He returns his attention to the others.

Naked. She feels naked.

"I wonder what the children are up to," she says, taking a step away. He doesn't follow. She notices his traveler's stubble has gone. The curls, too, have been cropped.

She hears him grunt softly to himself, then, after a few moments, he turns to face her. And there it is again, the sadness about his eyes, made more evident by his mouth forming a smile.

"Kate told me of these," he says. "I was rather afraid to see them. And now I have." He looks back at them. Smiles more fully. "She was right. They're very passionate," he says, "and *very* strong, Claire. When you have more, you should think of exhibiting." He nods to himself. "Perhaps that's what it is, Claire. The sense of the passionate in most of these that's lacking from the one."

"Are they passionate?"

"*Aren't* they?" He sends a flare of a glance in her direction. She looks away.

"I didn't ask—"

"You didn't ask for a critique. And I didn't come intending to give one."

He turns and leans against the work surface, his back to where the drawings are propped up and he smiles again.

"I just dropped in to collect the drawings I loaned you. I'm gathering my summer's work. As it seems you are. Must be the season for it. Harvesting."

Then there's reason to wish he would look at the drawings again, for his eyes are fully on her now, their paleness all the more strident since his tanned face is clean-shaven.

"How does it seem?" she asks, quickly.

"My summer's work?"

"Yes."

"Promising."

She busies herself with the drawing on the table, putting it back in the portfolio.

"Will you have a cup of tea?" she asks.

"No, no. Thank you."

"I'll just get your drawings, then."

"Thank you."

When she comes back, he's studying her work again and continues with it, ignoring her, so that she finds herself pottering around in the kitchen behind him, belatedly putting away breakfast things and maybe *he* doesn't want a cup of tea, but she thinks she will have one and she fills the kettle and switches it on and glances across at him: the line of his relaxed shoulders, the whiteness of his cropped hair, still trying to curl against his sun-browned neck, the softness of the corduroy shirt he's wearing; a very deep blue. Perhaps that's why his eyes seem all the more striking today. She takes the tea bags from the cupboard. He turns to her again. And, somehow, this time it's easy to meet his gaze. They smile at each other.

"Oh, here they are," he says, seeing his own drawings where she's put them on the table and crossing to them to renew his acquaintance.

"In what way were they useful?"

"I'm sorry?"

"In your note, you said having the drawings around had been useful."

"Oh yes, I did. Are you sure you won't have tea?" Claire asks, putting a couple of bags in the pot.

"Quite, thanks." He looks at her. "Well?"

She laughs and shakes her head. "I can't ever talk about this kind of stuff without feeling *ridiculously* pretentious . . ."

"Try."

"Pseud's Corner quote of the week?"

"Come on."

"I *can't*," she laughs.

"Try."

She throws the box of tea bags back into the cupboard.

"I don't know. Something to do with . . ."

She trails into silence.

"Yes?" Nick pushes.

Nathan rushes in.

"Damien won't let me have the ball."

"I thought you were playing hide-and-seek," Claire says, sweeping hair from the boy's eyes.

"It was boring. Now he won't let me have the ball."

"Damien!" Claire calls, then more quietly, "Would you like a drink, Nathan?"

Nathan puts his thumb in his mouth and nods. Claire gets milk from the fridge.

"Take your thumb out."

She looks across to Nick to shrug an apology.

"Oh *no*," he says. "You don't get let off that easily."

Claire laughs.

A football whizzes in through the kitchen door, followed by Damien. "What are you doing?" he asks.

"Footballs are for *out*side," Claire says firmly.

"I'm trying to get your mother to say something about these drawings and she won't," Nick says to him.

"Oh, it's all right," Damien says, recognizing the pieces of Nick's work he's been forbidden to touch. "She did like them."

"That wasn't quite what we were after." Nick grins.

"Nathan, don't you dare go anywhere near the table with that glass of milk in your hands. Go and sit on the window seat," Claire says. "Good boy."

"She said it had lots of . . . what was the word, Mummy?" Damien asks. "You said it was like when I jump up and down all the time."

"Energy," Claire supplies for him. Her eyes flick quickly to Nick's.

"Aahhh," he says.

"I thought it was a bit silly because everybody knows drawings don't jump up and down," Damien says, wiping his nose on his sleeve.

"Do you want a drink, Damien?"

"Yes."

"Yes, *please*."

"Yes, *please*."

She pours him milk and he drains it.

"What's this about not letting Nathan play with the football?" Claire asks, taking biscuits from the cupboard.

"He's too slow."

"I am *not*!"

"You must share with him, Damien."

"*Okay*," Damien drawls, grinding an imaginary, inch-high Nathan into the floor with the ball of his foot.

"Off you go now and be fair with your brother."

He dribbles the ball out of the room, then boots it from the back door, hard.

Claire sighs. She puts a splash of milk in her tea.

"You all right, Nath?" Nathan nods from the window seat.

"It's probably the thing I'm after most, in fact," Nick says, crossing the kitchen to pour himself a cup of tea after all.

"Sorry?"

Nick looks up at her. "A sense of vibrancy, energy. Landscape isn't static."

"Oh well, then. Not Pseud's Corner at all."

"Not unless I'm there before you," he smiles.

"So, seeing as you've bamboozled your way in here and told me what's what with my work, perhaps you'd be kind enough to invite me to view yours, sometime."

"No time like the present," he says, picking up her mug from the countertop and giving it to her.

"Now?"

"Why not? Bring your tea with you."

"What about the boys?"

"They can come too."

"I'll have to collect a key," Claire says, as they leave the room.

"Oh. You lock up, then?"

"I do now the Armstrong painting's here," she says, wryly.

"Very sensible."

"Don't you?"

"I do the studio. Not the house. Not unless I'm away for more than a week."

It feels rather like entering a forest. Big pictures hang, predominantly green. Vegetation and landscape, bold and very present, some figurative, some abstract.

The children are silent for once, standing back to back, rotating slowly to see round the room.

In one corner, there's a pencil drawing, in the style of the ones she borrowed, only much bigger. Claire goes close to the heavy mess of lines then steps away again, watching the image spring back into being. Part of the trunk of an ancient tree, sparse fern at its foot, the debris of the forest floor. It seems so gutsy; so sure of itself. Going close again, she can see the way the pencil line has been pushed hard onto the paper so that the surface is indented.

"You haven't seen my garden, have you?" she hears Nick ask the children.

"No," Damien answers.

"Did you know I've got a tree house?"

"*Have* you?"

"I have. Do you want to come and see?"

"Yes please."

"What about you, Nathan?"

"*He* doesn't even know what a tree house *is*," Damien says.

"Time he found out, then. Is that okay, Claire? I'll leave you to it for a little while."

"Will they be all right?" she asks, turning to them.

"I think they'll be fine. Even Sky hasn't managed to hurt herself on it."

"Oh well, if it's passed the Sky test."

"I'll stay with them. Just dig around as much or as little as you want. The ones on the wall are this summer's and there are more in the folio in the corner, waiting to be framed. Earlier work's through here." He opens an internal door and she gasps to see the racks of stored pictures.

"Won't you tell me about them?"

He smiles. "I rather hope they speak for themselves."

Well, that told me, she thinks, left alone.

In an angry upsurge of landscape, one house lodges fast, a speck of shadowed ocher stone. Sweeping greens and blacks speak of late evening, long shadows cast by a pale sunset from a bleached, empty sky. The tops of trees catch yellow and the color bleeds down.

There are several like this. The trees huge, often backlit, the color smearing from one plane to another. Sparsely placed buildings cling steadfast, tiny.

In a series of four; rooftops figure in the foreground, above them the outline of a tree-clad hill, above that, naked hill, above that, cloud, above that, the shoulder of a mountain, above that, a dawn sky lightening. The format is tall and narrow, the colors of early morning. The first of the four is figurative, progressing through to an abstract last. The figurative work seems to have been attacked with the same vigor as the drawing in the corner. The abstract work appears calmer, a smoother surface.

More drawings. Smaller. The corner of a stone plinth beneath an old water pump. A riot of vegetation grown around and in front and behind it. Studies of a rock outcrop; the same dense, frenetic line.

Claire pushes open the inner door. She wonders how long she's been engrossed in the work and how the children are behaving themselves. She probably ought to go soon. Just a quick look. She pulls a picture out from its place in the rack, then puts it back without looking at it. Shame to rush it. She'll let the first lot sink in before looking at more. And yes, they do speak for themselves, but it would be good to have Nick here. The thought of coming back again pleases her. This old building with skylights let into the roof, the squat dehumidifier in the corner keeping order, the treasury of pictures to be explored and, perhaps, next time, the guidance of Nick.

She looks round the pictures on the wall once more, then goes out into the garden. Snatches of laughter come from where the garden gives way to a wood. She can hear the high voices of the children and Nick's answering deeper tone.

Forty-four

Excellent, Elizabeth thinks, seeing Claira coming forward to greet her: the impression she had kept of the young woman *was* accurate. Really, an exquisite face. And grace. Even though her countenance is flushed with color today and her eyes seem especially bright, there is yet a quality to her movement that speaks of self-possession. Excellent.

And this is the husband then, she thinks as hands are shaken. A strong jaw and direct eyes. Pleasing face. Quite a lot older than his wife.

"Has Claira said, I am hoping she will let me paint her?"

"No," says Munro, surprised. "But I have scarcely been home half an hour, so we have not had time yet to talk of all that has happened while I have been away."

"I disturbed her last week, by the stream where she had been playing her violin." Elizabeth sees that Claira darts a glance at her husband. "She looked so lovely there. I hope you can spare her long enough for me to try and do justice to her."

"If Claira is willing, I see no reason not to," Munro says. "I should be pleased for you both, if it's what you want."

"Would you, Claira?" Elizabeth asks.

"Yes, I would like it," Claira assures her, warming at the thought of being able to see her new friend.

Tea is offered and accepted and brought to the parlor, the kitchen being chaos. Ellen and Hannah come through to say hello, then Beattie and William and Samuel. Claira watches Elizabeth watching them, the way she absorbs all. The painter catches Claira's eye and they smile at each other.

There are scones and jam and cream to be brought through and Claira finds Elizabeth is talking to Munro, listening with her head slightly to one side, her eyes full on him. Claira catches a snatch of conversation. Africa. Eadie comes in to see what she is missing and Claira introduces her to Elizabeth's mother. Coming back with the next pot of tea, Claira sees them in animated talk. And it's good, this activity, the buzz all around her.

Then, just as quickly, it's time for people to go and there's the rounding up of William and the things he brought and the bundling into carriages and won't Hannah and Beattie travel with Elizabeth and her mother as there is room in the carriage and they take the same road? Elizabeth gives Claira her new address in St. Ives and the women arrange a date for the first sitting. Then there are the thank-yous and good-byes.

And then it's just the three of them, Munro, Claira and Eadie, standing on the lawn by the front door from where they waved their visitors off, except that Eadie announces she must have a lie-down, she has quite exhausted herself with tea and talk. No, she will manage, thank you and she turns and takes herself indoors, so that then it's just Claira and Munro.

They glance at each other, then away.

Claira looks across at the sundial, then goes to it. Half past six. If it were a day for chapel, he'd be leaving soon, but it isn't. She traces a finger round the sundial's face.

Munro steps into her peripheral vision.

Claira looks hard at the dial.

A wren flits into the nearby hedge.

Munro clears his throat. "I liked Elizabeth."

"Yes, isn't she lovely," Claira agrees.

"Canadian," Munro says.

"Is she? I thought from her accent she . . . I hadn't really had time to ask her."

"No."

"I expect—" Claira begins.

"You will look forward—" Munro begins and their words meet and crash midair. Claira winces as the debris falls to earth. Munro snorts.

"What were you going to say?" Claira asks.

He looks at her standing there, slender, half turned from him, the sun on her hair—and back it comes: the punishing pattern of desire and denial. He had thought it conquered by his hours of thinking while he's been away, but no! Within minutes of being alone with her, here it is back again. And with it, the old temptation to turn and leave, to bury himself in checking round the farm—Heaven knows it's time he did, there must be plenty needs doing. He takes half a step away then stops, forces himself to remain. If the pattern is to be broken, now is the only time to do it.

"Claira," he says and she looks round in surprise at his use of her name, so that he has her eyes for a second. "I wanted to talk to you."

She holds his gaze, so he draws breath and continues, "What I did to you . . ." She drops her head. "No, please listen," he says and he takes a stride towards her so that he stands in front of her. His hands move as if he will take hers, but he folds his arms, then drops them again, shoving his hands in his pockets.

"What I did to you was a wickedness for which I can never forgive myself. And I want you to know that I have thought"—he gives a mirthless laugh and casts his eyes to the sky—"for many hours about it while I have been away."

He takes a pace away from her and another back again.

"I've sought God's guidance—and the guidance of men too, my brother and his minister—on how I can atone for such a deed as I sank to."

For the briefest moment their eyes dare to meet, then flit quickly away again. Difficult, difficult, hard not to flinch, to suffer this nakedness.

"And I have thought," Munro struggles on, "of what I have done in marrying you, of how it was my choice to marry someone"—he looks down, then at her once more—"someone not entirely of my persuasion and that I must live with that decision and find ways in which we might proceed here that are as easy as possible for us both.

"The Bible has guided me," he says, "although"—and he gives a self-mocking laugh—"although I needed Edwin's minister to point it out for me." Then, looking at her, he begins to intone, " 'And the woman which hath an husband that believeth not, and if he be pleased to dwell with her, let her not leave him. For the unbelieving husband is sanctified by the wife and—' "

" 'And,' " Claira says, taking over from him, " 'the unbelieving wife is sanctified by the husband: else were your children unclean, but now they are holy.' "

She gives a brief smile. "In a household such as the one I grew up in . . ." Her suggestion trails into silence and he kicks himself as he learns this latest lesson. He has traveled far, claiming new territory as his own, only to discover she is there before him, firmly encamped, terrain all charted. In a household such as the one she grew up in, this passage must have been the family motto. Obvious, obvious. So much for all his thinking that he had not made the connection.

"Indeed," he says.

Claira runs her finger again around the dial, then along the shadow of present time.

"I, too, have had time for reflection," she says. She gathers herself. "What you did *was* wicked. I spent much time trying to forgive it, but I don't suppose there is a way to entirely."

"I know it," he says flatly and draws breath to say more, only she looks straight at him and raises a hand. *She* will speak now, it says.

"One of the reasons it seemed unforgivable is the way you are with other people." Claira joins her hands at her waist and looks at them. "The kind attention you give Aunt Eadie, the way you are with Jed and Mrs. Jago who have worked for you for so long, the way they respect you and how you go about things here—and Michael does, too. And then I thought about the animals."

"The animals?"

"Yes. I thought about seeing you with them. About how, when you drive your cattle you do not shout or beat them, you just call to them—at most, you rest a hand on their haunches."

"Do I?"

"You do. As gentleness. And then I remembered how the horses turn and push their heads against you."

"They know me. I feed them."

"And see to them well and are kind with them. And the calves, too, come to you."

Munro flinches at a recollection she perhaps does not have.

"Even with the killing of pigs you make all effort to dispatch them swiftly."

"If they are to give their lives, it seems the least we owe them to—"

Again she silences him. Dark eyes hard on his.

"At first this made your action in . . ." She throws her hands down. "In hitting me seem all the more wicked. It seems you could find more compassion for your cows, than you could for your wife." She laughs. "So I spent a day or more in anger and then"—she pauses at the memory of it—"I woke one morning with the clear question in my head—Why? Why is such a man like this towards everyone and everything else, but not towards me?" She looks at Munro. "It was then I started to learn of my own wickedness."

"*Your* wickedness?"

"Yes."

"In what way, wicked?"

Claira pauses, arranging the words in her head. "A lack of attention to you. A neglect."

"But, your father, you were grieving."

"Yes I was. I still am. But"—she joins her hands again, looks down at them—"what began as a reasonable oversight . . ." She trails off. "I allowed it to harden into neglect." She looks straight at him. "I chose to neglect what you had a right to expect of me."

Munro returns the directness of her gaze, glad of God's earth, firm beneath his feet.

"So," she continues, turning to pace a little away from him, folding her arms across her midriff, then throwing them down to her sides again. "So, yes, *husband,*" and, from this greater distance, she throws the word at him, "your action *was* unforgivable. Try though I have, I cannot find it within me to pardon it." She stops pacing to look at him. "Neither can I pardon my willfulness that drove you to it."

For moments they look at each other.

"What then is to be done?" he says. It's almost a whisper and he wonders if it will carry to her.

She smiles a little.

"This," she says, gesturing with her hands the words that flow between them. "And actions. We have already started those."

Across the divide their eyes are on each other.

"The fiddle," she says.

He raises open hands and shakes his head. "Is the repair good?"

She nods. "It plays perfectly. I would not have believed it possible."

"The dent on the scroll," he says.

She smiles. "It will remind us."

She begins to pace again and he watches her bringing herself to something and he wonders what it is that comes next and catches himself thinking that he almost doesn't mind what it is as long as the connection with her is as good as it feels at this moment.

She stops again and looks at him; still the distance.

"I too," she says, "have begun to act."

"Yes?"

"Perhaps you have heard, perhaps Mrs. Jago wrote to you?"

"No."

"Or perhaps you have seen the minister."

Munro shakes his head. "No, I came straight here from the train."

"I attend chapel now," she says.

He feels his face open wide.

"Not every service," she says quickly. "I will not go to every service. You will not find me there on Thursday evening or Sunday afternoon, but I do attend on Tuesday evening and Sunday morning. And the minister has spoken to me about taking a Sunday school class, which I may well."

He turns away. He hears his breath sigh from him and only then knows how tightly he has been bracing himself. Briefly he closes his eyes. *Thank God. Thank God.* Tomorrow is Thursday, so she will not be coming. But on Sunday . . . He wants to laugh for the joy of it. He wants to pick her up and hug her and kiss her face with gratitude. He turns back to her.

"I cannot say how . . ." His hands fly wide then catch themselves together. "How pleased I am."

She smiles. Their eyes meet half a second.

He frowns suddenly. "The villagers?"

Claira looks down. "Aunt Eadie was kind. It is easier now."

He lets out held breath, seeking her eyes; shoves his hands again into his pockets; paces away from her.

The shadows are lengthening now, at the end of the garden.

"Mrs. Jago tells me you have had to tend the brindle cow," he says.

Claira looks up.

"She has had a touch of mastitis. She is a little better these last few days."

"Thank you for that," he says, stopping in front of her.

Their eyes chime against each other.

"And the hay all about has been cut and ours must be soon," he says.

"Yes."

Still they look at each other, eyes resting steady now.

"Will you walk with me while I check the animals?" he asks.

She smiles a little, watching him, then nods her head. They begin to move towards the yard.

And then Jed is there, coming from the byre with awkward gait and determination to greet Munro. They shake hands, warmly, Munro clasping Jed by the shoulder as he compliments him on the rick of furze so neatly made.

Forty-five

The Automobile Association drops the BMW at an approved garage. Claire thinks this is the best plan although she can't reach Howard on the phone and his mobile seems to be switched off. Guilt and pleasure mingle. The car breaking down means the boys won't get to see their grandmother. The car breaking down means Claire can go home to Howard. It seemed so ridiculous him being in Cornwall during the week Claire was due to be away. Now Providence has stepped in, allowing her to see Howard, to spend time with him. At that moment, her mind chooses to replay footage of Nick: turning to her in his garden, play-fighting Nathan in his arms. She stamps the image out. A silly attraction brought about by his kindness to the children and her loneliness.

Silly.

The children watch the spectacle of the BMW being let down the ramp, underbelly showing.

"Well, we *have* had an adventure," Claire says, bobbing down beside the boys.

"What do we do now?" Nathan asks.

"The AA man will take us home."

Arriving at Trethenna, Claire sees her Metro is there. Howard must be home already. She's surprised and checks her watch. It's only a quarter past three. She thought he'd have to be at the development in Falmouth all day. She hopes he's all right. The thought crosses her mind that he might have been taken ill in her absence and she thanks the AA man quickly and drops the case and the bags inside the front door as she calls Howard's name. There's no answer, but she hears movement upstairs. Checking the children in the garden, Claire sees the AA man is giving them something, stickers or badges. Nathan's got his pedal car out of the barn and he's towing it along in a breakdown.

"Howard?" she calls as she goes upstairs.

In their bedroom the curtains are drawn and Howard is standing by the side of the bed, doing up his trousers.

"Are you all right?" she asks and even as she hears her voice, the tightness of the atmosphere hits her and she hears an inner voice, too, and she doesn't want to hear it as she watches him fumble with his fly, but it repeats itself, louder and says again, *caught-with-his-trousers-down* and *don't-be-ridiculous* another voice says, but the first is insistent, *caught-with-his* . . . and she sees the gray of his face, then the flush on his skin and his fingers stumbling. He's saying something, Claire, Claire and she hears the rough of his tongue on her name and the room sways slightly, slurring into slow motion and there's a familiar smell she can taste. Sperm. No! It can't be, not here, not here at the cin-e-ma.

She wants to leave, but her legs don't move and the film flicks on and the soundtrack sounds like the thump of a heart and the rush of blood through ears. She scans the big screen and in the curtained half-light sees the mound of duvet twitch and mount and, from the belly of the bed, a creature erupts; the birth of a being from the marriage bed only full-grown and beautiful and perfectly formed. A naked woman. Beautiful. Claire feels the floor reel, hears herself gasp for breath round the tightness in her throat. There's something in her ribs, a pain as the wall comes up to catch her and locates her with the point of the metal door latch and she puts out a hand to try and keep the room still and her lips move and a voice groans, *"Oh God!"*

The woman on the screen turns and begins picking up clothes

from the chair at the side of the bed; it looks like Claire's chair where she puts *her* clothes, but the actress's body is brown and tight with taut little breasts and a flat belly. She turns and her buttocks look like firm fruit. Then it's as if she changes her mind and she puts the clothes down on the rumpled bedding and sits on the edge of the bed, raises her head and looks straight at the camera. She has an elfin face, sharp, and a tangle of long dark hair. Well? her stare says. What are you going to do about it? Focus shifts to the activity of the man who's coming towards the camera doing up his shirt. His face looks like Howard's face when he's angry. Claire is hot and she cannot breathe. She holds on for a second, her back hard against the swaying wall, willing the tilt of the floor to catch up with her. Sickeningly it moves and tips her out of the door.

The landing is more solid and as she reaches the top of the stairs, she looks down and sees Damien at the bottom, coming up.

"Is Daddy home?"

"Yes," says Claire's voice from a distance. "Yes, but he's not himself."

"What do you mean?" asks Damien, continuing to come upstairs.

"He's not himself, he's not well. Come away," she says, turning him by the shoulders.

"I want to see him."

"You can't. He needs to rest. We're going to see Kate and Sky."

He pulls away from her.

"Damien." She raises a hand to halt him. "Come away."

She sees her hands are shaking and drops them by her sides. The boy looks past her up the stairs, then at his mother before he turns and goes down ahead of her.

Claire sits very still. She wraps her arms round her knees and her eyes look downwards to the part of ground where the edge of the turf creeps over rock. The grass is thin and wiry and short and the peaty soil shows through. Darker rock is blurred at the edge of her vision and she concentrates on it without focusing. Letting her consciousness seep into out-of-focus no-man's-land, it's as if her body dissolves. Still and silent and out of focus.

The cloud is much higher than it was this morning. This morning it would scarcely have been possible to see her hand in front of her face, but now if she were to look from where she sits at the height of Blundle Hill, her view would be gray, but good. Claire does not look. Not yet.

Although the fog has cleared, the air's still damp and sometimes, if her mind must move from rock and grass, she looks at the beads of moisture that have settled on the sweater she is wearing. She can see them marking the outline of her arms where the wet has been brought by the wind at her back. She thinks that quite probably she must be cold, but that information is in the unfocused part. She knows, if she were to move and touch the beads of water, they would join together in a wet smear. She doesn't move; she leaves the droplets to settle as they would on gorse or on stalks of grass. As they would on the grass in front of her if she were not here.

Kate had said simply, "Claire, you look dreadful, whatever's happened?" Then she had shut up and quietly gotten on with what was needed: a drink for the children, a thicker sweater for Claire, who seemed to be shivering.

Claire had watched and waited for the children to settle. Nathan was determined that they should play breakdown with the pedal car he'd insisted they bring. Claire had had to carry the thing along the footpath that crosses the fields between the two houses, lifting it high over the stone stiles. Damien, directing play, seemed to have forgotten about his father. For now, at any rate.

"What do you need?" Kate had asked Claire quietly.

"Some time to think. Half an hour. May I leave them with you?"

"Of course."

The movement comes. It flickers at the edge of her vision; top left.

Look, then.

Her gaze drops down: *no movement there.*

There'll never be another chance.

She draws breath and looks up and the world slams into focus and into focus again as she locates, in the landscape's gray-green, two moving dots. At first it looks like one dot, but it divides into two and one goes back towards the house and then comes out again.

Forgotten the car keys. So like him.

She hadn't been sure it would be possible to see figures from here; she'd thought it would just be the bigger dot of the car that would give them away. But it's easy.

She drops her gaze back to the ground. An ant carries the dead down the grove at the edge of the soil. The way is barred by debris and the ant backs and veers and clambers up to drop down again, hurrying. Claire wonders where it's going, why it carries its burden, for food or burial or just to dump it. She wonders if she'll hear the car door close from here.

No, you won't. Look again. It's what you came to see.

So she does and she sees the lighter dot of the car, her car, already on the lane that winds below her round the shoulder of Blundle Hill; Howard and his lover in it. For a second she wonders if they might see her, but no, Kate's sweater is the color of bracken and they'd have no reason to look.

That's it then. All over. You can go home now.

The urgent message comes that her body must shift. Just in time she whips round as the muscle spasms grip her body and, in full vomit, throw her face to the earth.

The key clatters in the lock. Claire pushes into the block of stillness and the calmness of the house engulfs her. She rests against the door frame, looking in. Like untrodden snow, smooth to the eye, the peace seems far too soothing to mar. She walks down the hallway past an open door and stops at the different wedge of silence there, marked by the measured tick . . . tock . . . then she moves on and up the stairs, wanting to see now.

She slows at the bedroom door, her mind replaying the film. Frowning her face against it, she makes herself note the level of daylight she can see coming out of the room. They drew the curtains back at least.

It's true then, she thinks as she walks into the room: hands do fly to mouths at times like this. The mirror catches the cliché and gives it back to her. It's a helpful sighting, letting her read her body in this unfamiliar stance.

Look at yourself: from that gesture you can tell this really is happening to you.

Because the room wouldn't confirm it. That's the shock: the perfection of the room.

Claire's brushes and bottles on the dressing table are in exact array. The pair of trousers draped over the chair are just as Claire left them. And the bed is perfectly made, smooth downy duvet without a crease. The curtain stirs slightly and she sees the window has been left an inch ajar. She walks to the chair and sits down. She imagined it all then. Aberration.

"Knocked off balance by a near car crash and disoriented by a change of plan, mother of two, Claire Lattimer came home and imagined she saw her husband in bed with another woman.

" 'The images only lasted for about fifteen seconds,' Mrs. Lattimer said. 'And I feel much better now that I've . . .' "

Claire leaps and the chair upturns and she relishes the racket. The bottles and brushes are the next to go, crashing to the floor. Nothing there. She flings aside the cushion that's fallen from the chair. Nothing. She throws open the wardrobe doors, the line of clothes sway on their hangers. Howard's clothes. Claire's clothes.

Neat, ordered, perfect. The bed then. She rushes to rip back the duvet. Nothing. Pillows fly. Nothing. Nothing.

She throws herself down to sit, head in hands, on the edge of the bed. Her heart is thumping and she waits for it to slow. It does not. She forces herself to gulp deep breath; forces closed her eyes. She *must* stay calm. She'll have to pick the children up soon. *Get a grip. Get a grip.* Her breathing begins to steady. Her pulse rate begins to slow. *Better.* Her mouth tastes foul from vomiting, her throat raw. She takes another deep breath. She'll go and get cleaned up in a little while.

Infidelity. She wonders how long it's been going on. The business trips away. Howard lying to her. Her heart rate increases again and she blocks the thoughts, turning her concentration back to her breathing.

Breathe deeply, breathe slowly, calmly, calmly.

She drops her chin to her chest. *Better.* One thing at a time. She'll go and clean her teeth and wash, perhaps take a bath, yes, a bath would be good. Then she'll make up a bed in the spare room. That's what people do in this situation, isn't it? Move into the spare room. Then she'll go and collect the children.

She takes another deep lung-full of air and slowly opens her eyes. Cushions and pillows and bottles lie on the floor where she scattered them. She'll pick them up in a moment. Put them all back. Then, against the cream of the bottom sheet, something catches her eye. Protruding from beneath her hand, it looks like the loop of a hair. Quite slowly, she moves her hand away. It is a hair. Long and uniformly dark, tinged with red. Dyed. Curled into an "S" shape.

There's her proof, then.

She looks at it, there on the sheet.

Forty-six

Morning light creeps under the gap beneath his closed door and Munro shifts in his bed and sleepily rubs his face, then rousing a little, scratches his cheek more definitely where something irritates. A third time it tickles and he brings his hand up to move away what turns out to be a hair. He catches hold of it, idly pulls to get rid of the thing; only it doesn't end and through his sleepiness it occurs to him: this hair has something his doesn't. Length.

Suddenly awake, he sits upright in the bed. He pulls and the hair keeps coming and then he has it all before him and even through sleep-bleary eyes, there can be no doubt whose it is. Darker at one end and lightened at the other by the sun, even solo and in this thin light, it shines. The idea fights through and is formed: *Claira has been in my bed.*

Nonsense, the countering thought quickly comes. Been in the room to tend it, maybe. *Made* the bed, perhaps. She has never been in it. *Nonsense.*

Still holding the hair, he gets up and opens his door to let in more light and stands awhile in the doorway, running the hair between his fingers. Crossing to the bed, he pulls back the covers, lifts pillows and the bolster, searching for more evidence. There is none.

Do not begin this, his conscience chides him. Only last night as you shut yourself in your room you were glad to hear her go on up to the attic. A stability, you called it, as you heard her feet pass, a maintenance of separateness. An expectation of nothing. A breaking free from the snare. Well, you have broken free. Do not make yourself prisoner again.

He places the hair on the whiteness of the exposed undersheet. It shows darkly against it. She would have swept it away, surely, as she made the bed, seeing it there.

Wondering what to do with it, he sits on his bed and loops the hair through itself, round the brass bar of the bed-head. That's something else she could have been doing here: polishing brass-work.

He lets himself fall back onto the bed, his head on the pillow. Watching her hair as it hangs down towards him, he sees it move to and fro with his breath. He breathes in deeply and the hair touches his face and he thinks of her in his bed, how the mass of her hair would tumble down over him. He feels his pulse quicken. *Dear God. She has been in my bed.* He feels himself gathered tight, his penis flexed hard.

Jumping out of bed, he pushes the door to. With a clatter of the metal latch it shuts and he stands in the middle of the room, eyes closed and breathing fast. *To be carnally minded is death.* His penis pushes out his shirt. *To be carnally minded is death.* He struggles and smothers till his breathing settles, then, crossing to the bed he falls to his knees and begins to pray out loud. *I should renounce the Devil and all his works, the pomps and vanity of this wicked world and all the sinful* . . . at that moment he hears her coming down the stairs . . . *and all the sinful* . . . as she passes his door, he holds his breath and listens to her footfall . . . *and all the sinful lusts of the flesh* . . . his lips mouth as her footsteps fade.

"You were right about the weather," Claira says, minutes later as Munro comes into the kitchen. She casts an eye to the rain that spots, lightly, on the window, then smiles across at him.

"Not a day for cutting hay," says Eadie, at the breakfast table.

"No," Munro agrees. "Seems it will worsen, too. Barometer's still falling."

All day he is out on the farm. Claira hears his voice from time to time as the men return to the yard. She hears Jed's voice, too, lighter today, pleased to have the master home. Even the dogs seem more settled.

At midday he comes in. And she loves the feel of the room once he is in it, full of his presence. And she cannot help but watch him, the ease with which he brings buckets of water, tips them to fill the pitchers. Fluent, practiced movement; his body making beauty of the mundane task. Feeling himself watched, he looks up and their eyes catch and flare before she looks away.

Tending him at table, she finds her body lingers as she passes dishes from the dresser, aware only that the flesh of his arm is merely inches from her belly as she stands.

"Did we butter the potatoes, Claira?" Mrs. Jago asks.

"Yes, I think so," Claira replies. "Yes, I'm sure we did."

Putting food before him, she sees the grooved muscle of his forearms where he has pushed back his sleeves to wash. The skin has been browned by weather. She draws slow breath as if she might breathe him nearer; catches the scent of new sweat on him and the smell of fields from his hair still moist from the rain.

Turning; the fabric of her skirt brushes Munro's elbow and she draws breath again— involuntarily this time—as the shock of the contact floods through her body.

He works on through the evening, comes in tired and grimy. She is kneeling on the floor of the kitchen, stuffing feathers into a cushion she is making. They litter the floor round her, like daisies or dropped blossoms. She smiles, acknowledging the mess. "I should *not* be doing this in here."

Drinking a glass of water down, he sits and watches her, there at his feet.

She looks up again. "Have you eaten all you need today?"

He smiles. "Thank you, yes," and he cannot just sit there, watching her, so he goes upstairs to wash and change.

She is still there when he comes down again, gathering the feathers from the floor only it's difficult to do both, to hold the mouth of the cushion open and scoop the feathers up too, so he kneels by her, takes the cushion from her and holds it wide. Claira glances at him.

"Thank you," she says, rounding up feathers and though she has both hands now, somehow it's more difficult—the nearness of him. Her fingers fluster and miss the feathers.

Bending forward in her gathering, she smells the fresh linen he's put on and the scent of his soap. The neck of his shirt is open and her eye follows down the line of his neck where it plunges into the breadth of his chest and she sees the muscle there flex as he gathers the edge of the material round. Her heartbeat hastens. She had never thought to see his body tamed to such a task; the power of him brought to bear on such trivia.

"It is for the rocking chair," she says.

He looks up quickly. "Is it?"

She nods.

"Does it please you?" he asks.

The flicker of a smile. "Yes."

He gathers the edge of the bag again. Unnecessarily.

"I wanted there to be a chair that was yours. Somewhere for you to sit, away from your room."

Their eyes meet, briefly, a second, less, before she looks away. Iron gray, his eyes, flecked with brown.

Still he holds the fabric wide, so her hands must find feathers, and they do, fumbling and inefficient, moving between his hands to let the feathers go. She concentrates on the mouth of the bag, sees his hands move too, closing together so that she looks up at his eyes again and there it is. Unmistakable. Minutely her lips part and she feels her heart thump hard, but she holds his eye this time; sees the depths of his eyes seem to quicken: peepholes down to a maelstrom sea. The pull of them is overwhelming. Like an undertow they have her as his hand rises to brush against hers, as his fingers trace the outline of her knuckles, as his voice whispers, "Claira, Claira."

Tap, tap. Tap, tap.

They start.

Eadie's cane in the corridor.

In a second he has shoved the cushion to Claira and leapt to his feet.

"I'm off to my bed, then," Eadie says, coming into the room. "Oh, that *is* a pretty mess," she says to Claira on the floor, where spilt feathers fly.

Claira bursts into laughter. "Isn't it?" she agrees, steadying herself. "I really should have done this out-of-doors."

"Can I get you a glass of water, Aunt Eadie?" Munro asks.

"Yes please."

Munro turns to the pitcher and Claira gets to her feet and kisses Eadie on the cheek. "Sleep well," she says.

"Thank you, dear."

When Munro turns to give Eadie the water, Claira is not in the room.

He tries not to run as he goes to the parlor. Empty. He checks the dining room. Empty. His study empty.

The front door is ajar.

He pushes it to without looking out, not bearing to think of her gone. She must be upstairs. His room.

He takes the stairs two at a time, picturing her by his mirror, waiting in the shadows, pale and wide-eyed for him. He throws back the door and the silence of the room floods round him. The attic, then, and he heads for the little stairs, but, as he crosses the landing, her image burns into the corner of his eye. There she is. In the empty room—against the grayness of the mizzled evening.

He steps inside and his footsteps echo and she turns and paces, turns and paces so that he crosses to her and they meet in collision and his strength rises round her to hold her there, containing her: dragonfly in a jar. He feels her twist in his confinement, so slight in his grasp and fearing to hurt her, he loosens his hold. She slips from him and is gone. Across the landing he follows her—his room this time.

She does, now, stand in the shadows by the mirror, where he had thought her; but she is no pale icon. Two yards between them yet. He takes a step towards her but she backs farther from him, so he stills himself.

Quickly her fingers undo the buttons of her dress and slide it from her shoulders, letting it fall to the floor. He gapes. What is he to do, merely witness this? He steps to her again. She backs; maintains the distance. *Oh no,* her eyes insist. His lungs punch out pressured air, but he holds his position. Seeing him still, she pulls the ribbon of her chemise undone. For the first time he sees the curve of her breasts, the quick rise and fall of them. As she moves the fabric away, it catches, briefly, on a nipple. He clenches fists round frantic stillness, but cannot steady his quickening breath. Why must she do this? Surely they should just . . . Untying her drawers, she steps from them. As naked as Eve she stands, straightening herself to her full height. In the mirror, he sees the firm white flesh of her buttocks. Surely the pounding of his heart can be heard by her across the room, six feet. He looks to her face, trying to read her. She holds his eye. *Not yet;* she glances, stepping to the bed. *Not yet*, reaching, slender-limbed, to turn back covers. For a second more she stands, then slides herself onto the sheet's whiteness.

You may join me now, her eyes say.

In moments it is over. The tearing off of his clothes and the lying down on her, the desperation to be in her and the desperation not to hurt. Beneath him, he feels her spread herself wide, yet still he cannot locate her, so that she must help him and he gasps, pushing on in, hearing her yelp; giving his seed instantly.

Rolling from her, he gathers her to him, kissing her head. God, that she might be hurt.

"Are you all right? Are you all right?"

She raises her face to his kissing and he wants her closer. He will hold her and hold her and he brings her to his breast and—miracle—he feels her nudge into it.

In the dark room he wakes and does not move. There's warmth at his side. Claira. He squeezes his eyes closed as the flood of emotion sweeps up through his body. How can he ever be equal to the importance of this? His lips move in silent prayer. Thanksgiving. Then he listens and can hear her soft breathing, feels the rise and fall of her skin on his as she lies on her side against him. His penis rises and he wishes it would not. Her head is on his shoulder, her arm across his chest, her leg over his. So it goes on into sleep, then, this closeness.

She stirs and he holds his breath: don't wake, don't wake. He wants this moment for longer, to examine it and seal it in his memory. He wants to learn the weight of her arm; how far her hair reaches over him; the lie of her toes against his ankle; the warmth of her vulva at his hip. His lungs intake rapid air. And she takes deep breath too, only long and slow, stirring again so that he keeps absolutely still. But it's no use; she is waking. She pulls her head quickly away from him, says, "Oh," softly and lets her weight down again, nuzzling her face into his neck. Her breast is against his arm. He brings his hand up to cup her head, feels the skull small through the density of hair, presses it to him and holds it there so that she reaches her arm out across him, catches his farther shoulder and hugs him tighter to her.

He turns to face her, wondering if it's possible to die of the lump of tenderness that fills his throat as he drags air past it then buries his face in her hair.

Her hand falls to his chest now, then rests on his waist, then goes from there to nowhere and even as he thinks, surely she would not, his penis starts as her fingers touch the tip of him, the shaft of him and then her body's against him and he's pushing her over, pushing between her, pushing on into her, *Claira! Claira!*

The lamp splutters to life, grows dim, then surges brighter as Munro brings himself back to the pillow, then that's too bright and he reaches back to turn it down. But he must see her, see for himself she is all right and he turns to search her face. The sweat is on her still as she looks across at him from the pillow and there's something in her eyes he cannot read until suddenly her lips echo it and he breathes out his amazement. Her eyes are smiling at him. He has done this to her and she smiles at him for it. He traces the line of her lips with a finger, dislodges a hair caught at the corner of her mouth.

"It's no good," she says.

"What isn't?" he asks quickly.

"I shall have to go downstairs and clear up the feathers."

"What?"

"You know how early Aunt Eadie rises." Claira laughs. "She will think it very strange to find the feathers still there in the morning."

He grins and shakes his head. "I'll come down and help you."

And then, although the smile is still there, her eyes are serious suddenly and she is watching his eyes deeply as she reaches over and kisses him lightly, quickly on the mouth. Their first.

There's the difficulty of being out of bed together, naked, only she smiles and reaches under the bolster for his nightshirt and throws it to him and he puts it on while she finds his shirt from the floor and wears that. He laughs, seeing it come down to her knees, then, seeing her blood on the sheet, becomes silent, touching it.

"It'll wash out," she says. "Come on. Feathers."

Like recalcitrant children they sneak downstairs, carrying the lamp and trying not to giggle.

The clock in the kitchen says twenty past three, not long till dawn.

On their knees they gather the feathers in. This time it's quickly done and the big sack tied and the cushion tied too; for now, till she sews it.

"Will you have water?" he asks, resting a wrist on her shoulder and daring to finger her hair.

"Yes," she smiles and briefly kisses his hand. "I am hungry, too," she says and disappears into the larder while he pours two glasses of water.

"Those *surely* are not ready," he says, seeing her bring two small green apples from the bowl in the larder.

"I have not tried them."

"I know the fruit is ahead of itself this year, but it will be another six weeks at least before they're ready. They will be sour yet."

She holds the apples to her with a defensive toss of the head.

"It's so long since I had one," she says, then sniffs the fruit. "Mmmmm. They will be *perfect*," she laughs, taking a knife from the table drawer and a plate down from the dresser. "I can manage the lamp," she says, from which he learns this feast is to be eaten in bed.

He stops in the hall by the barometer and she holds up the light for him. They peer at the dial as he gently taps the glass and he wonders at their reflection, their heads together and the halo of light. The barometer needle has swung up a little.

"Good," he says.

"Hay Monday?"

"God willing."

"It's only the peel that's sour," she says, sitting in his bed with the plate on her knees, paring apples.

"Is it so?" he says, watching the turn of her narrow wrists and the quickness of her fingers and the lamplight in hair that tumbles forward as she looks down to her task. She smiles quickly up at him.

"Of course."

He gets into the bed beside her and she cuts the peeled apple into four and cores it, then gives him a piece and takes a piece for herself. They look at each other. Simultaneously they bite the crisp flesh. His mouth instantly dries at the sourness and she laughs, her face contorting as she chews.

"Quickly," he laughs, reaching back to the glasses he brought, "drink this."

And he hands to her the sweetness of water.

He feels taller, walking into chapel on Sunday. There's a little murmur, he's aware, and a slight drawing apart of people as they arrive. Before him, Jed helps Eadie. Munro has particularly requested it. Today it is his wife Munro wants on his arm.

All through the service he keeps contact with her, even in prayer as he thanks God for her presence and asks for His guidance in governing this strange, new knowledge of the flesh; even then he feels the miracle of the hem of her dress brushing against his ankle.

Anticipating Monday's Jubilee, Henry Pascoe beams today, reporting on the plans to parade the Sunday school banner and the preparations for the tea treat.

"When the time comes to chronicle Queen Victoria's reign," he says, "it will be found that there was no such green spot in all the history of England. Some of the greatest triumphs of our national life have been accomplished during the past fifty years and our queen has nobly and beneficiently played her part in making England what it is.

"She is also," he continues, "in the best sense of the word, a true Christian. We will all remember her description of the Sacramental service in the Scottish Kirk—so simple and at the same time so beautiful and with such a flavor of old-fashioned religious worship about it—it touched her heart, she said and made her weep."

His quick blue eyes seek Munro's.

"Her Majesty is one of the most liberal-minded Christians in the land," he says, allowing, then, his eyes to move on. "A thousand claims to reverence are closed in her as Mother, Wife and Queen."

Forty-seven

"Look, Mummy."

Claire's hands are automatic, lifting Nathan up onto the slabs of granite that form the stile. He feels heavy and she grits her teeth with effort. On the top stone the boy struggles and twists from her grip.

"No. Look!"

He bobs down and she forces her focus on the thing he points to, small tight flowers, he runs his hands over. White. Starlike. She wonders if Howard will be home when they get there. Home. Hardly that anymore. *Home sweet home. There's no place like . . .*

"Look!" Nathan says, shifting impatiently.

"Oh yes, Nathan. That's one of the ones we found in the book the other day. Can you remember what it's called?"

"No."

"Hurry up!" Damien shouts, ahead of them.

Not that it's ever been a home for Howard. *Home is where your heart is.* It makes sense now, his being happy for them to move first.

Getting them out of the way.

She purses her lips tight, reaches back for the pedal car she must carry. Her stomach feels knotted. Kate had given the boys something to eat, bless her. She should probably eat something herself when they get back. Her stomach heaves at the thought.

"No, I *can't,*" Nathan squeals.

"What?" Claire says, frowning; bringing her attention back to the boy.

"I can't me*rember* what it's *called,*" Nathan squeals.

"All right, Nathan. Don't be cross with me."

There's a flicker of film footage. The naked woman on the edge of the bed. Slender, taut body. Her stare at the camera.

Claire's face flinches. Her knees feel weak. She sits down heavily on the top slab; glad of the solidness of its support. She rests the pedal car on the next step. It grates a bit.

"Where have we found it?" she asks the boy.

"On the path to Sky's house, of course," Damien says, coming back to them. "Can we go now?"

The turn of an elfin face. The flick of long hair over a shoulder. Howard's face, angry.

"Yes, but where on the path?" Claire asks, hugging round her stomach.

"On the stile," Damien says, snapping grass stems from the hedge.

"Which is made of what?" she asks.

"Stone!" shouts Nathan, triumphant.

"Well done, Nath. Now that's a big clue to its name. Can you remember now?"

The boy shakes his head.

"This is boring," Damien says.

"Stonecrop," Claire tells them. "Do you remember? It's a plant that's tough enough to grow in places near stone, which other plants couldn't manage because there's hardly any soil. Remember now?"

Rabbit dangling from its mouth, the fox drops down onto the path, then scents and—unseen—sees them. Scarcely breaking rhythm, it rounds and doubles back over the hedge.

Forty-eight

Claira smiles, stirring awake in his arms. "Jubilee day," she murmurs sleepily.

"It is," Munro says, touching his lips to her forehead.

"Is it a beautiful day?" she asks, slurring words.

"Beautiful," he confirms without moving, marveling at the perfection of the curve of her eyebrow and the lashes against her cheek.

Sensing herself studied, she struggles to open bleary eyes.

"Is it late?" she asks.

"Sshhh," he says, bringing his mouth again to her face and kissing her eyes closed. "No. It is early yet."

She pushes her face into his neck. He hears her sigh and feels her breath inside the collar of his nightshirt. Of its own volition, his hand comes to cradle her head there against him. Softly it strokes her hair, once, twice, then rests its weight on her again. His hand has been doing that a lot recently, he's noticed. Acting as if it has a mind of its own; putting into practice the new language it is learning: the touching of her. He closes his eyes against tears. He must be turning foolish. Her head feels heavier against him now, her breathing slow and rhythmical in sleep.

Half opening his eyes, he lets his gaze focus out through the little window where he can see the low slant of early sun filtering through mist: making a golden haze of it. Silently he thanks God: for the love of this woman who sleeps beside him; for the day of sun that stretches out before him; for the gathering of good hay; for the knowledge his body will be strong for the labor.

His gaze drifts out of focus. He shifts a little; rests his cheek lightly on the crown of her head. Dozes.

"Shall I do that?" Munro asks an hour later, watching her struggle to brush the back of her hair.

"Yes," Claira says emphatically, handing him the brush. "Thank you."

He watches her in the mirror while she separates the sections she has brushed through already from the tangled parts she cannot reach; her hair so dark against the white of her nightgown.

"Do you think we might get to Newlyn today?" she asks as he begins to brush.

He purses his lips in a grimace of regret. "I cannot see that I shall be able to go." He catches her eye in the mirror and smiles. "Divine retribution," he says. "If I will go off when by rights I should be here seeing to the farm, then it seems I must forgo the Jubilee. You could go with your sisters, though."

She shakes her head as well she can amid his brushing.

"I think both of us should go, or neither," she says.

His hands stop their movement and he searches her eyes in the mirror again. She looks up at him, wide and clear. He smiles and shakes his head, separates the last tangled strand of her hair and begins to brush through it.

"Do hearts burst," he murmurs, "when they are this full?"

She swings round on the stool and hugs him fiercely round the waist. He puts the brush down. Lightly, his hand presses on her head, holding her to him, feeling the push of her face against him. She draws away.

"There's so much to *do* today," she says and begins quickly to plait her hair. "Hay to be gathered and butter to be churned."

He nods, watching her, then turns to find clothes.

"That ewe is still lame."

"Is she? I'll see to her today," Claira says, opening the wardrobe.

"There's no need for you to be bothered with her," Munro says. How little space her clothes take up compared to his. He must make sure she has more soon.

"I cannot have brought my bonnet down," she says and he is surprised, knowing she doesn't usually trouble with it around the yard, not seeming to mind her skin darkening.

"You don't mean to join us in the fields, surely?" he asks.

"I do, if you don't oppose it, once the dairy is done."

There's the thought of the pleasure of working alongside her. He chides himself for his selfishness. "It is heavy work you don't have to do now," he says, coming to the wardrobe for a shirt.

"My brothers will be here, and Beattie, too," she says. "It would feel strange, not to be with them."

He nods at the truth of it. "As you will, then," he says.

From his greater height he sees the bonnet at the back of the shelf and lifts it down for her.

Taking croust to the fields, Claira balances the basket carefully. A jug of lemonade and another of cold tea are both muslin-covered against flies. The weighting beads clink against china as she walks and there's the muffled clunk of cups wrapped in cloth. Lark song teems from the sky and Claira risks looking up to scan the deep azure, but she cannot locate him and she will not stop to search. She wants to find the hay makers.

They've raked this little meadow clean. Like huge mushrooms, the four-foot pooks of hay sit at intervals. The scarlet of poppies and blue of scabious left standing, nod from the hedgerow she follows. Thank Heavens for the breeze, she thinks, the midmorning sun hot on her back.

Down the dip at the edge of the field and through the gateway she goes. There they are. Jed is closest, standing under the shade of a sycamore, binding a wooden rake that has broken. Freed from the shafts, the horses graze nearby. The harness jangles as one horse stamps and shakes his head, ridding himself of flies. Hearing Claira approach, Jed looks up to say good morning.

"Good morning, indeed, Jed," she says, putting her basket down in the shade. She straightens her back from the awkward carrying and scans the figures raking hay. There's Munro, working beside Claira's brothers, Jethro and Samuel, and there's dear sister Beattie and there's Michael and two more lads from the village come to help.

Munro is the first to see her, closely followed by Beattie. Waving to her, Munro calls the others so that they all down-tools. As they walk towards her, Munro has his head tilted towards Samuel, listening to something his young brother-in-law is saying and it moves her to see his kind attention.

"Lemonade or tea?" she asks Jed, unpacking the basket.

Jethro climbs the loaded wain like a monkey. He turns round and grins down at them. "Come on, Beattie," he says, reaching a hand down to his sister.

She laughs. "I can't get up there."

"Yes you can. Give her a lift up, Samuel."

Samuel, Michael and the lads from the village descend on her.

"Use the wheel," Jethro calls down.

Beattie puts a foot on the hub and laughs as they half push, half lift her to a higher foothold and Jethro reaches towards her, pulling her up, making it more difficult, in fact, so that she lands facedown on top of the hay.

"Now you, Claira," Jethro calls.

"I can manage, thank you," Claira laughs, warding off their help and quickly shinnying up the load.

Jethro begins to clamber down.

"Are you not staying?" Claira asks.

"What? Stay with the hay queens?" Jethro says, grinning as he disappears over the side of the cart so that they must look down at him from their height. "Certainly not. I know my place."

"Fool!" Claira calls, grabbing a handful of hay and throwing it down at him. Then they must grab at hay for certain as the cart lurches into movement and the mass of the load sways beneath them, forcing them to sit. Claira shuffles to one side so that Beattie, too, can clutch the ropes that tie the cargo down. Once they are used to it, it's easy and the sisters relax, leaning back on their hands.

"Well, Claira Richardson," Beattie says, pulling a wisp of hay from Claira's bonnet, "something about marriage must please you. I have never seen you look so well."

Claira smiles at her and gives her sister a hug in which she brings her mouth close to Beattie's ear. Their bodies sway with the movement of the cart and she must hold her tight a moment to maintain their position. Claira draws breath. "It's *wonderful,*" she whispers and Beattie gives a little gasp and pulls away to read her sister's face to see if she's understood correctly.

"*What* is?" Beattie asks.

Claira says nothing, but grins broadly.

"Claira!"

The cart lurches into a rut and they are jostled and must hold on.

Claira laughs, so that Beattie laughs too. "It *is.* It is *won*derful."

Then Claira squirms, reaching inside the neck of her clothing where something irritates.

"Excuse me, but I am *not* comfortable," she says fishing out stalks and seeds caught in her sweat.

Rake and pull, step, rake and pull. Rake and pull, step, rake and pull. As the day goes on, the blisters begin to be a nuisance and the lines of hay won't fall so straight. Claira hopes it doesn't make it more difficult for Munro to pitch it. Jed is working opposite her.

Just the three of them now. Slowly the pooks of hay mushroom up. Rake and pull, step, rake and pull. Her body will ache tomorrow.

She breaks from the rhythm of it to go and help with the evening milking.

"Well," Munro says, coming later into the kitchen. "Have you energy left for Newlyn?"

"Now?"

"It won't be Jubilee day tomorrow."

"Isn't it too late?"

"I think there will still be things to see."

Claira smiles. "Yes, I would like to go."

"Good."

They stop in the lane outside Jed's cottage. Claira wants to persuade him to come as he had left by the time they were changed and ready.

Knocking on Jed's door, they hear the tone of his voice in conversation. It does not stop, so Munro knocks again before they let themselves in. Only then do they realize it is not conversation as such, but prayer.

In the dim interior they see Jed in profile, kneeling on the flagstones, open eyes raised to Heaven; showing no sign of having heard them; denouncing himself a sinner.

Munro clears his throat. Jed prays on for forgiveness and salvation, for fire to cleanse the wickedness in his heart. Claira feels as if she's spying and she catches Munro's eye and nods towards the door: *perhaps we should go*.

"Jed," Munro begins.

Unceasing, Jed prays. Claira thinks his eyes unusually bright.

". . . to scourge my sinful soul. I am not worthy of the good Thou givest, nor can my wickedness ever be atoned . . ."

There's a plate upon the table with a hunk of bread and a piece of cheese, untouched.

"... save by Your mercy. In me, all things are sinful, all light become dark."

Claira touches Munro's arm, but he stands, transfixed.

"I taint the very air I breathe with my unworthiness. In my breast the cancer of sin grows, fed by my misdoings." He clasps his hands together the tighter and his voice rasps, breaking up. "God have mercy on me, a sinner. My deeds are unworthy, my life shameful, my flesh foul, my thoughts corrupt."

Claira looks at Munro. Will he not intervene? She clenches her hands to stop herself going to Jed. Who is she to come between him and his God?

Jed draws breath. "Know me for a debased sinner ..."

Claira turns and goes out, leaving Munro to it.

From the hedgerow flanking the garden path she snatches stalks of grass, breaks them, finds her hands are shaking. In long shadows at Jed's gate, the horse lifts his head at her movement. The air is cool with evening. She takes a long, slow breath of it.

Munro is silent as he drives the cob along the lane. An old hand, the horse settles to an easy rhythm and the jingle rides well. The clear sky is luminous, tinging peach where the sun is setting. Another good day tomorrow. One bright star appears.

Claira looks across at her husband, who is staring ahead. She wants to ask him about Jed, about the quarter hour that passed before Munro came out, but she thinks better of it. He will talk to her when he is ready. She slips a hand under his arm and shifts a little nearer to him. He turns briefly to flicker a smile at her; squeezes her hand against his torso with his elbow; moves his leg closer against hers. She tucks the knee rug farther round them both, against evening air suddenly chilled.

When they reach the curve in the lane at the height of the incline, the view is revealed to them.

"Oh look!" she says.

Munro draws the horse to a halt. As usual, far below them, dim lights glimmer from the town and the anchor lamps of boats, close to the shore, but also today, on the ring of hills round the bay and beyond, beacon fires burn. They count them and can see seven, the last faint and far, on the Lizard.

Chinese lanterns hang in gardens lining the street. Red and gold they glow. Where the crowd begins to thicken, two boys run, holding medals aloft and singing a raucous "God Save the Queen." They catch up with their mother, who boxes their ears. Munro winces. They've definitely caught the end of the day. From the sports field, men come, hot from tug-of-war, laughing and drunk with fatigue, their shirts undone. Munro puts Claira's hand through his arm.

The drift of the crowd is towards the center of the little town, where there are more lanterns, some strung with bunting across and back across the street. In most of the windows, candles are lit and flambeaux burn in the hands of stewards. Banners and arches span the street decked with greenery, fading now. It's as if these stewards are marking a route. Of what? Claira wonders and then they hear it, the ringing of hand bells and the warning shouts: "Carnival!"

The pair of horses at the front are wild-eyed with the noise and made frantic by the light that beats against their bodies so that the driver has trouble holding them. One of the horses skitters and half rears and an "Oohhh" goes up from the throng as people scatter from the animal's path.

"Get someone to their heads," a man shouts from the crowd and a steward runs in causing more chaos as the horse—with a flare of red nostrils—pulls away from his burning torch.

"Not with fire in your hand," someone else yells, derisory, and a laugh goes round the crowd.

Struggling, the wagon passes. It has a boat on the back; a fishing boat. In all their gear, fishermen shoot their nets then, rhythmically, haul in their catch. Someone throws another's shoe into the net and the crowd cheers the bounty and its owner, who hobbles on one shod, one stockinged foot after it. Munro and Claira catch each other's eye and laugh. Then the crowds round Claira jostle and crush and Munro draws her in front of him, both hands on her shoulders.

All right? his eyes ask as she turns back to look at him.

Yes, she smiles, pleased to feel his greater solidity.

The white horse gleams in torchlight. He pulls a wagon with a model tin mine, lit, the big wheel working.

A well-to-do farmer has been usurped. Tied between the shafts of a light two-wheeler, he must pull his workers along as they recline, swigging pints of ale. Stopping, the farmer uses a huge handkerchief to elaborately mop the sweat from his brow and his workers whoop to him to move, cracking a whip above his head.

"Get on! Get on!" the crowd call.

Dancers next, clad in bullock skins; their faces and bodies blacked, dancing to the beat of drums and the bells at their stamping ankles. Outside the formation, isolates roam, posturing to the crowd, savage with burning torches. One such stops and challenges Munro, staring at him with eyes bulging, their whites clear in the flame light, against his blackened skin. Involuntarily, Claira shrinks against Munro and glances over her shoulder to see his face, sadly calm as he looks back at this spectacle inches from him. As the dancer wheels away, Claira feels someone touch her arm and, turning, she sees Elizabeth Armstrong.

"Are you all right?" Elizabeth asks.

"I think so," Claira laughs, greeting her friend.

Mrs. Armstrong is there too, and Mr. Forbes. Claira introduces Munro to him.

"We are feeling in need of a little time away from the crowds," Elizabeth says, "so we're making our way to Stanhope's rooms. You are welcome to join us if you would care to."

Claira looks towards Munro, who in turn waits for Claira's reply.

"Thank you," she says. "That would be lovely."

"It's very nearby," Stanhope says, "but we *do* have to cross the road."

The wagon that passes is decked out as a smith's shop. Fire is bright in the forge and there's the clang of red-hot metal being beaten on the anvil.

"Perhaps after this one," Munro says, seeing a greater gap behind this exhibit and that which follows is a troupe of boys forming arches and dancing thread-the-needle.

"Splendid," Stanhope says, and offers Mrs. Armstrong his arm to assist her across the road.

In the doorway of the dark interior, before the lamp flares up, there's the smell of something; heavy and pleasantly musky. As the glow settles, Claira follows the scent and traces it to a bottle of thick amber liquid on a bench next to a wooden palette scraped and oiled clean. There are scratch marks in the middle of the palette. Perhaps that's where he mixes the colors, perhaps with one of those funny knives, shining and placed in a row, catching the lamplight. Tubes of paint are laid out, neatly, some half used with curled-up tails, others turgid and untouched. Claira picks up the bottle and smells the neck of it. Even with the stopper still in, she can tell that's where the scent is coming from. Nutty. Rich. Lovely. She puts the bottle down and her fingers are a little oily. Absentmindedly, she rubs them together, standing in front of a small canvas on an easel. The oil sketch is half finished, the head of a fishwife. Even in that state, Claira feels she could reach out and touch the flesh of the woman's cheek and find it soft. Claira wonders what it's like, being able to put people down in paint, like this. Perhaps if she had been able to, she would have painted her father and would have his image now, like this one, almost touchable, as if about to speak.

"Looks as if we have lost Mrs. Richardson for a little while," Stanhope remarks to Munro.

"It does," Munro smiles, watching her.

"I was going to say come up to my rooms, but as your wife is so absorbed and if you are quite comfortable there, Mrs. Armstrong," Forbes says, turning to where Elizabeth's mother has seated herself on a rather forlorn chaise longue, "perhaps we could just have a sherry here."

"I don't suppose Mr. and Mrs. Richardson drink sherry," Elizabeth reminds him quietly.

"You are quite right, we don't as a rule," Munro agrees. "But it's not every day we can celebrate a Jubilee, so I think we should make this an exception."

"Good man," Forbes says, taking a decanter and glasses from a cupboard.

There are photographs of paintings on the wall above the bench. Looking at them, Claira feels a hand slip through her arm. Elizabeth. She jolts, rather guiltily, back to the present.

"*Their Ever Shifting Home,*" Elizabeth says, giving Stanhope's photographed painting its title. On foot, a gypsy woman carries a sleeping child. In the lane behind her, the rest of her family follows, then the vardo—driven at the rear of the cavalcade.

"I was wondering if I knew them," Claira says.

"Might you?" Elizabeth asks her.

"My father only gave up the life in order to marry my mother."

"Ah," Elizabeth comments, feeling that much has been made clear. The bewitching wildness Claira exudes, her particular brand of beauty, her lithe animality. "Wasn't that difficult for them both?" Elizabeth asks and Claira likes her directness.

"Yes. My mother's family are rather well-to-do apparently. Merchants in Helston."

"Do you not know them?"

Claira shakes her head. "They make sure we do not."

"Have you never even seen them?"

Claira laughs, remembering. "When I was a little girl, a carriage passed my mother and me in Newlyn one day. I can remember the coat of arms on the carriage door and the leather glove of the lady who stepped down and lifted my chin and looked at me. It was the palest leather I had ever seen and I remember marveling at how she could keep such a thing clean. She spoke severely to my mother and I wondered who had the right to do that. My mother told me later it was my grandmother."

"And that's the only time?" Elizabeth says.

"Yes. I did think perhaps it might be different now that . . . now that my mother is a widow, but there has been no word."

Elizabeth gives Claira's arm a little squeeze and turns her attention back to the photographs. "The painting was exhibited at the Royal Academy in London this year," she says. "It was well received, although Stanhope was disappointed. The one from 'eighty-five was such a success," she says, indicating an image of a fish sale on one of the local beaches.

"Was it?" Claira asks and immediately feels clumsy. "I mean, I am sure it's very well painted—even in the photograph you can almost smell the fish and the wet sand. It's just I didn't know they would like these things in London. Wet fish and gypsies."

Elizabeth laughs gently. "Ah, but they do." She leans closer and whispers, "For all their fine clothes and buildings, the city folk need to cast their eyes to us every now and then. They seem to think we keep them in touch with something important, which, of course, we do, something they feel they have lost, which, of course, they have."

"And you need them to do that so that you can sell your paintings," Claira adds.

"Quite right, Claira," Elizabeth laughs. "Don't let me get away with it entirely."

Claira's not quite sure what it is she's done, or what it is she is not letting Elizabeth get away with, but she doesn't much mind, sensing Elizabeth's laughter is kind and anyway, another photographed painting demands attention. Claira holds her breath at the strength of it. A woman, in a conservatory, in mourning evidently, chrysanthemums at her knees and feet. Behind her, windows arch onto snowscape. Instantly Claira remembers moments after her father's death. Frozen numbness in sunshine, the surprise that the sun *could* still shine.

"One of Frank Bramley's," Elizabeth says, observing Claira's attention. "*Weaving a Chain of Grief.* Again, very well received in London when it went to the N.E.A.C."

Claira is about to ask what the N.E.A.C. is, but stops, seeing a pencil drawing of Elizabeth, pinned to the wall. Detailed, exquisite.

"That was done with very much love," Claira asserts.

Elizabeth looks at the drawing of herself. "Dear Stan," she smiles.

The women look at each other, pleased.

"Of what does your poor Stan now stand accused?" Forbes asks, hearing his name and walking across to them.

"Of painting and drawing too well," Elizabeth says, turning to him.

"Have you exhibited in London?" Claira asks Elizabeth.

"She most certainly has," Forbes replies for her.

"Not to quite such acclaim," Elizabeth adds.

"Yet," Forbes finishes. "Perhaps the painting of you will be the one, Mrs. Richardson."

"Of me? You would think of sending it to London?"

Elizabeth raises an arm in protest. "I always think it very bad form to decide on a painting's fate before it is even begun."

"I know you do, Lizzie. Sorry." He hands the women the sherry he's brought across with him. "We're waiting to toast the Queen," he says.

"Oh," Claira says, then sees Munro has a glass in his hand and so feels able to accept one herself, though she's never drunk sherry before.

Munro helps Mrs. Armstrong to her feet and they raise their glasses in solemn salute.

"To Her Majesty," Forbes intones.

"Her Majesty," they repeat.

On the way home, Claira tries to add up how long the day has been. They were up at five and will need to be again tomorrow and the village clock at Newlyn struck eleven as they left. She's too tired to work it out.

The cob is swift, keen to be home. Claira feels warm inside from the sherry and from Munro, close next to her. On the hills, the beacon fires still burn and from Newlyn behind them, fireworks flare. Looking over their shoulders, they see how the brightness falls from the air.

Hanging the harness away, they come out again into starshine.

"It is *beautiful*," Claira says, stopping to look up at the spangled sky. They cross the yard, passing the hay they've brought home from the fields. In the still air, the scent of it tarries. Munro pulls out a wisp from the start of the stack, three feet high, feels the hay crisp, yet pliable in his fingers; says a silent prayer of thanks.

"I think I should like to sleep here," Claira says, sitting down on the edge of the rick then shuffling farther out towards the middle of it.

Sitting next to her, Munro laughs. "You would be cold, surely?"

"Not with you beside me and the hay to be among."

His fingers find hers among the cut stalks.

"It's very vexing," she says.

"What is?"

"Having to sleep. I want to lie here all night and watch the stars pass and then see how beautiful the dawn is and then be ready to do the dairy and bring in more hay."

"It'll be time for the dairy soon enough," he says, bringing her fingers to his lips. "It must be past midnight already."

Claira shifts towards the warmth of him and burrows her feet beneath the hay. "How was Jed earlier?" she asks.

"I don't think he can be well," Munro says.

"He is so *thin,*" Claira says. She feels Munro nod his agreement.

"Of course, he won't have it," Munro continues. " 'There's nothing wrong with me as hard work wouldn't cure,' is what he said tonight. Nonetheless, I think we should have the doctor to him."

"Did it take him forever to finish praying?"

"It did rather," Munro answers and she feels him tighten his shoulder muscles then relax them as if he's shrugging something off.

"He gave me a Bible," she says.

"Who, Jed?"

"Yes. A beautiful one, bound in white leather and cased in velvet."

"Good gracious," Munro utters. "Ebenezer always did say I pay more than a laborer's wage. *When* did Jed do that?"

"Before . . . before you went away."

They are silent a moment, remembering that time. So recent. He brings her hand between his own.

"Did you enjoy Newlyn?" he asks.

"Oh yes and I was so pleased to see Elizabeth. I do like her."

Munro nods. "She and Mr. Forbes make an impressive couple."

"Did you like the paintings?" Claira asks.

"When I eventually managed to get near them," he teases.

"I hadn't realized I studied them so long. Was it very rude of me?"

"Very," Munro asserts.

"And I hardly spoke to Mrs. Armstrong," Claira continues. "It wasn't very polite, was it?"

"Very impolite, I should call it."

Claira elbows him on the arm. "But *you* spoke to her."

"Had to," Munro tells her. "Poor woman would have been quite left out, otherwise."

"What did she talk about?"

"Methodists, among other things."

"Really?"

"One of the young artists was reckless enough to paint on the Sabbath and had his canvas slashed and thrown in the harbor for his trouble."

"How awful!"

"I don't suppose he will do it again," Munro says. "You rather missed out on Mr. Forbes, too. He has just finished a portrait of the elderly Mrs. Bolitho."

"That *is* an honor."

"Indeed. The family are pleased with it, by all accounts and he's been asked to paint Mr. Bedford Bolitho, once the election is out of the way."

Claira is silent, reflecting on what it is to have a portrait painted. She had said yes to Elizabeth so quickly, because she liked her, not really thinking about the painting that would come of it or what its fate might be.

"Did the carnival amuse you?" Munro asks.

"Mmmm," she says sleepily. "I was sorry not to see Jethro though. He was due to be leading the quarry horses."

"He was telling me he's hoping for an apprenticeship there."

"Yes," she says. Then she pulls back a little from him and tries to make out his face in the starlight. "Do you think they celebrated the Jubilee in Africa?"

"I'm sure they did in some way. Why?"

"I just wondered. Your family. Don't you miss them?"

"At times. My younger brothers. I miss my younger brothers."

"But not your elder?"

Munro pulls at hay. "Thomas was one of the reasons I left."

"And your parents?"

He thinks about it. "My mother I miss. My father and Thomas are alike as two peas. Why do you ask?"

She shrugs in the darkness. "I am part of your family now."

Munro murmurs his agreement, then is silent again.

"There was never room for my opinions," he says after a little while. "Kimberley—the mine in South Africa—was opencast. Easy at the beginning, then more and more dangerous as it got deeper and sections were undercut. After the rains it would be especially bad. Send down the blacks. That was their solution. Not just my father's policy. Every owner was the same. When it's dangerous, send down the blacks. Expendable." He throws down stalks of hay. "Any objection I made was me being womanly."

From the fields a fox bark rasps. In the kennel, dogs fidget.

"In the end I came home," Munro says. "It was hopeless trying to fight it and as I couldn't justify being part of it, I came home. We had had to sell our claims by then. The big companies had taken over, but my father had seen it coming and had already put other irons in the fire. He was good at that. I went into farming in South Africa with my younger brothers, supplying the company stores. It seemed more excusable." He laughs, wryly. "I understand my father now *is* the company stores." Munro pulls more hay from the stack. "We dealt in diamonds, too," he says. "I started it, in fact. When I sold my claim I bought fifteen hundred pounds' worth of diamonds."

Claira tries to smother the gasp that rises in her throat.

"I took them to Cape Town, Claira, and sold them two weeks later for ten thousand pounds."

"Good heavens."

"The return was never quite that good again, but it was still very profitable. It's how I bought Trethenna—and Edwin's farm near Truro."

The call of owls sounds in the valley.

"Why did Edwin not go?" Claira says.

"What?" Munro asks, though he understands her question.

"Why did your twin not go to South Africa?"

He sighs and moves to the edge of the rick and standing, he brushes hay from his clothes.

"Another day, Claira," he says, stretching out a hand to her. "You have worked hard, as you always do. We should be sleeping."

His arm is about her waist as they cross the yard to the back door and the dim glow from the kitchen where Eadie has left the lamp turned low.

The following week there are five more hot days in which the remaining acres of hay are cut and turned and turned and pooked and gathered and stacked in the yard. Munro and Claira work from early dawn, doing other tasks until the morning dew dries. On the fields by day; nine, ten, sometimes more of them work. Claira's body aches and aches, then gives up aching, growing stronger and tighter. Jed noticeably slows and Munro finds reasons to send him back to the farm, giving him lighter chores.

Rather than walk the six miles home each day, Claira's siblings stay at Trethenna for haymaking, Beattie in the attic room, Jethro and Samuel in makeshift bunks in the barn with the other lads from the village.

Finishing work at late dusk, even Munro forgos evening chapel.

Trethenna's in silence soon after sundown; the household in deep, motionless sleep.

On the fifth day, they collect the remaining pooks of hay and bring them home to the rick. All day they haul the harvest in, the weather making a race of it. Clouds gather as they transfer the pooks to the wain. Rain spots as they fork hay to the rick.

At evening time, while the women cook and Jed and Munro tend livestock, the young men begin to thatch the finished rick. The sky is dark with rain clouds now. Jethro wills his body beyond its tiredness, but as he climbs the ladder, his hands drop the reed and for moments he can only slump against the rung. Brought by a warm wind, big splots of rain hit the shirt already stuck to him with the day's sweat. *Come on, come on* he goads himself as his brother gathers the fallen reed.

Cooking—again—for twelve, Mrs. Jago, Claira and Beattie break a moment from their work in the kitchen, coming out for cooler air and to see when the meal will be wanted.

"It's as well the reed knows its business," Mrs. Jago laughs as she watches the lads attempting to arrange the stuff. Munro comes from the tending of animals and puts his helpers right, shinnying up a ladder alongside Jethro, working with him to straighten and pin down the reed. And Jethro likes him there: the steady stamina of the older man, the comfort of his body, bigger and broader than his own. Seeing his tiredness, Munro catches brief hold of the nape of Jethro's neck. *Not long now.*

"Supper in an hour?" Mrs. Jago calls up to him and Munro turns to answer her and catches Claira watching him, her head a little to one side, her lips slightly parted. Their eyes skim a meeting and a spark leaps through his body and with certainty he knows—as surely as this hay is gathered now beneath him—he will take her tonight, in bed, before they sleep.

"Excellent, Mrs. Jago," he calls back. "And I'm sure you will not stint us."

The reed in place, they move the ladders to the ends of the rick. Hammering hard, Munro drives blackthorn stays deep into the stack. The young men hurry to finish turning straw to make rope. Munro will need it any minute now. Jethro fixes a length of it to a long pole, ready to pass up to him.

Silently, Claira's lips mouth the grace Munro offers at table. Heartfelt, the words well up in her. God, she is grateful: grateful for the hay, safely in; grateful for her body, heavy in the chair, anchored with exquisite tiredness; grateful for the good food they will soon be eating; grateful for her good hunger and for the company she keeps. She glances up at the heads bent, her brothers and sister, the lads from the village, Jed and Mrs. Jago, Aunt Eadie and Munro. God she is grateful, most of all, for Munro. She hopes somehow her father watches.

The amen echoes round the table and Munro looks up to find Claira's eyes resting softly on him and he smiles.

"Let's eat now," he says and they take the lids from hot dishes on the table and Claira sees her brothers' faces through the steam that rises: faces reddened and browned by the sun and scrubbed for supper, except that Jethro's left a tidemark round his neck and she reaches out to him, ruffling his hair.

Forty-nine

"I don't *like* it," Damien says, pushing his plate away.

"Yes you do, Damie."

"I *don't.*"

"Well, you ate it last week."

"No I didn't."

Claire takes the plate away from him to cut the meat into smaller pieces and to remove the tomato he's unlikely to eat. The smell of food makes her retch and she moves the plate away to do the task at arm's length. Damien kicks Nathan under the table. Nathan yells and hits his brother, knocking over his own drink. As Claire grabs a cloth, the phone rings.

"Leave your brother alone, Damien," Claire says, moving him farther down the table, giving his food back to him, leaving the cloth beside the spill, answering the phone.

"Hello, dear, it's me," her mother's bright voice calls.

"Hello, Mother," Claire says.

"I'm so glad you got home safely, Claire. Was it a dreadful shock?"

"What?" Claire says, then, "Damien don't do that, eat your food."

"It must have been such a shock, the car breaking down like that. Loss of power in the fast lane. I remember it happened when your father was driving once."

Claire hears the Metro turning in to the yard. She feels the flurry of her pulse. Howard's come home.

"Did it?"

"You probably don't remember, you were only little. It was very scary. Someone ran into the back of us. No one hit you, did they?"

"No, they didn't. Mother, Howard's just arriving."

"Is he? I'm sure he'll be relieved you're home in one piece. Were the AA helpful?"

Claire's heart thumps fast as she hears the back door open.

"Can I have a drink?" Nathan says, banging his empty cup on the table.

"Hello, Daddy," Damien sings out as Howard comes into the room. "Are you better now?"

"What?"

Claire cannot look Howard in the eye. Her hand is sweaty on the phone and she has to hold on tightly. She sees his shirt is open at the neck and thinks of his skin next to the body of his lover.

"Were they, Claire?"

"Sorry?"

"Are you better now, Daddy? Mummy said you were poorly."

"Did she? I'm fine."

"The AA. Were they good to you?"

"Oh yes."

"Didn't keep you waiting too long, I hope?"

"No."

"Did they say what was wrong with the car?"

"The cam belt went."

She feels Howard glance at her as he registers this information.

"Can I have a drink?" Nathan says, banging his empty cup on the table.

"Oh. That's a big job, isn't it?"

"I think it is, yes."

Howard strolls across the kitchen. Wrists limp, he flicks through the pile of papers on the table till he finds the one he's looking for.

"Can I have a *drink?*" Nathan calls, swirling the edge of his cup through the puddle of the last lot.

"Nathan, don't be disgusting," Howard comments.

"Listen, Mum. I really have to go."

"All right, darling. As long as you're all okay."

"We're fine."

"Sure? Only you sound a little subdued."

Taking the paper, Howard saunters past her on his way to the sitting room. He's going to read the paper. In the sitting room. As he always does. He picks up his cigarettes and lighter from the worktop. Touching the half-full French press, he finds it cold, so he leaves it, goes out through the door.

"Sorry?" Claire says into the phone.

"No, I'm sorry darling, you've obviously got rather a lot going on down there. As long as you're all home all right. I'll phone again another time. Perhaps after the children are in bed."

Imagine that, Claire thinks, the children will go to bed. The day will end, as usual.

"Yes," she says. "That would be better, only perhaps not this evening."

"All right, darling. I'll phone tomorrow. I *am* sorry not to see you, but we must be thankful that you're safely home. Bye-bye now."

"Bye and Mum?"

"Yes, dear?"

"Thanks for phoning."

"Can I have a drink?" Nathan says.

The children *do* go to bed. Furthermore, they stay there: asleep. Claire clears up the aftermath of their meal and then—on autopilot—puts the kettle on. The cold coffee she empties circles as it goes down the sink and she pauses, watching the grounds appear as the rest drains away. Howard must have made that jugful, to share with his lover. Howard and his lover. Or perhaps *she* made it. Those may be her fingerprints, there on the glass. Claire rinses the jug under the hot tap, then shakes the water off and polishes it shiny with a drying cloth.

Howard is still in the sitting room, reading the paper and smoking when she takes the coffee through. The television is switched on with the sound turned down. *Coronation Street.*

"Thank you," Howard says as she places the mug beside him. She sits down opposite him. No coffee.

"Would you like the sound turned up?"

"No, Howard." He surely is not thinking of simply . . .

"Where did you say my car is?"

"I didn't."

He lowers the paper onto his lap and looks at her.

"No," he says quietly, "you didn't, did you?"

Claire looks down. "The AA took it to the BMW garage near Truro."

"Well done," he says lightly, shaking the paper straight.

"Howard, I . . ."

"What?"

She brings a cushion onto her lap and fiddles with the edging of it. Shouldn't he want to say something, too? She glances up again. Howard has returned his attention to the paper. A little muscle moves at the side of his face.

In a flicker of color and TV light, Ken Barlow remonstrates, mouthing what looks like indignation. It must be the last few minutes. The children are in bed early tonight. Ironic. She could so have used the distraction. She looks at Howard. His steady hand on the edge of the paper. She can't imagine how it will be now—knowing his capacity for deceit. That's it. How to proceed, knowing that.

"What are we going to do?" she says quietly.

"What?" Howard asks, looking up.

"What are we going to do?"

"What do you mean, what are we going to do?"

"Howard, I . . ."

"Claire, I *do* hope you're not going to be tedious about this."

"Tedious? I . . ."

Howard gets up, folding the paper and slinging it onto a chair where it lands with a thwack. Claire can't smother an involuntary jump. He stands looking down at her a moment, TV light filtering through his fingers. "Only I really don't want to talk about it. It's just unfortunate you came home when you did, that's all."

"And if we hadn't come home then, it would have been all right?"

"Precisely," Howard agrees, walking off. "Now, I'm going to take a shower."

From the night window, comes a lesser darkness; more discernible if not looked at directly. Claire sets her stare in the darkest corner of the room, wishing tears would come. They do not. The pattern of dimness in her peripheral vision is the same design as the one she is used to—rectangles of a tall sash window—but they're in strange relation now; seen from a different bed in a different room. Both hands cling to beading she can feel through the sheet at either edge of the narrow mattress. Her shoulders are rigid, holding herself tense against questions that bludgeon the barrier she's building. She cannot face them. Not yet. She battles her concentration out into darkness, running her sight round the window's shape.

See how it embosses the night. Like paper. Or like a watermark.

Look at the window—it disappears, look back in the corner, it's there again. Look at the window—it disappears, look back in the corner it's . . .

The children. However will you tell the . . .

The fog has gone, hasn't it?

She thinks it has. Just dense cloud now. No stars. No moon. There's the sound of wind coming up from the west.

His lover—a voice hisses—*who* is *she?*

You must have been neglectful, Claire. That's *why this whole thing's happened, of course. You've been neglectful.*

She shifts her shoulders under the duvet.

And—in any case—what have you been playing at with Nick? It's no different, you know. Worse if anything. Keeping it all inside your head. Not having the courage to act on it. Cowardice, not fidelity.

The leaves outside the window rustle.

Think Howard's was a casual affair?

The wind has been rising these last few hours.

Or did he plan it?

Hardly a breath when she came to bed.

Shunting his family off to the country so he could spend time in London with his lover.

The clock downstairs begins to chime.

One . . . two . . . three . . .

The window begins to rattle in its frame.

Going on when you were in London, probably.

Claire closes her eyes tight, closes her eyes, somehow dozes, dreams she walks in fields that join the cliff path; high above glinting sea. Damien and Nathan run on in sunlight; blond heads bobbing, their laughter carried back by the breeze. The path—funneled between two hedges—leads to huge slabs of granite arranged in a humpbacked open stairway.

"Careful, Nathan. Let me help you over."

As she takes Nathan in her arms to carry him across the stile, Damien is already tackling the climb. They catch him up and she is straddling the top stone when the dizziness hits, forcing her to sit abruptly. In slow motion now, she looks down, sees Damien on the stone below her, clinging on. Clinging. Why is it he is having to cling? Slowly the thought filters through: *this dizziness is not in my head, it's the ground that's moving. Earthquake.* She clasps Nathan tightly, his scream in her ear and in slow stroboscope reaches a hand down to Damien, desperate to claw him up as the massive stones supporting her begin to slide.

"Mummy!" The scream is high-pitched and she has tipped herself out of bed and is moving towards the cry before she's fully woken.

"What is it, Nathan?" It sounds as if he's on the landing. There's the danger of him falling down the stairs. She must reach him, too, before Howard wakes.

She finds the boy at the door of her old bedroom, catches him on his way in. The cold air tells her that her face is wet. She rubs the back of a hand across her eyes.

"It's all right, Nathan. Did you have a bad dream?"

"There's someone knocking on my *window*," he squeals.

"No there isn't, darling, it's just the wind. It's knocking on my window, too. Come and listen." She scoops him up, his body hot against her chilled flesh.

"Why are we going in here?"

"I'm sleeping in this room now." She takes him to where the wind pummels the window and a hard rain beats. She holds out his hand to feel the draft that whistles in.

"There, you see, it's a wild old wind tonight. But it's all right because we can snuggle down safely in bed."

"Can I stay with you?"

"Yes. I should think there's just about room for us both in this little bed," Claire says, thankful that darkness hides the tears which start at the closeness of him.

Still hugging him to her, she picks up the duvet, which has fallen to the floor.

"There you are," she says, lying down and covering them both. He pushes his head against her neck, his little fist across her breast, his warm knees curled against her belly. "There you are," she says, stroking his head.

"Why are you sleeping in this bed?"

"I just am for a little while."

"Yes, but *why* are you?"

She brings her lips closer to him.

"You know how you and Damien might have had different rooms?"

"No."

"When we moved here, do you remember, we said it might be nice if you both had a room each because you'd have more space to play in and more room to put your own things. Do you remember?"

He nods his head against her.

"Well, it's like that for Daddy and me. We just want a little more space."

"Oh."

The window rattles hard in its frame and Nathan pushes closer to her. Claire kisses the top of his head.

"It's all right, little one."

She brings the duvet farther up over him. Making sure there's still passage for the boy to breathe, she checks the rhythm of her own breathing; steadying it for him, calming him with her body. She feels the warmth build up between them, feels his body slacken towards sleep. Thank Heavens for him, she thinks, thank Heavens for the weight of him there on her arm. And tears do fall then, flowing from her, hot, to the pillow, silently so she will not wake him, they flow and they flow and they flow. It will never be the same for him. Poor little boy.

One . . . two . . . three . . . four . . . five . . . Downstairs, the clock strikes.

Being busy is good. She plays with the children all morning, then leaves them to finish their game at the table while she starts preparing a casserole for the evening meal.

"What happens when you land on a treasure chest?" Damien calls from the kitchen table.

"You have to throw the dice to see if you can open it," Claire says from where she stands at the work surface, cutting onions. "You have to throw a six."

"If not, does the opticus get you?" Nathan asks.

"That's right, Nath. The octopus *might* get you if you don't run away fast enough."

As she washes the beef skirt under running water, she hears the Metro pull in to the yard. Against her will, her heart thumps hard. She'd avoided Howard this morning, staying in bed until after he'd left, letting the children get in his way for once. What ever is he doing here, now, at midday?

"Daddy's home," Nathan sings and jumps up to greet him.

"What happens when you land on a skull and crossbones?"

Claire puts the meat on a board and picks up the knife. How is she supposed to greet him? What is her face supposed to say? She keeps her eyes on the meat. She feels her stomach tighten. The back door slams.

"Hello, Daddy. We're playing the pirate game," says Damien.

"Are you?"

The knife cuts into the flesh, which rolls beneath her fingers.

"Would you like to play?"

"No. I have to go to London suddenly."

Claire's hands falter. She's found a piece of gristle. The other knife is probably sharper.

She inspects the knife handles where they point at her from the block on the worktop. She's looking for the one with a chip in the end. She feels Howard walk behind her on his way to pack. She feels her skin tighten.

"I'll be able to pick the car up on the way back on Friday," Howard says.

She pulls the knife out of the block. And she's right. It's better. It cuts straight through.

Fifty

Damien watches the beetle climb; the beetle back shining like his teddy bear's eye. Feelers wave in search of the next move as the beetle takes slow steps up the stem. Little legs cling. Curled in a womb of undergrowth, Damien brings his face nearer, his nose only inches away. A recent scratch runs the length of his thigh—the price of entry into this secret world where bracken and brambles arch and conceal. His fingers, already stained purple with blackberry, worry at beads of blood that have congealed, relishing their stickiness against his soft skin. Reaching out through bracken, he plucks another berry, gets another scratch, too, pulling back his arm. He squashes the fruit with his tongue against his teeth and feels the juice burst in his mouth. The pips feel bitty and he spits them out. As he moves, he feels that wet from the ground has soaked through his shorts. He digs the heel of his trainer into the soft earth.

He wonders how it would feel to handle the beetle; have it caught between finger and thumb. Damien reaches out a hand then hesitates; the horror of beetle-face arresting him, but the desire to touch is greater and he plucks the beetle from the stem; upturns it. He watches closely the wriggle of legs, sees the underside, ridged and polished, like the plastic of his Batmobile, but softer; he squeezes and the body flexes. Much softer. Legs wriggle faster: they don't need whizzing on the floor to wind them up. He turns his hand round so he can see beetle-face. He doesn't much like beetle-face. He squeezes; feels the soft snap of beetle-body. And the legs stop. Instantly! Dud battery or power failure. Strength failure. He is the stronger. He wipes the dud beetle away on the grass.

He likes it in here. He can hear his mother calling again, but he won't go yet. His shirt is green and, if he keeps very still, he bets no one will find him. Besides, she would never come into this part. It's too wild. He leans back against the upright stone, enjoying the sunlight dappling through onto his body; indolent cat quite concealed in his lair. For several seconds he is still. Round the chapel and the trees, rooks caw. He watches them, circling black against blue sky. He senses their sharp eyes pick him out. They won't tell though.

He becomes aware of something digging into his back and, turning to the stone, sees it is the ivy that has grown up; fierce, hairy tentacles cling to the rock. He can see there are letters carved in stone. Most of them are covered by the ivy. He moves the leaves about and traces the letters with his finger, then spells them out loud. A . . . I . . . then . . . R. And what's that at the beginning? Is it L? He moves the stem with his fingers. C . . . L. That's funny. Isn't that . . . ? He tries to uncover the rest, but the ivy is denser, stronger and will not budge. He breaks a nail and sucks his finger.

"Damien. Will you come here, *now*!"

Her voice sounds cross. He supposes he'd better go. On all fours he crawls out of the cocoon, getting another scratch on the way out.

His body leaves a warm imprint in the sickly grass.

Negotiating his way through the forest of undergrowth, he arrives at the rusty gates and squeezes out between their unhinged slanting. Reaching neat grass, he runs to where his mother is, then stands before her, blinking at his rebirth into brighter light.

"I've been calling you for fifteen minutes. What do you think you've been doing? I brought you here to play on the swings, not on people's graves."

"Your grave is in there," he says importantly, swanking with the knowledge. He turns to point.

The sharp sting of a slap hits his leg. He gasps and gapes, then grits his teeth.

"Now get on home," Claire says, pointing to the stone stile that leads to the footpath they must take. She turns his shoulders and he shrugs her off.

"I hate you!" he yells, fighting tears and running off. "You're just stupid."

"I *beg* your pardon."

"You're just stupid. Daddy said so. That's why you're not sleeping with him."

By the side of her, Nathan bursts into tears. Claire feels the color drain from her face. Very quietly she says, "Let's just go home, now."

She ruffles Nathan's hair.

"Come on, Nathan, it's okay."

She picks the boys' jackets up from the bench and follows Damien who, tearful and furious, cannot manage the stile.

Fifty-one

The sound of the little stream running. Hidden among trees, birds pipe out song. Sunlight filters into the clearing. Morning air stirs about them; warm. It should be perfect and there is Claira, looking like a rabbit facing a farmer's gun. Elizabeth puts her pencil down. Usually models settle after a few minutes, but they have been here for nearly an hour and still Claira's tension is evident in every muscle. What is it? Elizabeth thinks of the fisher girl she painted in Zandvoort. Her easy assertion of self. The opposite is happening here; as if Claira feels the need to hide something. Disappointing.

Elizabeth smiles. "I think we need tea," she says, not at all sure she will like the milkless, cold version that Claira has brought, but certainly there is a need for diversion.

Claira relaxes as if she has been holding her breath for too long and falls to the basket she brought. Shyly she glances at the sketches. Elizabeth turns them to her. Studies of the face.

"Oh. You have not drawn the fiddle."

So *that's* it. She had thought when she suggested bringing the instrument that Claira had shown reluctance. Somehow holding it is what has been making her nervous. Elizabeth watches her, sitting, easily, on the ground, pouring out tea from the bottle, as if it were always woods she lived in.

"No. I've not started the fiddle yet." Elizabeth smiles, taking the cup Claira proffers. She sips the amber liquid. Finds she quite likes it. Where next then? How to get round this stiltedness? Abandon the violin? Her brow furrows.

"Will you play something for me, Claira? When you have finished your tea."

"Yes. If you would like me to," Claira says, smiling for the first time since they arrived.

"I would. Very much," Elizabeth says.

Her demeanor is so different now, Elizabeth thinks, watching Claira tune the violin. Her face has quite softened and her hands move about the instrument knowingly—with self-disregard. Elizabeth reaches for her sketchbook. Claira is not at all in the sort of positioning she had in mind for the painting, but to have her relaxed while she and the violin are drawn is the main objective for the moment.

Claira grins up at her. A different person.

"Do you mind what I play?"

"Whatever you would like to most of all."

She plays where she sits and for all her wanting to capture the image on paper, Elizabeth has to stop and listen. The sound is so pure and sure. She plays a light and silly thing, pushing out mischievous notes to her friend, so that Elizabeth tips her head back to laugh her admiration and Claira grins at her, eyes shining.

"I need to stand," Claira calls through her music.

"Please do. Where you were before, if you wouldn't mind."

Claira scrambles to her feet, still playing; slurring the notes to mimic her own movement. Elizabeth laughs out loud. This is theater. A violin version of Bottom's absurdity.

Elizabeth returns to the little folding stool, placed in a dip, three yards from Claira's feet. Through the sunlight, notes rain down on her. She looks up at Claira, bouncing and chopping the bow across the strings. This isn't just playing the violin. This is the stuff of a virtuoso. And what change! The animation of this moment compared to earlier frozenness. Some fear of being seen with the instrument completely banished by her confidence—so clearly justified—in her ability to play.

Claira ends. A strong, ridiculous, harmonized slide.

Elizabeth shakes her head. "I had assumed you could play. I had no idea how well."

Claira grins. "It is a lovely instrument."

"From which I could not get a single note and from which you play so many, so readily and with immense flair and surety."

"It is the way my father taught me. I am sure I could not paint."

"I am not at all sure *I* can with such excitement in the air."

"I should stop then."

"Oh no. I hope you will play more."

"Perhaps something which takes itself more seriously," Claira laughs.

"Yes. And if I see a particular position I would like you to hold, perhaps I may stop you."

"Of course."

For minutes Elizabeth draws while Claira plays. There is such a painting to be had here. When the light comes round more behind her. When the right position is found. Maybe this is it. This sketch that catches her with the bow pulling back towards its tip, the line of the bow and her arm, echoing the skyline visible on rising ground through sinewy trunks of trees. Yet still it is not the best it could be. The piece Claira plays now is more solemn. Quite, quite beautiful. Claira focuses more intently on it; enveloping the instrument, bringing her face more towards her body. That is the problem. It cuts the viewer out. Whatever is this music, Elizabeth wonders, pausing again to listen. Beautiful.

It ends. Claira moves the instrument down and looks out across at Elizabeth. Elizabeth gives a little gasp.

"There," she calls, keeping her voice steady. "Could you hold that?" *There* is the assertion she has been looking for. Senses alert, she gathers detail. Puts them, quickly, down on paper. Eyes first because soonest to lose the moment. Wonderful expression. The whole face. A self-confident radiance. Sure in the knowledge of a piece extremely well played. And the arm with the bow to one side still does the work Elizabeth wants it to in matching the line of the horizon. Perfect.

Elizabeth works with a will. Sketches done that day are worked on in the studio for the next two days; the canvas—made ready and waiting for the purpose—is brought to the woods the day after that. Claira gapes to see the size of it and again to see the speed and industry with which Elizabeth works.

For four weeks, she works long days, though not the Sabbath, or at least, not at Trethenna. On days when Elizabeth is working on the background, Claira need not be there, but they walk down from Trethenna to the woods one afternoon, Munro, Claira, Mrs. Jago and one of her daughters. Claira becomes quieter as they approach, not sure what Munro's response will be.

There is not much of her to see yet, on the painting. He studies the sketches for a long time. Claira sees him look at Elizabeth, nodding at something she says. Then he comes to stand next to his wife, puts her hand through his arm; holds it close.

They have brought Elizabeth freshly baked heavy cake and the cold tea she has now quite taken to, but although this feels like an outing to them, like a chapel tea treat, they leave her soon, sensing her desire to work on, knowing what it is to work out-of-doors; unsure if the weather will hold.

Other days, Claira must stand for her, long hours, though Elizabeth is careful to rest her. There is time, as she stands, for reflection on her new life. Time for frustration, too. All the things she could be doing at Trethenna. But she is pleased to see Elizabeth. Recognizes this as a special time. And it is a wonder—seeing the image emerge. How some essence of herself has been captured.

"Look at the time!" Claira says, coming, after a day of it, into the kitchen and putting Elizabeth's easel down. "Five past six and Munro will be gone to chapel by half past and there's no shirt ironed for him."

"I am sorry," Elizabeth says, carefully putting down the painting and her wooden box. Taking out a handkerchief, she pats her face; warm from the walk in the sun, uphill.

"It's not your doing."

"I have kept you for so long."

"Nonsense. I should have had the shirt done sooner. Mrs. Jago would have done it, if I had thought to ask her."

"Shall I do it?"

"No! I should be giving you tea in the parlor."

"Not at all."

"I'll put the kettle on anyway."

"Lovely, but a man must have a shirt for chapel, so don't let me keep you from it."

"Would you mind?"

"I insist. I shall read you snippets from the paper," Elizabeth says, seating herself at the table and taking a newspaper from her box.

Busy placing irons in the fire, Claira looks up in surprise. Although her father sometimes brought one home, Claira herself has never owned a newspaper.

"I'll just have a look at this first, though," Elizabeth says, turning to her painting, which she lifts then props up against the dresser.

Looking across at Elizabeth, Claira smiles to see her standing in that particular way again; focusing on the painting, her head on one side. Although Elizabeth's back is to her, Claira can visualize the expression on her face. She has seen it so much these last few days: a trancelike concentration. Claira wonders if her own face goes like that when she plays the fiddle. She rather suspects it does.

Thank Heavens that, despite the warmth of the day, Mrs. Jago has left a good fire and once the shirt is ironed, Claira crosses the room to stand quietly next to Elizabeth; experiencing again the difficulty in looking at this image of herself that is emerging. She begins at one corner of the picture, where the dark greens of long shadows stretch and are intersected with light from a setting sun—unseen. She follows their lead diagonally up to the edge of her dress, just a roughly sketched area now, a pale wash of color hinting at the burgundy it's going to be. Perhaps that is one reason Claira finds it difficult to look. She has grown so used to herself in black; felt strange changing out of it for this purpose, into one of the new outfits made for her.

Strokes of the brush, where the sweep of fabric will be painted, lead her eye on to the line of the arm and the fiddle, poised after playing. Hovering near the image of the face, Claira's own eye cannot help but follow the line of the instrument there. Yet still it's a shock: the lift of the head, the length of neck revealed, the way the eyes are *so* direct. Three quarters of the face catches the light and the outline of the sunward hair flames with it. But it's the expression that is really difficult for Claira to witness. Elizabeth had placed herself lower to paint, deliberately seeking out a dip in the ground in which to stand and set up her easel. So perhaps that's it, perhaps that's why the lowering gaze seems so self-assured.

Claira slides her eye away from it, down the arm that carries the bow, held wide and backed by the tinted sky through trunks of trees on a wooded horizon. The image of her wears the backdrop like a mantle, embracing and embodying her, till that, too, feeds back into the tracts of shadow and light.

Claira glances sideways at Elizabeth. She sees she is smiling.

"What do you think?" Elizabeth asks.

"I cannot say."

"Do you not like it?"

"Oh yes."

"Is it difficult because it's you?"

"Well, it isn't me. Oh, it is, of course," Claira adds hurriedly. "It looks very much like me, only . . ." She hesitates. "Only much stronger."

Elizabeth smiles and slips an arm through Claira's and squeezes it. "I am only painting what I see."

She turns from the painting. "I am hoping this will be finished in time for the opening of the art museum in Penzance. There's going to be a big exhibition."

"And you would want to show this?" Claira asks, surprised and considering again that the painting will have a future once it's finished.

"Yes."

The lid of the kettle begins to rattle. Claira goes to take the thing from the heat, wondering what Munro will think of a painting of her and the fiddle hung before public gaze and then, there he is, coming from the fields, behind time, into a kitchen tinged with the smell of fresh ironing.

"Miss Armstrong, good afternoon," he says. "You'll have to forgive me if I hurry away, I'm later than I intended. Oh!"

He stops and stares. The painting.

"Much nearer completion than when you saw it last, I think."

"Yes. Yes, indeed."

Claira folds sheets while he looks.

"You will be late for chapel," she says, taking down the ironed shirt she's left airing and crossing the room to hand it to him.

"Thank you," he says, staring at the picture still as Claira pushes the shirt into his hand. He turns to Elizabeth.

"Finished for today?"

She shakes her head. "Not quite. I want to go back in a while and see what the sunset does to the light."

"Ah," Munro says, studying the painting again. The clock chimes the half hour and still he stands.

"Oh, do listen, Claira," Elizabeth says, reading from *The Cornish*

Telegraph once Munro has gone. " 'Seeing that the average brain weight of women is about five ounces less than that of men,' " Elizabeth reads in a pompous tone, " 'on merely anatomical grounds we should be prepared to expect a marked inferiority of intellectual power in the former.' " She looks up at Claira and grins. " 'Moreover,' " she continues, " 'as the general physique of women is less robust than men and therefore less able to sustain the fatigue of serious or prolonged brain action, we should also on physiological grounds be prepared to entertain a similar anticipation.' "

"Who has written this?" Claira asks, not at all sure she fully understands the sentiment or what it is Elizabeth finds so amusing.

"George J. Romanes," Elizabeth says.

"Where does he live?"

"I am not sure, London, I think, or Oxford, perhaps," Elizabeth replies, somewhat surprised by the question. "One of Darwin's disciples in any case."

"Oh," Claira says, dropping her gaze to the ironing.

Elizabeth finds her place in the text again. " 'In actual fact,' " she reads, " 'we find that the inferiority . . .' Oh, did you notice? He's moved from the suggestion that we should be prepared to *expect* an inferiority to inferiority as indisputable fact." She moves her marker finger back a little way. " 'In actual *fact* we find that the inferiority displays itself most conspicuously in a comparative absence of originality and this more especially in the higher levels of intellectual work.' "

Claira slides one of the irons into its shoe and places it back into the fire.

"Oh dear," Elizabeth says, "I'm afraid it gets rather worse. 'It is in original work,' " she reads, waggling a schoolmistress's finger, "'that the disparity is most conspicuous. For it is a matter of ordinary comment that in no one department of creative thought can women be said to have at all approached men.' Oh well then," she says. "That's me done for. May as well cease any attempt to paint.

Never mind, there's a whole huge column next to it giving advice on 'How to Vary the Toilette.' It seems lace dresses trimmed with ribbons are what we should be wearing. Perhaps I'll take up dress-making instead." She laughs and drops the paper on the table and only then notices Claira is still and watching her.

"Oh Claira, what is it?"

Claira picks up pillowcases to fold.

"What is it?" Elizabeth repeats.

Claira shrugs. "I don't know." She looks up at Elizabeth. "Doesn't it make you angry?"

"The article?"

Claira nods.

"It might have done once. I'm sorry. Has it upset you?"

Claira looks down to the pillowcases. Smooths out a crease.

"Is it true what it says?"

Elizabeth smiles gently. "No, Claira." Her face breaks into a broader grin and she draws her knees up and hugs them. "Do you know what I shall do with it?"

"No."

"I shall cut it out and show it to Stanhope and he will go rather red around the ears and say, 'Oh, the fellow couldn't possibly mean you, Lizzie, dear girl.' And then, perhaps I shall send it to some other artist friend, Mr. Whistler or Mr. Sickert, and they will write back—with irony, Claira—and say, 'Good thing too, women should know their place.' "

Claira looks into her shining face and cannot help but smile back.

"Now then," Elizabeth says, picking up Claira's fiddle from the table and getting up to take it to Claira, "I hope you will humor me and put the iron down long enough to let me hear you play before I go back to my painting."

So then there's music too, sliding round the kitchen to bind them together as they look at each other's eyes and grin.

Fifty-two

Damien rushes into the kitchen and out of the back door.

"Where are you going, young man?" Claire asks, at the sink, washing up.

"To the beach, *of course,*" he answers, running back in and jangling his bucket and spade under her nose.

"Oh yes?"

"Is the picnic ready?"

"What?"

"Daddy said we could take a picnic."

What *is* Howard playing at? He hates the beach.

"That's *my* bucket," Nathan says coming in, tearful.

"No it *isn't,*" Damien argues. "Yours is the blue one."

"It's mine! It's mine!" Nathan yells, running out after him.

"I thought we could go to the beach," Howard says, striding in from upstairs. "The boys are ready when you are."

"They might find a change of clothes helpful, Howard. Perhaps a towel or two."

"I'll just go and clean the car while you're getting ready, then."

Claire places a mug down on the draining board. She notices her hands are shaking.

"Howard?"

He stops in the doorway. "Yes?"

"When are we going to talk about this?"

"Talk about what?"

Claire fidgets at the sink.

"Talk about *what*?"

She hears him begin to move away.

"This!" she says, turning towards him. "This state of things between us. Your lover." She flings the word at him. "The woman I found you with in our bed. Remember?" Fighting tears, she hears the note of hysteria rising in her voice. "Well?"

"Mummy, Damien won't give me my bucket," Nathan says, running into the kitchen. "Oh. Why are you crying?"

"She's just upset about something, Nathan," Howard says. "I do hope you're not fighting with your brother again."

"What?" Nathan says, staring at his mother, crying by the sink.

"It's all right, Nath," Claire says, quickly mopping her eyes. She crosses over to the child; crouches down by him.

"Now then," she says, straightening the collar of his shirt. Howard leaves. "I think I saw your blue bucket in the garage with the fishing nets. Why don't you go and have a look? Daddy will be out there. He's gone to wash the car."

They've only been to this beach once before. It's quite small, with rocky cliffs that curve into an amphitheater. The beach is fairly busy. People making the most of the Indian summer, the last weekend before school starts.

Claire stops and takes off her sandals, letting her feet sink into pale sand. Nathan slips his hand into hers. She breathes in sea breeze, keeping her shoulder turned towards Howard; shutting him out; wishing she were here with just the children, or perhaps with Kate and Sky. She shades her eyes with her hand and looks out at sunlight glinting off the water. The sea is beautiful, a pale aquamarine.

"Can you manage, Nathan?" she asks, bending to him where he struggles to take off his shoes.

"I can *do* it," he squeaks and she straightens again. She can feel the weight of Howard behind her. She focuses out to sea. The waves are quite big from recent wind. Several surfers are out there among them. Squinting against the sun to watch one surfer riding in, she can see the tousle of blond hair to his shoulders, his lithe body flexing, encased in black, stark against the blues of sky and sea, a wave breaking white to the right of him. The sea really is an extraordinary color. She finds herself thinking of Nick's eyes and blots the image out.

They find a place to settle. Claire watches the children. They're old hands at this now. They love it. They don't even ask if they can go to the sea. They've looked and know it's too rough for them. Claire likes that. Nature's discipline.

Howard's eyes fall on Claire. She is lying near him on her stomach, her arms folded on the sand in front of her with her chin resting on them. Her face is turned away from him, directed towards the children and the sea, and he lets his gaze fall on her back; on her rounded, familiar body. She has lost weight recently. She is still well rounded, though, at her shoulder and thigh where the elastic of her costume is too tight. He wishes she wouldn't . . . *abandon* herself like this. Facedown. Oblivious. He can see her shoulders are reddening. She's going to burn, he thinks.

Claire thinks the sun is wonderful. She rests her forehead on her folded hands as she used to at school, only this time, the tiny cocoon that's revealed is not the desk with its grain traced by ink, but a cocoon of sand. There's a similar feeling though: a shutting out of the world.

It doesn't look like ordinary sand. Without breaking the hide, she moves her fingers across the surface inside it. It seems to be millions of pieces of broken shell, pounded and smoothed by the sea. Yes, each piece has evidence of shell about it. A white underside, the remains of a ring or a line. The sun steals in through her hair and the particles of smoothed shell stick to her fingers, pale pinks and yellows and the faintest mauve.

There's music too, a cacophony of sound: the waves and the

voices of children all roll into one and the breeze wafts the sound across her sun-warmed body. She can hear her own children playing close by her.

Howard's presence feels like a weight pressing on her shoulders. She eases her muscles against it and looks up to check the children. Damien's hat needs putting on straight. She reaches out an arm and makes the adjustment.

"All right, Damie?"

The surfers are still out there. All in the water now, waiting for a good wave. This one? This one? Yes, one of them is up again. The blond man she watched earlier has caught the motion of the wave. It's like watching a bird. He's like a bird skimming across the water, playing dare with the waves. She rests her chin on her hands and spends time just drinking him in, the movement of the waves mirrored by the dip and rise of his slender body, the delicate balance, arms wide. Then—in cruciform—he tumbles and is engulfed so that Claire holds her breath till the sea releases him.

The sun is hot on her skin and it occurs to her to go into the water. She turns to Howard and is immediately aware he has been watching her.

"Will you swim?" she asks him.

He shakes his head. "No."

"Damien," she says, smoothing more sunblock onto his skin, "Mummy's going to go for a swim. Be a good boy and look after Nathan for me."

"It's too rough," Damien says.

"It's all right for me, I'm bigger."

She smooths cream onto Nathan, too. "All right, Nath?"

And then she does it. She just gets up and walks down the beach, leaving the children with their father. She doesn't even look back, just walks towards the sea until her feet feel wet sand and then the water.

The shock of cold as it bursts against her legs makes her draw breath sharply and suddenly it seems ridiculous—the waves so much bigger from here, more hostile. They crash down hard onto the beach. Perhaps she should turn back. Cold water swirls round her knees now, sucks the sand from beneath her feet. She has to keep moving to keep her footing. The waves draw back down to the sea, drawing her down with them, fiercely. The cold! Her body shrinks from it, contracting as the water meets her belly, forcing her to gasp air, her eyes stretching wide with the shock of it. *I cannot. I cannot.*

"It's all right once you're in."

Claire looks up to locate the voice. It belongs to a head bobbing on the waves a little way out to sea. It is the head of a woman who has to be seventy. She is wearing a bright green rubber bathing cap. "Really dear, it's all right once you're in. Getting out through the surf's the worst bit."

Claire erupts into laughter. At the sea, at her fear and at the woman's green head bobbing. Apple in a bucket. And even as she thinks, *I can't do this,* her body takes over, contradicts her and she feels herself launch into coldness. Cold water closes round her hot shoulders and she gasps and splutters and doggy-paddles, but she's in. She's in and it doesn't seem she's going to sink. She tests it. Stretching out, she takes a deep breath, gives a strong single kick with her legs and feels herself glide on. It feels like flying, the depth of water beneath her now, the height of sky above. Her body tingles and contracts; sings with the water. She glides in the water. And grins.

Turning onto her back, she looks towards the beach. The people are colored dots on the pale sand. Heaped rocks tower hugely above them. She wonders which dots are her family, but cannot tell. Perhaps Howard is thinking of his lover—their deceitful little screwing.

Let him.

Rolling onto her belly, she kicks again and glides on, feels herself lifted by a wave, gently, then lowered, feels the pull and power of the water she swims across, turns to watch the turquoise sheen rumble into whiteness as it rolls to the sand.

Fifty-three

"He seems a very fervent believer," the doctor says, sitting at Trethenna's kitchen table to write up his notes.

"In what way did you notice it?" Munro, watching him, asks.

Without looking up, the doctor gives a short laugh. "I would have been hard-pressed *not* to notice," he says. "Seems the man must pray all the while."

He does look up then, thinking of it.

"He seems to have little rituals. Prayer at the doorstep before we went in, prayer as he put water in the kettle, prayer before the drinking of tea, prayer as I took my leave."

"Jed was always very pious."

"Oh, but *very,*" the doctor says. He resumes his writing. Munro cannot help but watch his hands, thinking of the time they tended him when, tired, misjudging, Munro had put the sickle in his leg, letting the blade bite into flesh that must be sewn back together. Good hands they had been then, unwavering, compassionate.

"There is no prospect of a woman to wive him?" the doctor asks, writing still.

"No."

"Does he eat here with you often?"

"On occasion, when we are busy. And Mrs. Jago sends him something on baking days."

"And he eats well, here with you?"

"As far as I am aware. I think so. Yes, I would say he does."

"You see," the doctor says, putting down his pen, "I have given him a good examination and can find nothing wrong with him, but that he is very thin. I suspect he may be forgetting to feed himself."

"Simply that?"

The doctor stands, gathering his things together. "Perhaps simply, perhaps not. We will only be able to tell that if he has good access to food all the time."

"To eat with us more often, you mean."

"That would probably be the best way round it."

"It would be an easy thing for us, but we might have trouble persuading Jed to it. He is always quick to take himself home at mealtimes."

"Well, I'll leave that to you to arrange as best you can. Probably best if you tackle it first and not as a health matter. If he is not to be persuaded, let me know and we can try another approach."

"Is that the sum of it then, that we must be sure he eats well?" Claira asks, that evening, propping herself with one elbow on the pillow.

"It seems it is, for now," Munro answers. He reaches from the edge of the bed where he sits to move a strand of hair from her eye. "I shall feel very foolish if that is all it is."

"But, you pay him well enough. It is not your place, surely, to check Jed has eaten his meals every day. And why ever would he not eat?"

Munro looks at her hand, resting on the counterpane, traces the line of one of her fingers with his.

"I suppose there are many reasons why a man will deny himself."

"*Are* there?"

"Yes."

She looks at him, her eyebrows raised.

"Our religion, for example, urges a certain self-constraint."

"But *not* a denial of food," she says.

"No, but then"—quietly, he laughs—"perhaps the idea of

denial can become a habit with all things, especially if life gives you reason to believe it best."

He looks up at her.

"I am thinking out loud," he says. He drops his gaze again and she watches him ponder, the lamplight catching the side of his cheek. How she has grown to love his face.

He is tracing, again, the line of her hand. He looks up, eyes resting on hers.

"My brother Edwin's first child was born out of wedlock."

She feels her eyes widen. "Oh, I . . ." But she trails into silence not knowing what to say.

"Edwin was eighteen."

"You must have felt it very keenly, being his twin."

Munro nods. "I did. And one of the things I felt was that it would never be my experience to father a child in that way."

"And so a sense of denial began?"

"Yes."

"But you could have married."

"I could, but then the move to Africa meant I met fewer women likely to be a wife to me and by the time I moved back, the habit of being single had grown and there was so very much work to be done on Trethenna."

"I remember it."

"Do you?"

"Yes."

"You can only have been a child, or little more."

"I do remember it though. The people who lived here were French."

"They were! They built it, then, after a few years, returned to France. It's why the building is unusual—their influence."

"Is it unusual? Well, I had always wondered at the huge stones that have been used."

Munro nods. "Yes. And the attic. Which other farmhouse can you think of near here which has an attic?"

"I suppose that is true. I had not thought of it."

She upturns her hand to hold his fingers.

"Is that why Edwin didn't go to Africa?"

"Yes. He felt he had responsibilities here. And my father was very indignant at the disgrace. Of course, they are married now. Their other children born after their marriage. So, now you know, Claira, our family's shame."

"Well, I am very pleased," Claira says. "You might never have waited for me otherwise."

"Dear Claira," he laughs and kisses her on the forehead, then stands and before moving away, turns the lamp down very low. Claira feels the leap of her heart. She wonders if he is conscious of this signal he gives: the turning down of the lamp. Not a night, it says, for talking in full lamplight nor for falling straight to sleep in the dark. Her eyes follow him as he moves about the room. He does not look at her. By the window he bows his head in prayer. For a minute or two he remains thus. Then he goes to the washstand, pushes the braces from his shoulders and unbuttons his shirt. He pours water into the bowl.

As the shirt slides from his shoulders, she sees his skin is dun in the lamplight, except at his neck and forearms where it has been made darker by the sun. His body is tight from recent haymaking and now the cutting and gathering of corn. The muscles at his shoulders ride proud as he moves his arms in washing. The line to his waist is lean. Watching him, Claira stretches out her body in the bed and the rustle of bedding is in the room, meeting the sound of water trickling, squeezed from his sponge.

He is still a second: listening.

She sees a small movement of his elbows, the slight flexing of his upper arms as he unbuttons his trousers—one . . . two . . . three . . . four . . . five . . . six . . . before he slides them down, stepping from them and his underclothes. The honed muscle of his buttocks flexes as his moves to drape his clothes across the chair.

Claira sighs, so quietly, yet he stills again, his skin alive to her.

With a rhythmical turning of the cake of soap, he makes a lather on the sponge then begins to soap himself, the small of his back, his buttocks, his genitals, his feet. All the while his back is to her. With the sponge, he rinses the soap away then takes the towel and makes himself dry. He reaches sideways to the rail where he usually drapes his nightshirt when he washes. It is not there. He hesitates. Claira feels under his pillow. The garment is still where he put it that morning. She thinks of throwing it to him and chooses not to. She sees the rise of his shoulders in breathing and waiting. She will not rescue him. He will have to face her.

He turns and, as she thought, his penis stands huge. He leans back against the washstand and dares to look across at her. The striking of eyes is like a tidal wave flooding and straightaway he feels himself swept up in it. "I do not want to hurt you," he hears his voice say as he crosses to her.

"You will not."

"Claira, I . . ."

"Come to me."

And he does, though he scarcely knows whose body it is that slides into the bed beside her, scarcely knows who it is that lifts up her nightdress, scarcely knows whose knee spreads her thighs wide, whose hand reaches round, spanning her buttocks, lifting her up to him, whose flesh it is that pushes so deeply into hers, so deeply, whose flesh it is, whose heat, who draws and is drawn. *As God is my witness, how else do we multiply?* And he cries out, clasping her, holding him, giving, taking, giving his seed.

Through the window at dawn, the gentle colors of early sun are swathed in mist. Man and wife wake in each other's arms. Claira opens her eyes to see their image reflected in the belly of the lamp: the rounding of arms and shoulders; the closeness of heads. Circles mirrored in the dulled brass orb. She wonders if he has woken and pushes her face, minutely, against his neck. Minutely his embrace tightens round her. She feels her face expand into a smile and nuzzles closer to him.

"Will you manage without me again at harvest?"

"No."

She draws away a fraction.

"Must I tell Miss Armstrong she may not paint me today? I would be pleased to help with the grain," Claira says, relaxing her weight against him again. "It doesn't suit me to do nothing for so long."

He brings his hand up to her head; resting the palm across her forehead and cheekbone. She presses her face against the strength of it, seeking the familiar roughness of his skin, reaffirming the measure of his span against the smallness of her skull.

"No, of course you must sit for her. We can manage the harvest. It is only that I will miss you, being gone a whole day." He smiles at his own foolishness and she kisses the corner of his mouth.

"Do you mind the painting?" she asks.

"Mind it?"

"Yesterday. You stayed such a long while looking at it."

He shakes his head. "No, I don't mind it. I find it remarkable. Beautiful."

"Miss Armstrong says she wants to show it when the art museum opens in Penzance next month."

He is quiet, digesting the news, then says, "The event will be the richer for it."

She kisses the palm of his hand, then catches hold of it with her own and draws it down beneath the bedclothes. Closely he watches her face on the pillow as she brings his hand to rest on her belly.

"I cannot be certain," she says, straightening his fingers against her and looking deep into his eyes, "but I think there is a baby."

She sees his eyes open and flare before he closes them tight and clenches her to him.

"Praise God," he whispers, his face in her hair, covering her head with kisses.

Fifty-four

"This is outrageous," Kate says, staring at her.

Claire nods. "In a way, it is."

"You mean, he won't talk about it at all?"

"We haven't managed to yet."

"But, you are *sure*?"

"Oh perfectly sure," Claire laughs wryly, thinking of the things she is sure of these days and the things she is not. The certainty that Howard has a lover has been such a solid presence these last few weeks. There's a splash of milk on the table, left from breakfast. Claire circles through it with her little finger.

"It's probably not just Howard who won't talk about it. I wanted to talk it through at first, but I find it impossible now."

"But aren't you *furious,* Claire?" Kate asks, shoving a hand back through her hair.

Claire looks at her in surprise. "What good would that do me?"

"It might help you decide what to do."

"I already know what I want to do."

"Which is?"

"Maintain a stable home for the children."

"So Howard gets away with it?"

Claire shrugs. "What *can* I do?" she asks quietly.

"Throw him out."

"What? Change the locks and refuse to open the door? Have a slanging match through bolted doors for the children to witness?"

Claire shakes her head. "Not what I think of as providing a stable home."

"You could tackle it through a solicitor. I know a very good solicitor in Truro. A woman."

"Well, perhaps, if that time comes. Thanks, Kate."

"Oh, *Claire*," Kate sympathizes, reaching across the corner of the table to squeeze Claire's shoulder. "And I thought it was just first-day-at-big-school that was worrying you. I think I was far more concerned about it than Sky was this morning. How was Nathan?"

"A bit tearful as we left home. This thing with Howard has come at a bad time for him. He can't understand why Mummy and Daddy don't sleep together anymore. It's a shame. He'd done so well at playschool *and* he'd enjoyed his few days at the primary last term *and* he's got a brother there to look out for him. Should have been plain sailing for him, really—and now this."

Kate rubs the flat of her hand across Claire's back. "He will survive, Claire.

"Do you know?" Claire says, sitting back from the table. "I actually hit Damien the other day."

"Did you?"

Claire nods.

"Well, you wicked mother," Kate says. "I bet that's something you do at least every other day."

Claire feels tears rise at her friend's supportiveness.

"Bless you, Kate," she says, rubbing the back of her hand across her eyes.

"Well? How many times does that make it?"

"That was the second time ever."

"Fist in the face, was it?" Kate asks, looking round for something for Claire to mop her eyes with.

"Kate!" Claire exclaims, recoiling at the image.

"Well?" Kate insists, handing Claire a piece of kitchen roll.

"A slap on the leg."

"I expect he'll live."

Claire blows her nose rather noisily. "Yes, but I still feel dreadful about it."

"Of course you do, but it's difficult when you're having to filter all the shit. Some of it gets through to them sometimes."

Claire nods. "I don't think I've ever hit Nathan at all."

"Really? I'm sure I've bashed Sky often enough."

"Wonder how they're getting on."

Kate looks at the clock. "Twenty to ten. I should think Sky's got them well organized by now."

Fifty-five

Claira has never been in a room so large. She gasps at the breadth and height of it and is glad of Munro's arm. She tries to guess at the room's dimensions and estimates its length at seventy or eighty feet with a breadth of perhaps half that. Light floods in through windows high at the edge of the curved ceiling. Everywhere the walls are hung with paintings.

And there it is, quite quickly noticeable, Elizabeth's painting of her. Claira feels the sudden urge to turn and leave, only Munro is walking on and she goes with him.

In its framed and finished form, the image is more than ever striking, the green and burgundy chiming out across the room the strong assertion of the pose; the self-possessed insistence of the gaze. Self-possession. What would the minister say? Claira stands in black before it, her hair tightly braided beneath a little hat from under whose brim she peeps. Two women nearby nudge each other and—for all her disguise—nod in her direction. *Isn't that the woman in the painting?*

"Can we not go and see some others?" Claira whispers to Munro, leaning her weight away.

"Of course."

Their Daily Bread, Claira reads. In a St. Ives street, a young child—a girl—struggles to carry the weight of a loaf of bread.

Her first ever errand, the faces of mother and sister announce as they watch from an upper-story window to see how she fares. It is signed Stanhope Forbes. There are two more of his here. One another Bolitho portrait. Mr. Edward Bolitho this time. Strong, straightforward, none of the challenge Elizabeth has painted.

The Jubilee Hat. Mother adds the final trimmings; young son at her side leaves his toy boat to admire her finished work. Frank Wright Bourdillon.

Claira finds some of Frank Bramley's work. Roses she feels she could pluck from the canvas. And a study of a girl's head—*Simplicita*. Turning to speak to Munro, Claira sees Frank Bramley himself walking towards them.

"Doesn't Miss Armstrong's painting look well," Bramley says to Munro once Claira has introduced them.

"Doesn't it," Munro agrees.

"Miss Armstrong has been so pleased to have had the chance to paint the picture. She was here earlier, have you seen her?"

"No."

"What a pity. She will be sad to have missed you. Have you seen the Langley yet?"

"No," Claira says smiling at Bramley's obvious enthusiasm.

"Quite exquisite. May I show you? It's over here."

He leads the way and places them before it and straightaway Claira is lost. Or at least, at first she resists the painting's pull, busies herself with reading the plate. *But Men Must Work and Women Must Weep, Though Storms Be Sudden and Waters Deep and the Harbor Bar Be Moaning*.

An interior of two figures. Subtle pinks and blues and browns. A young wife of a fisherman weeps over the swaddled child she nurses on her lap. Behind them, the grandmother stands, gazing out through a window suggested by the way light floods in. A death then. A fisherman drowned at sea. Son and husband and father.

The fabric in the basket in the right-hand foreground looks like a bedspread, waiting for repair. The swirl of material leads Claira's eye to the blanket in which the babe is wrapped and so on to the mother's arm, her head in her hand and thence to the grandmother's hand resting on the younger woman's shoulder. Having been so swiftly moved, Claira wants the journey to continue, but the path divides now. One way leads to the ancient head, staring out. Claira's eye follows the path and flounders at the edge of the image, feeling pushed out by it: made to face the cruelty of an unseen sea.

She brings her gaze back to the comfort of the picture, starts the journey again, from the sweep of fabric to the old woman's shoulders and then down the second path to the ancient woman's other hand. Again Claira's eye is arrested. This second hand is on the table, heavily. It seems that one ancient hand rests to give comfort, this second to take support. It, too, points towards the sea. Claira looks at the balance of those two hands. It's almost as if the woman is weighing something. The hand taking support is lower—as if that has to come first, before there's strength to give out comfort.

Claira's eye wants to make the journey a full circle, but the image only lets her trip down bumpily, from table, to footrest to floor, before starting again the smooth ascent. And then another thought forms. The shape of the picture is making her feel what the people in it must be feeling. The smooth ascent speaks of a connectedness in grief. The uncompromising halt leaves her, too, floundering in the knowledge of the power of the sea or in the need to grasp at what little is solid in the face of such knowledge.

The blood rushes to Claira's face. She turns and strides back across the room and looks at Elizabeth's painting again, only full on this time, eye to eye. Yes, actually. It *is* a painting of her. In some vital way raw. She wheels round to cross again to the Langley. Images of hats and girls with bread blur.

Back before the Langley, she tries the journey again. The sweep of grieving unity leading inexorably to thoughts of the cruelty of the sea. However many times the journey is made, that is where it will always end. Even if the eye stops in the ancient woman's holding on; her hand points only out to sea.

Another presence catches Claira's attention and she looks aside. Munro talking to Bramley. Bramley, watching her, wears a knowing smile.

Fifty-six

"Why don't you play outside?" Claire calls as the boys race through the kitchen once more.

"It's raining."

"Not that much, it isn't," Claire says, peeling Sunday-lunch potatoes. "Put your jackets on and go outside if you want to run around."

By way of answer she hears their feet thunder up the stairs. Howard comes into the kitchen and she feels her face mask itself. She's almost getting used to it: being cheery with the boys and switching to neutral for Howard. Difficult when they're all together, but otherwise she doesn't even have to think about it anymore. He passes through the kitchen, saying nothing. She wishes her stomach wouldn't churn every time she sees him. Perhaps it won't soon. She hears the BMW start up. He must be going to buy a Sunday paper.

"Yes please, Howard," Claire mutters to the carrots. "We are a little short of milk. If you could get a couple of pints that would be really helpful."

There's a knock at the front door.

"Could you answer that, Damien?" Claire calls, in the middle of scooping up vegetable peelings. Screams and giggles from upstairs tell her they haven't heard. There's another knock as Claire rinses off her hands. The boys' feet thump on the upstairs floor. She hears them race up to the attic.

"Hello," Nick says with a grin, standing in the drizzle and looking ridiculously handsome in a tatty cagoule with a pickax and spade slung over his shoulder. Then he frowns a little. "Are you all right?"

"Yes," Claire says, tucking stray hair away from her face, "just surprised to see you."

"I'm a little early," he says. "Kate will be here soon."

"She will?"

"Yes." He swings the pickax and spade to the ground. "Didn't she say?"

"No."

There's the clatter of children's feet coming down the stairs.

"She's bringing the ready-mix."

Claire laughs. "The ready-mix?"

"Ready-mix. Freddy-Bix, whoever's Freddy Bix?" Damien chants, pushing past his mother and bashing into Nick who catches him one-handed and twists him round in a fearsome armlock, pinning the boy against himself.

"Stuff to make concrete with," Nick tells his prisoner. "I think we can succeed in our mission, but only if you're prepared to help. What do you say, number one?" he asks.

"Aye-aye, Captain," Damien giggles out.

"Good man," Nick says, releasing him.

"When's Freddy Bix coming?"

"Soon, but we've got to dig the thing out first and then dig a hole."

"Nick, what *is* this all about?"

"Didn't Kate say?"

"No."

"The sundial. She said you wanted the base putting in properly."

"I did, I do, but it's not exactly a priority."

"What? She told me it was essential to get it done immediately or the world would come to an end."

"Will it really?" Nathan asks from where he stands behind Claire.

"Hello, Nathan," says Nick, squatting down. "How was school?"

"Okay," Nathan says, sucking his thumb.

"Just okay? Which was the best bit?"

Nathan thinks about it. "I took Dobbo to school."

"Oh *did* you?" Nick replies, looking up to Claire and mouthing, "Who's Dobbo?"

"The hay horse you made," Claire supplies.

"Oh, *Dobbo*. Did Dobbo have a good time, too?"

Nathan nods. "He had carrots for lunch."

"Brilliant!"

"Kate's here," Damien calls, running to meet the VW that is trundling into the drive.

"Oh good," Nick says, standing and offering Nathan his hand to hold while they go to meet the car, "Freddy Bix has arrived."

Kate and Sam and Sky tumble out.

"This is a conspiracy," Claire says, following on.

It's almost worth a photograph, Claire thinks, coming out of the house to see six bottoms sticking out of a bush as they contemplate how best to get at the base of the sundial.

"Sky, this might be easier if you weren't in the way," she hears Kate say.

"Nathan, you come out too," Claire calls.

Hearing Claire's voice, Kate backs out, hauling Sky after her.

"Go and play with Nathan," she says.

"Here you are, Nathan," Claire says, holding out the jacket she's brought for him.

"I don't want it."

"It's raining."

"Come on," says Sky, grabbing Nathan by the hand and running off towards the barn.

"Sky!" Kate calls and is ignored. "Oh, but my daughter is so *willful*," she says. "She just must *organize* everybody."

"Can't think *where* she gets it from," Claire says, watching Nick and Sam with pickax and spade beginning to dig round the base.

"Ah, well," Kate says, grinning. "Have I been found out?"

"You have."

"It seemed more constructive than coming round and punching Howard on the nose, which was the only other thing I could think of doing. Where is the ragbag, anyway?"

"Gone out for a paper, I think. Kate, you haven't told Nick, have you?"

"About Howard?"

Claire nods.

"No, Claire, no," Kate says, catching Claire's arm in emphasis.

"Only I really don't want him to know."

"I haven't said a word. And all I've said to Sam is that I wanted to demonstrate a little solidarity." She puts an arm round Claire's shoulders and gives her a brief hug. "Now then, where would you like the dial to be?"

"Hello," says Howard, returning with the Sunday papers.

"Good morning," says Nick.

"It seems you've been invaded," says Sam.

"So I see," says Howard.

"Time for the sundial to be reinstated," says Kate.

"Well done," Howard says, walking in out of the rain.

"Well it's such an im*prove*ment," Kate says once Howard has gone, drawing back with a grin, and nodding to where the sundial base is now in place and looking a little silly—like a soldier on guard, only—without the dial—blind: studiously directing an unseeing eye towards sky and rain; waiting for the cement to set.

Fifty-seven

"You'll be walking, I expect," Aunt Eadie says, pulling on black gloves.

"I do intend to," Munro replies, "although I have not discussed it with Claira yet."

"It is his custom," Aunt Eadie explains to Claira, "though don't ask me why. We have perfectly good transportation, but no. Come harvest festival your husband finds he must walk to chapel."

Munro smiles at her teasing.

"And will I walk with you?" Claira asks him.

"I would love you to, if you wish it."

"Heavens, now the world *has* gone mad!" Aunt Eadie exclaims. "He goes over hill and down dale and your dress will be in shreds before you get there."

"I shall be very mindful of her dress," Munro promises. "Only, we should set off soon. Will you be happy to bide here alone, Aunt Eadie, till Jed comes for you?"

"I should think I shall be much the better for it, for who can tell whether or no this madness is catching. Walk to chapel indeed." With a wave of a clawed hand she dismisses them. "Get off with you then. And I hope you'll not be late."

At the height of Blundle Hill they stop and look back. Trethenna's land below them is a patchwork of fields; those harvested now lighter than those where sheep and cattle graze or mangolds grow. Ricks of hay and corn fill the mow hay.

Standing behind her, Munro puts his arms round Claira's waist, looking out over her shoulder. His lips move in a prayer of thanksgiving and in her thoughts Claira adds her own thanks: for the harvest and for him.

"It is a wonderful thing to look out and see the work all done, all good harvest safely gathered," she says.

"Isn't it?" Munro agrees, inviting her weight further into his embrace. Putting his hands to her shoulders, he turns her and, facing her, strokes a wisp of hair from her eye. "But never more so than this year, Claira," he says, kissing the side of her face beneath the bonnet, drawing her close to him, kissing her mouth.

Resting her face against him, she hears the steady beating of his heart. Then, on the road below, the movement of the jingle catches her eye. Jed and Aunt Eadie on their way to chapel—and another vehicle behind theirs: Ebenezer and his family.

"They will be there ahead of us," she says nodding towards the vehicles.

"Oh, we cannot have that," Munro says, releasing her a little, resting his hand on her shoulder still; kissing her mouth again.

Together they turn and begin the descent.

Grass where their feet pass springs back. High on the hill, jackdaw land.

Reaching level ground, footpaths join, all leading on to church and chapel. Others are on them, hastening; families together, all wearing their best. The breeze brings snatches of sound.

"Isn't that the harmonium?" Claira hears one woman ask her husband.

"It is."

Calling them in through chapel doors thrown open.

The husband shakes his head.

"Sounds more like a fairground than the Lord's house."

" 'Tis said they had entertainment down Scilly, with their tea. Violins and a cello, I 'eard."

The man lets out breath.

"Well there'll be none of it here and that's for sure," he says, then, as Munro and Claira pass, "Oh, good afternoon to you, Mr. Richardson. Mrs. Richardson."

"Good afternoon, Alfred. Hettie," Munro says, raising his hat.

Walking on, Claira cannot quite hear what it is they whisper.

Sheaves of wheat and ripened apples, flowers and, long, plaited bread; sprays of soft fruit; bunches of grapes. Wherever have those come from? And there is the butter Claira has made, Trethenna's stamp upon it—a sack, too, of Trethenna's flour. And there's greenery, soft asparagus fern; interwoven ivy.

"I'm not so sure 'tis seemly, all this deccer-ashun."

"Well now. I don't suppose there's any harm to it."

The minister moves through the congregation, like a boat in the bay: parting waves, proud wind in his sails.

"What do you think, Aunt Eadie?"

"Well isn't it lovely? And what a to-do. I shall be pleased when it's time to sit down for my tea."

And it's Mary Bellham, isn't it? At the harmonium. Who is it she watches as her hands move across the keys? Claira follows her gaze to where Munro stands. Really, she watches him so intently, her face left blank in her absorption except that her lips move, only a little, as if she tries across the distance of the crowded chapel to follow what it is he is saying.

"But the quality is there in the grain, Ebenezer."

"So it is Munro, but 'tis the *quantity* that's down. And the straw, see? Short, stubby stuff 'tis this year."

Munro nods his agreement. "I was saying to Jed, we may need to cut bracken."

That's all, Mary Bellham. The quality of harvest. And why would you want to know it? Feeling herself watched, Mary jumps and flashes her gaze across to Claira then down to the keys. All the time, the hymn tumbles out and she doesn't miss a note.

The voices seem stronger today, the singing livelier. *We thank Thee then, O Father, for all things bright and good*—there are children in front of Claira, shiny hair braided—*The seedtime and the harvest*—it moves her to hear their higher voices—*our life, our health, our food*—next year she will bring her own son or daughter—*Accept the gifts we offer*—perhaps, next year, another—*For all thy love imparts and, what Thou most desirest, our humble, thankful hearts*—she feels Munro at her elbow. God that she might live to stand here with this man and her children, grown beside her. She wonders how many they will have. Musing, she loses the hymn. Jolts back near the start of another.

All is safely gathered in,
Ere the winter storms begin.

Fifty-eight

"Are the rabble coming round this weekend?" Howard asks, buttering toast.

"I've no idea," Claire says, packing Friday school lunches; annoyed with herself that she hasn't challenged Howard's nickname for her friends before now.

The boys are still in bed and Claire and Howard busy themselves on different sides of the kitchen, their backs towards one another. Generally they miss each other altogether in the morning, but Howard is down later than usual. Recovering from a few days away.

"They do seem to have tucked you under their wing," Howard continues.

Claire scrubs hard at two apples. She supposes they have been round quite a lot recently, Nick and Sam and Kate and Sky. The sundial is cemented in place now—and then there was the weekend they all did some drawing together and the weekend Sky came to stay. It's nearly half-term. That's not so often, three or four times in a half-term.

"I must say, I *do* find them something of an invasion, Claire."

Claire stops cutting bread rolls and looks at the back of his head and waits for the irony of his words to become apparent to him.

Howard undoes the marmalade.

Feeling her heart race, Claire puts down the knife.

"Rather less of an invasion for you than your lover was for me," she says.

He plugs the kettle in, his back still to her. She hears his short, hard laugh. "You really are going to keep throwing that at me, aren't you?"

"What would you *suggest* I do with it?"

"Forget about it," he says, opening a new packet of coffee.

"*Forget* about it?"

"Yes," he says, reaching a mug down from the cupboard. "Probably ninety percent of marriages are like this."

"Oh, *are* they?"

"Yes."

"Like *what,* exactly?" Her heart thumps hard now.

He shrugs his shoulders and pours cold coffee down the sink. "Like this. Like ours. After the first few years they just plod on. People inevitably get distracted."

"Oh, *do* they?"

"*Yes,* Claire."

"*Really,*" Claire says. She knows the pitch of her voice is rising. She tries to keep it lower and fails. "Then it's a wonder people bother at all," she cries out.

"Yes, isn't it?" Howard says, calmly; spooning coffee into the jug.

"And what of the children who result from these marriages that people foolishly *do* bother with?" she stumbles and spits.

"What about them?"

"What happens to *them,* exactly?"

He shrugs again. Behind him the kettle boils and makes steam, then there's a click as it turns itself off. He reaches into the fridge for the milk.

"They grow up and make the same foolish mistakes."

"Having been set such a *splendid* example—"

"By an hysterical mother," Howard finishes for her, in quiet monotone, turning and leaning back on the work surface to look at her. Then he says, pleasantly and looking over her shoulder, "Good morning, Nathan."

Pale-faced, the boy slips into the room.

Fifty-nine

Claira's in the yard when the postman comes: late today. Putting down the last pail of milk, she waits to take the post from him.

"Good morning!" she calls.

"Good morning, Mrs. Richardson."

Only he doesn't look at her. Hands her the post with his head a little down.

"My condolences to Mr. Richardson. And to yourself," he says, turning away.

Claira's about to question him, then sees the letter he's left on top. Addressed to Munro; the envelope is black-edged. News of death. There's something different about the stamp. Looking more closely, she sees it is from Africa. One of his brothers then. Or a parent.

It's in a dip, Rocky Park, so at first it's just Munro she sees with horses and plow working along the rows of potatoes. Then as she follows the cart track, she sees Jed, too, shaking potatoes from the overturned stems, throwing the stems aside into piles. Michael and the boys from the village come into view, bent double and placing the crop in baskets. It's all so ordered. Though he is working towards her, Munro hasn't seen her yet, the difficult ground needing all his attention and anyway, he's in that state of mind, the calm concentration he has when he works the horses. She loves to see it. Hands kindly on the reins, the quiet and occasional word. And here she comes bringing bad news from Africa; letting it close in on him. She thinks about turning back—leaving the letter for him to read at midday. Too late. He has seen her and is bringing the horses to a halt.

Eyes on eyes as she walks towards him. *What is it?* his ask. *Soon enough,* hers say. Then he sees the letter she passes.

The kettle on the fire begins to sing. Most probably he will want more hot in the bath. Claira plays her hand through the water next to his torso. The water is cooling a little. She catches the sponge and brings it up to soap his back again, making slow circles of lather on his shoulders, then squeezing the sponge out to trickle and stroke the suds away.

"Don't move," she says, touching his neck to ask him to stay leaning forward while she reaches for the kettle. On her knees again, slowly she pours, stirring new water in behind him.

"There."

Munro leans back and looks at her. A little smile, rather grim and not echoed in his eyes. Perhaps it is not a good idea after all; tending him in the bath. He loved it last time. She starts to move away, but he catches her hand.

"Don't go."

She smiles and kneels again.

"Unless you have to," he continues.

She shakes her head. "No."

There are suds left on his neck and she slides her fingers through them to rinse them away. The clock ticks solemnly on. Evening sun fills a tall narrow rectangle made by the door ajar. It strikes the flagstones then runs up across her body and he sees the fine downy hairs on her moving arm; gold in the slanting light. She sits back on her heels, in the shadow again. His eyes watch her as she reaches towels from the back of the chair.

"It seems very cruel," she says quietly, looking at him, the towels on her knee.

"What does?"

"That you had no chance to say good-bye. At least with my father, I had time to talk with him, knowing he would die."

Munro shakes his head. "It wasn't like that for me, Claira. *Not* wanting to talk to my father was one good reason to leave Africa."

"All the more reason, then, to see him before he died. A time to make good."

"No, no," he says, more emphatically. "We were irreconcilable. Everything about us, our beliefs, our motivations, everything was different—no, not just different, in opposition."

He sits upright and cups water in both hands and brings it to his face and as the water splashes down he runs his fingers to and fro along his jawbone, then stops and looks at her.

"There's more," he says. "His death is the least of it."

"What sort of thing?"

He reaches for the towels and stands, wrapping himself in them and stepping from the bath so that she gets to her feet in surprise at the quickness of his movement.

"What sort of thing?"

"It seems we shall have to leave here," he blurts out.

"And go where? Africa?"

"No, no. Not Africa."

"Where then?"

He shakes his head.

"I don't know. I don't know where we can go."

With the end of a towel he rubs hard at his hair, leaning his head to one side.

"You had better read my mother's letter. Here."

He flings the towel across his shoulder and plucks his trousers from where he has left them draped across Eadie's hearthside chair, then plunges his hand into the trouser pocket. Wrong pocket. Flipping the garment over, he plunders the other one, locates the letter, takes her by the shoulders, tight.

"As God is my witness, Claira, I swear to you I did not know."

He turns and walks away a pace.

"I swear it. When I married you, I knew nothing of this."

And he goes from the room, leaving the letter there in her hands.

My Dear Munro, Claira reads; the hand spidery. *I must write with the news of your father's passing which sad event happened two days before the writing of this letter and what with the distance and all, by the time this letter reaches you he will have been in his grave two weeks or more. I know there was little love lost between you and now that he is gone I feel there is things to straighten out before I follow on.*

It is the matter of us leaving Yorkshire as I think you should know of as your brothers here do though not Edwin till I write and tell him too which I will.

Struggling to make sense of it, Claira is surprised. She had assumed Munro's mother would have a good turn of phrase—but no. It strikes her that she could have written better herself. She reads the sentence through again, drawing the meaning from it.

It is the matter of us leaving Yorkshire as I think you should know of as your brothers here do though not Edwin till I write and tell him too which I will. Only you did ask me often as a boy why it was we upped and left for Cornwall and I never told you an answer that was all the truth. It was in the past and I thought it best to leave it there only now, what with your father gone and your brothers knowing, it seems right to tell you of the accident as happened in the Yorkshire mine your father owned that left twenty men dead and near as many women widowed and I never did know how many children left without a father.

Twenty dead! Claira feels the breath escape her.

They was paid compensation but it seems it wasn't good enough for some who wanted more besides on account of the accident being caused by rotten timbers which ought to have been replaced they said and how it was your father's duty and only his mind on profit which stopped him. Our lives was made difficult living where we did in the house beside the village I expect you will recall the fire, so we decided we should sell up and move a bit away though we never meant as far as here only Cornwall didn't work out what with the price of tin and all. I think it made it hard for your father when you used to take up against him about the miners here and say some of the things that people in the village used to say only you wouldn't know it being too young to remember, but nonetheless it would give him a turn thinking he had come all this way only to hear the same again and from his own son. It was one of the things that made it difficult between you only you couldn't know it probably thinking it was always your religion he wasn't party to that vexed him—that and you with your learning and liking of books. So there it is and I hope this explaining will help you know now why it was sometimes difficult between you, not that I didn't often think you right save that mining is a hard life for anyone and I might have come back to England after you but that a wife's duty is to her husband and where the most of her children are and now I am too old.

I thought too you would want to know that your father died quickly and with little pain being about his business only the day before he was took poorly. We will miss him here. Being not so strong as I was your brothers see to me to the best of their natures. You and Edwin was always the kindest of them and I miss you sorely because of it though you must not think me uncomfortable. Your father has supplied us well and I have the things I need about me though the company mayn't be all I would wish it.

Henry's daughters grow up strong as do John's three boys and as for Thomas's two, well they are all growed up and there's Nancy likely to marry soon.

I hope your marriage is well for you and the farm and all and that you will think kindly of us in our loss.

God bless you

Your loving mother.

"Is bath time over?" Aunt Eadie asks from the door.

Sixty

She's done this once or twice recently, it occurs to her. When the boys are out with Kate or amusing themselves for once, she has brought a mug of coffee through to the sitting room and has sat, in fading, evening light, long after the coffee is finished. The phone has gone twice this evening and she has let it ring, listening to the way the bell shrills out through silence, hearing its dying afterfade, letting her consciousness reach out to the painting again.

At this hour, lowering sun comes through the tall sash window. Its slow sweep highlights the Armstrong painting a section at a time. When Claire first sat down, the rectangle of low orange light was on the violin in the woman's hand. It has traveled now, lengthening and slanting across the slender turn of her body, burgundy chiming under amber. Because of the angle of the sun, the light never quite reaches her face, but it really doesn't matter as the lowering sunlight in the painting makes the image so much brighter there and, curled in her chair, Claire can make out the face quite well. Even when the day's sun has quite dipped below the horizon, the light in the painting remains visible, glowing dimly through dusk, making trees and hair it flares through darker, making dark eyes deeper, darker. Claire—her breathing long and steady—likes to try and identify a moment when the sky's light matches the light in the painting. And there was a time, last week, when the colors seemed to blend entirely, pouring into the room and pulling out of the painting, and she held her breath then, wondering if the painting was crafted at this time of year, in these weather conditions, with this much cloud, with this angle of sun; wondering—at that enchanted second—if she could get up from her chair and find herself walking in the painting's era.

The sounds from the boys' room have settled into sleep. Outside, the sound of blackbird song. Is it the beauty of the light that is so calming? Or perhaps it is the beauty of landscape, overlaid with trees; the depth of forest soon to be in darkness; overtaken by night. Transience, then, making the moment precious. Or perhaps it is color that is calming: the harmonization of her dress's deep reds with the deep green of the glade. All of those and something more. Something caught in the face and body that's more than the beauty of those things. No, no. If she fixes her mind too tightly to it, it flies. Something about the struggle she had—the painter and the painted—that links to her own creative struggle. What was it Nick said? Something about Forbes's disapproval of Elizabeth's association with Whistler and Sickert. Their influence on her. Their ideas too radical for his rooted Victorianism. And yet Elizabeth kept on; did what she must, despite the man she loved, who loved her. And here's the evidence, embodied in this painting's existence and—*and* in the image, too. In the assertive, lowering gaze. In the way the head is held with proudness. That's it, isn't it? Talented women doing—with talent—what they must. Regardless. Despite.

You're going a bit batty, Claire. Sitting in near dark, communing with a painting.

Still, it is *such* luxury, having this beautiful thing in the house.

En-rich-ment.

She must get her own work back on the rails soon. And it's good now, that she can think of it in that way. Work. Her own work. As if it might be of value.

You may have a sham of a nuclear family, but you do now have your own, valuable work. And yes, you may well smile in the dark.

Claire stretches in her chair and shivers. The night air coming in through the window is cool now and her flesh has chilled. She gets up and goes to push the heavy sash window closed, fingers fastening the latch by feel. There are others open upstairs she should shut and she pads out of the darkened room.

In the bedroom, she closes the little window, the squeak of its weights and rollers loud in the still of the evening.

Sixty-one

The little sash window slides down, the squeak of its weights and rollers loud in the still of the evening. Claira looks out onto the yard, a soft breeze lacing her face. He must still be out there. She waits till her eyes adjust to the dark. Yes, there the shadows move and, there, the paleness of his shirt is picked out. She thinks of calling, but doesn't. He will come when he is ready. She draws the cream curtains closed wondering if he looked up from outside.

The lamp is lit and she spends a minute tidying round, slowly, wiping the slate of the washstand, placing his shaving things just so, not wanting to go to bed without him or until they have spoken. She does though, turning the lamp down low and sliding between crisp sheets and even smiling at the strange weight of her breasts, newly swollen.

Stillness in lamplight; just the curtains stirring minutely at the open window. She feels her breathing steadying. There's the sound of the back door scraping to. He's in then.

It's several minutes before she hears his feet on the stairs, then the click of the metal latch and the opening door. Thinking her sleeping, he pads quietly in and Claira lays still, watching him in the dim light. Keeping to custom, he crosses to the window to pray and she wonders what it is he prays tonight, staying longer there than usual. She tries, again, to link the content of the letter to his statement they must leave, but simply fails, again, to understand.

He moves to the wardrobe and begins to undress, changing into the nightshirt she has put out for him. His movements seem slow and she wonders what slows them most: the news, or his wanting to be quiet for her. It is when he moves to the bed that he sees she has been watching him; sees the gentleness of her mouth.

"I thought you sleeping all this time," he says, getting in beside her.

"No."

He says nothing. Puts an arm back to straighten the pillow. Looks toward the ceiling.

"So," he says, without looking at her, "is it all to regret now? This marrying."

"No!" she says, drawing herself up onto one elbow. "Why should you say it?"

He pushes three fingers hard against his temple.

"Twenty dead, Claira." He turns to look at her, his eyes dark. "Twenty—like your father—crushed underground."

Her face flinches at it.

"Only this time it was neglect for sure. My father's neglect."

"You cannot know that for certain."

Munro snorts. "Oh yes I can. Beyond any doubt, I know it."

He raises his arm from the bedding, his eyes intently on hers.

"As I know this is my arm, I know it. Twenty dead and all this"—he waves his arm to indicate the house—"all this is built on them."

"How is it?" Claira demands.

He looks at her in surprise. "Do you not see?"

"No, I don't."

"I would not be here, but for it. The money that funded this came from that."

"The money that funded this came from Africa."

"And the thing which caused the move to Africa? The thing which funded that move?"

Claira says nothing and the question rings out into the silence. He throws the covers aside and gets out of bed.

"How can I rest? All is tainted now. All poisoned. All to no good."

In haste he begins to dress.

"You were three years old!" Claira says, sitting up in the bed.

"What of it?" he retorts.

"It is not then, of your doing."

"The sins of the fathers, Claira," he says, buttoning his shirt. "Your fiddle. The legacy of music your father left you."

"It is a strong and joyous thing."

"It is. And there are some legacies which are not. Some seem like worthy opportunities. I thought this one such. To toil here. To look well to the land and animals."

"So it is."

He shakes his head. "There is no cloak now for this sin."

Claira bounds from the bed to confront him.

"There are some who name my music sinful. The voice of the Devil some call it," she says.

His eyes slide from her. "They are misguided."

"And so you are here," she says, her hands on his shoulders, her eyes seeking his.

With his face tilted forward, slowly he draws her hands away. He lets out breath.

"I care very much that I have brought this upon you. It is the last thing I would have wanted."

"Don't then! Don't bring it upon me. Your mother is right. It belongs to the past and is best left there."

Eyes down still, he gathers her hands in his before pushing them from him.

"Go back to bed, now," he says.

Listening to his feet on the stairs, she hears the clock below, striking the hour. One o'clock and they must be up at dawn.

She does sleep, eventually: wakes in the dark to find him getting into bed beside her. From her warmth she reaches out and feels his flesh a little chilled.

"Here. Come here," she murmurs, hugging him to her, lifting her head to kiss him on the mouth, placing her thigh over his belly, pressing her body tightly to him.

Gently he takes her arm away.

"Claira." Gently he moves from beneath her thigh. "Claira."

She feels his body taut.

"Claira, we should stop this."

She feels his body back away.

"Why should we?"

He touches the back of his hand on her belly.

"We can think of something which will not harm the child," she says, warming to him still.

He takes her arms.

"But there *is* a child. We have done God's will."

"But . . ."

"Sshhhhh," he breathes, placing a finger across her lips. "Sshhhhh," he whispers, briefly kissing her forehead. "Sleep now," he says turning her by the shoulders, away from him, to hug round her and smooth down her hair. "Sleep now."

Munro's spoon scrapes round the bowl. Eadie and Claira have finished, but he is slower and they sit to the sound of his scraping and the tick of the clock. For days he has been like this: slow; his countenance grave. He has talked no more of leaving. Neither does he gladden. They breathe better once he has gone to the parlor to check the fire they have lit against October chill.

"I never thought he would take it so badly," Eadie says once Munro has left the room. "It's not as if he was close to his father."

Claira takes a breath and risks it.

"It isn't so much his father's death," she says, gathering dishes from the table, then stilling herself to look at Eadie. "His mother wrote of the accident in the Yorkshire mine."

Claira sees the old face grimace.

"I should have thought all that was best forgot. Why ever did she trouble him with it?"

"Seems she thought it would help him understand the difficulty his father had in speaking with him."

"Psshh," Aunt Eadie says. "And now Munro has taken it all upon himself."

Claira nods.

"Well, he mustn't you know. 'Tis not for me to speak ill of the dead and him my blood, but my brother was a stubborn man and which one of us is always right?"

Sixty-two

Claire turfs through the pile of logs left, unwanted, by the previous owners. That piece is interesting. A section of branch with a bend in it: an arm with a gnarled elbow. And what's that, lodged in the earth of the barn floor revealed by the logs she's moved. The chunky metal handle of something. She kicks with her toe, scrapes muck away with her heel till the stuff yields it up: an old flatiron.

She reaches down and pulls at it. The weight! She'd thought the heaviness was the drag of silt, but no, the thing is freed now.

"What are you doing, Mummy?" Damien asks, padding into the barn, barefoot and in his pajamas.

"What are *you* doing?" Claire replies, discarding the flatiron. "It's school tomorrow, Damien. You should be in bed by now."

"I'm not tired. What are you doing?"

"I'm looking for things to draw," Claire says, taking the section of branch and beginning to walk from the barn. "Now, go to bed or I shall never be able to wake you up in the morning."

She stops to choose a piece of granite from the pile in the corner of the yard. Old walling materials, perhaps, or field clearance. She'll need to find a piece she can lift. And oh, look. Ivy. What about that? She struggles, without success, to break off a spray. She'll come back out in a moment with pruning shears.

Absentmindedly, Claire picks up the mug of coffee. It's halfway to her lips before there's room in her head for the message to reach home that the coffee is cold. What? Impossible. She only made it a few minutes ago. She looks at the clock. Twenty past ten. It can't be! She checks it against her watch and finds, if anything, the clock's a little slow. She's been drawing, solidly, for two hours. She gets up from the table to look, sitting the drawing board in the chair she's vacated.

On the table there are the beginnings of the first drawing she had to abort—the one of ivy. She may not be all that conscious of what she's about, but, whatever it is, she knows with certainty she has no desire to be a botanical illustrator and, drawing at this close range, she'd felt the danger of slipping into that; of being seduced by the desire to put down, exactly, the delicate intricacies of leaf shape and shine and vein. Won't do. The softly textured ground of Ingres paper is helping, steering her away from too much exactitude, but even so.

She looks at the second, more worked-through drawing. The image of the branch trails across the page, the shape of the granite rising large and rounded behind it, the outer edge of one, leading the eye to the outer edge of the other, all the way round and back down the opposite side, till the second runs, again, into the first. Quite simply drawn; the emphasis is on shape and size, the encompassing of one by the other. That seems important. Shape and relation. She finds herself wondering what Nick would have to say and as soon as she allows thought of him, her mind piles on detail: the weight of his eyes on her, the turn of head as he laughs, his warmth with the children, his kind directness with her, the touch of his hand on her shoulder as he left the other day. She sighs out breath. Gets up from the table.

Filling the kettle, she plugs it in. Busies herself with making fresh coffee. Turns her mind to the present. The drizzle of the day must have settled into fog. She can hear the low drone of the foghorn. The weather here is quite extraordinary. So changeable.

It's little more than a week since they went together to the beach and now all this wetness. She wonders where Howard is in all this fog on a Sunday evening. He went out hours ago . . . *Perhaps she lives down here, after all. Perhaps he's seeing her now.* The kettle starts to boil and she clicks it off in advance of itself. She is *not* going to torment herself. She's hardly thought about it all evening. Like the bashing of heads on brick walls. It's so good to stop.

She turns back to the drawing. She's tired, but she doesn't want to finish yet.

She moves the branch section away from the table and looks at the granite left there. She reaches out to feel the surface of it, feels her fingers find slight purchase: as climbers do. Once this would have been molten. How long ago? Ungiving cold now and for millennia. She feels the contrast of her own vital warmth. Flesh and rock. She grins. Not just shape and relation at all, then. A whole process of something. What? Her fingers trace the texture. Something to do with her brief vitality at one end of a scale and this enduring grit at the other.

Hurriedly she unpins the drawing she's been working on and places a new sheet on the board. She sits to draw, stands again, heaves the piece of granite nearer, sits and yes, she can now leave her left hand upon rock while she draws. She feels the flurry of her pulse, draws breath to calm it. *Alertness not excitement.* Her eyes flick to her hand on stone, pick out an echo of knuckles in the rock's outline. And there look, the smooth line of stone—like the line of her forearm.

Drawing breath, she draws.

See the way skin molds round bone; is stone like bone, thrusting out through the flesh of earth? See the way tendons pull skin tight, landscaped valleys and hills. Here veins flow through, blue; here rock creases at knuckles, the crevice between fingers and—focused—the room is lost in peripheral nothingness. Only the clock anchors her . . . tick . . . tock . . . tick . . . tock . . . seconds spill from it, stroke down her hair, land at her feet, build up like layers of snow, soothing as she works . . . tick . . . tock . . . tick . . . tock . . . Thump! Her pencil stops. It's the sound of his car door slamming. Twenty to twelve. She'd meant to be in bed by the time he came home. However did she fail to hear the engine? She thinks of hurrying away, but does not. And then he is there in the kitchen; his hair a little damp from the fog.

For the first time for a long time now, she lifts her head and looks him full in the face. He raises his eyebrows.

"Didn't expect to find you up. Is the coffee hot?"

"No," she says, returning her attention to the drawing, "I don't suppose it is."

Heavens. She's done a lot. And she's pleased. The vitality of it, not tight like the drawing on the table, she thinks, taking it in at a glance.

"Don't you want any?" Howard asks.

"Sorry?"

It's difficult to know how much more to add to the tonal quality of this one . . .

"Coffee. Don't you want any coffee?"

. . . because it's really exciting to see how the interplay of *line* works. Perhaps she should just transfer what she feels she's learned here onto another, completely fresh . . .

There's the bang of the kitchen door as Howard goes through into the hall.

. . . onto another, completely fresh drawing. Perhaps without the Ingres . . .

His feet thump up the stairs.

. . . perhaps without the Ingres paper this time. It was kind of Nick and it's been useful because it's something to rule out—the textured ground has really only confused the issue and she feels she wants to what? Put what she's learned into practice with the minimum of interference from the medium. She grins again. A few months ago she could hardly find the courage to make marks on paper and now this impatience with materials coming between her and her intention. She gets up from the table. God, but it's going to be exciting following this line! Taking this principle out-of-doors. She'll have to ask Kate if she can borrow her as model again, and soon, what with autumn fast approaching. And scale. She wants to work larger now. Begins to find this small-scale stuff claustrophobic. She wonders if she can remember how to make her own canvases.

Claire stretches tall and sighs. It's rather late. Howard is probably in bed by now. Or perhaps in the shower. She listens briefly, but can't hear running water. She yawns. She really ought to go to bed herself, she thinks, then grins, watching her hands mutiny against this good sense as they unpin the sketch. She reaches behind the dresser and pulls out a pad of paper: very large, white, untextured.

Sixty-three

During the quartet by Fesca, Elizabeth leans her head towards Claira and nods to indicate the violinist.

"She *is* good, isn't she?" Elizabeth whispers.

"Yes."

"But Claira," Elizabeth continues, leaning nearer, "you are—by a very long way—better."

Claira blushes. "It's not the sort of music I have played."

"Not yet."

"I cannot read music."

"No," Elizabeth whispers. "But I thought perhaps you might like to learn. Stanhope has found someone who might teach him the cello. I thought perhaps you might learn to read music, too."

Claira thinks of it. Of how it would allow her to explore completely new areas of music. Perhaps even play at events like this. She wonders how Munro would receive such a notion.

"I am not sure," she whispers to Elizabeth. "My work about the farm. And then—I have not told you—we are to have a baby."

"Claira!" Elizabeth exclaims, too loudly, so that Stanhope and Munro look across, eyebrows raised at her din.

The music over, there are the paintings to see once more before the exhibition closes.

"Will you have a ticket for the draw?" a seller asks as they make their way through the crowd. On Munro's arm, Claira feels him bridle with resistance.

"Thank you. No," Claira says, before Munro can answer. "Our religion does not permit it."

Over the heads of the crowd the image of Claira ranges. Standing before the painting, among the little knot of people it attracts, Claira surprises herself; feels it a good thing, seeing it there.

"Oh Claira," Elizabeth says, "let me introduce you to Norman Garstin. Norman, this is Claira Richardson and her husband, Munro."

"And there was I thinking, Elizabeth, that you must have exaggerated the beauty of your model," Garstin says, shaking Claira's hand, resting gentle eyes on hers. "I see now you did not."

"No, I did not," Elizabeth says. "And you should hear her play, Norman. More beautiful still."

"I should like that."

"Mr. Richardson also spent time at Kimberley," Elizabeth says.

Garstin winces at the name.

"I hope you fared better at it than I," Garstin says, shaking Munro's hand. "Fate did not smile kindly on my time there."

"I am sure I know little of Fate," Munro says.

"Providence," Claira finds herself blurting out. "We tend to think more in terms of Providence. Each outcome as part of God's greater plan."

"Ah, indeed," Garstin says, kindly.

Claira is sitting at the bedroom mirror when she feels the baby move. She stills to feel it, her hand to her belly, warm through the nightdress. Sometimes she tells Munro of it, shares it with him, this movement. Not today.

There's a sound outside the room. His feet on the stairs. She reaches out. Turns down the lamp. Turns her head away from the door—towards shadows. She lifts the bulk of her hair forward, so that it flanks her face; like a hood. She draws the brush down the length of her hair. There is the sound of his feet at the door. The click of the latch.

He stops a second, seeing her.

Her hair is tangled and the brush cannot cope. She picks up the comb to try. Starts at the ends. Works up. No good. Hearing him moving in the room behind her, she places the comb down; tries the brush again, bringing it down through her hair, through the good bits; the gloss and glide. Then there's the tangle. The brush stops and stays fast and she cannot get it loose, so she must tease the hair out of it, a strand at a time.

"Can I help?"

She shakes her head. Once. He moves to the washstand. She hears the tip and pour of water.

Freeing the brush, she pulls it through knots. Hairs snap.

He's in bed before she has brushed her hair through. She carries the lamp to the bedside, to the mound of his back, rounded away from her.

In the dark she lies. Separate. Listens to the slow rhythm of his breathing. Listens, with her body, to the new life that grows within her. They will be grown up now: the children whose fathers were killed in the mine. The same age as Munro, or older most likely, with children of their own.

Sixty-four

The primer soaks in; lays down its covering like snow. Lush, pristine layer on canvas soon to have her paint upon it. A virgin canvas. Like the body of a lover, waiting to be touched.

Stop grinning—idiot.

Six feet tall, this lover and very trim—even if she says it herself. No wrinkles on *his* corners, she thinks, slurping the brush right to the edge. And very nicely toned, she notes, drawing the brush across tight-bellied canvas. The body of the brush is glutted with paint and she feels the soft give of fabric beneath it as she works the unsullied surface. No one would guess the configuration behind the cloth: corrugated nails bashed into roughly mitered corners; triangles of hardboard hammered over each join and then the canvas itself adding more support; stapled tightly round and now the primer, helping to shrink the whole thing tighter. A technique learned on the foundation course she took and never followed up—and probably it's time she graduated to a more sophisticated method, but she's not sure what. She wonders what the physical makeup of the Armstrong painting is like, hidden beneath canvas. Not corrugated nails, that's for sure.

"Mummy, I'm hungry!" Damien yells up the little stairs.

"Okay, Damien. Have an apple for now. I'll be down in a minute."

More primer smears on her hands as she grips the canvas and upends it so she can paint over the remaining area. And it takes effort to turn the thing, the tall, broad canvas causing her to work herself.

"You're quite a hunk, aren't you?" she says to the canvas out loud.

Batty woman in the attic, Claire.

The last part is quickly covered and quickly she gathers her things together, moving the primed canvas to stand next to the other two she's already made.

"You're the biggest and most beautiful and I shall use you first."

"Mummy, I'm *hungry*!"

"I'm just *coming*, Damien. Please don't *shout* at me."

Shove lid on paint pot. Scrunch up used newspapers from the floor. Grab paintbrush to take down and clean. Footsteps resonate as she leaves.

Sixty-five

"Come by, come by," Munro calls. The workhorses lean their weight into the turn. A glance to the inner horse; to the shoulder. Sweating up now. The harrow clatters the corner. On the western horizon, mares' tails streak blue sky. So that's why he has been rushing them. Seen the gathering warning. Wanting to get this finished before bad weather comes.

"Steady," he calls out, gentling their power. "Steady, now."

Wrong of him to push them for work which will wait.

By late afternoon the sky is dark; the wind whipping up rain to spit. The empty basket placed at Claira's feet is whisked away to tumble and roll across the yard so that she must chase it, her skirts and hair all blown before her.

And "No you may not walk the way home, Mrs. Jago," Munro says as evening rain sets in and a hard wind blows heavy, "I shall drive you."

It is as if the house crouches, Claira thinks, crossing the yard in the dark to stop the barn door from its banging. She crosses quickly, her shoulders shrugged to her ears, pausing to toe straw out of the channel it has blocked, holding her light low as she peers through rain for the glimmer of his lamps on the road. He cannot be long now. But there is nothing to see and the weather, blowing against the way he will come, all there is to hear.

Close tight the curtains and the doors against the wildness. Go to the room farthest from it. The parlor with its heavy drapes and warm fire burning. It's as if the house crouches, keeping its head down.

Lamplight catches her needle. Her stitches are small and even and neat. How is it he did this? He must have caught it as he jumped down from something. The cart perhaps. The tear is a long one: from the pocket to well down the trouser leg. The material is good though. Strong enough to hold the patches firm.

A freak flurry of wind flings rain against the window as if someone has thrown a handful of pebbles.

Dozing; Aunt Eadie stirs in her chair.

"Is it all right?" she mutters through her sleep.

"Yes, but that you will crick your neck, Aunt Eadie," Claira says, securing the needle in the fabric then getting up to place another cushion behind Eadie's head.

The old woman wakes more fully, straightening and stretching her neck. "You're quite right, I shall," she says. "Time I took myself to bed."

The second patch is nearly sewn when the back door is heard to blow hard to. Safely home, then. Claira pulls the thread up tight. With the push of her foot, sets her chair rocking. A log shifts on the fire. She hears the latch of Eadie's room trip. Munro checking the old lady is all right. He never misses. Claira feels her lips form a smile.

Bursting into the parlor, he brings with him the smell of rain and wet heather. Water glistens on his face, the ends of his hair are slicked to his neck, his skin rosed with the pasting.

"It's a long time since we had quite such a night," he says, his eyes on hers with a brightness that has been missing for a time. "The road from the top of the hill is awash."

"Are you wet through?" Claira asks.

He feels under his jacket to the shoulders of his shirt.

"No. Dry enough."

She sees his trousers, from the knees down, are soaked.

"And Mrs. Jago is safely home?" Claira asks.

"She is," Munro says, pacing to the fire then away again.

Claira watches him. Usually he would sit, now, with the Bible.

"There will be wetted harness for Michael to clean tomorrow," she remarks.

"Hmmm? Yes, there will," he agrees, absently, pacing.

Claira draws the needle steadily through. Another little stitch. Neatly. Then another.

He flings himself into the chair opposite her. "I had no trouble on the road."

"Good," she says, stopping her sewing to look at him.

"Even in weather fit to take all your senses; still I had no trouble." He gets up from his chair. Paces again. His eyes dart a look at her. "It's because I know it well. The road, I mean."

"I expect you must," she says.

"Every turn, every gradient, each boulder and dyke on the way. And I thought, as I drove that good horse through weather we could scarcely see in, I could probably find the way blindfold or in sleep. And then I got to thinking of the land to either side the road, the hills and the valleys and, as we came alongside of them, I thought of Trethenna's fields."

"What of them?"

"I know them too, in any weather, or darkness, like the back of my hand, like your hands. I know them in the way I know you."

Claira feels her eyes widen a little.

He looks hard at her: testing. "It is as if I were married to them also in a way, to have and to hold, to love and cherish, to honor and keep until death."

"Yes?" she says, holding his eye.

"I thought of the time I have spent with the land, how it has fared since I bought it, the betterments I have made. I think I have done quite well by it," he says, pacing away again. "No. Well," he continues, "I think I have done well. I think I tend well, and take good care. I think."

"Have I not said as much?" she asks.

"Yes," he says, letting his eyes rest a moment on hers. "And beyond doubt, I love it. As part of me. Or you. There is the hand of God in it. In the form of it. In the strength of seasons. Of growth. And I love it the more for that." He throws himself again into his chair. It occurs to her that she has never seen him so agitated. "I feel myself so *bound* to it," he continues. "To leave would seem . . ." He pauses, searching for the word. "It would seem like a divorce," he says, looking with realization at her. "The dissolution of what is a healthful marriage. A violation of God's will, His order of things."

Claira picks up her sewing again, spreading the fabric flat on her knee. "And there was me thinking I would have to let out all our chickens to the fox," she says.

It is his turn now to widen his eyes.

"After all," she continues, beginning to work the fabric, "if—as you suggest—all is tainted here, then the chickens must be too, so they may as well go."

She swings the rocking chair into gentle motion.

"And then I thought, perhaps I should not do the dairy, tainted milk after all, never mind how sweet it might taste. And then cooking, perhaps I should not trouble with that either, nor the kitchen garden."

Munro shifts in his chair.

"Then I wondered on the baby," she continues.

"Claira!"

She rests a hand on her belly and looks at him.

"You did say *all* was poisoned."

"Yes, but I—"

"Only, I didn't know quite how to stop growing him."

Munro thumps to his feet to begin his pacing again. "This is lunacy."

"Is it not?"

"You cannot say this other matter is of *no* importance. Twenty dead, Claira."

"I know what it is to lose a father to the mine," she says quietly. "And I feel for you," she continues, looking up at him. "It seems a heavy and undeserved burden that has come upon you and so unexpected. It will take some adjusting to, knowing now the past was not as you always thought it. To say nothing of the nature of the event."

"Despicable at best," Munro supplies.

Burning wood gives way; letting a log fall to hot ashes. Claira looks to her sewing; pushing the needle to, pulling it fro.

"What, then, is to be done?" he asks.

"It needs to be made good in some way," she says, not troubling to look up.

"In what way?"

Wind and heavy rain gust past the window.

"Compensation perhaps. To individuals or the community. Perhaps a chapel, or schoolrooms."

"You have been thinking of this."

"Of course."

"Buy myself a clear conscience, then."

"Some would see it that way."

"And you?"

"I believe if you think there is a debt—you should pay it. If not—leave it alone."

"Simply that."

She looks up at him again. "Yes."

His eyes rest on hers, searching. "A chapel."

She shrugs. "Perhaps. Or perhaps the community already has one. Perhaps some of the families have moved away. You could trace them. Perhaps some went to the workhouse."

She sees him wince.

"It is possible," she says.

"I know it."

She folds the finished repair work, picks up the baby's garment she has started.

"I suppose there must have been a solicitor involved," Munro says, "to manage the compensation."

"Almost certainly."

"He would have a list, would he not? Or those who came after him might still have one."

Claira nods. "Aunt Eadie might recall which solicitor it was. Although she has trouble with the happenings of today or yesterday, her memory is good from that time."

"I shall draft a letter," he says and he is up and gone from the room.

Again she is in bed before him, waiting in low lamplight while he wrangles with the letter he must write, so that it's late when he comes to bed beside her and reaches across her to turn out the lamp. He pauses briefly to touch his lips against her forehead and she wants to hold him to her and knows he will not let her.

"God keep you," he says, resting back on his pillow.

She says nothing. Lies on her back in the dark next to him, listening to the weather battering the house. She thinks of it, the ground soaked and the gorse, thrashed by wind. The cattle will be huddled against the hedge. Warm to one another in a place you would scarcely know the wind is blowing. She thinks of the hay and corn ricks, tight against the weather. And the furze rick, tight, too. She thinks of the horses safely stabled. And he has written his letter, so that is under way. Little wonder he can just lie there then, when all is so well. Inches from her.

Her eyes feel hot.

"There is one area you have not tended," she says, the words out before she knows it.

"What?" he says through the darkness.

"An area you have neglected." Her throat feels tight.

"Where?"

"And another you force me to neglect."

"What do you mean?"

"How can I help it if weeds begin to grow? And they *do* grow," she says, tears on her face now; her hands—fists on the sheets. He hears the break in her voice.

"Claira, what is it?" he asks, reaching across her again for the tinder; not finding it; fumbling.

"Only you did *vow* it," she says, pushing his arm away from her where it stretches across her face, pushing its weight away into darkness so that he draws back. "You did vow it, so why must I ask you?"

"Ask me what?" He moves to hold her shoulders, finds her rigid.

She draws breath. The lump in her throat enlarges.

"What, Claira?" he says, urgently.

"Must I say it?"

"Yes."

One by one she forces out the words.

"I . . . need . . . to . . . feel . . . my . . . nakedness . . . next . . . to . . . yours."

He lets out breath. She holds hers, clenched tight, her whole body tight. The blast of air and rain around the house. A second. More.

"Claira, I—"

"You did vow it before God."

"The baby—"

"Needs to feel the love of you, too. Needs to know he is not *tainted*," she thumps the word and her arm against his breast.

"Claira, Claira." He tries to gather her to him; but cannot for her body is taut with the fight of it, her arms pushing against him, but it is nothing to him. The shift of his shoulder contains it, the rounding of his arm about her.

"Sshhh now."

An effortless lift.

"Sshhh now."

Bringing her in close.

"There is no harm done."

"Ah, but there *is*," she says, her body tensed.

"No, no." Leaning over her, containing her enough. Has she gentled a little? He eases off. Feels her move away; her fist to her face, pressing eyes. Gentled a little then: not so much as to risk letting go. His mouth in the dark, finds her face: the kissing away of tears from eyelids. "No, Claira." He feels her breathing, short, torn. "No harm done."

Finding her mouth with his, he feels her whisk her head away. The ridiculous bumping of noses. "Sshhhhhh." He rests his head down. Rests his forehead on hers. Wait awhile. Contain her. He will wait all night if he must. He nuzzles his face into her hair, drawing her ankles to him with his foot, tucking her knees beneath his thigh. He sighs out air; shifts himself lower in the bed; pushes his face against her neck; feels her draw in breath. He matches his breath with hers, and his penis rises. Minutely he shifts away. He will wait all night if he must; resting, breathing her in, breathing at the same rate, the same air; their bed adrift in the pounding weather.

"Do you think we shall have a roof left in the morning?"

"Yes," she says and he brings his face to rest against hers and—there—she moves her face minutely to him, doesn't she? Yes. He sighs out, feels her move her face till she finds the place where the contours fit. She moves again, her mouth to his ear.

"Is it that you would teach me to love you and then cast me out?" she says, her voice so low and near to him he cannot, for a second, be sure if she has spoken, or if he has simply thought the words.

He brings his head from the pillow. "Never that."

"What then?"

In the dark he finds the buttons at the neck of her nightgown. His fingers cannot manage the smallness of them.

"Take this off," he says, moving from her. In the dark he waits. The window rattles with the push of the weather. She moves and among the rush of wind he picks out the rustle of fabric as she pulls the garment over her head, so that he discards his, too, finds her again in the warmth of the bed, skin against skin, breathing deeply the softness of her, tightly held in emphasis of his words:

"Claira, I am learning still."

He feels her sigh out, nodding her head against him.

"And I."

Sixty-six

The weather is foul, windy and wet and Claire dresses the children warmly, then—in the last-minute dash to get them to school—runs upstairs for an extra sweater for herself.

Howard's bedroom, where some of her clothes still are, reeks of cigarette smoke. At least she doesn't have to put up with that anymore. She grabs a sweater from the drawer and then sees them—stumps of tickets in the ashtray, discarded from his pocket. Ephemera—so much of nothing—yet her hand reaches out. There's something else too—a small cash-register receipt. She knocks the ash from them and stuffs them in the pocket of her jeans.

"Good-bye, darling," Claire calls, but Nathan runs off too busy with friends to answer. It's good that he's settled so well. Perhaps she'll go down and try the job center again.

Back in the Metro she digs out the scraps of paper from her pocket. Pale green tickets, the lion and unicorn crest, Royal Opera House, Covent Garden. The receipt is for drinks in the interval, itemized, with a number for collection. One gin and tonic and a dry martini. She looks at the pieces there in her hand.

A gust of wind pushes at the stationary car, succeeds in rocking it. She looks up through the light spit of rain on the windshield.

Reaching down, she starts the engine. The job center will have to wait.

Claire always slows as she drives over the brow of this hill. She likes the shock of the way the road plunges to the sea, the land falling so steeply to the water. Today she comes to an absolute halt. The waves are simply massive. She looks towards where she knows the little harbor is and can scarcely identify the harbor wall for the sea running over it, then streaming white as the waves pull back. She has stood on that wall with the sea far below; now even the lighthouse at its end is being pounded, hit by waves that ricochet white-high above it. Last night she'd woken and heard the wind howling, she hadn't realized it had been this bad.

She drives slowly on down the steep descent. At sea level, the stone cottages press back against the hill, their small windows facing one another, shoulders huddled to the sea. The street is empty and she drives on over seaweed and sand thrown up onto the road.

Driving by the slipway, she sees gray water seethe in the harbor. The little boats have all been winched up high onto the sand. Two fishermen in yellow oilskins stand by the dark doorway of a hut, looking.

The tiny parking lot is tucked away between cottages. Claire puts on the pair of old wellies she's learned to keep in the trunk and walks to the stone steps that lead to the coast path. A woman scuttles down the wet street, clutching at the scarf round her head.

Claire usually takes the path to the west, but perhaps it's not safe today. Climbing the steps, she can see—where the cliff bows out beyond the village—the waves are hitting rock and crashing high. As she hesitates, a man hurries by below her, dressed in red oilskins. He glances up.

"That way would be madness on a day like today," he says without stopping.

"And this way?" she asks after him, indicating the path to the east.

She sees the shoulders of his jacket rise in a shrug.

"Better," he calls back. "Better still at home."

"Sorry, mate," she mutters. "I need the air."

The stone steps give way to the eastward path. Where it has eroded to rab, grit crunches underfoot.

Pressed under the thumbnail of the hand she stuffs in her pocket, the corner of a piece of card digs in. Used tickets to see the opera.

Wind needles in through her jacket.

He has no intention of stopping, you know.

She takes out her hands to do up the zip of her jacket. Still the wind comes through the cloth. She ought to get a better one, something that will cope with this kind of weather. Something like Nick has. Like *Nick* has. Sheltering. Capable even in this milieu. She shoves her hands back into scant warmth.

Ninety percent of marriages are like this after a few years.

Her foot slides on loose grit.

Why should Howard stop—believing that?

Flick, flick, flick, the tickets in her pocket.

He may have been out with someone else. A business contact to entertain. It might not have been his lover.

Whipped off the sea by the wind, white foam is flung up onto the cliff where it lies, splattered on wizened gorse. Claire stops and faces the chaos of waves, the angry gray whiteness, the heavy air. She runs her tongue across her lips and tastes the sting of salt.

Don't kid yourself, Claire.

She looks up at the footpath stretching out before her in a long rise. There's an apron of rock buttressing the cliff here, reaching out into the sea, keeping the footpath safe. She's glad she came this way. She turns and begins to tackle the climb.

So what of the future then? What's supposed to happen now—this marriage in tatters.

Boom!

Claire's leapt before she can register the noise.

Whatever . . . ?

And then again, boom!

An explosion? A gun? She turns back to face the village below her, the toy-town cottages, the threatened harbor, all as it was. She walks on a few paces, keeping out the cold and then turns again to see a car hurry to the harbor, like the scurry of a beetle; another close behind it. She can see the tiny dots of men running to a building. The lifeboat house. Surely they're not going out on exercise in this? No. Just practicing their call-out procedure, probably. That must have been what the bangs were. Maroons, she thinks they're called.

Walking on again, she nearly misses it, just turns in time to see a more than ever whitened sea where the hull of the lifeboat plunges in. Her face widens to witness it, the vessel emerging unbelievably from such maelstrom. She holds her breath as the boat struggles to punch through waves. Will it not simply be flung back against the slip? For seconds it seems in the balance—then a lapse in the waves allows the boat headway and she finds herself breathing again. For minutes she watches, sees the boat clear the harbor wall and begin to make progress along the cliff edge; worryingly close. She holds her breath again, sees waves dump down on the cabin roof.

Just as the movement of a figure on the footpath catches her eye, so, too, comes the sudden sound of a helicopter. From above and behind her it throbs into the wind and for the first time it occurs to her: this is no exercise.

She scans the sea for other boats. Nothing.

The figure approaching on the footpath is a woman. Fifty. Rounded beneath her red waterproof. Fragile mousy hair blown out from beneath a woolen hat pulled on tight. Her face is set, grimly.

"What *is* all this?" Claire asks.

The woman stops—catching her breath.

"A climber."

"In *this* weather?"

The woman nods.

"Where?"

The woman makes a broad gesture over the sea.

"They're searching for him. Swept off the rocks here," she says between breaths and pointing ahead. "I've come as extra eyes. Three others with him. Lucky they didn't go in too."

She nods at the lifeboat as it lurches and slams.

"My husband and son are on board."

Overhead now, the helicopter drowns out conversation. Blades of sound cut down hard through the air. Claire thinks of the climber out in the water. His clothed body immersed in the cold. Here. Now.

"How long has he got?" she asks as the helicopter moves away.

The woman shakes her head. "Minutes."

They walk on together, all the while their eyes on the sea. Claire wills him to come into her vision: twice translates the tumble of water as the roll of his body. The white-gray mass moves before her eyes. An arm! An arm! Surely! Surely a shoulder. They see it together and clutch each other, pointing. The woman shakes her head. Through binoculars she confirms it. Fisherman's rope.

Minutes drain.

"How long will they search?"

"Till dark, probably."

"Even though there's no hope?"

The woman nods. She's sitting on a rock by the path, her weight heavily there, binoculars trained on the lifeboat now. Suddenly Claire feels she's being intrusive. She glances at her watch. They've been looking out for half an hour. There's no chance. Her only role now is voyeuristic. Not for this woman, her family at risk, but it is for Claire. The time for giving lifesaving signals is over. Without question he is dead.

"Shall I bring you something?" she asks. "A flask of tea?" Someone in the village would probably let her have one.

"No, dear, thank you," the woman says, not taking her eyes from her vigil. Claire rests a hand on the woman's shoulder in farewell.

"I hope your family get home safely."

"Thank you, dear."

The woman's hand in fingerless gloves touches Claire's briefly.

As she walks downhill, it's difficult to warm. Claire can feel that the flesh of her buttocks and thighs has quite chilled. She thinks of the climber's flesh, tumbled by the water; chilled to the core till the life's pushed out. Still her eyes search. Futile.

The village streets seem the same; wet, deserted. In the parking lot, she takes the pieces of paper from her pocket and lets them fall into a bin; her eyes sliding over the shine of wet slate roofs.

Driving by the harbor this time, she sees there are five fishermen in a huddle by the hut. A door into the lifeboat house gapes through to daylight, cavernous now the boat has gone.

Sixty-seven

Used to going straight on along the flat to Penzance, the horse tosses his head when asked to stop to let Claira down at Newlyn Bridge.

"Will you find your way?" Munro asks her.

"Surely." Claira smiles up at him. "Elizabeth said in her letter it is very near. Are you sure you don't mind?"

"Oh. I shall manage," he smiles back at her. "In two hours then."

Setting off, she turns to watch him leave, the horse at a spanking trot, Munro's figure tall above the churns in the back of the cart, the cheeses and the hen coops. He turns, too. Raises his arm to her.

Stepping out through November sunshine, Claira heads towards the harbor. Fishwives call good morning to her, pausing from their work to watch her pass in her fine coat and trim hat, her good boots on the cobbles. Probably the same women who chased her off as a child, polite now to this well-dressed figure.

The Fisherman's Institute is easy to find. Claira hesitates at the doorway, then, on hearing Elizabeth's laughter, goes in.

"Good morning, Claira," Stanhope calls, as Elizabeth takes her to the upstairs room where the painting is going on. "Will you forgive me if I continue a little longer?"

"Of course."

Under the sloping ceiling, several people are gathered. Two men pose as if frozen. One seated around his cello; the other, standing to the cello player's right and slightly behind him, holds a violin, the bow raised in his hand, doubling as a conductor's baton.

At a table, three boys loiter, playing shove ha'penny. Two other men peer round the painter's shoulder.

Forbes stands in front of a large canvas that Claira guesses is four feet by six. Going round to join those who watch him paint, she sees the image he makes of these two men, startling in its realism. She sees them in context, too, the other figures who will be in the painting sketched in beside the two: musicians and singers.

Elizabeth indicates the preparatory drawings on Forbes's left and Claira goes across to the side table to see the detailed pencil studies: confident, solid, sure of themselves. Sheet music is also there, discarded. Claira leafs through it, wondering what kind of melody is represented.

"I have been thinking of what you said about learning to read music," Claira says to Elizabeth. "I was thinking, I would like to. I have yet to mention it to Munro, but if—as today—he could spare me for an hour or two while he takes produce to market, it would be possible."

Elizabeth is beaming at her.

"Of course," Claira hurries on, "once the baby is born it will be more difficult."

"But that is not for a little while yet," Elizabeth says evenly.

"I did think, perhaps I could make a start at least."

"We shall have to ask when Mr. White would be able to begin," Elizabeth says, nodding towards the man who poses with the violin.

"Is he the man who would teach me?" Claira asks in surprise.

"I'm sorry, Forbes," Mr. White says at that moment. "I'm going to have to move this arm again."

"Oh, please do. Remiss of me," Stanhope says, pausing to pull out his fob watch. "Good Heavens, yes. Very much time I rested you."

Before protest is possible, Elizabeth is talking to Mr. White, looking across at Claira, beckoning her over.

Claira is not sure she will like him, his lips thin, his dress so very clean, his eyes behind glasses that glint as he lowers them to peer over at her.

"Yes, well," he says to Claira over a bony, brisk handshake, "it is always lovely when the ladies *do* learn to play an instrument."

"Oh, Mrs. Richardson already plays well," Elizabeth insists.

"Oh?"

Claira finds herself blushing and looking down.

"My father taught me," she says.

"To play, but not to read music?" Mr. White inquires.

"Might we borrow the violin a moment?" Elizabeth asks sweetly. "Mrs. Richardson could play something to you."

Mr. White hesitates. "Well, I don't usually . . ." he begins, holding the instrument to him. "It's a Stainer, you see."

Elizabeth leans her head towards him.

"She really is rather good," she whispers in his ear.

"Oh, well. I don't suppose . . . I suppose . . . Just this once then."

It's strange to hold a different instrument. Claira's fingers fumble as she takes it from him and she sees his eyes widen in alarm, sees his expectation she will drop it.

She turns her back on them, wanders down the length of the room, nestling the thing against her shoulder, checking the tuning, learning how the instrument differs from her own: the neck a little more curved, the pegs easier to turn.

"Where are your thoughts?" Munro asks her on the way home. Their shoulders sway with the motion of the vehicle, lighter now with the produce sold.

Claira's smile widens. "I was thinking about something which happened this morning."

The recollection of their faces, seen once she had stopped playing. Forbes transported. Mr. White, his mouth wide. She giggles at the thought. How Elizabeth had grinned at her. Claira had begun a reel to contrast the lament she had bound them with and the three boys had leapt to a dance—a different magic to break the spell of the other. People had come from the room below to find out who it was that played.

"Well?" Munro asks.

"Mr. Forbes was painting a picture of musicians. A violinist among them. I played for them a little." Claira glances at him.

"And?" Munro persists, looking aside at her. "How were you received?"

"Well enough, I think."

"Well enough for what?"

Claira takes a breath.

"For Mr. White—the violinist—to think me worth teaching to read music."

"Ah yes. Elizabeth mentioned to me that she thought you should learn."

"Did she?"

"She did." He laughs. "Gave me quite a talking to, in fact."

"When?"

"At the concert last month. Said you had an extraordinary gift and what a shame it would be if you were not to have the chance to develop it fully."

Claira gasps. "She said that?"

"She did."

"And what did you say?"

He frowns. "I don't recall what I had to say on the matter. Besides"—he laughs again—"I had the impression Miss Armstrong was not seeking my opinion."

The vehicle rides on a moment. The day has clouded over now, a freshening wind pushing towards them. He pulls the knee rug from under the seat and she spreads it over them.

"And will you?" Munro asks.

"Learn to read music?"

He nods, looking at her.

"If you would not mind it."

"I would not mind it, Claira. Not that Mr. White of Newlyn would particularly be one to 'fully develop your extraordinary gift,' " Munro says, tilting his head in a way that is immediately Elizabeth, so that Claira cannot help but laugh at his mimicry.

"He would do, to begin with, would he not?" Claira asks.

"I don't know. It is always easier to learn something properly in the first place than to learn again something which has been taught incorrectly. Not that he will teach you badly, I am sure, but he may not be able to teach you much. And I think Elizabeth is right. You do have an extraordinary talent—or so it seems to my ears."

He glances across at her.

"Every time I hear you play, it strikes me again how . . ." He searches for the right word. "How *vital* you make the music sound."

Claira is silent. Whatever will he say next? This begins to sound like approval when the most she had hoped for was his tolerance.

The hooves of the horse pace rhythmically on.

"Who, then, should teach me?"

"That is the problem. I don't suppose there is much of real quality to be had locally. There may be in Truro. And certainly in London."

"London!" Claira has only been to Truro once. London is scarcely to be contemplated. "Our lives have nothing to do with London."

"They could have."

Claira balks with amazement.

"But what of the farm?! Your sense of belonging here?"

"It would not have to be forever," he says calmly.

"Our child, then."

He nods. "That might be more difficult, but not impossible."

Claira laughs her astonishment out loud.

"Wait, wait, wait," she says, placing her hand over his and easing back on the reins so that the horse comes to a halt in the narrow lane, in a tunnel made of high hedges and a canopy of green.

"It's a holdup!" Munro says, laughing his objection.

"It is," Claira says, shifting herself on the seat so that she can face him. "What *have* you been thinking of? Are you trying to bundle me off to London now?"

"Never," he says, immediately. "Or not without me."

"What *have* you thought about then?" she insists.

"A combination of things, I suppose. What Elizabeth said, certainly."

"And?"

"And your evident ability."

"And?"

He looks down. "And your forthcoming motherhood."

"What of it?"

He looks at her again.

"You are very young, Claira, to be a mother."

"Not so young."

"But, so much younger than I."

Impatient to be home, the horse stamps a hind foot. "I suppose I have been thinking that I have plucked you from your home life and now, here you are at twenty—"

"Twenty-one."

"Twenty-one, then, about to be a mother. At thirty-seven, it is timely for me to be a father, but I thought, the other day, of myself at twenty-one."

He lays the reins flat across his hand.

"Whatever my time in Africa did or did not turn out to be, it *was*—at least—exploration and discovery and . . . and a *fulfillment* of something."

"It is not the sort of thing that women tend to do."

"Elizabeth did," he says. "She came from Canada to Germany and France and Holland and England in order to be a painter."

"Elizabeth is an exception."

"Both an exception and exceptional," Munro asserts. "And you are too, Claira. It is the thing which drew me to you, though I did not realize it at the time." He grimaces. "Endeavored even to lessen your differences before I learned the value of them. But, be that as it may, it seems—simply because of our *age* difference—there may be things that you would want to do that you have not yet. And, God willing, we will have the rest of our lives to live at Trethenna *and*—if a time in London would allow you to achieve some of the things you would wish for, things that cannot happen here . . ."

He raises his eyebrows to question what she thinks, but she says nothing, her dark eyes watching him.

"It would be interesting for me too," he continues, "to spend time in a city again and to see how you fared."

A gust of wind tousles the trees above their heads. Still she says nothing.

"This horse will get cold," he says, allowing the animal to walk on.

"I cannot understand," she says at last, "how you can say all this now when I have been made to feel I must keep my playing to a minimum and away from you."

She sees his face in profile wince.

"Your music is a powerful thing, Claira."

"A *good* and powerful thing," she insists quickly.

"I know that now."

The lane takes a turn uphill and Munro lets the horse trot on.

"You heard the couple on their way to Harvest Home say that violins had been played in the chapel rooms."

Munro nods. "I have heard, too, that they are played now in chapel upcountry and no doubt the custom will be spread here."

"So that now—what I do—is all right after all."

He purses his lips. "It isn't that."

The vehicle rides on, the horse in a rhythmic trot. She slips an arm through his.

"I am sorry. I do not mean to be cross. It is wonderful that you have thought of this on my behalf. Thank you."

He squeezes her arm against his side.

"We will talk more of it," he says as the vehicle emerges up above the tree line into wind, which flings rain at them.

Sixty-eight

"Hello?"

The interference on the phone is so bad she can hardly recognize the voice.

"Howard?"

"Yes. Listen, Claire. You've heard the news?"

"The stock market?"

"Yes and this *bloody* hurricane. We've only got the tail end of it and it's still mayhem. No trains running yesterday. No traffic getting through at all. London was like a ghost town. Meantime share prices falling through the floor and no one could get in to sort it out. *Still* no phones. Can you believe it?"

"It's been bad here, too. Someone died from the cliffs yesterday."

"What?"

"Nothing."

"*Nothing's* working at the office. I've had to drive miles to find a phone box that works and so many roads are blocked and then—when I did find a phone, I had to queue for half an hour. Listen. I need to know—"

Crackle. White noise. A buzz that makes her ear hurt.

"What? You need to know what?"

"I need to know if there are any faxes for me."

Oh. So that's why he's bothering to phone home. "No."

"Nothing at all?"

"No."

He starts to say something, but the white noise is worse. Wipes out his words.

"What did you say?"

"I said—you do understand what this crash is going to mean, don't you?"

"I don't know that I do understand, no."

"No more Cornish . . . *buzzzzz crackle* . . . we'll all have to move back to . . . *crackle crackle.*"

The voice sounds tinny, tiny, could be imagined, just a thought she is having.

"To London? Why?"

"Cornwall's too much the end of the line, Claire. Risky even in a buoyant market. No one's going to . . . *Crackle. Crackle. White noise. Buzz.*"

"What? No one's going to what?"

"No one's going to want to invest after this. *Crackle* . . . *Buzz* . . . *Buzzzz* . . . Cornwall's such . . . *Crackle* . . . extremity. Too geographically removed from . . . *crackle* . . . *buzzzzz* . . ."

She thinks of the climber's body in the water.

Cold biting extremities first.

The heat drawing back to the core.

Draining life from the least essential.

"*Crackle* . . . Are you there, Claire?"

"Yes."

"The retirement apartments should . . . *buzzzz* . . . all right. They're mostly signed up, thank . . . *crackle crackle* . . . but there'll be no more plans . . . *crackle buzzz crackle* . . . country clubs. You may as well start packing . . . *crackle buzzzz* . . . not viable for Clarendon to stay in Cornwall. Anyway . . . *buzzzzzzz* . . . faxes do come in, perhaps you'd . . . *crackle crackle crackle.* Claire?"

Sixty-nine

Claira puts eggs for Munro in last so they will be done the way he likes them, their golden yolks still a little soft. She checks the table, laid for only six this morning. Sarah, one of the milkmaids is away, poorly, and a tray has already been taken into Eadie who said, first thing, that she needed to rest more today.

In the larder, the crocks are full of salted pork, new from last week's pig-kill. And there's fresh bread from yesterday's baking. They will have to go sparely with the marmalade, though. She steps on the little stool to reach down an unopened jar. Only two more left and the oranges not due till after Christmastime. Taking off the lid, she tuts to see that mold grows in half a circle where rucked waxed paper has not covered. She scoops round with a knife, puts the spoiled part with scraps she'll take to the chickens.

Here he is, coming in at the back door. She plucks the towel from the hook for him, his hands and forearms wet where he has washed at the pump. Munro's eyes weigh on hers as he dries himself. She gasps at the coldness of his hand at her neck as he bends to kiss her.

"Jed is here," she laughs, pulling away as she hears the back door open again. She skitters across the room to lift eggs from the poacher. It's Mrs. Jago, in fact, come in from the dairy, Molly and Rachel behind her.

"Where's Jed?" Claira asks.

"I'll call him," Munro says, going again to the door.

"I've done nothing to deserve this sort of breakfast," Jed mutters, after grace is said.

"So you have, Jed," Munro says. "And eat up, we have plenty to do and there is no time to waste sending you home at mealtimes."

Molly and Rachel look at each other.

"Perhaps you would kindly pass Jed the butter," Claira says, her words, to Molly, clipped.

Munro opens the post on his way out. Raises his eyebrows as a newspaper cutting tumbles out. Sits to read it. Snorts at the content.

"How very kind," he says to Claira as she clears the dishes. "It seems Mary Bellham is concerned for the company we keep, lest it corrupt us, no doubt."

"The letter is from her?"

"A very brief one. A newspaper article is the most of it. She was concerned we might not have seen it. Which we had not. It seems the writer has been put out by our painter friends in Newlyn and has seen fit to publish his angst."

"Really?"

"Shall I read it to you?"

"Please do."

" 'With the advent of lady artists, gentleman artists, their sisters, their cousins and their aunts, have come to Newlyn, things—actions, manners, customs—to which the unsophisticated inhabitants of that place are strangers. Our visitors manage differently to us *old fogies*.' Dear me," Munro interrupts himself, "the man is put out. 'They have no regard for the proprieties—we beg pardon—the formalities. They romp, they sing at most ridiculous times of the night, they flirt, they spoon, they sketch. In fact, their "Bohemian" ways—as our worthy MP called them—astonish us! And that's the candid truth.' "

Munro pulls a face at Claira who has come to pick up the envelope.

"It is not both of us she warns," Claira says. "The letter is addressed to you. It is me she warns you against."

"Claira," Munro says, disclaiming.

"Of course it is. It is you she writes to, knowing my greater involvement. What does she say?"

" 'I thought you would want to know,' " Munro reads, " 'what is being said of the Newlyn artists, knowing your recent association with them.' "

"Knowing *my* association with them, she means. And what a pity she did not send us the article on the exhibition. It was so favorable."

"It is possible she means this as an act of friendship."

"To you, certainly. Not to us both or she would address it to us both," Claira says, casting an eye over the report. "She thinks I lead you astray," she adds, shaking her head.

"As you do, wickedly." Munro smiles. "We will not let it upset us, Claira," he continues, "which, as you suggest, may be what she, knowingly or not, intends."

He looks up at her, his eyes steady.

"I saw her, at Harvest Home," Claira says. "She was watching you."

Munro raises his eyebrows. "Was she?"

"Yes, she was. Strangely watching you. And jumped when she found I noticed her watching."

He gives a little, grim half-smile.

"Well. She has developed something of a habit of watching, over the years. Though I never wittingly gave her reason to. And I suppose we cannot stop her; there being no law against looking.

"We will not let it trouble us, Claira. Indeed, perhaps we should thank her for her warning," he smiles, more fully now. "Perhaps it would be best if *you* were to thank her. You could leave it to me to talk of the gentle manners of Miss Armstrong and the courtesy of Mr. Forbes.

"In the meantime," he says, picking the paper up to crumple it, "the best place to put this, is on the fire. Good Heavens. That reminds me. Is it Thursday?"

"It is."

He leaps from his chair. "We must let the fire out."

"We must?"

"Yes. Quickly," he says rushing to rake aside the burning fuel.

"Whatever for?" she asks, amazed to see him there in the hearth, hopping around hot ashes. Let the fire out? When the day is cold and there is cooking to be done?

"I had quite forgot." He glances at the clock. "They will be here in an hour."

"Who will? And why ever must we let the fire out?"

He grins.

"Time will tell."

Arm in arm, Mrs. Jago and Claira stand and stare. Minutes pass.

"Big enough to take two jam pans, I shouldn't wonder," Mrs. Jago says.

"And to think, no more raking ashes out of the cloam," Claira says.

"Oh, but how those ashes did get in your hair, never mind which cap you were wearing."

They listen as the kettle begins to sing.

"How *quick* that was," Claira says.

"Spreads the heat more, I suppose."

"And perhaps coal burns hotter."

"Oh, I think it does, once it's going."

"We will keep the furze for when the range is out though, won't we?"

"Oh, I'm sure. If it's just a kettle that's needed."

They hear the back door close to.

"Of course, it'll need to be blacked and to have the brass done."

"I could do that," Claira says.

"Well, it would be no trouble for me to do it."

They laugh. "No doubt the novelty will soon wear thin."

"I suppose it will," Claira says, going forward to stroke a finger along the smooth, warm, black metal; to open and close again the oven door. Astonishing. A metal oven with a metal door.

Coming into the room, Munro laughs to see them still standing there. He grins across at Claira.

"How is it?"

"Perfect."

Seventy

"Going *back*?" Kate says, lifting her head to look round at Claire.

Claire flinches at the drawing disturbed.

"Sorry," Kate says, "but you can't drop a bombshell like that and expect me to keep still." She rests her head back down and attempts to settle herself as she had been. "You *can't* be serious," her muted voice continues. "You've only just *arrived.*"

"I know," Claire says, continuing to work the drawing.

"*And* the children are really settled."

"I know."

"*And* I thought you liked it here."

"I do."

"*Why* then?"

Claire looks at the drawing. It's daft trying to do this. Naked Kate on the beach in October. Flesh against rock. Even in the sun they have today, it's much too cold to ask her to sit for long. She has the feeling again, the one of clawing against time left. This should have been done next spring or summer.

"Five more minutes and then get dressed and have a hot drink and we'll chat about it."

"Okay," Kate concedes.

Reaching over, Claire moves Kate's hair to expose the line of her shoulder again.

"Can I do some photos, now?"

"Sure," Kate says, her face in her folded arms.

Claire frames the torso and the outline of rock that echoes its shape so precisely; the flesh of the shoulder, the rounding of rock. Click. She zooms in on the waistline, the dip where the waves have pounded. Click. The rise of buttocks, the thrust of stone. Click.

"You must be frozen."

"Wouldn't do it for anyone else."

"I know."

The line of shin and the rounded calf muscle, the smoothed boulder. Click.

"Nearly done."

She turns the camera through ninety degrees, zooms in to the waist again, but this time gets rock below and above. Like a sandwich. It's remarkable, the creases eroded in the stone like the tucks between the arm and the rib cage, then the stone again. The stone has paler veins that run through it. Claire reaches out and touches Kate's shoulder. Chilled flesh.

"We must stop, Kate."

"Sure?"

"Yes, come on. Here," Claire says, picking up Kate's clothes and giving them to her. It is as Kate stands about to dress, her back to the sea that the unexpected image comes and Claire hurries to sketch again: the figure against the breaking waves, rocks from the cliff line rounding behind her, light from reflected sun bouncing off the water.

"On second thought, I'd always heard it's best to get wet if you really want to warm up," Claire says.

"You mean you want me in the sea?"

"Could you bear it?"

"Thirty seconds maximum."

"You're *such* a star, Kate. I'll use the camera." Then she's on her feet and Kate is squealing with the cold as she backs into the water and waves roll in behind her as Claire takes the photographs, four, five, six—"Enough, Kate, out now"—seven, eight, but Kate throws her head back and laughs, "Oh God, it's cold!" as a big wave hits, nine, ten.

"Come out! Come out!"

She throws the camera down and picks up Kate's towel.

"Come on, Kate, out now."

And seeing that Claire has finished with the camera, she does come, running through the surf, her wet body tight from the cold, so that Claire flings the towel round her and rubs her back hard.

"Apart from anything else, there's an anorak and his dog coming."

"So there is," Kate shivers out. "Wouldn't want to give him a turn."

"Or anything else," Claire adds rummaging in a bag for the thermos.

"Okay, why then?" Kate asks, moments later, dressed and huddled in blankets and drinking hot tea.

"Why what?"

"Why do you have to go back to London?"

Claire shrugs. "Howard's business. The stock market crash has made things very difficult here."

"And you have to run along, too?"

Claire looks down. "It's probably a case of being grateful to have had any time here at all."

"Do you *want* to go?"

Looking for pencils in the sand, Claire busies herself packing drawing things.

"There's really no choice, Kate," she says looking up to meet Kate's gaze. "Clarendon can't stay. We can't. Simple."

"And that's more important than your life here, is it? More important than uprooting your children again? More important than Nick?"

Claire looks quickly up. "Nick? What has Nick said?"

"Nothing. He doesn't have to. It's so obvious he was drawn to you from the word go. And I rather thought you were drawn to him, Claire."

"I was. I am."

"Well then. That's simple." Kate raises her eyebrows and holds Claire's eye a moment, then shivers. "It's no good," she says, "I shall have to run."

And suddenly she's gone, leaping from the blankets and casting them aside and running off down the beach, jumping and flinging her arms wide and sending a shouted whoop to the sky. And Claire has to grin as she goes, and stops her packing awhile to watch Kate's running form.

Moments later the wind brings the wail intact.

"Claire, Claire! Oh, *God*!"

There's a quality to it that has Claire on her feet and running towards Kate at the water's edge where she stands, face in her hands.

"Claire, oh God, Claire!"

"What *is* it?"

Claire puts a hand out to her, but Kate catches her by the shoulders, braces her tight.

"What?"

Kate turns her head a little to boulders at the water's edge and, following her gaze, Claire sees.

"Oh God," she says quietly.

Pushed up by the waves and draped between rocks now, face-down, the body of a man. In the water two weeks, the harness is yet snugly round his hips. A wave comes and raises the hand. The flesh of the fingers has been eaten, leaving bones. Part eaten too, and beach-grazed, the gouged flesh of the sodden face; visible as the lapping waves slowly shake his disbelieving head, tapping the safety helmet gently against rock—as if in party-game mimicry of a chicken picking at corn. Claire closes her eyes.

"The climber," she says.

The men are very kind and insist the two women sit in the little office and drink scalding tea with lots of sugar. And when there's time to remember their things left on the beach—oh no, Nick's camera, lent for the afternoon—one of the men goes to collect their belongings for them.

They see the ambulance arrive. The men with the stretcher going down, grim-faced.

"I'd like to go home," Kate says.

Staring at the curled edge of the tide table pinned onto chipboard, Claire nods. The air is hot and thick from a portable gas fire.

"I had no idea he would come back to the same beach that he . . ."

"May not be him, of course," says the man with fish blood on his shirt.

The rotund man in the blue Guernsey clears his throat.

"Most likely 'tis though. There's a circular current out in the bay, see," he explains to Claire. "Sometimes we 'ave flotsam, barrels and the like, goin' round for weeks. 'Course, he *could* of been taken off, never can tell."

Claire nods.

"I'd like to go home," Kate says.

But then the policeman is there, the darkness of his uniform pushing its presence into the little room; the crackle and voice of his radio muffled through his jacket.

Seventy-one

Ten for supper. Across the warmth and glow of Trethenna's dining room, Claira smiles. Young William, on Beattie's knee, is nearly asleep. As he came earlier, into the room, his eyes had widened in wonderment at the lit candelabra placed on the table ends and at the way fire and lamplight reflect in silver's entwining. Now the candles are half burned and wax runs and Stanhope amuses Samuel by sketching Jethro, while Munro and Ellen talk and Hannah shows Aunt Eadie her sampler.

Claira supposes they could abandon the meal's debris and go through to the parlor, but that everyone seems happy enough here.

And there's Elizabeth, leaving Beattie and William to come round the table and place a wooden box in Claira's hands.

"A little present," Elizabeth says.

"For me?"

"Yes. A thank-you for sitting for the painting, which is sold now. I wanted you to have something."

"Is it sold?"

Elizabeth nods and smiles.

"I met the gentleman who has bought it. A doctor who visits the Academy every year. I understand he has a lovely house overlooking the Thames and the painting now hangs there."

"Oh," Claira says, trying to imagine what the image of her would look like in such a place, "well, that is good."

From the box, Claira withdraws a sphere of brass, the silky metal pierced into an ornate pattern.

"Oh look," Jethro says, across the table, "a shadow ball."

"Is it?" Claira asks, thinking what she holds is a pomander.

"It is," Elizabeth confirms.

"A what?" asks Samuel.

"A shadow ball," Jethro says, getting up to see, so that his pose for Stanhope's sketch is broken.

"Sorry," Elizabeth mouths to him, but he smiles to dismiss her concern.

"Open it up," Jethro says, only just able to stop himself taking the sphere from his sister.

Claira's fingers find the little catch and open the lid of the thing. Inside, the hemispherical lamp swings in its three-ringed gimbal. Claira marvels at it, the way the lamp keeps an even keel however the sphere is moved.

"How wonderful," she says, passing the thing for Munro to see.

"May we light it?" Jethro asks, beside himself at their slowness.

"In a moment, Jethro," Ellen says.

William strains open sleep-heavy lids to find the room has turned into a forest where sunlight filters through. Is it a forest? Or is he at the harbor with sunlight coming up off the water to dapple and fleck against the wall?

The waves sound like voices.

His sister's breast is warm.

The waves sound like music. He struggles to open his ears. It is music, isn't it? The drag of waves over shingle sounds like clapping.

"You have done very well, Stanhope," Munro says, "to learn so much so quickly."

"I am afraid there is another," Stanhope says from behind the cello.

"Two more," Claira corrects him. "Miss Rossetti's, too, after this next one."

"Excellent," Munro says.

And they begin again, Claira with the tune on her fiddle, Stanhope a simple bass line on the cello.

"I know this," Munro says quietly to Elizabeth.

"It is from Mozart's *Magic Flute,*" Elizabeth whispers. "Claira said one of Wesley's hymns is set to it."

"It is—'Behold the Servant of the Lord'—only this version is much more beautiful."

"Mr. White said such pieces are often simplified when taken for hymns. Claira requested it especially. She thought it something you would be pleased to hear her play. There is another by Wesley, set to Handel—only," Elizabeth smiles, "Stanhope's part is not quite ready."

Munro watches Claira play across the room, the edge of her form flecked with light from the shadow ball, her face lit from below by the lamp that shines on the music she reads. Or sometimes she reads, sometimes closes her eyes to play, effortlessly, holding the tempo for Stanhope too, even when he fumbles and stops, she grins and keeps time, points to the place where he has lost the music, hums the notes, while pointing, she has missed, picks the tune up again, surely.

Munro looks at the other faces, too. His house, filled with faces. Such wondrous change she has brought him. And, in a few months, by God's grace, a child will be born. He shakes his head. How his cup overflows.

Seventy-two

"Are we going to sleep in there all night?" Nathan asks, pointing in through the flap of the tent.

"We are," Claire says.

"Or that's the idea, anyway." Kate laughs.

"*All* night?"

"Yes. Is that exciting?"

Nathan looks at the tent, then back at his mother.

"All of us?"

"You, me and Damien in this one," Claire says, indicating the three-man Vango they've borrowed from Nick. "Sam, Kate and Sky in the green one and Nick in that one, there."

Nathan looks at the semicircle of tents round the fire. He grins and throws back his head and jumps up and down.

"Look out, Nathan," Kate warns. Claire catches his arm.

"Mind the guy ropes, Nath," Claire says, pointing them out to the boy. "And no going in the tent with your shoes on and be really careful with the fire, okay?"

"Okay."

"Good boy. Could you take these over to Nick for me, please? Only it's such a brilliant fire, I bet those potatoes will be done soon, so we need to heat these beans."

With both hands and lip-biting concentration, Nathan carries the saucepan across. Kate and Claire smile to see him.

"Well done, Nathan," Claire hears Nick say. "Won't be long now. Are you hungry?"

Claire is, she realizes. Not for food, but for this moment. There's a quality to it of which she has felt starved. She drinks it in, trying to gauge the flavor of it. Long shadows cast by sun setting through trees on the skyline; the tents semicircled in a dip round the fire, beyond the fire the stream. She can hear the trip and trickle of water; the trip and trickle of Sam's mandolin. From trees around the clearing, where ground rises, comes the chime of children's voices—Damien and Sky—in endless play. Then there's the pleasure of Kate beside her, sketching—muttering about the fading light. And then Nick. She watches him. The easy agility with which he stands to add more wood to the fire. Closing her eyes, she listens to his voice as he chats to Sam, too quietly now for her to hear his words, but still she listens, feels herself gentled by the deepness of his tone, the warmth of it. Nick. Nick. It's begun to feel like suffocation: the need to touch and be touched by him.

She forces her mind to the chill of the air, reaches into the tent for their jackets. They'll be glad of the fire later.

"You warm enough, Kate?"

"Just about," Kate drawls, not taking her attention from her drawing.

"Here," Claire says, placing a coat round Kate's shoulders and then standing to find Nick watching her, his eyes gentle, unblinking, and she looks down, as if for foothold.

"Claire," Kate says, suddenly. "You know *the* Painting?"

"Elizabeth Armstrong's?"

"The very same."

"What about it?"

"Look at this," Kate says, scrambling up and proffering her sketch pad, then taking it again from Claire's gaze to indicate the sweep of the clearing and wood around them. "Better still, look at this, the landscape. What does it remind you of?"

"Oh God."

"Familiar?"

"Yes, but it can't be. It's a hundred years. The trees—"

"The trees will have come and gone. Although some will have stuck around," Kate says, indicating the thick trunk of an oak. "But barring bulldozers, the lie of the land won't have changed. And see where the sun is setting in relation to that dip? It *is*, you know. It is. Nick! Hey, Nick!" Kate waves him over. "Come and stand here."

"What is it?"

"Kate thinks she's found the spot where Elizabeth Armstrong did the painting." Claire grins.

"What do you mean 'thinks,' ratbag? I'm certain. My feet are standing where famous feet have trod. I only hope she brought a cushion to use while painting because my bum's numb. Stand here, stand here," Kate says, maneuvering Nick into position and then Sam, who has wandered over to see what all the fuss is about. "Look, look," she insists. "I can't think how it took so long to dawn on me that what I was sketching was amazingly familiar."

"Oh *yes*," says Nick, bobbing his head down to the height of a woman sitting on a stool to paint.

"Don't *you* start," Claire complains.

"Why *not*?" Kate demands to know.

"It could be anywhere," Claire protests. "It could even have been done from imagination."

"I don't know, Claire," Nick interjects. "The *plein air* ethos was very dear to the Newlyn School. It's true, she did delve into legend later, but even then—"

"Listen," Kate chastises, "never mind the art-babble. Just tell me if you think it looks like the bit in Claire's picture."

"I do. It does," Nick says. "Remarkably like it."

"I think so, too," agrees Sam.

"Sorry, Claire. Well outnumbered," Kate gloats. "And just look at the sun setting by that blip in the horizon just so," she continues, with a theatrical wave of her arm, and then, in tight imitation of Earnest Natural-History Commentator, "as every bit as precisely in place in relation to the sun as the stones at Stonehenge."

"Oh, bollocks!" Claire shouts with laughter. "You can't even *see* the sun in the painting. It has dropped from the sky. Out of sight. Below the horizon. It is no more. It is a *late* sun. It has *gone* to meet its *Maker.*"

"Well, you can *imagine* where it *would* be," Kate persists, though her sides shake with laughter.

"Bollocks!" Claire repeats.

"Claire!" Kate laughs, her arm round her friend's shoulders. "You are no longer the lady you were when you arrived."

Darkness closes in; gathers them to the fire. And why is it food tastes better out-of-doors: the salads they've brought, the potatoes half charred, the fish from Sam's catch he has watchfully cooked, the wine they drink. "All right?" Nick asks Claire as they pass each other, fetching and carrying food and wine, the light of the fire on them, his hand so briefly, so lightly on her back she might have imagined it.

"No," she laughs, though she means it. "It's too lovely."

Then on the lane, a Land Rover stops: the shocking sweep of its lights through the darkness. Dennis, the farmer, who has said they could camp, come to share a bit of fire and company and the brandy Nick has brought. Approaching, his boots snap twigs on the floor of the wood, his torch swinging a pool of light before him, so that Nathan goes quickly to Claire to know who it is.

"It's only Dennis," Damien says, scathing and from the safety of his position—sitting beside Nick and leaning back against him, warm beneath surrounding arms, where he has been for half an hour, so that Claire has another image-she-would-keep.

"Come on, Damien," Claire says. "Time for bed."

"Oh!"

"No ohs. It's past ten o'clock and besides, you have a tent to sleep in and it's only here. You can keep the flap open if you like, but I want to see you snuggled down."

A cocoon of bedding to bury into; heaps of it. The boys squeal as they dig their way in and Claire has to laugh, the chaos of heels and elbows and flickering flashlight.

"Cozy?" Nick asks, crouching to peer into the tent. "Is that torch all you've got?"

"It is," Claire says.

"One moment."

He reappears with a small brass cylinder that telescopes out to reveal a candle behind glass. The boys watch as he lights it, so—there's another image for Claire to store—their three heads grouped round candlelight.

"It goes on a loop in the middle of the ridge," Nick says indicating where they can hang the lamp by its chain.

"Oh yes," Claire says, taking the light he passes to her. Her fingers fumble.

"Oh, *I'll* do it," Damien says, scrambling up.

The brandy and the fire burn warm; notes from Sam's mandolin chime out from darkness like the night's stars do; twinkling through trees as branches stir in breeze. Claire hugs her knees and grins. Her focus slides to Kate next to her, laughing at something Dennis is saying. Her laugh is warm and rich and full and when she tips back her head, her throat is beautiful and her hair tumbles over shoulders like the stream over rocks. Sam grins too; his fingers picking out the tune.

Nick. She ought not be looking at Nick. Not after wine has left her unguarded. Perhaps just a glance. Nick in firelight. Mellow. He's wearing a thick, padded jacket now—mountaineering stuff. The jacket falls open at the front. Underneath he is wearing the scruffy blue sweater she loves. He's sitting on a rug, one knee up, his arms round it, a glass cupped in one hand. She loves the ease with which he sits.

Stop this.

Think Howard.

No, no.

Think the boys, then. Think maintaining the nuclear family. She turns to look at the tent, can see their heads, snuggled down in sleep at last, she must blow the lamp out soon and oh! Nick has moved, has come to sit next to them, offering more brandy.

"Thanks, but I'm going to turn in now," Claire says, her voice strangely normal.

"Ohhhh," Kate sighs out, stretching and getting up. "That's probably a good idea, Claire, while we're still warm."

She reaches down a hand to pull Claire to her feet.

"Sleep well," Kate says, kissing her lightly on the cheek.

Wander off into the wood for a pee, mind low branches, hand out as one catches face, fumble through layers to find button and fly, crouch and feel hot water pass, looking back at figures round the fire, up into spangled blackness, at stars tangled in branches, giggle at them caught there, *you should be more careful,* voice chuckles to stars, chill air fingers for flesh. No chance. Stand up. Wrap up, keep core hot, the pumping of blood quick with pleasure and alcohol, the bundle of bedding soon to clamber in, Nick in the tent next door and but for thin fabric you could reach out and touch him he will lie so close, stumble a little, steadying hand on a tree, *Shame on you, Claire,* voice says, *you've had too much to drink.*

Ssshhhhh! Look!

The silent sweep of an owl, ghosting, gliding—the white of

underwing—mouth opens to tell, eyes follow. Gone.

He is there when she returns. Dennis has left. Sam and Kate turned in already. Only Nick. Making safe the fire. She hears Kate's giggle from inside their tent, Sam's overlapping talk and laughter, subdued to let the children sleep. Claire checks the boys, tight asleep in their bags, then goes to Nick in the circle of firelight, where he smiles to see her.

"There you are," he says, pushing soil in to smother the edge of the fire. "Has it been a good evening?"

"Lovely. Will the fire be all right?"

"Yes. It's settling well. Any more of this?" he asks, proffering the brandy bottle he's about to pack away.

Claire shakes her head. "No. Thanks. I think I've had enough already," though she feels suddenly sober, here with just Nick.

"There's water if you would like some."

"That would be good."

She finds two cups to hold while he pours from a bottle, and they drink the water down, standing in darkness and fading firelight.

"More?"

"Please," Claire says and shivers, so that—as he pours more water for her—he steps close beside her; gathers her, too, into the warmth of his open jacket; great downy thing, made for the mountains.

And she laughs as he pours, not daring to move. "Careful, careful! I'll spill this over you."

"No you won't," he laughs, nestling her nearer. "No you won't."

Their clothes smell of wood smoke and outdoors: the scent of centuries of leaf mold beneath their feet; rising with the damp of night air and why ever would she move from him when his closeness feels as guileless as the embalming air; as easily round her as this darkness; licit like starshine. They make their seat the fallen log, dragged earlier down to the fireside, where he sits astride now, easing her to lean her shoulder against him and when the fold of his jacket isn't enough, he reaches to unzip his tent—don't move—hauling out his sleeping bag to snuggle round them; throwing more wood onto the fire, after all.

"Better? Warm enough?" he asks, his arm round her.

"Yes, Nick. Yes." And she brings her fingers to his face, feeling his features as if she were blind: the curve of eyelid, the height of cheekbone, the tautness of cheek, the day's rough stubble, the firmness of lips that kiss her fingers, once.

He brings his face to rest gently on the top of her head. "What do I do with you, Claire Lattimer. You are so out of order."

"What?"

"Barging into my life—"

"Doing *what*?"

"—just when I had it all worked out. Paint. Exhibit. Travel. Teach a bit—just to see what thoughts are up and coming, mostly. No women. No hassle. And then you arrive. It's quite out of order."

"Sorry."

"So I should think."

"Still. It won't be for long."

"*Won't* it?"

She pulls away to look at him. "We have to move back to London."

He chokes a short, hard laugh. "Are you calling my bluff, here?" He studies her face. "Oh God. You mean it, don't you?"

She nods.

"When? Why? Not this stock market thing?"

"Yes. The stock market thing. Anyway," she continues, leaning back to him again, "I'm a married woman, remember?"

He tucks the duvet jacket round her, draws the down bag round, hugs her to him. "I remember."

The trickle of the stream seems louder, now, Kate and Sam silent;

the night deepening. She thinks of Howard, alone at Trethenna, not wanting to join in the silliness of camping. Just up the lane—a quarter mile. Miles and miles and miles away.

"I don't believe in degrees of fidelity," she says.

"How do you mean?"

"Oh, I don't know," she says, wishing she wouldn't think out loud; letting the weight of her head sink to his shoulder more.

"Howard has a lover, Nick."

"*Does* he?"

"Yes."

"Did he tell you?"

"No. I found them together. In our bed."

"Claire! When?"

"A few weeks ago. No, longer. It must be longer."

He leaves a silence, then says, "The shock of that . . ."

"It was a shock. And at first I couldn't get my head round it and then when I did begin to get some kind of grasp, it was about Howard's infidelity and deceit and all the things he'd inflicted on me."

"I can understand that. It's . . ."

"It's only half the picture." She shifts her weight again on the log, where she's stiffening, sits to face him after all, closely while he throws the sleeping bag about her shoulders and she drapes it to cover his knees. Under its warmth, fingertips touch. "I'm sorry. I don't mean to go on about it."

"No. I want to hear. What do you mean, only half the picture?"

"I hadn't thought about my infidelity."

"You've been unfaithful, too?"

"Yes. No. It depends on your definition of what it is to be unfaithful." She gives a wry laugh. "There's a painter guy. You might know him. Lives in the cottage down the lane from us. Teaches a bit at the art college. Goes off traveling every year."

"What about him?"

"Ever since I first saw him, there's been this *bloody* attraction."

"I felt the same, Claire. One of those from-the-first-moment things."

"I know and it's a *damn* nuisance—as you say—barging its way into our lives and I've tried to pretend it's not there or to stifle it and I can't. So there's my degree of infidelity. A very different form from Howard's, but just as bad. My heart has not been with him for a long time. In fact, I've wondered lately if it ever was."

"The office pregnancy."

She nods. "Exactly. Looking back, I can see how it happened. Howard got the hots for his dad's personal assistant. Having just broken up with my previous lover, I sincerely resisted his attentions. I really did *not* want to know. Unfortunately Howard—as I now realize—is one of those men who is only incited by refusal. He's also bloody determined. It's one of the reasons he does so well in business: his persistence. When—a year later—I eventually succumbed, I fell pregnant—as they say. I mean straightaway, our first time."

"You didn't think of termination?"

"Yes, I thought about it. By that time, I was beginning to convince myself it was love."

"And now?"

"Now there are children, Nick. It may be a cliché, but it's a truth, nonetheless, that they don't ask to be born. And having inflicted life upon them, I have to do my best for them."

"And that means moving back to London, does it?"

"They deserve stability. They need to know who their father is."

"And that means moving back to London, does it?" he insists.

"I think it does."

He nods.

She sees his eyes, by firelight, look weary, and she sighs out, "It's a bit of a mess, isn't it?"

He draws her back to him, closer, facing him still and she wraps the bag around his shoulders, too, a cloak or cave about them both, heads resting each by each as a dog-fox rasps its bark through the valley.

Seventy-three

There is movement in the room behind him. No matter. Probably one of the urchins from downstairs. They do come up from time to time; put their heads round the door to stare at his painting.

The fall of the tablecloth to amend. Let the brush slide down the canvas. Scrutinize. Better. Another such stroke, where it catches the thin light from the window. Scrunch eyes to scrutinize. Better. Mix a shade darker to blend into shadow. He hears the hushed voices of adults. Not an urchin, then. He supposes he must stop. Turns to see who it is.

"Frank, dear fellow, we have called at an inconvenient time and we shall take our leave immediately."

"Stanhope!" Bramley says. "And Elizabeth and Mr. and Mrs. Richardson. Come in." He stops a moment and frowns. "Come to think of it, am I not expecting you?"

"You are," Elizabeth laughs. "Or so we believed."

"You wanted to show these people the painting before it goes to London," Bramley recounts.

"Indeed."

"Well, here it is then," he says, stepping aside, though they could not help but see it, the tiny cottage is quite dominated by the thing.

"I'll make us some tea."

Munro has already found Claira a chair, where she sits to catch her breath after the hill; her body full to brimming with the baby.

It's madness, she thinks—her heart thumping—to come as far as Newlyn, the farthest she has been for weeks and the baby due so soon. A woman's harsh voice rasps from the floor below. Chastising children.

Elizabeth comes to stand beside Claira.

"Are you all right, Claira?" she asks, resting a hand on her shoulder.

"Yes, thank you."

"What do you think?"

They look, together, at the painting. A cottage interior: *this* cottage interior; poor, the household objects utilitarian, minimal. The subject matter is similar to the Langley Claira saw at the art museum. Two women grieve the loss of a fisherman. But here there is a sense of space you could move in, the bare floor of the cottage taking up—Claira estimates—perhaps one third of the canvas.

Enlivened by her quickened blood, the baby kicks. Claira rests a hand on the side of her belly; shifts her weight on the chair.

The line of the table—laid with a simple and untouched supper—and the shape the grieving women make, both lead the eye to where the sea is visible through the window, gray and disturbed under a similar sky. It's almost like a triangle, the line of the table, the women and then the sea above them as the dominant point. Beneath it the rough emptiness of bare floor.

The pain that has troubled her these last two months twinges again at her side. Claira gets to her feet. She'll be better standing.

"Well?"

"It is beautiful," Claira says.

And it is, she thinks, the soft light of it, the flow of the form the women make. It is. It is.

While Stanhope gallantly helps Bramley with the tea, Munro stands in silent contemplation. He takes a step nearer the canvas. In shadow on the painted wall, a print. Isn't that. . . ? It is. Christ and St. Peter. The giving of keys to the Kingdom of Heaven. And there the Bible open. He wants to read the page, but cannot, so looks round the real room, only to find the huge book has been moved aside and closed. On the painting's window ledge a candle burns its last moment, feeble against the gray of the sea that holds the man these women grieve.

Especially curious, seeing the painting *here,* the representation so true to life he feels he could walk into it. As he already does, being in the room it mirrors.

Forbes, with tea, is at his elbow.

"Do you like it?"

"Quite beautiful. And you, Stanhope?"

"I think it is excellent indeed," Forbes says, pulling his moustache. "The dramatic interest so wonderfully balanced. And then so finely painted. There will be no questioning Bramley's stature after this has been to the Academy."

"Do stop, Forbes," Bramley says, across the room.

"Do you have a title for it?" Munro, turning, asks him.

"A Hopeless Dawn," Bramley says.

Munro nods. "And it is to go to London soon?"

"It must in a week or so. I shall have to stop fiddling with it and allow the paint a proper chance to dry."

Munro looks directly at him.

"If it is not extremely well received, then London is not worthy of you."

"Sit down, you *stinking* elephants!" the woman's voice yells from below.

Forbes grimaces. "How ever you have managed to produce such a wonderful thing in such conditions, Bramley, I shall never know."

"Sorry?" Bramley mutters, intent again on the canvas.

"Get in here!" the woman's voice shouts. Her running footsteps sound at the side of the cottage. Bramley's door is pushed hurriedly open.

"Oh, I'm sorry, I'm sure, Mr. Bramley," the woman says. "I didn't know as you 'ad comp'ny, only one of the infants 'as runned off and I was thinking 'e might 'ave come 'ere."

"I am afraid not, Mrs. Barret," Bramley says, managing to take his eyes from the painting.

Claira sees—with shock—the woman has no arms. Under one stubbed armpit, she clamps a stout cane. A draft comes through the opened door. Cooled now after the uphill walk, Claira shivers. There is no warmth in the day's pale sun. The fire in the hearth is almost out.

"Do you think we might go home soon?" Claira quietly asks Munro.

She dozes against his shoulder on the way. Wakes cold as he stops at the forge for the plowshare the blacksmith has repaired.

"I hope Mrs. Jago has built us a good fire," he says, as he steps back onto the vehicle, wrapping the rug further round her, sending the horse off, fast.

The rocking chair is almost too wide for the door. Claira giggles as Munro brings it into the bedroom.

"I am so spoiled," she says. "A fire lit in here for me and now furniture brought."

Munro grins at her, places the chair next to the fireplace.

"Thank you," Claira says, seating herself, beginning to unpin her hair. "And it was *so* thoughtful of Mrs. Jago to light a fire here for me."

"Wasn't it? All we need now is tea."

"Here?"

"I'll just get it. Mrs. Jago has gone early."

"Oh, of course, her son coming home."

He turns from the doorway. "Are you all right, Claira?"

She tilts her head a little to one side. "Yes. Thanks to you."

"I was worried earlier."

"Just a little cold and uncomfortable. I'm sorry if I made a fuss."

"You didn't," he says, resting his eyes on hers a long moment, taking her in, there by the fire in the rocking chair, the color returning to her face, her hair falling about her shoulders.

In dream she walks again in childhood, the steep, narrow garden behind the cottage. There's a hiding place among arched greenery and she crawls in, her youngest sister, Beattie, behind her. Peeking out, they look down over rooftops to the glint of sun on sea. Gulls call. She can feel the sun, hot on her legs.

Look, Beattie, strawberries! she says and stands, a giant, breaking through the green canopy to reach the wild berries that grow on the wall. The tiny things are sweet on her tongue. And there is her father's voice, calling her, *Claira,* softly, *Claira.*

"I didn't know whether to wake you or not."

Claira smiles, moves her too warm feet farther from the fire. Lifts her mouth upwards to kiss Munro's face where it hovers above her.

"I've brought tea," he says and she kisses him again.

"Warmer?" he asks.

"Very much," she says, turning the chair away from the fire, taking the tea he passes her. "Thank you for this, Munro."

He smiles; comes to sit on the rug at her feet, so that she gets out of her chair to sit with him.

"Careful," he says, holding out a hand to her.

"It's all right."

He tends the fire, making it flame. Like cats they bask, drawing the heat into themselves.

"Is Jed busy?" Claira asks.

"Yes. Attaching the plowshare, then I've asked him to dress the millstone."

"So Michael will help him."

"Yes."

"And Mrs. Jago has gone home and, doubtless, Aunt Eadie is dozing by the kitchen hearth, as she does at this hour."

He raises his eyebrows at her. "What of it?"

She drops her gaze a moment, then grins up at him, her eyes dark under dark lashes.

"I have a terrible backache."

He feels his eyes flare wide.

"Claira, it's the middle of the day."

"So it is," she grins. "But then backache is no great respecter of the hour."

She gets to her feet, so that he does too, offering an arm to her, which she uses this time, more than she needs, leaning against him.

"It is *very* persistent, my backache," she says, undoing his shirt.

He feels his penis rise, as it does, so quickly for her.

"There is *work* to do," he laughs, pulling back a little, feigning resistance.

"There certainly *is,*" she says, still busy with his buttons, so that he laughs again, gathering her face in his hands, kissing her.

Watching her undress, he marvels again at her litheness, how it has remained with her, the slender length of her limbs. "You have a waist still," he says, seeing her, there by the fire, naked and three quarters to him.

"I do not think so," she says, pausing to run a hand down the side of her body.

"You have."

"I shall like it the better when I have a proper one again."

"Not long now," he says reaching out a hand as she walks to where he sits on the edge of the bed, pulling her to him, closing his eyes at the skin-on-skin of her.

"Now, where is this backache?" he asks, falling under the covers, drawing her after him so that she lies on her side, facing away from him.

"You know where it is."

"Here," he says, his hands on her hips, pushing both thumbs up the small of her back.

"Yes."

"And here," he says, circling the pressure of his thumbs towards her spine.

"Wonderful," she sighs, closing eyes at the relief he brings.

"Too hard?"

"No."

For minutes he kneads her flesh, till she reaches out behind her, behind him, bringing his pelvis forward against hers.

"Are you sure?" he whispers, his mouth to her ear.

"Oh yes," she says, shifting to align his penis against the rounding of her buttock. There. She clenches muscle against him, feels the tip of him against the small of her back, hears him draw sudden breath.

"Sure, Claira?" Pushing against her.

"Mmmm."

"Sure?"

Her skin sings with the pressure of him, pushing back hard against him. Leaning over her, he kisses the side of her mouth and she arches her neck to turn her head back to him, then he pushes her down again, hard to the pillow and there, there, there, the hot spurt of his seed, high on her spine. She grins against the pillow and giggles so that he falls close behind her, laughing in her hair.

"This is an outrage," he whispers against her head.

She laughs again. "You had better get up, then, and be about your business."

"And you are *very* wet," he says, reaching to the night cabinet for the towel they leave there now.

She lets him towel her dry, then turns, impatient to face him. Dark eyes on his.

"I love you, Munro Richardson."

He smiles down at her. "And I you."

She grins. "Now hurry and get dressed before Jed comes looking for you."

"You didn't say what you thought of the paintings," he says as he dresses.

"I didn't, did I?" she says from the bed, her hands folded behind her head.

"Well?"

"I thought Stanhope's *Village Philharmonic* very accurately painted and . . ." She pauses and Munro glances at her. "And very *jolly,*" she says, stressing the word.

He shouts a quick laugh.

"I know what you mean, it was rather *jolly,*" he says, grinning and then puffing out his cheeks and she laughs, recognizing the painting's player of the double bass.

"That is it," she says from the bed. "Not that the musicians *were* grinning."

"No. Rather solemn in fact, I remember."

"Yes, but the feeling was somehow jolly."

"Or jaunty."

"That more closely has it," she says, grinning across at him.

"And the other?"

"Aahh."

She brings her arms from behind her head. Smooths the sheet down on the counterpane, the image of Bramley's painting in her mind. She sighs.

"I thought it exceptional," he says, buttoning his shirt.

She nods.

"The space and the low light," he continues. "And the elements Bramley had balanced. The hope and the hopelessness."

She looks at him, his face quite fired as he talks of it, his eyes unfocused while he thinks of the picture.

"Where was the hope?" she asks.

"The print on the wall—the promise of Heaven in the hereafter."

"I didn't see it."

"And the Bible open, too."

"Aahh."

"I was surprised," he says pulling on his jacket. "Perhaps we should tell Miss Bellham of it. Our Bohemian friends depicting a little piety."

"In a very subtle way," Claira adds quickly.

He laughs. "Indeed. Did you not like the painting?"

"I thought it *extraordinary,*" she says.

"I felt I was in the presence of something that will reach out across *decades,*" Munro says. "Centuries, perhaps, and him living in such tightened circumstance."

She nods. "Mmm."

"And?" he says, crossing to the bed.

She rests a hand on the bump of her belly beneath the covers. "Perhaps it is because I am so full of new life. I did not want to be reminded of its end—or the dominance of nature."

"Nature?"

"The sea that has taken the fisherman. There and in the Langley we saw at the summer exhibition."

"I remember. I had thought of it more in terms of God."

Claira shrugs. "God through Nature. Nature through God. I know the life of this child I bear is finite, I suppose I did not want to think of that today."

He nods. "But in general?"

"Yes. When I stood before the Langley I did not feel troubled in the same way. I felt *exhilarated,* in fact. I know that must seem a contradiction—their subject matter so similar, my response so different."

"It does. Why did the Langley exhilarate you?"

Claira frowns. "You know how it is to lie on a hill in heather and watch the clouds race by and feel the soil at your back and all the air above you, and you—just a slip of a thing between the two that one day will no longer be there."

He laughs. "I think so."

"That feeling that you are only a small part of something much bigger and more important."

He nods. "Oh, I see, yes. I sometimes feel that drawing water, wondering from what distance it has come and where it will go to once I have had my use of it."

"Do you?"

"Or plowing, seeing the soil turn."

"Yes? Well that is what I felt about Mr. Langley's painting. Even though the sea was not visible, still you could not escape its presence and the knowledge that . . ." She searches for the right words. "The knowledge that it is so much stronger, so much more *enduring* than we are."

"And did you not find that troubling?"

"No," she says, her eyes flashing to him. "Not then. It was exciting to be reminded of it. It made—it *makes* now seem so valuable."

"As it is," he says, his eyes across the room, on hers. "As it is."

Seventy-four

There is some sun suddenly, a few defined rays push their way down through gray clouds onto the cliff. Her brush hesitates. It's a bit of a cliché, really: petulant sky with chinks of brilliance. But see how the focused light fires the rock face, enlivening ochers and greens, burning bright the siennas of spent bracken and—where gorse flowers remain—a vivid, windblown splattering of yellow. She reaches into her box of paints; becomes aware of another pair of walkers who stop to loiter at her shoulder. She twists the lid off the tube, squeezes out the color she needs onto her palette. The luxury of it. Paint to use. She glances at it only quickly, her eyes following the force of light over rock, of light on water, of light through the spray from waves.

The brush loaded with paint, she works the surface of the canvas again, the cut piece of canvas, primed and pinned to her drawing board—sketches in oil in preparation for the big canvas she's left at home. She doesn't like working on this hard surface, but she'll have to lump it; not having found an easel or the courage large enough to handle the big picture in public. She glances down the length of beach. The walkers who stopped by her are specks in the distance.

She sketches quickly, changing canvas often before the light changes; loosening up to the task, knowing she can take this experience home and use it to range over larger ground. A sketch there—where water in shadow pounds rock face, there where rock glistens as the sea draws back, there the contrast of rock in sunlight, there the tumble of vegetation and all the time, thoughts of where to place the figure and of the force this seascape, cliffscape, brings to bear.

At a pause, she steps back to view her work. The cuts of canvas she has worked on are spread out on the ground around her, weighted with stones at their corners against the breeze that would lift them. She pours herself tea from the flask, sits on the stony beach amid her work, hugging her knees to warm them.

You couldn't have done this six months ago. Painted like this. The sense of rightness and purpose and sureness of direction.

A sense of arrival then—she purses her lips—*just as it's time to go back to London.*

The note is through the door when she gets home from picking up the children. *I've been meaning to tell you*—it says, in Nick's hand—*but perhaps you know already, there's going to be a big exhibition of Newlyn School paintings soon in Truro. Work coming back from all over the world. The organizer—Naomi Johnson—is a friend and very interested to hear that I know of a major piece by EA that's recently come to light. She wanted to know if you would think of loaning it? What do you reckon?*

"Well," Claire says, out loud to the Armstrong painting, "show time."

Seventy-five

The point of the pickax thuds again to wedge between root and earth. Rammed deep, it sticks. Munro thrusts his weight against the handle, pushing to rotate the device, then levering. Nothing. He grabs the thing at the crosspiece, hauls it out and swings it high, driving the head on down. The metal bites into root this time. Gaining purchase, he hears it splinter, draws the pick out, swings, thuds; draws the pick out, swings, thuds. The piece that comes away is small. Not a foot long. Less than half the diameter. Swinging the pick, he works afresh. His back screams for rest, but he will not.

He glances again at the window. No sign.

The stump went easily enough, parting to his ax like butter to a knife; and the trench to follow the root was soon dug. Now, at the heart of it, his jacket's tossed aside, his sleeves rolled and the spiteful easterly is as nothing to his sweat.

He glances again at the window. Nothing.

Changing tack, he drops down into the ditch. Swapping the pick for the ax, he straddles the root; rains heavy blows down on the length of it.

Merciful God. She is only tender.

Merciful God. Let it be soon.

Then he's out again, gaining ground with the pick now, forcing it home in the gash he's made. It splinters and widens, but does not give.

He glances again at the window. Nothing.

Then there's Jed come up the lane to begin the day's work. Huddled in his coat against the wind, he walks into the walled garden, come to find what it is he must do. His brow puckers—why this old root? Why now when there's all there is to do elsewhere?

"Jed." Munro nods, hardly breaking his rhythm.

There's a tapping from the upstairs window and turning to find out why, Jed sees Mrs. Jago there, holding a bundle of something. Another woman stands at her shoulder. Oh. Isn't that the midwife?

Jed turns back to say, only Munro has gone, halfway to the house already; the ax and pick left where they were thrown.

Bringing mud on his boots, it is not the baby, but Claira's eyes he seeks out. *All right? All right?* Through her sweat and his, their eyes strike each other. She flares hers, rests her head askew on the pillow. At her side on his knees, he is unable to touch her for the grime he brings.

"Are you all right?"

She nods. Gives a little smile.

"You have a lovely boy," Mrs. Jago says, bringing the baby.

Glancing, Munro sees already he has a thatch of Claira's dark hair.

Seventy-six

Toes in sharp detail, as many as three perhaps and the rounding at the side of the foot, the rest obscured by the flurry of surf, but, those three toes will be important, the metaphor she's working with: a coming out of the water, a contacting with solid ground. Quickly she works the pencil on paper. The rest of the foot and ankle and much of the lower leg will be obscured by the wave: the sea coming up behind this figure to wrap round it, to ricochet out from it so that the body has to brace and balance against its force. Claire glances again at the photos of Kate she took on the beach. She has put them up on the wall of the attic, next to the oil sketches on cut canvas she did the other day. She reaches out to swivel the nearest spot-lamp, so light flares more fully on the photo she's looking for. That's it, the one where the water has been molded by being forced to stream round the body. It's beautiful, the rounded, gray flood, breaking to whiteness on the beach. Then here—her pencil demarks—the weight of water, here the surround of towering stone: the cliff face. She'll think through use of light more, once she's working in paint.

She steps back from the easel, wonders what time it is. Three o'clock in the morning when she crept up here with more lamps and a plug board for them all. She must have been here at least an hour, maybe two. She hasn't got her watch on.

You'll be tired in the morning.

What of it?

Haven't thought the figure through well enough yet. That arm outstretched looks fine, not sure how much else to obscure with water—the face? Some of the torso? Kate has beautiful breasts, shame to obscure those entirely, especially if they could help to demonstrate the force of water.

Look away for a moment, come back to it.

She shifts the latch on the little window, slides the top half downwards and puts her head out into the night air. Waiting for her eyes to adjust to the darkness, she wills the gleam of light to be there farther down the valley, the one that comes from Nick's studio, knowing that sometimes he, too, paints in the night. It would be wonderful to know he was there now, working as she does. But there is nothing to be seen, a cloudy night, no stars, just the faint sound of the stream. He must be tucked up in bed. Very sensible.

Closing the window, she turns and is faced afresh with her work and—oh, it *is* coming together now. With a quick pencil she alters the figure, the turn of the head, the angle of the shoulders and—if you don't like the oh-so-threatening white of this canvas you are going to move onto soon, then give it a wash of a different color, idiot. And before she knows it, she's thinning paint with turps, mapping out areas of color on canvas with a wide brush and oh God, but it's wonderful when the work goes ahead without any intervening sense of the self.

Seventy-seven

"I hear she is took poorly," a voice whispers as Munro passes.

"Claira Richardson?" a surprised voice asks.

Eyes widen. *Not so loud!* A head scarcely nods.

"But I 'eard she was doing well. And the baby."

"So she *was.*"

"What now, then?"

Lips are pursed. A head shaken.

"I 'eard it, too, that she was bad."

"Well, *you* didn' say nothing."

Shoulders are shrugged.

"Proper poorly, I 'eard. Like the woman at Rilla Mill."

Quick breath is drawn. "Never!"

"Well they buried 'er last Tuesday!"

"She, from Rilla, was poor as a church mouse. Ony 'ad the doctor to 'er once. Richardson won't spare no expense."

"And 'e 'aven't, neither. Doctor 'as been up Trethenna four times since Sunday and that's just by my reckonin'."

"There's no money will help if it's fever she's taken with."

A head points direction. Eyes turn to where Munro stands with the minister.

"'E's lookin' peaky 'isself."

"No wonder, poor man."

"Poor man, nothin'. 'E should never 'ave 'ad 'er, I say. "'Tis retri-bu-shan."

A throat is cleared. Behind a hand a voice murmurs.
"There's someone won't be sorry."
Eyes indicate.
"G'd evenin', Miss Bellham," one says as she passes.

Seventy-eight

Getting to grips with sea spray. Letting the paint build beautifully, this layer of seawater bounding back from the body it impacts. Seawater streaking green-gray as it ricochets up to the white tumble of frothed foam that forms a mantle around her; whose fringe thins to a rain of droplets, exploding skywards and lit from behind: luminous beads of speeding water.

The face, turned aside, is masked by a race of sea green streaming past the head and shoulder. Only the smeared shape of the mouth is visible, open with shock and cold and letting the air and water out. The torso, too, is slightly turned; tautly braced against the onslaught, which strikes one side of the body sooner, lifting the breast on that side high on the force of water under an outstretched arm. Balance in danger, one foot comes forward, contacting, hard, the gritty beach.

Downstairs the telephone rings.

Let it.

No, no, it might be the school. Damien was a little unwell this morning.

Seventy-nine

In dream he travels again from Africa, prisoner to sickness and the boat's confines. As he nears England, the sense of homecoming swells in him, till he feels his body choked with it. God, to touch the greenness again. God, to feel his feet on Cornish soil. God, to be beneath kind skies.

The steam has broken down once more and, in calm seas now, the sail hangs slack and the sea's slap is like the slop of his stomach, his body on the bunk, his neck, half wrung, pressing his face to the porthole, to get the first glimpse.

At dawn, through mist, the Lizard slides by; a snail's pace.

Safely in next. Carrick Roads. Only somehow the boat grounds. The sickening tear and graunch of rock. The cabin lurches so he must cling. Men shout. Feet thud the deck. Urgently, a bell clangs out.

Tide drains. He jumps from the tilted vessel, the water only to his knees. He will walk the rest. Others do. From the corner of his eye he sees them. Women, floundering, held by wet skirts. Men with eyes strangely set. Why is it they stare so? It is no distance. There is the town, the church on the hill. He steps on, staggers, his feet caught in soft mud beneath the water. No distance. He looks up. There is the town.

No.

There is where the town was.

He looks round, but the mist is down. He calls out.

No answer.

All gone.

The vessel gone.

He steps on, only the water is deeper. A glimpse through mist before it closes again. The green of land he strives for. He steps. Water to his chin. Feet sucked down in mud. The green. Of water. Of underwater. He tips his head for air. His breath is panic! His feet! How can he? Tips his head for air. Cries out. Wakes himself. Dark. Sitting in a chair. Hard-backed. Only a dream. Cold. Heart thumping loud through the silence. His hurting neck. The tight sickness of his stomach. Why is he sitting in a chair? Which room?

Oh God!

It floods back. Like the deadweight of water pressing on him.

Out loud his voice sobs, "Oh! God!"

In what relation sits the chair to the bed? He reaches out with a foot. Sweeps a low semicircle. Nothing. The darkness complete. The lamp must have burned itself out of oil. Feet, cold, to the wooden floor. His arms reach out. Blind man. Fumbling out in the hope he will not find; in the hope he will find differently.

There. The bed. The counterpane.

Across it his hands pat.

The sense of sickness in his stomach tightens.

He heaves himself out of the chair. Old man. The blanket falls from him.

Where is she? Not gone?

Another day and she must be. The grave already dug.

Another day and she must be. The grave already dug.

His hands are halfway across the bed, his knee on the edge of it when his hand touches hers.

Cold as stone.

He is woken by hands, gently, on his shoulder, then the slide and clink of the curtain drawn. He blinks open swollen eyes to the trimming of lace at his dead wife's shoulder; his own body cold, fully dressed and curled in a ball on the bed. He presses his eyes closed.

"It's near nine o'clock," the voice of Mrs. Jago says from behind him. Her feet sound on the wooden floor.

"You must be cold," her voice says and he hears the rustle of her skirts as she picks up the blanket from where it's fallen; feels it placed over him.

"There's breakfast kept hot for you downstairs."

Claira's hair is next to his face. They wanted to plait it and he would not let them.

He feels a hand on his shoulder. Then Mrs. Jago's voice again, low.

"They are coming for her at ten this morning."

He manages to nod. Pushes himself to sitting. His eyes dance, not daring to rest on her face. In snatches, his brain picks up her image. Death has its own version of white. Her face so lovely he feels it as pain. Tears well.

"Is Jed with the cattle?" he says, squeezing eyes closed, not turning round.

"Yes."

"And the dairy?"

"They are all come and work without chatter for once."

He nods. Hears her turn to go.

"Mrs. Jago."

Her feet stop.

"When they come for her . . ." He pauses. "In case I should not hear them arrive, I wonder if you could let me know they are here."

"I'll come up as soon as may be."

Her feet again.

"Thank you. And the baby?"

"Doing well with my daughter."

"Thank you."

Eighty

In the attic, getting ready for packing, pulling out boxes and cases. On all fours, Claire hauls out things she put there less than a year ago, throwing them in a heap behind her. Flat-pack boxes that will do for the children's toys again. Boxes for kitchen stuff. May as well get used to the idea.

From outside, the shouts of the children drift up to her and she gets to her feet to look through the little window to the yard; sees the boys in the meadow now, running in play against the breast of the hill. Howard is downstairs on the phone to his lover. Or at least Claire gathers as much. His tone of voice as she walked through the kitchen: rounded, warm, conspiratorial; the face he turned to her with blinded eyes; his commentary on the phone as she passed, "Yes. That's *very* astute of you. No, no. Gone now."

Sighing out, Claire turns back to the cupboard . . .

When you get back to London, he'll just be nearer to her.

. . . a low cupboard, under the eaves . . .

Going out every time he feels like a fuck.

. . . then drops to her knees again to check if she's left anything in there and sees the edge of some light-colored thing, caught under the framework and goes in after it and pulls out a piece of paper, opens it and reads her name, *Dear Claire.*

A letter to her?

She doesn't remember leaving letters there. Who's it from? For a fleeting moment she thinks it might be Nick—there's something familiar in the slope of the hand. She backs out of the cupboard and sits on the floor, looking at the document and only then notices the thickness of the paper and the mustiness of it and the discoloration of age. An old document, then. Not addressed to her at all. She locates the signature. It looks like *Munro.*

Dear Claira, she reads, oh, Claira, not Claire at all. *I have asked Mrs. Jago to give you this letter in the morning, by which time I will be gone from Trethenna . . .*

Gone from Trethenna—from here—a letter written from this place.

. . . I must go away tonight and think about what I have done and pray for God's guidance and forgiveness. I do not know how you will ever be able to forgive me. I certainly shall never forgive myself.

I shall stay with my brother, Edwin, near Truro; Mrs. Jago has the address. If you want for anything out of the ordinary, you should send there for it. I cannot tell how long I shall be gone. I have spoken to Jed about the farm and with Michael and Joseph to help he should manage. Mrs. Jago will see over the dairy. I know how hard you work, but, Claira . . .

—Claira—

. . . my only wish is that you should rest and return to health. I have asked Michael to take word in the morning to your Mother that you are not well although I have not found the courage to own what ails you.

As God is my witness, I swear I shall never again do such a terrible thing. I have never before felt so sorrowful for something I did.

And then the signature. *Munro.*

Claire turns the paper over. Nothing. She looks at the signature again. It is Munro. She rereads the last couple of sentences and wonders at the nature of the "terrible thing." An infidelity perhaps.

She puts the paper on the floor and hugs her knees again, rocking and looking at it.

Dear Claira . . .

She thinks of Howard downstairs.

I have never before felt so sorrowful for something I did.

Concealing, bolstered; shutting her out.

And, *of course* Howard doesn't feel sorrowful. For him there *is* no terrible thing.

But for me there *is,* Claire thinks, with sudden clarity. I *do* think it's a terrible thing. Not his infidelity per se. If his affection—his *attraction*—is directed somewhere else now, then he *should* go. Only *really* go. Leave the family to establish itself on a new footing, not in this limbo with its effect on the children, this tension, this deceit, this pretense at marriage.

As God is my witness, I swear I shall never again do such a terrible thing.

But—not seeing what he does as terrible—Howard *will* repeat this pattern. Again and again and again.

. . . my only wish is that you should rest and return to health.

What, she wonders, would Howard wish her?

She bites at the skin at the border of her fingernail; thinks of the questions Nick asked her, last thing on the night they went camping, before they'd gone, with sadness, to their separate tents.

What are you going to, Claire, if you go back to London? What of the children and how they love it here? What of your painting?

A piece of skin comes away in her teeth and she sighs out—her mind replaying part of that evening, the tenderness of his arm about her, the warmth of him, his understanding. She has not to be selfish about this, but God, she will miss him. Plus he's right, of course, with all his gentle questioning. He has a point. If not several. What *would* be waiting for them all in London? What *is* the least disruptive action for the children? Damien has stated categorically he does not want to go back and as for being deprived of Howard, already they hardly see him. And her painting? She gets to her feet, then, going through to the second attic room to visit the work she's finished now: tackling the easiest issue first.

Seawater and foam and sunlight and shadow and a figure at a critical point of balance and the rock of the cliff face towering high, the paintwork both free and dynamic, loose and structured and she *is* pleased with that, to have found that style so soon, to have found that voice.

The content is pretty derivative, Claire. It's the Armstrong painting all over again.

In some ways, perhaps. The next ones will move away from that.

Next ones?

"Claire." Howard's voice calls from the belly of the house. "Claire!" He must be on the landing below. She remembers the door at the bottom of the little stairs clanging shut behind her, so he probably won't think of looking up here.

"Claire!"

The sound of Howard's feet can be heard in the room below—her room—and then out again. *"Claire!"*

His voice sounds as if he is annoyed.

Standing before the painting, Claire draws a long, slow breath, then lets it out, slowly: feels Howard slipping from her. Her lungs empty, she draws another breath, then breathes Howard out again; releasing the tension of him so that she hardly notices the sound of his feet going down the stairs.

The letter is still in her hand and she turns it, letting the paper spring back round its creases.

Then there's the sound of the BMW starting up—round the corner of the building. Howard going out, then. Crossing to the little window, she catches sight of the shine of the car roof as he drives round the side of the house. And when the phone rings, she knows for certain it's Nick and nearly falls, racing down the stairs to answer.

Eighty-one

Dear Mr. Richardson, the letter reads, *We write to inform you that works on the roof and the installation of new pews and other refurbishments of Wetherington Wesleyan Chapel have now been completed in accordance with your instructions.*

Munro's eyes move mechanically from one word to the next. Slowly, because to fill his thoughts is good. Take time; let each syllable sound in the head.

Also in accordance with your instructions, no member of the community has been made aware of the identity of their benefactor nor of the link to your father's previous ownership of the mine.

His eyes slide down the page after all.

. . . that we have met all bills arising from the monies you made available and enclose the accounts thereto. You will see that, after all is discharged, the sum of £37.17s remains and we look forward to receiving your advice on what should be done with said amount.

We take this opportunity to report that the many attenders of the chapel feel themselves most fortunate to have the benefit of the improvements made and—knowing me to be their benefactor's agent—have asked that their grateful thanks should be sent to you. The circuit ministers similarly send their thanks and report a growth in attendance since your interest in the chapel was shown.

You did mention in your letter of the 17th November 1887, that you would consider coming to inspect the completed works and should you wish to undertake the journey, it would be my pleasure to welcome you and your wife to . . .

His eyes focus on nothing. The hand holding the letter rests back onto his lap. He becomes aware of the slow tick of the clock. It times exactly with his breathing. From the yard he hears the rattle of pail handles. Molly crossing with milk to the dairy. He should be out there, helping Jed and Michael. Tick . . . tock . . . tick . . . tock . . . tick . . . He pulls in deeper breath, reaches for the padded cloth that hangs on the slab and uses it to turn the hot brass handle. Opening the fire door, he places the letter in.

There are two more letters. Local. The paper smooth to his fingers. Taut. He could open them. Tick . . . tock . . . tick . . . Why is he still holding the oven cloth? He looks down at it there, held in the hand that holds the letters. Of course. She stitched it. His fingers close further round it. Sitting in the parlor she stitched it. Soon after the slab was put in. Stitching the thing he now holds in his hand. He wants to look at each and every precious stitch and dares not. His breathing halts round the tightening of his stomach.

The letters are getting crumpled. Better open them. His fingers fumble the paper. What does the signature say? *Frank Bramley.*

My dear Richardson,

It is not possible to say what sorrow I felt at the news of your dear wife's passing. That so radiant a light has been quenched so soon is beyond understanding. I send you the John Ruskin piece which accompanied the painting—The Hopeless Dawn—*which you saw. Although little comfort is to be had at such a time, I send it in the hope you find some solace in it.*

My thoughts are with you.

Frank Bramley.

Munro turns to the quotation copied out onto a second sheet of paper.

"Human effort and sorrow going on perpetually from age to age; waves rolling for ever and winds moaning, and faithful hearts wasting and sickening for ever, and brave lives dashed away about the rattling

beach like weeds for ever; and still, at the helm of every lonely boat, through starless nights and hopeless dawn, His hand, who spreads the fisher's net over the dust of the Sidonian palaces, and gave unto the fisher's hand the keys of the kingdom of heaven."

A shout of laughter escapes him. Short. Hard.

No! No. Don't.

He clamps his breath round the ugly noise. These dear Bohemian friends who point him now to his faith. The laughter threatens to bubble up again. He pinches, hard, the bridge of his nose and thinks of his wakeful, starless nights, his hopeless dawns, seeking—in desperation—His hand, His voice, His sign. Nothing. Nothing like never before. Nothing as the welter of grief dragged him under. Nothing in the relative calm of exhaustion, staring for hours into darkness. Nothing.

He realizes he had thought—at some dark stage—of Bramley's painting; drawn comfort from it, even. The form of the women mourning. Their abandonment in hopelessness, a sense he now shares. There was the comfort, knowing his grief has common ground.

He puts Bramley's letter on the table. There is no doubt it is kindly meant. He must answer it. He will put it with the others in the study. The pile of them to answer. The sorrow of Elizabeth's. The solicitous warmth of Forbes's. The robust compassion of Ebenezer's. And all of those from chapel. Perhaps thirty altogether. He will answer them when he can.

Whose is this last then? He scarcely has the appetite for more. Spreading the page, he reads the signature. *Mary Bellham.*

He lets out breath. Skims his eyes over the words.

. . . the sadness of a young life lost . . . gone to a better place . . . knowing God will give you strength to bear this loss . . . the strength of your faith will bear you through the . . .

And then, among the platitudes, two sentences that halt him.

The future of the child is all. Even knowing your great capability, I hope you will let those of us who can help you with such women's work.

So, there it is, set out for him. The thought that has been surfacing when he does from his grief and even in it, even at the depths from which it seems he will never again break through to air, there has been the pull of connectedness, a lifeline sense he must do what he can for his son. She is right. The future of the child *is* all. And much of it the work of women. Of course the child must be where he is now, able to suckle with Mrs. Jago's first grandchild. But what will come about once the baby is weaned? It will need the presence of a woman. Constantly. Here in the house. And Eadie is too frail. He must make some arrangement.

He pushes the chair back, takes the letters through to the study, paces back again. He will see his son soon. Today. He has daily reports of him from Mrs. Jago, but he has not been to see him these last three days. How could he not? Never mind that the baby grows ever more like his mother so that it wounds him to witness it. He will go this afternoon. Every afternoon. They must manage here, afternoons, without him.

He folds the little padded cloth, places it in the breast pocket of his shirt, pressing it to him. Lacing his boots, he hears the back door open and there is Jed, come to find him. Munro sees his eyes are still red, as they have been since her death.

" 'Xcusing me," Jed says, fiddling with the cuff of his shirt, "but did you mean us to take dung to Laney Strait and all?"

"I did, Jed, and I'm coming to give you a hand," Munro says, straightening to rest an arm briefly on his worker's shoulders. Through the jacket, Munro can feel he has more flesh on him now.

Eighty-two

A young woman in black mourning garb sits in a conservatory, binding chrysanthemums one to another, a sea of fallen leaves at her feet.

"I hadn't met this one before," Nick says. "I'd only seen reproductions."

"What's it called?" Claire asks, searching for a nameplate that's not yet in place.

"Weaving a Chain of Grief."

"This other one of Bramley's I've seen in the Tate," she says. *"The Hopeless Dawn,* isn't it?"

"That's right."

"Mind yer backs!" the workman calls, backing towards them, a shared load of a painting in his hands, then, "I've told Naomi you're here. She's just on her way down."

"Thanks," Nick says as they move out of the workmen's way. "We just wanted to check a painting that Claire has loaned."

"Who's it by?"

"Elizabeth Armstrong—or Elizabeth Forbes you might have her down as."

"Oh, she's through there," the workman says, indicating the direction with a nod of his head, so that Claire half expects to see Elizabeth herself appear in person. "Not the next room, the one after."

"Is she?"

"Yep," he confirms. "Through there with her husband."

Claire didn't think she could be surprised by this painting anymore, thought she had spent long enough in its company to know it by now, but here—in the unfamiliar space and light—it catches her out again.

"It looks so different," she manages at last.

"Nicely lit," Nick says from behind. And Claire supposes that's it—the good light emphasizing color: the lilt and flow of the woman, backlit in landscape; the fluidity of movement caught in accord with the terrain. In this light, the fiddle seems edged with fire.

"Anyone who played a part in salvaging that *has* to be a star," Nick says from behind her, bringing his arm, briefly, to her shoulders.

The Zandvoort fisher-girl holds your gaze. Calmly resolute and hand on hip, she has you as surely in her easy grasp as the dish that's tucked against her waist; as surely as the fish on the plate whose languid weight drapes over the dish's rim.

"Somehow Elizabeth always identifies the dignity of her subjects," Nick says.

"Doesn't she? Such a self-containment here. And the girl must be all of thirteen."

"And not the most glamorous of occupations."

"No, yet her sense of self-worth is really evident, but subtly so. How does she *do* that?" Claire asks with a laugh.

Nick shakes his head. "Her use of backlight, the serenity of the girl's face, her eye contact, the use of height relative to the viewer. All of those, I suppose, yet still the whole seems greater. Some essence of timelessness caught."

They browse the others, about fifteen of Elizabeth's in all and Claire keeps returning to a picture worked in pastel. Children on summer hay fields that slope to the sea, where fingers of distant land reach out and the sun is nearly set. In dusk, blue light, five children link hands in a circle game, their bodies leaning outwards in play, their collective shape fitting perfectly into the roundness and angle of the hay mounds they are among. Light makes colors merge, the landscape, the sea, their clothing, their limbs as the smaller children raise their faces to the older ones.

And then Naomi is there, still managing some calm in the face of all the last-minute things, reaching up to give Nick a hug, then flicking her black hair back into its neat bob and shaking hands with Claire.

". . . who found the Armstrong painting, Nick tells me, you clever thing."

"Complete fluke," Claire says, shaking hands.

"Well, it's wonderful of you to loan it. And isn't it fabulous?" Naomi enthuses.

"You've done a great job with it, Naomi," Nick says.

"Well, thank you, Nick. It's every bit what you said it was. There's bound to be some media interest in it, Claire. It's a valuable painting you have here and found in such unusual circumstances. Would you mind if I mentioned it to the TV people? They'll be covering the exhibition in any case, so in a way it'll be difficult not to draw attention to it."

"I hadn't thought."

"Well, let me know, would you?"

"Yes, of course," Claire says.

And then the workmen are back again: a big painting.

"Naomi, I think we should get out of your way."

"You'll come to the private view?"

"Can't wait."

"Thanks for seeing so well to the painting. Oh look, Nick, *The Health of the Bride*," Claire says, indicating the painting just brought in and amazed to see this piece of history moving in men's hands.

Nick smiles. "You can see why it made Stanhope's reputation. That's Elizabeth, by the way."

"Where?!"

"The bride. She posed for him."

And Claire has to go closer to see this image of the woman who painted the painting she now owns. Elizabeth Adela Armstrong. The quiet strength of her extra countenance; kind, calm.

"Mind yer backs!"

So they drag themselves away through rooms of Tuke and Gotch, the brilliance of Langley and the latest arrival come in from New Zealand. A Frank Bramley procession of young girls and women in white, with flowers, along the harborside, the funeral of a child: *For Such Is the Kingdom of Heaven.*

Eighty-three

Morning sun on the baskets of strawberries and the blond head of the child who minds them.

"Half a pound, please," Elizabeth says and smiles to see the little face, puckered with concentration as the correct brass weight is hunted out before the fruit can be placed, ever so carefully, one piece at a time to swing the scales into balance.

"Are you in a hurry, dear?" the child's mother, above leeks and lemons at the next stall, asks.

"No. Don't trouble," Elizabeth says, smiling, enjoying the color and the sun on her back. She lets her eyes drift down the slope of the cobbled street. By the stone stairway, bandy-legged farmers chat. From the hand of one, two chicken dangle, live, upside down, held by the feet. Youth has a gathering of its own, vital in sunlight. Confident in newly broadened shoulders and the slimness of hips, they laugh. The quietest one catches Elizabeth's eye, uncertain. She smiles at him. Recognizes the gentle mouth of sensitivity. Women with laden baskets trudge up the hill, heads together. And, isn't that Munro Richardson? The sun shines on the surface of the cobbles so that Elizabeth must half close her eyes to see. It is him. Carrying a wire tray of eggs, his eyes on the stalls as he walks up the hill towards her and there, he has noticed her, the pleasure of recognition flickering to his face. She has not seen him since the funeral.

"Elizabeth," he says, shifting the eggs to one arm so he may shake her hand, "how lovely to see you."

"How are you?" she asks.

"Well," he says, dropping his eyes a second. She sees the new scattering of gray at his temples and when he looks up, the tiredness of his eyes.

"And young William?"

Munro laughs. "Aah. He keeps us perfectly busy and—at sixteen months—knows very well his own mind. And how are you?"

"I am well, thank you."

"And your mother?"

"Well, too."

"You are painting still, I hope."

"Oh yes."

"I was so sorry not to attend the private view the other month, but as I said in my letter . . ." He trails off.

"I understood," Elizabeth insists. "I am afraid you missed a very good show though. But, come next time. It will be an annual event now. Stanhope surpassed himself this year and the Royal Academy thought his painting quite the finest thing to come out of Newlyn. And they are right, too."

"The subject?"

"A wedding toast. *The Health of the Bride.*"

"Aahh."

"He caught the moment so well," she finds herself hurrying on, "and composed the whole thing with so much subtlety and painted it all so beautifully, the light sources, the characters."

"As he did in the *Village Philharmonic*," Munro comments.

"Yes, but this is very much the better. Really, altogether a superior thing," Elizabeth says, then looks down to the hand that tugs her sleeve to find the child has come from behind her baskets to bring the strawberries to her. She laughs and bobs down, finding the pennies from her purse and giving them to her, so that she takes them and shows them to her mother to check they are right. The women smile at each other.

When she stands again, she finds Munro's eyes, gray, on hers.

"I have been thinking, Elizabeth."

"Yes?"

"The painting you did, of Claira."

And she notices the way he says the name, his voice carefully round it, like the handling of porcelain.

"Do you know where it is?"

"I know who bought it. I could find out where it is."

"I was wondering if they might think of selling it." He looks at his feet. "Our wedding was not a day for photographs and I never thought to have any taken after, so there is no recent likeness of her at Trethenna for the boy, when he is older, to know his mother by."

Elizabeth nods. "I will write and inquire."

"Thank you. Well then, I must take these eggs before the custom has all gone. Will you send my congratulations to Stanhope for his painting?"

"I will."

"And tell him from me, enough of painting about it—when are the two of you to marry?"

Elizabeth smiles. "Next month," she says.

It is not so much a lie, he thinks, letting his horse trot his way home, to say he wants the painting for the boy. For certain, he *does* want it for William. Even more, he wants it for himself. Already he has the place thought out where the painting will hang. The wall in the parlor. Already he has spent long moments there, staring at the space, imagining it filled by her, the warmth of the thing, the power of her gaze. To think of it. The house with her in it again. He blinks his eyes against tears.

Good that the horse, then, knows well the route: rolling the track away beneath his hooves.

Eighty-four

Claire watches Nick at the counter, standing apart so she can see how it is with him, how he reacts with others, trying to keep a little distance, but it's hopeless. Even the way he handles small change is perfection; the beauty of his fingers finding coins to help the girl behind the register, who's young and flustered and hasn't got the right money to give him. How can she not love him: this tender, talented, beautiful man.

She sees the girl brought back to smiles by his empathy and compassion.

They take a table by the window where the sun comes through greenery and the view is of the riverside. As they drink their coffee in silence awhile, her head is full of the pictures they've seen, until she notices he is watching her.

"And so, is Trethenna sold?"

"Yes."

He says nothing; keeping eyes weighted on hers.

"The house is sold, but I'm not going back, Nick. The children and I will stay in Cornwall."

She watches his face, which does not alter, only something in the depth of his eyes seems to change.

"And what does Howard think about that?"

Claire looks at her watch. "Not sure that he knows yet. Oh yes, I suppose he does. Just because we don't get our mail delivery until noon, here. I forget that it arrives so much earlier in London, so probably he will have got my letter by now. I've really no idea how he'll react. With relief, I should think. He should get my solicitor's letter in the next day or two. That might not please him quite so much."

"And your plans?"

"Stay in Cornwall, love my children, paint."

"You should, you know."

"Should what?"

"Paint. You have some seriously good work emerging. You should think of collecting it towards an exhibition. Is the figure at the edge of the sea finished?"

"Yes."

"Pleased?"

Claire looks at him. "I think it has some merit."

He nods and their eyes lock solid a moment.

"Where will you live?"

She laughs. "Well, that's a minor detail I shall have to attend to. I've no idea. I only made the decision to leave Howard a few days ago. I can't do it all at once."

"You can rent my second cottage if you want to," he says, levelly. "I've been thinking about getting a full-time tenant."

"Is that a good idea?"

"Too close?"

"Isn't it?"

He shrugs. "Before we know it, it will be summer again and I shall be in Nepal."

"Will you?"

"I will, which is also my way of saying I know you're going to need space. The unraveling of a marriage takes a long time."

"Does it?"

He laughs. "I don't know. I just know it took me three years after splitting up with Helen to even be able to contemplate a serious relationship again. I had flings. Several of them, immediately after Helen left. Distraction therapy. Nursing the hurt."

"And after that?"

"As I said, nothing for three years, then I did meet someone and saw her for a year or so, but it didn't work out."

"No one since then?"

"No." He stretches in his chair and grins. "Lots of painting and lots of travel and other such selfish pursuits. Being single can be perfectly blissful."

Claire laughs. "Sounds as if you don't want a woman in your life at all, let alone one with two children."

"Don't know if I do," he smiles, his eyes softly on her. "Wouldn't mind one living next door, though."

"You out*rage*ous man."

"Probably, but come and see the cottage anyway. See what you think and then at least you can add it to your list of options."

Eighty-five

Mrs. Jago locates him, at last, sitting with his son in the parlor, after all. Opening the door she finds they have the lamps out, the better to see the flecks of patterned light cast by the shadow ball.

"*There* you are," Mrs. Jago says. "I thought it was Molly minding the boy."

"I sent her off," Munro says, then to William, "Mind now, it's getting hot."

He whisks the lamp from the boy's reach. On walls and ceiling, shadows dance and flail.

"Try very gently," he says, lowering the ball again. "Hold your hand near, but don't touch."

Gingerly the boy does as he is told—curls his fingers away when he feels the heat, looking up at Munro with Claira's wide eyes.

"I came to see if I should put the boy to bed before I go," Mrs. Jago says.

"Yes, yes, thank you, I'm sure you're right. It's high time he was in bed."

Munro places the shadow ball on its stand; picks the child up to embrace him.

"Go along with Mrs. Jago, now," he says, setting the boy down next to her. "God bless you, William."

She comes back to say good night and though half an hour has passed, still he stays in patterned light. The box of gritty earth with the diamonds sits idly at his side. They must have been hunting through it again. She worries about the game, knows how quickly little hands put things in mouths to swallow. Perhaps she should say something, then she sees the face he turns: how tears catch even faint light. Her face softens and she sighs to see him. More than two years, now—and still he weeps. Sometimes it is best to leave him and sometimes . . . which is it today?

Softly she crosses the room and he silently turns; buries his face in her skirts that she may stroke down the shaking of his shoulders.

Eighty-six

She wakes to the gentlest stroking of her shoulder and daylight colored by unfamiliar curtains.

"My God—the children," she murmurs as she stumbles through wakening.

"It's all right. It's all right. It's only two o'clock," Nick whispers, enfolding her again in sated arms; smoothing her shoulder in the rhythm of her breathing; nuzzling his face against the nape of her neck.

"It's only two o'clock."

Wakening more, she laughs. "God, that was wonderful."

"You referring to the sex, or the exhibition?" Nick murmurs, so that she laughs again, turning to gentle her face at his breast.

"The exhibition. Obviously."

Eighty-seven

A throat is cleared.

"I 'ear she is no stranger up at Trethenna these last few weeks."

"A man cannot help it if a woman will call and, besides, 'tis timely now, comin' up two years since his wife took ill and died."

A head is leaned forward.

"If you ask me, a woman should know better than to go callin' on a man, 'specially if she is not asked."

"Who says 'e never asked 'er?"

"Did you 'ear 'e 'ad then?"

A face is turned aside. Eyes watch.

"Bless 'im. See 'ow 'e do linger by the grave."

"And 'er and all."

"One to grieve, the other to gloat," a quiet voice sings.

Sharp breath is drawn.

"Miss Bellham is a *kindly* soul!"

"Who always 'eld a torch for 'im and is *not* about to see 'im lost a second time," lowly, a voice insists.

"She does keep beside 'im uncommonly close."

"Always 'as." A mouth is puckered. "It's been *years.*"

Figures at the graveside turn and move on. Eyes follow.

"Weddin' before long, then."

Eighty-eight

West Cornwall
1989

The grounding of flagstones holds heavy air, undisturbed; cooler than the spring day outside. Empty rooms resound to their voices and the whisper of their shoes on stone, sending echoes to the attic. Deeper in, the air is dank, a patina of mold on the kitchen's wealth of wood. Claire runs a finger through it on the surface of the dresser.

"*How* long since they moved out?"

"Only a month or so, but we've had so much rain."

In the hall, a sense of heaviness, of stone and wood settling under the weight of its era and the front room is all wrong somehow: granite newly plastered and a hideous stove put in and the place where the painting hung conspicuously bare.

"They've made a good mess of the place, considering they were only here a couple of years."

"They have a bit, although nothing that can't be sorted. Would it be strange to be back without the Armstrong?"

"Yes, it would. The only way though," Claire says, amazed all over again at the possibility of being able to buy back Trethenna if she were to sell the painting. "Do you think our work will ever sell for that much?"

Nick laughs. "Long after we are dead, perhaps."

The clatter and slam of the front door and Damien runs in, as tall as his mother's shoulder now and laughing as he calls, "Nick, Nick! The kite's stuck in a tree."

"Where's Nathan?" Claire interjects.

"Climbing up after it."

"And you let him? Damien, what were you thinking?"

"Come on, Damien. Which tree is it in?" Nick says, going out with him.

Claire goes over to the window that looks out onto the garden—and there's Nathan—not really *up* the tree, just balancing on a lowering branch, a couple of feet from the ground. And she wonders if Damien exaggerated on purpose—an excuse to call for Nick. The boy is seeking him more and more these days, getting to the age now, when men really matter; beginning, even, to block her out.

She watches the little performance a moment: Nick and Damien crossing the lawn, Nick countering the boy who shoulders into him, pushing for a play-fight; Nick grabbing and containing him, mock-tripping him, breaking his fall. They're just so lucky he's been there for them, she thinks as he lifts her younger child down from the tree; all the while, Nathan pointing, from Nick's arms, to where the kite is.

Nick finds her again in the attic where she's gone to put Munro's letter back.

"Better?" he asks, coming up into the room.

"Yes. I shouldn't have taken it away with me. The letter belongs here, even if we decide we don't."

"Got a verdict on that yet?"

"Don't know. We could certainly use the bigger space. What do you think?"

"I've always loved Trethenna. And it could soon be made beautiful again."

"I bumped into Howard on the stairs."

"Did you? There's only one way to exorcise that sort of ghost." He grins. "We just have to make love in every room in the house."

She laughs. "I said he was on the stairs."

"I daresay we could manage something."

They go down to the floor below to the windows at the front of the house to look out at the boys in the garden and he puts his hands on her shoulders: gathers her to him.

"What's the bother?" he asks gently, his face against her hair.

"I'm being really crabby about this, aren't I?"

"You are," he confirms, so that she laughs into his shoulder.

"It would mean a lot of extra work, I suppose."

"And you're still not ready for the St. Ives exhibition and you've just said you'll do more hours at the bank," he suggests.

"And you're due to be in Patagonia in three months' time and I doubt we could move before that," she adds.

"Could cancel."

"Don't see why you should. Don't see how you can if you want to fulfill your commitment for the Italian shows next spring. You said you would be pushed for time in any case."

"You trying to get rid of me?"

"Yes. In the short term, if it's what you need to do; if it lets you come back to us long-term."

"Might rather spend the summer moving in here with you."

She pushes her face against his neck, not wanting to be lured by the idea. "What about the Italian series?"

"I expect I'd get some work together."

"That doesn't sound like the 'cohesive whole' you were lecturing me about with mine the other day."

"You take notice of some things I say, then?"

"Well, does it?"

They are still a moment, a warm core in the coolness of the house.

"Do you know what?" she laughs, her body against his, still. "These are *nice* problems."

"I think so," he agrees.

She moves away from him a little then and they turn towards the stairs.

"What's our best bet, Nick? That's all I want to identify."

"Sorry?"

"Our best bet. For keeping this thing together and as good as it is now."

"You're sure, not marriage?"

"Yes. Positive. If you go to Patagonia and come back to me, or if we move in here together, or if we stay as we are living next door to each other—"

"It's hardly that anymore, Claire. I knocked a couple of doors through, remember?"

"You did, but there's still separate space if we want it. That's the point. We still have our own space—away from each other, I mean. You know if you just want to paint for two days, you can."

"And you can."

"To an extent, children permitting."

"I hope I've helped with that."

"You have, wonderfully. But not marriage, Nick. Whatever scenario we come up with, I want to know you go with it because you want to, not because we have some legal piece of paper."

In the hall now, he kisses the side of her face, his hand at the nape of her neck.

"I don't know, then, Claire. What is our best bet?"

She laughs. "No idea."

"We'll think about it, hey?"

"Starting with a bottle of wine this evening," she agrees, pulling the key out of her pocket to lock the door behind them.

At the shadow of the closing door, a beetle in the hallway scuttles, and from the insect's scampered passing, specks of mortar fall—a dusting rain—down to the flagstone floor.

Eighty-nine

West Cornwall
1889

Munro waits at the rear of the chapel. A particular shine is on his shoes. A particular crispness about his shirt. He peers through the finely bubbled glass. Heavy rain clouds gather and the light is failing. It will be dark an hour before time. No matter. All at Trethenna is orderly except that which will wait. He straightens the cuff of his shirt, sees the new minister glance aside at him. What is it he spies? Aahh. The cuff links: African gold.

There must be something about December, Munro thinks, looking again through the window at the darkness of the day. For months this wedding was just a possibility, a sometime in the future. Then suddenly December drew near and he woke one morning to find things different: an urgency upon him. It must be to do with the season—a time for bringing indoors all that will. A time for gathering ever closer together; for the weathering out of storms.

He had come down that day and seen William, no longer a baby and Mrs. Jago, there ever earlier to be with him when he wakes and Eadie, enlivened by him, but frail and tiring, too. And then his own sleep broken.

Mary Bellham, of course, cannot be at the harmonium. They have had to bring someone in from Penzance. A large woman he does not know. Anyway, she plays well enough, he thinks, listening to the way the sound settles over them.

Not so many here as last time. Less approval, perhaps.

He takes the watch from the pocket of his waistcoat. Five minutes yet before his bride is due.

He thinks of Claira in the chapel yard. Bones now.

He thinks of Claira in Heaven. God keep her.

He thinks of Claira in his soul. Safely. Safely. He has consulted her long. Has her blessing in this marriage. A mother for her child.

He does not know how it will be for him: all the fumblings of a new marriage. He feels his lips purse tightly at the thought. It is a thing of fondness, not of passion. Separate rooms to begin with. A bed already bought for her, made up in one of the rooms that has been empty so long. Perhaps together later. Perhaps not. Although the marriage must surely be consummated, mustn't it? Otherwise, not a marriage, in the eyes of God. Yet—as she is a few years older than he and unlikely to conceive, consummation could—in the eyes of God—only be the satisfaction of carnal desire, couldn't it? It is a dilemma that has occupied him increasingly as this day has drawn nearer. There is no one to ask. Not this new minister, so much younger than himself. The Bible has yielded nothing and God has not said a word. But then, God does not say much these days: only in the fields now, or when he goes to the height of the hill to look down over Trethenna. Only then, silently, Munro breathes His presence in, feels Him pump round with His blood and he is grateful and humbled.

William has done well. He looks across again at his son's dark head, where he sits between Mrs. Jago's daughter, and Eadie. For once he has made no sound, in awe of this special time. Elizabeth and Stanhope Forbes are seated behind them. Good of them to come. Good, too, the painting of Claira was not for sale. It would not have been fair, he sees it now, to have the thing hanging in the house for his new wife to live with. Perhaps one day the owners will let him go to see the painting. When William is grown, he could take him to London to stand before it. And he pictures them there, William, as tall as he.

And, oh!

He almost says it aloud, for here she is with him suddenly: Claira, at his elbow waiting with him for his bride, her presence so nearly and so absolutely not tangible.

He feels the warmth of her suffuse him.

In instant response, the surge of his love.

The push and flood and flow of his love.

"Here she is," the minister says, his cheeks suddenly pink.

Munro looks through the window. So she is. And, watching his bride, he sees she, too, has a certain self-possession. He recalls how she answered him when he asked her to marry him. Not yes or no, but why? And she had made him list the reasons. The mother she has made for William, her steadfastness over the years, her utter reliability, the fondness these things generate in him. And even then she would go away and think about it. No, she had not let him off lightly, Mrs. Jago.

He watches her walk to him, the minister gone to his place. For the first time it occurs to him, he cannot call her Mrs. Jago now; will have to get used to calling her something else.

He tries it in his head. Florence. Florence Richardson.

About the Author

Hayden Gabriel lives in the southwest of England. She is a graduate of the creative writing M.A. at the University of East Anglia, and *Where the Light Remains* is her first novel.

Touchstone Reading Group Guide

Where the Light Remains

1. Though their lives are separated by a century, Claira's and Claire's lives correspond. Describe the connections between their lives and the ways in which their paths intersect. As characters, how are they personally similar or dissimilar?

2. How does the author shape the novel so that the connections between these two stories feel vital and immediate, despite the hundred-year gap?

3. While Claira and Munro eventually become true husband and wife, their match is initially disastrous. What obstacles prevent them from coming together for so long? As the marriage grows stronger, how do they both learn from and enrich each other?

4. What do you make of Claire and Howard's relationship? Why do you think Claire stays with him for so long? Did you sympathize with her decision? What finally allows her to leave?

5. How do Claira and Claire express themselves creatively, and how do the men in their lives respond? What does the story ultimately have to say about women's artistic expression, both in the past and today?

6. Why does Claira's portrait have the power to inspire and influence Claire in a way nothing else had been able to? How did you feel at the story's end when you learned it had been sold? What do you think its sale signals about Claire's future?

7. What roles does religion play in the story? How do Munro and Claira each approach their faith, and how do the ways they observe it change as their relationship deepens? How do Jed and his fervent observance fit in to this story?

8. What different associations does the phrase "where the light remains" bring to mind? Do you feel this is an appropriate title for the novel?

9. How do Claira and Claire individually make the house, Trethenna, their own, piece by piece? What effect does Trethenna have on them?

10. Claira and Claire each has a strong female role model in her life: Elizabeth and Kate. How do these women influence them artistically and personally?

11. In addition to engendering creativity, the natural environment elicits a range of responses from the characters. Identify examples from both narratives. What comparisons are there?

12. At the end of the nineteenth-century narrative, the painting of Claira is in London, while at the beginning of the twentieth-century story, the painting is again in Cornwall. What does the text suggest about how this might have happened and what does it confirm about the character involved?

13. What compels Munro to take the burden of his father's sins onto his own shoulders? How do you interpret his change of heart, his realization that he is as joyfully bound to Trethenna as he now is to Claira? What legacy will he leave?

14. Discuss Claira's and Munro's unique reactions to the paintings they view at the exhibitions, Langley's *But Men Must Work* and Bramley's *A Hopeless Dawn*. Why do you think they experience the scenes depicted in them in such different ways? How do their responses foreshadow the events to come?

An Interview with Hayden Gabriel

1. How did you become interested in writing about life in Cornwall, England, at the ends of a two centuries?

I lived in West Cornwall for about fifteen years and was profoundly affected by the experience of living near the end of a peninsula which is exposed to the vagaries of weather that comes, predominantly and without interruption, from the expanse of Atlantic Ocean to the west. The peninsula has been inhabited for thousands of years, with many ancient historical sites still surviving, so the sense of antiquity is strong. Consequently, thoughts of those who have gone before were frequently evoked, especially as I lived in an old house. I found myself wondering whose feet may have worn smooth a stone step, whose hands may have erased the pattern from a brass bellpull, who may have glanced at a particular sundial. In addition, as a writer, I'm curious about universalities of human experience and how—despite the passage of time and changes in culture—some fundamentals are constant. Using story lines set one hundred years apart allowed me to explore what some of those fundamentals might be—with the timelessness of the Cornish landscape as a consistent element in both narratives.

2. Why is landscape so important to you as a storyteller?

In his epic poem *The Prelude,* William Wordsworth describes his upbringing in the dramatic landscape of England's Lake District as being "fostered alike by beauty and by fear." Similarly, in West Cornwall, the landscape can be both beautiful and awe inspiring. Almost every year there are fatal falls from the cliffs, the same cliffs that are stunningly beautiful when swathed in sea pinks, overlooking azure seas. I find living where natural landscape dominates is both a humbling and inspiring discipline—a constant reminder of human frailty which for me engenders a balanced sense of place and emphasizes the desire and need to seize each day. Sense of landscape is equally vital to me as a writer. *Where the Light Remains* could not have happened—the characters would not have acted as they did—without the beauty and fear of landscape.

3. *How did you discover the nineteenth-century Newlyn School paintings? And why did you choose to write about Elizabeth Armstrong?*

The nineteenth-century Newlyn School paintings are a well-established part of the culture of West Cornwall and beyond, as these paintings have made their way to galleries and private collections in many parts of the world. (I most recently bumped—unexpectedly—into two such paintings in a gallery in Sydney, an emotional moment, as one of the paintings of a girl playing a lute was by Elizabeth Armstrong and until that moment unknown to me.) During research, my attention focused on Elizabeth Armstrong because I found myself fascinated by her persistent creativity in the face of cultural and—to an extent marital—containment if not opposition. Elizabeth's artistic association with Whistler and Sickert was, for example, actively discouraged by Stanhope Forbes, whose apparently solicitous nature led him to observe in one of his letters that when he and Elizabeth were married, he would see that she didn't work too hard.

4. *What kind of research did you do to develop the story and to make the characters so realistic?*

Six large boxes of letters written by Stanhope Forbes, held now in the Tate Gallery Archive in London, provided good insight into Forbes's character, idiom, and value system. Plenty of research and consultation with art, theological, and local historians helped hugely with those respective aspects of the work. An archive of local newspapers from nineteenth-century West Cornwall provided cultural detail from the time, including the article on female creativity by George J. Romanes, which I reproduced verbatim in the text. The diary of a nineteenth-century farmer provided agricultural detail, as did other agricultural works of the day. Local museums supplied details of domestic life and clothing; an antique dealer gave details of furnishings. And, of course, tracking down and viewing as many Newlyn School paintings as I could was vital. It seemed essential to me to do this groundwork in order to identify the cultural phenomena that would have influenced and informed my characters. Even for the twentieth-century narrative, there was still research to do—the way a real estate entrepreneur operates; the exact timing of the stock market crash and its links with the tail end of the hurricane that hit the UK at the same time; the search patterns used by air-sea rescue, and so forth. And when information couldn't be found in archives, it was a case of finding people to help with detail—the staff at Covent Garden Opera House to describe what a ticket would have looked like in 1987; a pathologist to describe the condition of a body that has been immersed in seawater for two weeks, et cetera. There's a tendency to make a fine art out of gently pestering people.

5. *What are some of the challenges you have found as a novelist trying to create characters and settings that propel the story and entice the reader?*

There are so many! Using historical fact to influence the story line in a way which is appropriate to the book's themes; balancing the work's internal logic; acquiring a detailed knowledge of a character's way of being; what to include in the text and what to leave out. Every time I sit to write, or every time I think about an episode, there are a host of questions to be answered.

6. *When you started writing did you have a path in mind? Or did it evolve as you started to create the story? Which comes first for you, character or story?*

The only definite ideas I had at the beginning pertained to structure and landscape and a curiosity about shared human experience. I soon became interested in character, which necessarily sparked research. A process of evolution followed in which I found myself becoming ridiculously fond of these people, some of whom died before I was born and many of whom never existed. I remember wading through nineteenth-century newspapers in a cellar of a private library in Penzance and feeling utterly bemused about why I couldn't find an announcement of Munro and Claira's marriage. I hunted for several minutes, feeling certain Munro would have placed a notice in this, the only local newspaper at that time, before realization dawned. Definitely time to get out of the cellar!